I0692967

All Fall Down—Copyright 2016 © F. Bradley Reaume

This is a work of fiction. Any resemblance to actual people or events herein described is purely co-incidental.

Penshurst Publishing   **First Edition—August 2016**

ISBN 978-0-9734452-9-9

For Judy

All Fall Down

A Novel

the end of the world as we know it

By F. Bradley Reaume

May 29th

A battered oil tanker slipped through the waves toward the Verrazano Narrows, now visible from the bridge control tower.

The ship was streaked with grime and rust and salt, the badges of long service. Driving through the churning sea, a glint of sunshine on the curl of water kicked up by the hull, the old ship looked almost jaunty as it plowed its way steadily to port.

The ship and its crew of 14 were making for New Jersey bearing a load of oil. New Jersey was not its usual port of call but the ship had made this run before. Twelve miles out the radio crackled to life.

"Port Authority to Sea Merchant, what is your destination and ETA?"

"Hallo Port Authority, we are expected at Pier 72 - New Jersey. We should arrive in about 2 hours."

"Once you clear the Narrows the harbour pilot will board to assist your docking procedure."

All large ports insisted on their own pilots commanding ships once they entered the tight local confines of port. Local conditions were too difficult to keep up with, even for the most seasoned captain. Using local pilots also help speed the ships into port as they did not have to consult charts or ask as many questions of the movements of other ships.

The Sea Merchant slipped under the Verrazano Narrows bridge and, as promised, it was met by a Port Authority tug. The pilot boarded without incident in the calm waters, said hello to the crew, several of whom he recognized from previous trips. He headed to the bridge and took control.

"Pier 72? That's further up the harbour than usual. I thought you were carrying oil?"

"We are, but it's not for the refinery, it's fuel oil for the Port Authority. Your manifest should show that. You guys pay better than the refineries," the Captain laughed. He was an experienced seaman, and his face showed the life he'd lived, it was sun-baked, wrinkled with cares and sporting its usual two days growth.

The pilot flipped through his papers, "Yep, there it is. Okay, Port 72 it is. It's gonna take us a bit longer. The current in the river is usually pretty strong at this time of year."

"Sea Merchant to Port Authority Base, the ship is due for Port 72 Jersey with fuel oil. I've assumed command. Am proceeding."

The Sea Merchant's captain offered the pilot a steaming mug of coffee.

The ship cleared the Narrows and the pilot turned it toward Staten Island to keep out of the main current. The Jersey shore was so built up with new construction that it almost looked like Manhattan, except Manhattan was right beside it, dwarfing the Jersey side with a certain familiarity thanks to hundreds of establishing shots in films and television shows. The Statue of Liberty grew out of the harbour as the Sea Merchant moved closer to the river narrows. Ellis Island lurked behind it.

It was a lovely, warm late spring day in New York. The local weather was noticeable to the crew once the ship entered the inner harbour where the sea winds no longer held sway.

Everything was proceeding as expected and the pilot turned to take a final swig of coffee. "PA Base, Sea Merchant is moving out into the Harbour heading up river to initiate docking manoeuvres."

He switched the radio frequency to that of the pier's master and ordered the helm to move half turn to starboard which swung the large vessel out into the main section of the Upper Harbour.

The radio crackled. "You are expecting to come in stern first I see. Best to swing a little further up the river and let the current assist with your movement backwards into the north side of the slip. Once half the ship has cleared the river channel the current will have little effect." The pilot could sense the Port Authority controller watching the movements of the ship through binoculars, anticipating his movements and knowing what he would be trying to do.

"Roger that, 72."

The pilot reached past his coffee for the manifest. Three muffled shots thumped out in rapid succession. The pilot fell to the floor with a fourth thump, never aware that his life was in danger.

The captain motioned a few crew members to move the body.

"Allahu Akbar, my brothers. Make your preparations. I will signal you. Do not fail Allah."

Three crew members exited the bridge and made their way quickly into the hold. Under a large hatch they made their mechanism ready. One of the crew went immediately to a large cylinder perched on a cradle. He fiddled with controls embedded in it and then patted it, before moving away.

The Sea Merchant continued on the path set by the now dead pilot moving through the Upper Harbour between the Statue of Liberty and Govenor's Island towards the middle of the Hudson River. It cleared the southern tip of Manhattan.

The captain had increased the ship's speed to maximum and the ship churned against the current, making its way remorselessly up river. Minutes passed.

The radio crackled to life.

"Sea Merchant, you should be reversing engines to initiate your move to stern. Report."

The captain let the message repeat twice before picking up the radio.

"P-72, we have radio problems. Your signal is not clear. Is it time for reverse engines? Please confirm."

The captain reached for the controls and pressed a button which set the hold cover in motion, once engaged it would open up the cargo bay exposing machinery stored under the deck. The whine of the motors hauling the heavy metal cover away from the large opening in the deck could be heard throughout the ship. Several more minutes passed.

The Sea Merchant had cleared the tip of Manhattan and was passing the North Cove Yacht Harbour.

An explosion on the bow stunned the ship. Small explosions and shrapnel ripped through the bridge followed by a roar of jet engines. Two F18s flared out over head, now visible through the shattered glass of the bridge as they made their way up the Hudson. They made to turn for a second pass.

The captain grabbed the internal radio control. "Fire!"

The F18 pilots had located the ship, their first rocket had hit the bow in an attempt to disable the screw. As they passed they saw the opening in the deck. The fighters fired their first close range volley into the control tower to attempt to kill anyone there and further disable the ship. Two Port Authority speed boats were making their way to the Sea Merchant as the jets passed overhead.

Since Rome and the near miss in London the previous year, western port operations were sensitive to anomalies in procedure. The F18s could be on scene within minutes of getting the call. Other defensive measures were also engaged.

The jets wheeled around to challenge the tanker ship again. Both pilots expected to again pepper the control tower, and then swing around to fire rockets at the screw, just under the waterline in the stern. However, both pilots had seen the open hold and the strange contraption inside.

"Shit, Red Leader what was that?" the question was unnecessary as both pilots knew what they faced.

They had to target ship's command and the hold on their second pass. They made calibration adjustments as they turned to bear down on the Sea Merchant.

The planes took deadly seconds to turn around. As the fighters approached the ship, the large metal cylinder in the hold was flung skyward by the contraption it was resting in. The first F18 pilot couldn't target it as he was locked in on the ship and was too close to recalibrate his target. He fired anyway, as he had no other shot. Two rockets exploded against the bridge and two more entered the hold area.

The rockets hit amidships, into the open hatch and exploded convulsing the deck. A small dingy was nestled under the ship's port side and a few men had jumped aboard. Red Leader had seen the men flee the tanker and wondered for a moment what they were doing.

A Port Authority speedboat approached the Sea Merchant and shots pinged off their boat. They returned fire to the deck edge of the ship and swung around the larger cargo ship to see men boarding the dingy. They squeezed off a few rounds before more shots came their way, causing them to duck and take cover as they rounded the bow.

The second fighter pilot was also targeted on the ship but with more time to react as the cylinder rose he flipped quickly to manual and let off a stream of rounds aimed at the cylinder as it climbed into the air. His desperation, coupled with the speed of his jet and proximity to the new target guaranteed his miss.

The metal cylinder, about seven meters in length, and not quite two meters in diameter, glinted in the sun as it slowed, reaching the height of its upward thrust. It looked like someone had flung a piece of sewer pipe into the air.

Some New Yorkers with a view of the river watched the dance between the jets, the ship and its cargo with only the faintest idea of the drama that was occurring. A few knew what they watched and simply held firm, unable to take their eyes off the drama. Most New Yorkers only heard the sounds, which reminded them of the September 11th airplane attack.

The cylinder hung over the river, pausing briefly as it lost the last of its upward momentum and began to fall back to earth. The second F18 pilot exhaled as he banked his plane over the Statue of Liberty and turned towards the Jersey Shore, now two miles away from the river, then three, then four.

The Red Leader F18 pilot had banked the other way over Brooklyn and had turned back toward Manhattan when a sunburst filled his screen. He was flying at nearly the speed of sound directly into a nuclear fireball. He pulled on his controls in a hopeful but ultimately inconsequential attempt to survive.

The second pilot was moving away from the explosion when he saw the flash of light coming from behind. He continued to fly away from the scene waiting for the inevitable shock wave.

As the cylinder rose against the backdrop of Manhattan, the crew screamed "Allahu Akbar". The captain clicked off a text message . . . "It is done." As he pressed 'send', the bomb exploded.

The presence of fighter jets had alerted many New Yorkers to the drama in the Hudson. Many thousands could see the ship and witnessed the attacks from the fighters. Many saw the cylinder rise from the ship and could feel their chests tighten - not really knowing why, but fearing the worst.

The cylinder had reached just over 400 feet in altitude, falling back about 35 feet before exploding. Watching from the upper floors of many Manhattan skyscrapers the skirmish on the Hudson was small and far away given the vast scope of the city spread out beneath them. The cylinder reached up only as high as some of the smaller skyscrapers in its vicinity.

Millions were vaporized as the air itself burned. With temperatures rivaling the center of the sun, metal and glass melted, the water in concrete and mortar boiled and exploded. The air itself was consumed with the resulting shock wave, first pushing everything outward and then rapidly pulling it back in as the air itself rushed in to replace that which was consumed.

The southern half of Manhattan was utterly destroyed. The huge buildings were shattered and tumbled like children's building bricks and what wasn't vaporised was pushed into the East River. Buildings provided a backdrop against which the shock wave pushed and the rubble piled up against rubble. The southern tip of Manhattan was stripped clean. The built up section of the Jersey shore suffered the same fate.

In Mid-Town, Brooklyn and the further Jersey Shore the stripped land gradually gave way to rubble and remains, with construction materials pummelled, crushed and pushed out from the center of the blast. Temperatures set everything on fire with much of the fire damage confined to the fringes of the damage zone leaving Queen's, Brooklyn and large parts of Bayonne, Jersey City and Union City a raging inferno quickly devoid of most of the millions who had lived there.

"New York control to Delta 455 we are handing you over to the JFK Tower - on Radio five - zero -niner. Safe trav . . . "

"Oh my," said the Delta captain as he saw the flash wash across his windshield from the south of his plane's approach. He signalled his co-pilot, "Raise New York control." He began a turn to the south.

"New York this is Delta 455 we just saw a huge flash . . . oh my God," he trailed off, the beginnings of a mushroom cloud were rising in the distance.

"Try them again and if there is no response try JFK."

Still several dozen miles out the pilot quickly swung the 747 northward. He could hear the clatter of flying bodies in the passenger compartment. He scanned his instruments not really knowing what to look for. As the plane flattened out he reached for the public address system.

"I am sorry for the quick turn but there is an emergency situation in New York. Please fasten your seatbelts and let the attendants deal with anyone who is injured. We will not be making any additional rapid turns that I am aware of, but please be prepared for significant turbulence. Remain belted and seated until further notice. There is nothing wrong with the plane and we will be seeking a safe place to land."

Meanwhile the co-pilot had come up with nothing.

As the mushroom cloud rose from the blast - planes coming into New York's three airports had seen the flash in the distance.

"New York control, New York control, do you read?"

"Do we have enough fuel to get to Boston?"

"Can we land in Philadelphia?"

"Switch to the emergency frequency and see what you can pick up. I'll replot us a course for Boston."

"My fuel calibration suggests we don't have enough fuel for Boston, it's a significant backtrack. Are there any other runways nearby that are long enough?"

"I think we can buzz JFK to scope it out and still get to Hartford if it's a problem. We'd have enough room to land there, barely. We may not be able to get it out again, though."

"Not sure we really want to end up in New York anyway, if what I think I'm seeing is for real."

The captain shrugged.

"This is your captain speaking, there has been a problem with New York airports. We will try to get down in the city but we may be forced to another airport. I will keep you posted."

The pilot looked to his co-pilot to see if he acknowledged the rising commotion coming from the passenger cabin. The younger man simply stared straight ahead.

"I think we've gotten past the shock wave, our airspeed increased a fair bit. I think we were far enough out that it was the only effect. Keep trying to raise JFK and maintain the emergency frequency."

The co-pilot tried the standard frequency but didn't even get static. He moved immediately to the emergency frequency.

"All planes New York bound continue on flight paths until further notice," stated a shaky voice. "Planes bound for New York - La Guardia and Newark alter course for New York - JFK and await further instructions."

The captain turned the plane around in a slow sweep after giving his passengers ample warning. They had all seen the mushroom cloud rising dramatically in the distance.

"Delta 455, come in Delta 455," came the request from the radio.

"Emergency air control, Delta 455, come in."

The pilot reached for the radio control. "Emergency Air Control, this is Delta 455 from Paris to JFK New York. We read."

"Delta 455 - good to hear you. Please advise fuel status. Proceed to JFK with Hartford as your back up destination."

"We have enough fuel for that but not much more. Will need landing status in Hartford if we must divert."

"Copy that Delta 455. Proceed to JFK and report. At this time plan for Hartford divert."

They would soon know the status of JFK. The pilot plotted a course to arrive at JFK from the east and swing past it to the north-west. He initiated the wide turn, a complete circle to make his approach as planned. He had planned a nice New York get away on the three day layover. Those plans had changed radically. He glanced at his co-pilot. A younger man, they had flown together for several months. The younger man was ashen. Despite his very deliberate movements on the controls he was shaken deeply. And they still had to get the plane down.

"Josh, you okay?"

The younger man started to talk but he couldn't get his thoughts out. Then he stopped trying, nodded, and just watched the controls.

Chapter Two - Two years later

"Tourists and scavengers. That's what's there."

"What about San Fran?"

"'That's altogether different - different disaster, different future," he said. "They're rebuilding. They figure they've got 100 years until the next one," he laughed. "And all those LA refugees are looking for a place to live."

"I'd like to go to New York, but I wonder what you can actually see. I'm guessing anything that could be moved has been moved - and the rest is derelict. I mean how many Planet of the Apes reactions can you have?" he grinned ruefully.

"I was there. About six months ago. It is interesting . . .for about six hours . . .then its creepy. It's not what you can see that's interesting, it's what you can't, and the little bits of life that have sprung up. Take a tour. First you go by boat and then they take you through Central Park to the Battery. The city actually still functions, well, some of it anyway. Midtown and South Manhattan are giant reclamation projects. The Bronx is largely intact and Brooklyn suffered significant damage, about half is damaged beyond use."

"Is it even worth reclaiming or rebuilding?"

"Oh yes, the city is huge and much of it is intact. It's just got a giant hole in the center now. Remember it is one of the most desirable geographic locations in the world - and now the slate is clean. Hiroshima was rebuilt."

"Ok, New York is solved. What are we going to do about Texas?"

"Solved, not really. The President has some ideas but there are a number of hurdles to jump. Regarding Texas, there is nothing we can do. They've always had the right to secede. Now they are going to exercise it. I'm pretty sure we'll be on good terms though. The real question is, does Oklahoma try to join Texas?"

"If that happens the battles could turn violent. The Red River makes for a natural boundary and frankly, there aren't a lot of natural boundaries around there. If Oklahoma is allowed to go, then what about Arkansas, Louisiana, or at least parts of them? And at least half of New Mexico is already functionally Texas territory."

"The Sabine is our best chance to keep the borders intact. Northern Louisiana has more than a bit of Dixie in it. As for the west, there is little demand for border definition as the area is pretty empty. 'There be dragons', and all that."

The two men, clad in suits, each held a paper coffee cup. They stood in the atrium of a moderately sized, modern glass office building in Washington, capital of the United States of America, once the most powerful country on Earth, now, two years after the destruction of its largest city, truly an E Pluribus Unum - one out of many. Still a nasty opponent in a fight, it had been crippled. It's enemies were taking a longer view.

The last few years had been awash in change. The two men, Pennsylvania Senator Tom Findlay, tall, strongly built, with short dark hair punctuated with a hint of a wave above his brow; and a shorter man, a bit older and impeccably dressed, down to the watch chain crossing into his left jacket pocket was Massachusetts Governor Jim Grange. Both had been Representatives in Congress and had become acquainted then. They still spoke often.

Senator Findley, a confident of the President, was trying to manage the horrendous change to the advantage of the United States, as he intended to run for President in the next election cycle. Governor Grange was interested in the United States but only insofar as Massachusetts was part of it, or what remained of it.

Rome had been similarly attacked before New York so much of both men's efforts were to prepare for future attacks and clean up from the ones that had already occurred.

Poor map drawing after World War One and a failure to recognize festering cultural, religious and historical issues had been major causes of the upheavals that left the world shattered. They had fuelled a movement to a new order of government in North America and ultimately around the world. There remained a sizable number of variables that contributed to the catastrophic change, forcing people like Findlay and Grange to deal with the aftermath and leave the history books to be written decades in the future, when time might provide some perspective.

"And in New York of course there are two types of scavengers. Those on contract with the insurance companies and the 'independent operators' who are looking for metal, and other easily removed valuables," said Findlay.

The world had been changing slowly even as far back as the 1970's and there had been warnings in the scattered violence of embassy attacks, explosions of military personnel and equipment and assassinations. The first seismic shift had occurred on September 11, 2001 with the destruction of the twin towers of the World Trade Center, the two tallest buildings in New York. Despite the shock of that event, the shift continued its movement toward change with grinding slowness, and even though many people could feel that change was happening, a clear vision and understanding of it did not emerge. Murky connections, murky motives and the obvious conclusion of a clash of civilizations continued to be resisted.

Only after the tip of Manhattan had been destroyed by a rudimentary nuclear device on May 29, along with simultaneous attacks on Los Angeles and other US targets, did the world move fully into a new era. It was an era that still had not been completely defined as the endgame for all participants had not been identified much less achieved. A political, cultural and economic equilibrium was still some time in the future. The moving parts of society and civilization had slowed but they were still moving.

It took the United States government only 72 hours to respond. There had been much handwringing and debate on the proper response to the destruction of Rome with little actually happening as a result. The United States had been on hair trigger alert since the nuclear attack on Rome a year before New York, and had issued warnings of dire consequences should an attack on a US target occur. In some circles there had been optimism that the eventual attempt on another western city could be stopped, after all the British had thwarted an attempt on London a few months after Rome.

That optimism was misplaced as ships delivered simultaneous nuclear hits to New York, the US Naval Base at Norfolk Virginia, and Los Angeles within one hour of each other. Within an hour of the attack on New York, defence forces had managed to sink a ship headed to Boston, another headed to San Diego and another in the Gulf of Mexico whose target was believed to be Tampa or New Orleans. In their frenzied defence they sank several ships just to be sure, finding out after the fact that they'd been right about three of them. Intelligence gathering found chatter that San Fran had apparently been spared only because a large earthquake had caused significant damage in that city a few months earlier. The ship bound for Frisco had been diverted to San Diego to target the large naval base in that city but was sunk as it lagged behind the appointed hour of attack.

Islamic State had taken credit for the bombings. So had Hezbollah, Al Qaeda and a dozen other shadowy groups of Muslim fundamentalists.

The bombs were crude. Not that it mattered, but they were flung up in the air several hundred feet essentially by large catapults and then detonated. South and central LA was destroyed in a ring centered on the blast at Long Beach's port facility. It produced a wasteland for several miles inland. Destruction did not quite reach the de facto downtown section of LA located in the north west of the heavily populated Los Angeles basin. Sheer distance and the ring of mountains served to compress the blast effects.

San Diego narrowly avoided the same fate and more importantly was able to retain defense assets of the Pacific Fleet. The damage in Norfolk was not as bad as may have occurred as the ship was challenged as it approached the Naval Station. It detonated on the Atlantic side of the harbour managing to take out thousands of inhabitants and badly damaging two aircraft carriers the USS Forrestal and the USS John F. Kennedy. Several heavy cruisers were also affected. The major issues were with the station which was no longer in any shape to house and refit the Fleet as was required.

Three detonations. Millions killed. Millions more maimed and many more yet to die from radiation. Economies, food, transportation, jobs, livelihoods all destroyed. Truth was, two years on, most of those who would die were already dead. Many thousands were still in temporary housing and were left to their own devices as to what to do with their future. A trickle left each day to start a new life, usually hundreds of miles from where their lives had been put on hold.

With two major cities existing now with holes blown out of their centers and a third urban area also largely destroyed, the United States had undergone convulsions, both in the immediate wake of the attacks and in the months that followed. Two years later the recriminations and finger pointing still had not stopped.

The once mighty United States Dollar had been hammered as the rest of the world began to use other payment methods in the wake of the attacks. The process of countries moving away from the US dollar had already been underway prior to the attacks. Knowing the US treasury would simply print more greenbacks to help the rebuilding process, the once strong dollar had taken a beating.

Within a few months, significant military retaliation had restored some of the faith in the US dollar as the currency of last resort. While the US economy had taken a huge hit, there still remained a giant country and 300 million people to feed, house, and employ. In most of the country it was only the ripple effects from the attacks that had impacted the populace.

In the uncertainty, the financial world shifted its focus to a new unofficial gold standard, with several major currencies pegged to gold and minor currencies floating against the Chinese Yuan and the Swiss Franc. British Pounds, US Dollars and the Euro were forced to peg themselves to something tangible in order to retain their perceived value - they chose silver.

The currency issue was flip flopping about in turmoil almost every week. Though with every wide swing up and down the next swing was smaller until the churning valuations had flattened out.

Washington still controlled much of its former national territory; the Northeast, the Mid-western rust belt, the northern plains and much of the central west. However, Texas chafed under Washington's yoke and invoked their right to secede as Washington refused to clean up or abandon the Federal Reserve system and could not spare the resources to stop illegal immigration.

Without a whimper Washington acceded to the demands of Texans by giving up federal jurisdiction to the Texas legislature but making it easy for Texans to use US currency and other manifestations and institutions of the old US.

Oklahoma was so tied to Texas it wavered on joining with Texas. Northern Texans welcomed them. Southern and western Texans were ambivalent. Similarly southern Oklahomans were very interested in maintaining ties to Texas while other people north of Oklahoma City did not have strong feelings.

Dixie and the Old South had also risen up and effectively succeeded as US senators and other elected officials took to sitting in a Dixie-only legislature concurrent with their US obligations. Succession was being achieved without any grandiose announcement, and was becoming more accepted and permanent with each day the Dixie legislature went unchallenged.

Washington had no ability to attend to the needs of the southern states. Those States had met initially as a southern caucus to get southern Congressmen to put pressure on Washington for help. It soon became evident that Washington couldn't help and the caucus was more of a regional government. It began to take on more and more senior level authority, but it walked a careful line as no independence had been announced. Southern leaders knew the further along they marched the more natural their new regional government would become until it was the de facto national government that it was rapidly becoming.

Florida and western Louisiana were wavering. Dixie could not function fully independently as it simply melted into the United Sates at various places in Virginia. North and eastern Virginia remained with Washington, as federal money was pouring into coastal Norfolk to rebuild. The hoards of federal bureaucrats who populated the southern hinterlands of Washington, extending deep into northern Virginia cemented the US federal government's hold on the region.

The question of Kentucky wasn't settled. Many in the state thought themselves as southerners because they weren't hillbillies and they weren't Yankees. There were significant groups in favour of joining the New South.

Tennessee's two US senators had joined the New South caucus early on. Florida had so many northerners in residence that the State Legislature could not muster enough support to join the New South caucus. Northern

Florida agitated for closer ties with Atlanta. Southern Florida grew closer to Cuba and Mexico thanks to large expatriate populations from both those countries. A significant northern US presence in the south of Florida, from New York retirees to the federal military, kept that part of the state close to Washington.

The central part of the state was very sympathetic with the old US, as many residents had ties to the Northeast, the rust belt and the Upper Mid-west. While there was tension, the federal presence in Florida and a lack of desire for huge change kept official Florida from taking any action at all.

Louisiana was half of a mind to join Texas, and eastern Texans would have taken them. Western Texans were not so sure. The rest of the state liked the idea of a defensible Sabine River border that already existed for most of the distance between the two. The same issue occurred with Oklahoma - a well defined river border already existed but the Oklahomans were functionally more than half Texans anyway. Some Oklahomans were content with Washington while others simply wanted to play Washington and Austin off against each other. Northern Texans cared, others did not and Washington was prepared to do what it took to keep Oklahoma on side.

California was increasingly given over to Mexican influence. The earthquake in San Francisco and the bombings had cowed the Southern California population, many of whom were moving north to the Bay Area or leaving the state. The Latinos had nowhere else they wanted to be and so remained, gathering more and more influence every year. Southern California was becoming functionally a province of Mexico even if it was still part of the crumbling US.

Survivors from southern California were moving up to the San Francisco area despite the earthquake which had spawned fires rendering large areas of the city uninhabitable. The quake, a massive 8.4 on the Richter Scale, left much damage to San Francisco and other cities surrounding the

Bay though outside of San Francisco damage was limited to smaller areas and older buildings.

The biggest consequence of the quake, was a huge change in the local topography isolating the City of San Francisco. The fault had opened up a fissure between San Andres Lake and the Bay just north of San Mateo. The fissure continued northwest until it connected the southern bay to the Pacific Ocean just north of Pacifica. Effectively San Francisco was an island. As in 1906, San Francisco had been greatly damaged by fire. This time though fire damage was contained more effectively leaving a huge clean up, and many damaged and destroyed buildings. However, much of the city was repairable given enough time and resources.

The business center of the US had shifted to Chicago in the wake of the destruction of Manhattan. Certain economic activity still occurred in New York but it was small scale and mostly local - dealing with the needs of the surviving locals and with the clean up and rebuild of the city.

The US response to the attack had been a rain of death to those nations which appeared culpable. Within 72 hours of the bombings, Mecca, Medina, and Riyadh were smoking ruins. After warnings given a year earlier after the destruction of Rome and the near miss on London the US government and its western allies had agreed that any further attacks would set off a chain of retribution.

The US government provided 48 hours notice of the imminent attack, quickly pulled out American personnel, and rained nuclear destruction on Tehran, Tabriz and a number of other Iranian cities. NATO also announced its retribution policy was still in effect for nations connected in any way to future attacks.

The Israelis had already destroyed Karachi, Islamabad and a dozen other large cities and several dozen small cities in the aftermath of the Tel Aviv attack which occurred at the same time as the one on Rome. Israelis identified the weapons as being of Pakistani construction though they were less sure exactly who delivered them.

Given the small size of the country Israel itself was mostly a wasteland after the nuclear attacks, with only a small number of Israelis holding out. But they were heavily fortified and bunkered in and were essentially immovable - heavily armed, willing on a hair trigger to launch more nuclear weapons. Nearby nations, battling their own problems, gave them a wide berth, essentially forgetting about them as much of the land between them was poisoned desert. News reports throughout the Muslim world reported the bombing of Israel and suggested the country was no more, and had become simply a nuclear no-go zone. It's enemies celebrated its destruction and the world moved on, more concerned about other issues.

As expected, in the aftermath of the attack on Israel, western nations merely hummed and hawed, issued statements of condemnation and did nothing. They had long before come to the conclusion there was almost nothing that could be done as the necessary deed of complete eradication of the enemy was not on the table and anything less was only further provocation. Little did they realize that no further provocation was necessary.

In the wake of the eventual reprisals after the attack on the US, Muslim nations that cried foul were warned once with a general warning that any retaliation in any form would be met with a hugely disproportionate response. The threat served to quiet what was left of that cultural belief system. Mosques in the US and most of western Europe were under significant scrutiny; tracing worshippers, their backgrounds, those who preached and their travel histories. The process was begun to deport non-citizen Muslims out of the US, France, Germany and the UK. Mosques with ties to violent or incendiary leaders were closed and torn down.

Americans had a difficult time rationalizing their decision to reduce the footprint of Islam. With a long history of separation of church and state and religious freedom and tolerance it was only when they realized Islam was not tolerant of them, did they turn.

First all non-citizens from a range of nations were expelled. That many of these nations were Islamic in nature or deed was not coincidental. No citizens of those nations were allowed to travel to the United States and soon after Canada, and the United Kingdom. Demanding that citizens of specific countries, rather than members of a specific religion be under the ban, did the trick to quell the inevitable liberal backlash and the public easily shifted their approach.

That left the US with time and space to rebuild. Rome was a ghost town - the Catholic Church was uncertain of its future given that most of the curia had been vaporized. The Cardinals had met in Avignon, France to raised eyebrows around the world. The remaining Cardinals decided to let the issue of Rome stew for a while and had elected the aging Silviano Piovanelli the Cardinal of Florence as Pope to preside over the regrouping period.

The British had completely reversed their immigrant programs emptying out their inner cities. They had deported any non-citizens from any countries other than Canada, the United States, Australia, New Zealand or South Africa or India. All citizens who were not born in the UK became subject to carrying identification papers and submitting to bi-monthly meetings with immigration control to ascertain their employment status and financial health. Citizenship could be revoked in extreme cases but the British never used that provision, they just pressured those without means to leave the country.

The British Navy and Air Force conducted constant patrols of Britain and all approaching ships were stopped at sea and inspected prior to being allowed within the 12 mile international limit. The British had scuttled two ships after inspections and had turned away several others. One ship had been commandeered and taken into Portsmouth under Naval super-vision where it was stripped and eventually sold for scrap. The govern-ment would only say that it was a military convoy and contained offen-sive weapons and war making material. Some speculated about another nuclear attempt, others about chemical or biological weapons meant for activist groups within the country.

Most of the western world remained nervous and wavering in their commitment to significantly liberal positions. The pendulum had swung, but as is usually the case, it had swung back a long way.

Chapter Three New York

"That is the price we paid for electing a closet Muslim bent on ending US dominance in the world," said Tom Findlay, US Senator from Pennsylvania, looking at the ruin of Manhattan. He was standing on the upper deck of a tourist boat which ferried the curious to the old crossroads of the world - Manhattan. People were cautioned to remain on the island for only a few hours to avoid residual radiation. Most of them wanted to go much sooner than that.

Jim Grange looked at Findlay, "Tom, I know that everyone believes that but I'm not so sure we just didn't believe that unicorns and rainbows really would result from refusing to be world police."

"What is, is. People in decades to come are going to try to put this together. We lived it. We have some responsibility to at least call it as we see it."

"History will be written by whoever remains. All these years of turmoil between catastrophic events will be compressed into their essence - any nuance we struggle with today will be squeezed out of future accounts. After our retaliation I'm not sure we've won but we certainly hammered them back to the 7th century. They will be there for a long while."

"Problem is, in a lot of ways, they were already there."

"It's like a donut," said the Governor of Massachusetts. "New York is a city with the center blown out of it. It's really a series of peripheral ring cities now."

"You've got to stop talking like that. It's in our best interests to rebuild New York. To do that we have to keep it functioning while we reorient the city and clean up the damage."

"It might be in Washington's best interest. It might even be in Pennsylvania's best interest to restore New York, but many New Englanders believe it is not in their best interest."

"Washington can be persuasive."

"Come on, Tom. I'm not a Dixiecrat but all those threats do is force more people to want to end Washington's control. I'm walking a very narrow tightrope here, my friend. My Senators and those Senators in New Hampshire, Maine and Vermont are calling for a regional meeting. They've stopped short of caucus, but the intent is there. And look how that worked out in the South. I see the benefits of staying with Washington but they are not immediate, there is a cost, and the benefits are increasingly more difficult to defend in that light. Especially if Washington is determined to throw its weight around. People will not forget the idea to turn Boston into a Naval station. Expropriation on that scale would start a second revolution."

"That's what I'm trying to prevent Jim. We need to fill the hole in the donut and restore New York to its central function - the lynchpin of the Northeast. A naval station there makes good sense once we work out the insurance payouts and land ownership issues. Without rebuilding New York, I'm afraid the center will not hold and New England, Pennsylvania, Virginia and the old mid-west will be flung off the merry-go-round, more interested in their own local agendas than the greater national agenda. Remember, E Pluribus Unum."

"I hear you. But I must admit, I never quite got that; E Pluribus Unum - 'One Out of Many' or is it 'Out of Many, One'. That's two very different things and is dependent on punctuation, something the Latin doesn't emphasize. Anyway the local agenda is all anyone wants to fix. Why not make New York a Naval Station? Or at least Jersey. It's a good idea. Military is about the only possible use for the next 50 years - even if the danger is gone I think people will want to avoid the area."

"Hiroshima bounced back pretty quickly. I do like the Naval Station idea. Can you find a quick way to unravel all the property and insurance claims?"

"An 'Act of War' takes care of the insurance claims and a declaration of 'Eminent Domain' should take care of the property claims. Grease the complainers with a few bucks to settle their more litigious natures and voila - Clam Harbour, Atlantic Naval Station - NYC."

Findlay let that one go. However, he thought, maybe it was not as crazy an idea as it first seemed.

After leaving the Bronx the tour boat chugged slowly toward the shattered Brooklyn Bridge, its tall piers still standing but its bridge deck damaged beyond use. The hulk of the United Nations building, its windows all shattered stood behind the bridge piers. The building had been sheltered from the direct effects of the explosion by the large number of buildings between it and the epicenter.

"I can't say as I am sad to see that go. The bridge will be rebuilt but the UN never worked as advertised."

A number of recognizable hulks remained in southern Manhattan. The bomb that had been detonated had been flung up in the air about 400 feet, according to investigators, from a boat that was just off the western side of Manhattan near the North Cove Yacht Harbor south of Vesey Street.

The blast had been deflected by the huge buildings on Manhattan which had spared much of the Bronx and Brooklyn. Southern Manhattan was blown out. While some great hulks remained in Mid-Town they were lifeless. They were being torn down one-by-one with the materials used where they could be for rebuilding that was taking place.

The construction and deconstruction industries boomed.

One advantage of the destruction that nobody talked about was the terrible loss of life. It was estimated that 7.3 million people were killed by the blast or in the immediate aftermath. There was no need to find, feed, or otherwise care for all those people. Unfortunately many were the best and brightest in their fields in the world. Medical research, finance, business, entertainment were all hugely affected by the loss of talent and skill.

Most people were incinerated immediately. Hundreds of thousands succumbed to injuries and hundreds of thousands died quickly from massive radiation exposure. Thousands more died in the following few months from lingering radiation. It was expected that many who had survived would have much shorter lives. A surprising number had survived without any problem as they were buried in debris which shielded them from the fallout. Survivors of the initial blast, many of these people had died days or weeks later as their supplies ran out and nobody was able to find them.

As building hulks were torn down and removed it was not unusual to find knots of these short term survivors buried with access to supplies in New York's underground shopping areas. One or two had even emerged alive several weeks after the blast.

The boat tied up at the pier and the tourist groups disembarked. Grange and Findlay, each accompanied by a security man discretely following behind, and an aide walking with them; started toward Central Park. They were headed for the Metropolitan Museum of Art on Fifth Avenue.

The building had been stripped of artifacts but being on the park side of

Fifth Avenue, and having a low profile, it stood out as a landmark in a cityscape which had almost become devoid of them. Lower Manhattan was a no go zone, except for a few routes that tour companies used and a few deconstruction roads that scavengers used.

"Washington wants to restore the Museum as soon as possible. A symbol of New York and the renaissance we expect in the next 10-20 years," said Findlay.

"You can rebuild if you want but not on the backs of Massachusett's tax-payers," said Grange. "Already Washington's tax plans are causing some to start talking of throwing tea into the harbor."

"I wish you people could see the big picture . . . "

"We can," interrupted Grange, "the US dollar is nearly dead. Now that the initial shock of all this cleared the US dollar started to decline against other major currencies and it hasn't stopped. Only the Chinese are keeping it from complete collapse and they have less and less reason to do it."

"It's still the world's reserve currency," said Findlay weakly.

"It was used primarily for international oil payments and those have essentially ceased. Oil has become a local business to almost everyone - even us."

"The Texans have pledged to use it, and they . . . "

"The Texans will use it out of convenience for a few years. They will move away from it once things settle down as well. I'm told the Texas buck will be pegged to the dollar so both are usable for payments. They will go away from the US dollar as soon as it makes sense. Dixie will do the same thing. They just haven't thought it all out yet. Mayor Gentle has already said the South is all about local governance and keeping out of Washington's shadow. Can't think of a more shade producing thing than the dying dollar."

"Look Jim, I am trying to keep the Union together, at least the parts of the

Union that can be mutually beneficial. I doubt very much there will be any open hostility between parts of the old country and maybe we can put it back together again."

"I would keep that last wish very quiet if you value your office," said Grange. "Too many people are dead set against that, at least in the former way it was put together. You might get some traction on a looser alliance."

"Work for your own constituents first and then for the larger whole, keeping in mind those people who put their trust in you," said Grange. "That's my advice. We are outside of normalcy bias. If we don't do that people are apt to react quite unexpectedly. In my world a lot of people are blaming this on Washington's lack of foresight."

The group toured the building waiting for a delegation from Long Island to arrive after a tour of the demolition sites.

"Why do they say they are from Long Island?"

"They don't want to be identified with Brooklyn. Brooklyn was destroyed in the blast about two miles inland and another two miles away from Manhattan due to fires, and the ensuing fire storm. Sections in the south and east are still functioning, in fact almost back to some kind of normal. Queens is okay but they all want to be out of New York - for appearances. People there are calling their town Hampton, and lumping in all the functional sections of the Island. Brooklynites are not bucking the trend."

"Look here come the Islanders. Oh, and that's Mike Stile with them, he's about all that's left of Jersey City. It was destroyed in the blast too, just nobody noticed for two months until old Mike returned from an extended vacation with the US government - he spent two years upstate for embezzling. Nobody takes him seriously - but he was the brother-in-law of the mayor - rest his soul. He thinks he has some authority but he's all that's left of the place."

Once the two groups mingled for a short time they all stepped inside where a large entry hall had been rebuilt.

"Thank you all for coming," said Tom Findlay. "I am here at the request of the US government to kick off the rebuilding and restoration of this world renown museum, a centerpiece in our efforts to restore Manhattan, and ultimately New York as one of the pre-eminent cities in the world."

The delegates clapped quietly.

Chapter Four   **New Jersey**

"They're moving the plant to Mexico. They will close us down in 15 months."

He hung his head. It wasn't the hard times ahead that caused his feeling of defeat and resignation, it was the hard work he put in that was now trickling away. He had seen most of the neighbours take a hit, lose one job or sometimes two, each time finding something that paid less while grinding them down more. Cheryl was always upbeat, but he knew that she was worried.

"Called everyone into the loading dock - Preston got up on a couple of skids and told everyone. He cried. Said it was the decision of the board of directors. Either reduce our labour costs, move, or go out of business."

"He cried? What about him? Has he lost his job?"

"Yeah, I think he has, though he'll likely be kept on longer than the rest of us. I did hear some talk of an employee group resurrecting the plant. We'll be competing with Mexico but at least we could sell our stuff as American made."

"I'll give you credit, you told the Union guys this would happen," she said.

"Yeah, and they thought they won when they got all the company concessions in the last contract."

"It's not like we're the first on the street to have to find something new, heck we might be the last. The Henderson's have both had to look more than once and Gerry around the corner has probably had four jobs in the last three years."

"This one-way free trade with China and Mexico, neither of which have labour standards or environmental standards, is killing our manufacturing. They have an endless pool of low skilled underemployed and they can pay peanuts as they don't have to finance any concessions to labour."

"Preston even told us our jobs could be reclaimed in Mexico but the pay would be lower and the benefits essentially gone. We all are supposed to receive a payout based on years of service, but I think it's just the standard package."

"It's one thing to get done in by the destruction of New York and the loss of five million customers, it's another thing entirely to lose to government policy," said Cheryl. "This whole downward spiral has got to be obvious to the politicians. Why don't they reverse course?"

"I'd guess that while it isn't working to prop up the previous system, it is working to create a new one, and it's that endgame that policy makers want. They want a new system. You have to admit, the cost of many things has dropped considerably, especially if you take inflation into account. Electronics, cars, most manufactured goods are very inexpensive compared to 20 or 30 years ago. Put tariffs on goods coming into the country and all of a sudden nobody could afford a smart phone, or a microwave, a television set or a vacuum cleaner. And the Chinese would be particularly upset as their whole economy is dependent on selling things to us."

"But what's the end game? asked Cheryl. "How are we going to keep everyone contributing to the economy?"

"There is a shift into new types of employment and a shift into small business. In the end, changes to the tax code, changes to commodity prices and changes in attitude among Americans will create a new economic reality. Already most young people realize that jobs are not for life, that marketable skills matter and the soft liberal arts degrees are of little value in the new economy. The soft jobs those people used to fill are still necessary, though at a reduced rate of pay. The real bottom falls out of the economy when people can no longer afford to pay the taxes that keep the soft government services coming. It's a quality of life thing, as those taxes allow for social engineering to provide those services to everyone. It's why the poorest pauper lives better than the mightiest king of a 1,000 years ago. The problem is, the hard working guy who is looking to provide a bit more for his family is stymied by much less opportunity. It creates a haves and have-not world rather than the sliding scale of success our economy used to have, with lower middle, middle and upper middle classes, for want of a better description."

"Well, thank god we managed to get this far along, two kids through college, the house paid for, some money in the bank, before the roof caved in," Cheryl said. "We'll manage."

Hank went back to the plant the next day. Several of the guys scheduled for the morning shift simply didn't appear. Hank was irritated but not surprised. As shift foreman he made a few quick calls and got a couple of guys in to cover - he put on a pair of goggles as well and jumped into the line.

The talk at morning break was pretty bleak. Most of the guys were determined to hang on to the bitter end, knowing they would be hard pressed to find anything better, especially those who'd been around the longest. A couple figured it was an early, forced retirement and were worried about the company's commitment to their pension funds. Some of the young guys were talking of heading back to school to upgrade skills.

"After what I've learned here, I figure I could learn to be an electrician pretty quick. There's good money in that," chirped Ethan Robertson, who'd only been working at the plant since he graduated high school a year before.

"Good idea E, its gonna take you a while, but it will pay off. Me, I'm screwed. Not enough time in to retire, and a bunch of bills to pay that won't go away. I knew I shouldn't have bought that fishing boat this summer. She sure was sweet though. Maybe I can sell it and go back to fishing off the dock."

"Hey Mark-man, you got that thing used, so you should be able to turn it over for pretty much what you paid for it. Unless you're gonna go fishing for a living. You know a little guide work, maybe a fishing school, fishing products. Next thing you know you'll have a fishing show on local cable. You can show us how to cook 'em too. You'll be huge."

The older man laughed, "Humm, I hadn't thought of that. I'll need a company name and a name for the show - how about 'The Fishin' Marksman'? - you know, me zoning in on all them swimming dinners."

The whole group laughed. Maybe it wasn't going to end up so bad thought Hank. Change is always difficult but it does bring opportunity. Some of these guys would come out the other side of the change as winners, some as survivors and a few as losers. He just hoped he wasn't one of the losers.

"Back to work, boys. You don't want to piss off the foreman. I heard he's a real bastard."

As they were walking back across the plant floor, Paul the sub-foreman walked with Hank. "You know little Ethan is on to something. Each guy just has to assess the situation and make some adjustments. I'm hearing more about a possible employee run company - Preston is asking around. Seems he wants to get into the more high tech electronic products. Stuff like retina scanners, basic smart phones with a limited array of uses for normal people that only use them for a few things."

"Yeah, like me. I'm not sure I like the idea of nodding toward the cash register in order to pay. With the way Cheryl looks at stuff to buy these retina scanners could cost me a lot of money. Cheryl loves to window shop. With a retina scanner, just thinking about buying something is going to put it in your pocket," he laughed.

"Well we've got 15 months to figure it out. That's some time. You got any ideas, Hank?"

"No, not yet. It's really hit me hard. I've been around here a while. One side of me knew this would happen and the other hoped I would dodge the bullet. Too busy living day to day to think too much about the bad stuff. Now it's here and I can't get my head around it yet. Best not to panic. A few months with a new mindset should do wonders for my clarity of thought."

"I'm liking the employee owned company idea. Guess I gotta hear the details first. Like how much less they are going to pay us . . . I mean, how much less we are going to pay ourselves."

"Time will put a bit of meat on the bone for all of us. We'll have a better idea of what will work best for us. You know, some of the near-retirees might be best to move to Mexico and finish up their service time even at a much reduced rate of pay. Even me. I'm a few years removed from it likely making sense, but you have to consider all the possibilities. Don't want to dismiss anything without knowing how it might work."

"Hey, I heard that the board of directors might lend Preston some capital to get things going?"

"What? So they'd own the new company?"

"I guess. Or maybe they are just talking to keep the rest of us from revolting. They are still 15 months away from moving their production to Mexico. Gotta keep the natives happy."

Chapter Five   Atlanta

"Ms. Gentle? Ambassador Rodriquez on the phone. I think it's the Mexican Rodriquez."

"Thank you, I'll take it in my office," she moved around the big desk, a view of downtown Atlanta spread out before her, thanks to the two-storey windows behind her formal desk. She hated taking calls sitting at the desk. She preferred to stand and if necessary to match her verbal jockeying in conversation with her movements around the spacious office.

"Hello Ambassador, tell me good things about your country," she said cheerily into the phone, gazing out over the city.

"Ah, Ms Gentle, the City Cathedral of Mexico is no longer sinking, according to recent measurements. It appears as if our water table issues have been solved for now."

"Well, that is nice to hear Mr. Ambassador. I can share with you that our decision to build an underground freeway should alleviate much of the traffic congestion we currently face. Phase One should be built in about five years and the whole thing will be fully completed in 10. Of course that's what the engineers tell me, I'm guessing it will take considerably longer."

"That is good, that is good. I look forward to a more restful way to get into your great metropolis for a visit."

The Mexican ambassador was a genial type. An old world businessman who had spent much of his time in Spain and Argentina where he represented family business interests prior to his political appointment. He had made himself known to governors and big city mayors in an effort to smooth local relations for Mexico and various commercial interests.

"Ms. Gentle, I am calling today on a delicate matter."

"I imagine that all ambassadorial conversations are delicate."

"They usually are," he replied. "Today is particularly so. I have heard through diplomatic channels that your Dixie is about to announce a complete break with the US dollar. We in Mexico are particularly concerned about the pressure that announcement would have on our US dollar holdings and our trade agreements. Mexico respectfully requests that you do not completely break with the US dollar but that you take your exit one stage at a time - in the manner of Texas."

She made a face that the ambassador could not see through the telephone. She had not heard any such rumor and knew she would be privy to such talk should it be occurring.

"I think you should be speaking to our Assembly Speaker, Mr. Vernon Clemons."

"Ah, Ms. Gentle, that is the delicacy I referred too."

"Mr. Ambassador, I see. You refer to Mr. Clemons remarks of yesterday?" She paused.

"I can assure you that Mr. Clemons will act in the manner best for the people of Dixie. He has a long term view. Surely you have made your concerns known to him."

"We have, Ms. Gentle, at several levels of government. However, Dixie is not an official country, yet. We have no formal process. That is why I have called you, one of the few officials in official government that I know well. In all cases Mr. Clemons has said that he will act only for the people of Dixie and as you may have heard in the video of his remarks, and I quote, 'If the god damn Mexicans want it - it can't be good for Dixie' end quote. We were hoping that you would have some insight you could share or might be willing to take our concerns directly to him."

Anne Gentle breathed in deeply and audibly. It wasn't the first contact she had had regarding the 'national' issues of Dixie. Clemons was notoriously impolitic and determined. The fact he was not a politician probably had something to do with it. She found herself playing Dixie politics even though she was only a mayor. The mayor of the most important city in Dixie, true, but not able to speak for the whole emerging country. Only Clemons could do that and he was particularly circumspect - he believed that time would grant Dixie its sovereignty not bold declarations or sabre-rattling. Not that the Yankees were likely to burn Atlanta, but there was a history, and as he would say, it is possible to be burned without fire.

"I can speak to Mr. Clemons but he will want something for his consideration on this." She went out on a limb, "I expect he will demand recognition by the governments of Mexico, Spain, Chile and Argentina. I'd throw in Portugal and Brazil too, as that's what he'd ask for, but I think he'd settle for the first four."

"You know I do not have the power to compel Spain, Chile or Argentina, or even Mexico for that matter. I have already acted for Spain in their concerns about Dixie but I do not speak for them, I only convey what they ask of my government."

"Of course. And I cannot speak for Mr. Clemons but I can convey what I know to him. I will speak to him. Can I say Mexico will diplomatically recognize the independent government of Dixie? Can I say you will speak through diplomatic channels to Spain, Chile and Argentina?"

The ambassador drew in his breath. "Yes. For a slow withdrawal from the US dollar, of at least a decade in duration, Mexico will make such a declaration. I will speak to the others but they have fewer concerns with the status of the US dollar."

"Once these negotiations have been completed. You will need to meet with Mr. Clemons. I can assure you he is actually a very nice man. I expect that his somewhat inflammatory remarks were caused by something that touched him off," Mayor Gentle said.

"Perhaps you might arrange a less formal meeting in advance. Even a chance encounter at a grand opening or something might be all that is necessary?"

"An idea Mr. Ambassador. Perhaps I can put something together. How committed are you. Do you have a preferred time line?"

"For you Ms Gentle, I am available whenever you require."

Roaming around her office during the conversation she now found herself right up against the window. She walked back to her desk chair and turned it around to face the window with the sweeping view of Atlanta. She sat down. She smiled knowing that the Ambassador would do just about anything to keep her door open in his quest to improve relations between Mexico and the Dixie.

"I will be in touch Mr. Ambassador."

A large aircraft, slid across the sky at the top of her view through the double storey windows. It left a contrail behind it, obviously flying very high. Every time she saw such a plane, she wondered why planes would fly over airports rather than fly around them. Obviously it was the three dimensional nature of flight paths at work, but was the savings in flying direct worth the danger of being so near? And she wondered, at what point in distance from the airport did the altitude of arrivals and departures from the airport intersect with the high flying passersby?

She turned back to her desk and began to look for Clemons private telephone number.

Chapter Six   Buffalo

It could work thought Peter O'Neill. Almost 50, dapper, coiffed, he was standing in an abandoned warehouse on the Lake Erie waterfront. Tall, spidery with a full head of thinning hair, he stood in the muted light in an overcoat and stylish but sensible shoes with good thick soles. He had visited enough industrial buildings to know a bit of extra sole was often the difference between a slight misstep and an injury.

His wife liked him well dressed, always insistent that he would get additional respect from whoever he encountered merely for wearing nice clothes. In his younger days he had pushed back against such elitist notions, nowadays he dressed the part instinctively no matter where he was expected to be. And as she said, you never knew what you would encounter at an industrial site, even one long abandoned. Thick soles were insurance against things he might walk on. The dapper appearance insurance for things he wanted to walk over.

"It won't take much to get this going again," he thought, looking around. A few machines and viola, a cold rolled steel finishing plant. He had already made arrangements to get new production from Dofasco across the border in Hamilton, and was in talks with US Steel which owned the old Hilton Works in that city and the more modern Nanticoke Steel plant across the lake.

"There is going to be a huge demand for steel when it comes time to re-build," he said to his wife of 24 years, standing beside him. "Now all I have to do is get the scrap steel from New York City to Buffalo. We'll be rich."

"We're already rich," she said.

"Okay, we'll be richer. It's kind of a figure of speech."

"Is that necessary?"

"No, but I like the sound of it. It's that eureka moment that everyone wants to have. Anyway, we will be doing our part to rebuild. Somebody has to do it and somebody will make money doing it. It might as well be us. We can put it into philanthropic works of our own choosing."

"Okay," she said, "as long as our own choices are effective choices for the community."

"Absolutely, I see it now, the Peter and Amanda O'Neill Cancer Center of Greater New York City."

She made a face.

"Okay, the Amanda and Peter O'Neill Cancer Center of Walla Walla, Washington," he joked.

"How can you even make jokes about other people's suffering?"

"It isn't a joke about suffering, it's a joke about you and I don't think you are suffering. At least not too much, except perhaps with my optimism." He smiled sweetly.

"You have to be aware of how other people perceive your words, that's all."

"Believe me they will perceive my words very well when I hire them for hundreds of new jobs here in Buffalo and for the medical facilities we build in Manhattan. In fact, Senator Findlay has already conveyed his appreciation and invited us to the White House to meet with the President."

That stopped her in her tracks.

Peter O'Neill wandered around the property taking stock of all the necessities of the site. He figured they could be in production in three months. He had already put plans in place to buy the scrap from Norfolk and New York.

The O'Neill's had been residents of New York City, the east side of Mid-Town actually, but had been on holiday in the south of France when the big bang came. Most of their possessions, their friends and some of their business interests were destroyed in the explosion.

Peter O'Neill had been well insured but the payouts were minimal as the destruction was ruled an act of war, and there really wasn't much dispute. He had managed to diversify their holdings outside of New York in the wake of the Rome disaster and had largely completed that process. They lost a small manufacturing plant and adjoining warehouse in Brooklyn and of course their east Mid-Town apartment and much of their lifetime collection of stuff.

Their lack of interest in material goods meant that the most devastating loss was their photo collection and a few bits and pieces of memorabilia from their travels that could not be replaced.

They had moved to Buffalo after a time in a holiday home they owned in the Finger Lakes near Watkins Glen.

It had been many months waiting for litigation to be solved, for various government agencies to figure out how to resettle all the internal refugees.

"When do we go to Washington? Amanda asked as they reached their car to leave.

"Tomorrow we'll drive down and we are expected at the White House the next day and at a gala event celebrating rebuilding efforts the evening after that. We can do a bit of sight seeing."

He looked at his watch.

"Right now we are meeting with the Mayor to see if he can grease the rebuild of the plant and ease rezoning requirements. One part of our site had been rezoned parkland but he said the other day he thought he could have that shifted. He said something about the Mayor of Fort Erie, the Ontario city on the other side of the Niagara River, joining us in the meeting."

Chapter Seven   Texas

The land was parched. Heat waves roiled up from the ground making it look much hotter than it actually was. The land rolled away to meet with small plateaus before rolling away again.

Jeb Ryan spat. He always hated the dust clouds that followed his pickup and then caught up to it and engulfed it when he rolled to a stop at this time of year. He waited for it to settle in the heavy air. There were a few cattle in the distance and a bit of dust kicked up in the air over yonder hill which indicated some of his herd were in the dell beyond it.

Exiting the truck he wandered over to a little blackened pile surrounded by a few rocks. Obviously the remains of a campfire and it looked like it had been out for a couple of days, no rain had muted the embers and it last rained only three days before. The rocks were unusual as they were fairly large and not really native to the immediate area. Smooth and rounded they must have been hauled here from the dry riverbed about two miles south. Almost as if the haulers had known they would need them and known they would be back again to use them. Hauling those stones was a lot of work and not likely to be undertaken for a single traveller.

Jeb poked around the site and soon saw the tell tale signs of illegals. A wrapper with Spanish written on it. A discarded water bottle from Mexico.

He shook his head. The illegals had stopped coming briefly in the wake of the bombings but had picked up again as California had stopped prosecuting them. He wondered why so many still moved through Texas, figuring that it must be that it was the established route they were familiar with. And not everyone wanted to go to California, especially the California that existed now. There weren't a lot of jobs available in the barrios of South Central anymore.

Ryan moved back to his truck and started to roll down the dirt track towards his cattle when there was a noise and the herd started toward him. These runs were something he enjoyed as the cattle moved in unison until they ran out of energy. He waited until the stampede had passed on both sides of his truck before moving toward the hill where they had started.

Then he saw them - about a half mile off - a small group of travellers surrounding a slaughtered cow.

He wasn't sure what to do as he had never caught them red-handed before. He pulled his shotgun from under the passenger seat and took aim through his window. He was still several hundred yards away and the illegals had been too interested in their prize to notice his truck. He fired. The buckshot wouldn't kill anyone from this distance but it might inflict a couple of nasty wounds as the little pellets found their mark in ones and twos.

The shot caught the group and they started to run. There really wasn't anywhere to go in the vast open country. Jeb made a quick call to the local sheriff and simply trailed the travellers at a distance in his truck.

Half an hour later the sheriff caught up to him and after a couple of quick questions went after the slowest of the escapees. He bound them hand

and foot and moved off after the next group. Within 90 minutes he moved backwards to round up the bound fugitives.

He explained to them what would happen, even though none acknowledged understanding English, he could see the tell tale signs that they understood. A twist of the head, a movement of the lips and a raised eyebrow gave him all the evidence he needed to know they understood him.

"First you will be processed, photographed and fingerprinted. If anyone is found trying to enter Texas again they will face much stronger penalties than simply being deported," the usual spiel triggered the usual low level of awareness.

"I warn you all now, with the new government of Texas taking on this matter at the first of the year, penalties will likely be much harsher. I understand ranchers will be deputized and allowed to shoot to kill anyone on their land without permission."

At that several eyes lids were raised, confirming that most of this group understood English as well as he did.

Texas was through playing by Washington's rules. Alamo dollars were being used in conjunction with the US dollar. The legislature had set up the currency backed by several million acres of Texas ranch land. The ranch was operated by the state and profits of the enterprise were the only way new currency could be created. It gave the Alamo buck some credibility and its relative rarity compared to US dollars led to its rapid acceptance in Texas as a legitimate currency. Outside of Texas it was viewed with suspicion, kinda like discount coupons with an expiry date and limited acceptance.

Jeb continued his drive around his large spread. Everything else seemed in order though he did find two more spots where illegals likely camped. There was no evidence of animal remains leaving him at least pleased about that. There was talk and a few news reports that more Mexicans were surfacing in Florida having crossed the Gulf. So far that news had produced only a low level hum but it was something that might cause more fissures in the old governing structure.

Jeb was due in San Antonio the next day for a meeting of large landowners. They were interested in getting Texas to commit to a more robust plan to keep out illegal immigration. While they all liked the idea that they had the state's blessing to shoot interlopers on sight, they were looking for ideas that kept their costs down, enforcement up and had a bit less room for interpretation. The former laws of the US, its politically correct policies and long time efforts to discourage but not punish law breakers had wormed their way in deep to even the Texan's psyche.

Certainly the shoot on sight rules had made a difference. Jeb wasn't opposed to the approach, he just wanted to know what to do with the bodies and who to give the survivors to. Deep down he knew it was a human migration, almost unstoppable and that until Mexico was able to produce a more equitable society, where opportunity and economic mobility was increased, people would flock north for a better life. He just didn't want them flocking at his and his herd's expense.

"I'm going to have to shoot somebody dead and then send the survivor's back with the message," he thought to himself. "Why don't they just cross into California - there is only a token barrier there now anyway."

He had heard stories of the migration into southern California. It was a ragged society but a resilient one that was scavenging Los Angeles for scrap and rebuilding. The migrations had caused significant numbers of people of European extraction to move north into the overcrowded areas around San Francisco Bay. San Francisco itself was a mess, being rebuilt by Europeans from the outside in, with big money being made in reprocessing materials and manufacturing housing.

Of course there was a huge loss of life in the nuclear blast in LA and the preceding earthquake in San Francisco. Millions more died in Southern California within six months of the blast. In Los Angeles more than five million were vaporized with an additional 3 million dying within six months. The death toll from the San Francisco earthquake was a more modest 42,000 split between those who died in building collapses and those who died in the ensuing firestorm.

Southern California had experienced a creeping Mexicanism. While it still operated as part of the US - its southern border remained virtually open. It was anchored by the Naval Station in San Diego, but virtually all positions of influence were held by Hispanics. San Diegans of European extraction were fewer and fewer as the Hispanic influence grew, it pushed out the European influence as people felt there was little future in the area. The idea of Aztlan, an Hispanic California homeland, seized by the United States in the California gold rush, and now ripe to be seized back, was strong amongst the working population.

Central and Northern California were still American in spirit but people there had more of a "Don't Tread on Me" approach than even the independence minded Northern Californians that had existed before the upheavals.

The Bay Area was a cauldron of independence, Yankee ingenuity, California entitlement and a fierce determination to not be southern Californian. The battle lines were being drawn along the southern boundaries of Monterrey, Kings, Tulare and Inyo counties. It wasn't terribly defensible but the counties were already on a map and formed the boundary in the mind of most people. There were a number of people in the southern sections of those counties that were flying the California Republic state flag where they might have flown the Stars and Stripes. Functionally Mount Pinos served as a forward border point with the Mohave Desert being firmly in the South even though it was partly in Inyo County. At almost 2,700 feet in height, Pinos provided a good aerial observation point and an obvious outpost. Drones did much of the surveillance work and locals were drawn into the web of watchers who scanned from the skies for interlopers.

Texas and California were being invaded, slowly. In Texas many of the illegals moved through on their way to other places. In California they began to get a firmer grip on southern sections of the State.

Chapter Eight

They had gathered. It was a room located in an old industrial warehouse - most likely a lunch room and employee gathering space. Above the main shipping floor the large room had a high ceiling and muted lighting, as not all the fixtures contained bulbs.

They came in one at a time, sometimes so quickly they met on the stairs. The faces were all familiar but the ritual required acknowledgement. They gathered tightly around the large circular wooden table. Each man laid his left arm straight out, towards the center, palm up.

And each arm had the mark. A small cartoon battle axe, tattooed simply in sailor blue and positioned closer to the wrist than the elbow. It featured a little notch in the blade and was inscribed with the letters AUW.

There were a few moments of silence to give everyone the opportunity to glance around the table, to ensure themselves in legitimate company.

"Gentlemen, look to you left and look to your right, ensure each of us our legitimacy," he intoned the ritual beginning to the meeting. He paused a moment and then continued more conversationally, "I trust we are all satisfied. In fact I can certainly vouch for everyone here, though I know there are meetings you will attend where that is not necessarily the case.

Let us proceed."

AUW - Advanced Urban Warfare - had been formed as a modern version of the Road Runners, a group of ex-military personnel who, in the shadow of World War Two had been brought together to provide for the rule of law in war torn areas when civil authority refused to exercise it. Originally an outlaw group, vigilantes, the lawless bringing law to the unchallenged, they charged themselves with maintaining law and order - despite their supra-legal status. Because of the contradiction their internal checks and balances were carefully maintained. They were very much an enigma wrapped in a conundrum. Eventually they went mainstream, unofficial but well known to official authorities.

The original group had used small tattoos of the cartoon Road Runner character because of their slippery nature, their quickness of action, and willingness to defy conventions, and because a cartoon would not give away the nature of their group to inquiring authorities. Some underground units in France during the war had used the symbol and it stuck after the war. Many times the Road Runners were behind the outcome of incidents which appeared to be getting out of control but which magically appeared to work out. In such incidents invariably the Road Runners were behind the satisfactory turn of events.

The group had fallen apart only when college kids in the 1980s began to appropriate their identification tattoo - rendering the group's members indistinguishable from drunken college kids. In fact a single incident where a college student was approbated into an operation by a Road Runner who mistook his tattoo in the heat of the moment, was enough to effectively kill the organization. But something was sure to rise from its ashes.

In the end, the regrouping was not a bad thing as it gave the Road Runners an opportunity to start fresh, to take on a more professional aspect and to renew inside contacts who were privy to Beyond Top Secret information. These inside connections helped to legitimize the organization, which was given operations that could not be carried out by visible means or by those official groups or agencies which might be subject to investigations.

The symbol they now used was a simple cartoon battle ax that had to be in a specific spot on the left forearm, oriented in a specific attitude and accompanied by the AUW letters. They referred to themselves as Gold-T the 'T' being for tungsten, with its chemical symbol 'W'. Tungsten has the highest melting point of any metal and is extremely hard.

"You have been summoned as it appears your services will be needed. Intelligence reports suggest that our enemies will concoct a very bold attack on us. An attack not aimed at any victory or material gain, but aimed at punishment, terror, a final blow against us, a last direct attack before they regroup and approach our conflict differently."

"You will be called on to act. To reduce the impact of their attack but not to thwart it save in specific instances where high value targets must be protected. We must allow their rampage to be seen in all its horror if we are to move our own people to act decisively to end the threats."

"You must be ready as it is expected the attack will come without warning, that our response must come quickly and without an overall battle plan. Simply put you will be required to kill, and to do it without fear, without forethought and at almost any time. We have guidelines assembled on our approach - essentially we will protect the innocent - children. We will be less concerned with those whose decisions have led us to today - those who have encouraged undocumented immigration, who have mindlessly allowed our nation to be overrun and who believe that all cultures are equal."

"Additionally we are planning a larger, less violent approach to dealing with our enemies on all fronts. Our operatives are approaching key decision-makers, public officials and major commercial interests to secure their co-operation with our plans. This is a multi-pronged effort to convince the fifth column in Western nations that their way of life is under attack."

"We have only small windows within which to act. We must be prepared. Until further notice, due to the seriousness of the conflict, we will not be accepting any new members of our group - anyone who claims to be a new member and to have joined within the last year is illegitimate."

The leader of the group added, "We will move into smaller groups, discuss each aspect of our operations, and then rotate everyone in attendance into each discussion so we are all clear on the intent."

Group members began their task.

Chapter Nine   **Switzerland**

Europe was a mess. People were on edge as lone guerilla attacks were frequent and indiscriminate. Economic activity was scant in the face of that uncertainty. Unemployment stalked the lesser skilled. Discontent hung like a mist in the streets. Heavily armed police and military men wandered urban areas in small groups.

"This cannot go on," was the universal refrain. But it had gone on, grinding month after month in the wake of the destruction of Rome. It had become the new normal. There were bright spots in the gloom. Attacks and violence were scaled down and but still happened too often for a sense of comfort to fall. Everyone was wary always. Even an unexpected knock at the door was reason to fear.

Governments, once the upholders of minority rights and tolerance had begun to take steps to unwind their immigration problems, as the minorities they protected had no thoughts of tolerance of other minorities.

Faced with an existential crisis of its own making, Europe decided to become European - restricting entry based on cultural background rather than ethnicity. It had been a slow process as people conditioned to a multicultural approach had to be weaned off it. After a generation of social engineers hammering away that all culture was equal, they now had to embrace the truth, that all culture was not equal or even worth tolerating. The decision to ban religious practices and any other demonstration of faith outside of places of worship had begun to turn the tide. national sentiments were gaining ground and the Euro project scrambled to keep European unity whole while reacting to the growing divisions.

"We did it in England. It wasn't as difficult as it seemed it might be. The people making all the noise were few and once public opinion turned away from conceding to their demands the protests just fizzled. Some immigrants simply went home. Others, people who had been in the UK for a time, adjusted and kept their overt cultural and religious practices to themselves. Of course the Swiss never really let the multicultural swamp happen. They stood up to much of this stuff early on. The French, being French, quietly started to dismantle any support for it. No sense making a big hue and cry, they simply stopped defending exceptions to the French approach. Now you Germans have to get on board," said Edward Spenser.

"You know how difficult that is for some, really for most of us," said his dinner companion Franz Bergenheiler. "We are so afraid of the slippery slope of the 1930s that we have almost committed hari-kari to avoid it today."

"I think I speak for our shared Saxon heritage when I ask you to take charge of your future. It isn't so black and white as all that," said Spenser.

"The German mind doesn't process shades of grey well," laughed Bergenheiler. "To us, its beer or its not beer. There is no Pilsner, Porter, Ale or Stout. And certainly no lite. Coors may sound like a German name but I'm guessing they were Austrian or maybe Prussian."

"You Germans need to develop a reasonable approach that you can live with and then implement it without delay and avoid the hand-wringing reconsiderations. That at least should work to solve your immediate problems."

Spenser and Bergenheiler sat in a small restaurant in Sion within site of the twin hills which defined the city. Both businessmen, they often met in Sion to discuss their shared commercial interests and to share war stories of their struggles dealing with the changing face of Europe. They even occasionally did business with Spenser buying goods from his German friend for export to England.

Spenser, a man of average height, his hairline receding slightly, had changed to comfortable shoes, and while he still wore his suit jacket, he had undone the top button of his shirt collar and loosened his tie. Bergenheiler, tall, blonde and in the bloom of his life, was already dressed down, having spent the day inspecting a small manufacturing plant he regularly did business with.

Since Rome there had been a great reset occurring across Europe. The entire economy was being re-engineered. Across Europe many millions of immigrants were being displaced leaving jobs undone, service businesses without clientele and without the labour to grease the economy.

"We are removed from all the turmoil here in Switzerland, in fact it feels like we are here pre-Armageddon," said Spenser.

"Oh how I hate that name for all the troubles," said Bergenheiler. "It makes it seem so biblical, predictable and as if it isn't over and with an end game that awaits us that is most unpleasant."

"I'm not sure what to call the whole clash of civilizations thing, as it all seems interrelated but certainly has its distinct subplots. The attack on Israel wasn't a surprise, save how many years of threats led up to it before the actual deed. And I suppose there were people who figured the Israelis would pull the trigger first - though I must admit I wasn't one of them. They needed a provocation. They got it. It was the Israeli reprisals on Pakistan that caught me by surprise. The fact that the Israelis are so dug in shouldn't have surprised anyone but somehow I didn't see it ahead of time. I must confess, I figured they'd be nuked, they'd fire back and then they would quietly disperse, mostly to America."

"This whole Masada thing shouldn't have been a surprise, they'd been planning for this for decades, probably since the very beginning."

"And the opposite is true of us and our American brothers. We saw it coming but played ostrich and kept thinking it would just work itself out. I'm half convinced that the US figured the Muslims would be satisfied with doing Israel. I always figured they'd go after Rome as well," said Spenser. "They want their Allah to conquer so they have to go after the other centres of faith."

"The immediate issue appears to be that Muslims, Catholics, western civilization and a few others are too big. They are so widespread that they cannot be completely destroyed. It isn't possible even if there is a will to do it."

Bergenheiler looked around and gave a vague wave, "One thing is certain, they'll never attack Switzerland. This place is an armed camp with facilities built into mountains, a wary, watchful citizenry and a good bit of paranoia. A decade ago it seemed a bit creepy, now it appears prescient."

"In some ways the Swiss are the perfect westerners. They are open and accepting and willing to look the other way on a lot of stuff - but they are the first to cry foul if your exercise of rights interferes with their exercise of rights. Sort of an intolerance for the inevitable clash of civilities."

"I'm here with some frequency," said Spenser. "It is certainly the best place to do business. The Swiss are reliable and your goods are not likely to be firebombed or stolen, at least not until they cross the border into France, Italy or even Germany. In fact I'm taking delivery tomorrow of two boxcars of chocolate and two more of leather goods by way of Italy. Our hosts have given up on insuring delivery past their borders. Now I have to do it and insurance is difficult to get. In fact I often only insure half the delivery. That's why I'm taking chocolate and leather, losing half to terrorism is not quite the devastating financial blow it would be other-wise."

"At some point all of this will settle down and we will be able to put our attention to rebuilding our societies. Despite the problems that came from a lack of assimilation, there were benefits, mostly economic, that will have to face a significant reset."

"Another beer?"

"Yes, one more. I have to be up early tomorrow for the shipment. It goes at first light. More likely to get through that way. Terrorists appear to like their sleep."

"What about the Netherlands? Have you had any problems there?" asked Bergenheiler.

"That's actually where I run my warehouses, though I usually move the goods in and out within a few days. The Dutch figured this whole thing out before the rest of us and were actively pressuring immigrants to move on even before this Armag. . . . these troubles. Not that things don't happen there, they do, but not on a large scale and not very frequently."

"I don't like dealing in France but with the size of the economy and the closeness of travel I still do it often. It's dangerous with bands of armed men roaming the cities. Deliveries are pretty safe outside the big cities, especially in the north, but in the south and in cities in the south I have trouble getting insurance if my trains are scheduled for a stop. It's getting better though, fewer attacks. But you know how hard it is to counter per-ception. Plus the insurance guys put in a bunch of new rules to reduce claims, then the claims go down and they think they are geniuses," said Spenser.

"It's better in America I'm told," he laughed. "That's the old saw. My sister lives there - in Atlanta. She says they cleared out a lot of the non-citizens pretty quickly. They just used a few of the idle cruise ships, packed them in two families to a cabin and in three or four trips to Beirut, Turkey and

Morocco they had disposed of a significant part of their problems. The immigrants flooding Turkish ports looked good on the Turks. Those Turks appear to be on everyone's side at the same time but are really only on their own."

"She says it isn't widely known there in the US, but any resistance or trouble and people are just taken to a temporary tent camp in northern Florida and told to make ready for departure. I understand the cruise ships will need significant overhauls after the trips thanks to the damage inflicted by their guests, but there are not too many people taking holidays anyway given all that's happened there."

"My contacts tell me that people who aren't citizens are given 30 days to get their affairs in order and are told to make their own arrangements for travel or to report for transportation. If they want to make their own arrangements they are free to do so, but must let authorities know their departure date," said Bergenheiler. "Of course that comes from contacts I have in the Boston area. It might vary place to place."

"I've heard rumours that some Muslims had warning to get out of the big cities prior to the May 29th. I haven't heard of any concrete evidence but rumours often have a kernel of truth to them."

"I know the Americans struggled with their belief in the separation of church and state and their history of religious tolerance. They were only able to change when it dawned on them that the religion they were concerned about was more than half a political system and in either case it wasn't being tolerant of them."

Chapter Ten Southern California

"Senor Octavius?"

The tall, well dressed Spaniard turned from his light conversation, where small talk held sway. He enjoyed the small talk as it often yielded little bits of information he could mine and file away for future use. These type of conversations were Miguel Octavius' stock in trade. He was a diplomat, an envoy of the Spanish government which had numerous interests, family connections and historical interests in much of Mexico and South America. His special interest was in Mexico but he was deeply aware of many interests throughout the Americas.

He was attending a gallery opening in Palm Springs California. Still a very well to do community it had been changed and was changing still due to 'the troubles'. Untouched by the nuclear explosion in Los Angeles if you ignore a week of fallout and a few months of fallout fears, Palm Springs was largely protected from the blast by the mountains between it and LA.

Many long time residents were slowly selling their properties to well off Mexicans and Hispanic locals who survived the blast.

Well known Mexican - American artist Hellenga was showing some of his paintings as the featured guest of the gallery opening. The gallery was owned by Senor Cartenga, who was well off through his construction business prior to the blast, but whose expertise had made him millions through the clean up and reconstruction throughout the LA area. He owned the gallery with his wife Margita Cartenga, who also operated it. It was she who was as much on display in the grand opening as Hellenga.

"Senor Octavius, I'd like you to meet Hellenga. Several of his paintings are on display here today."

Octavius turned with a smile and opened his little circle to Mrs. Cartenga and Hellenga who stood behind her, a little uncomfortable with the stiffness of the introduction.

"Ah, Mrs. Cartenga," he smiled. "So nice to see you again. And a pleasure to meet you sir," he nodded his head and stuck his hand out to the artist, motioning inward with the other. "Come you two, please tell us about the gallery and of these two magnificent paintings just above us."

Margita beamed at the graciousness of the diplomat. She was dressed in a formal gown befitting her standing and wealth. Hellenga was dressed in studied casual - his usual attire, a nice pair of shoes his only concession to the elegance of the event.

"Galleria de Baja Nord is very happy that Hellenga is able to attend and gracious enough to bring several of his works. I should let him tell you about them. He is a well known artist specializing in Aztlan, the culture and history of northern Mexico. A native of California he consistently uses native touches to give his work its poignancy and depth. Please tell the Ambassador and his friends about your work, especially what they can see."

Hellenga lifted his head and raised his eyes to meet with Senor Octavius. He nodded slightly.

"The large painting just behind you sir, is very representative of my more recent work. The landscape is taken from Joshua Tree National Monument which is not far from here. To that I've married some elements

69

which tell in a quiet way of the turmoil that has engulfed this whole region in recent years. You can see the large cactus is damaged slightly but beginning to grow again and repair itself but in a different way than it was before the damage occurred. There are hints of a disturbed civilization in the landscape which I'm afraid is very common in California today. I have tried to be subtle in the representation, in fact I saw something very like this composition while hiking at Joshua Tree but it was almost over the top in terms of symbolism. I had to draw it back a bit or people would accuse me of being too political."

"Aren't all artists political," asked one member of the group, with a touch of haughtiness.

"I suppose we are, if everything you see reminds you of a political stance or message," said Hellenga refusing to be drawn in. "I try not to be political but to simply represent reality, which can lean either way politically but always focuses on how people perceive their world."

"What is the focus of the picture? asked Octavius. "I found myself at first drawn to the broken cactus and then to the bit of plastic bottle in the distance."

"Aye, Senor Octavius, that is the focus. It is whatever you perceive it to be. Looking at this painting, you should be able to draw out of it those things which are important to you, and understand a bit more about yourself having seen it."

"So you're saying I'm particularly political if I choose to see the political aspects in it," said the haughty man with a smirk.

"No, I'm saying you choose to be political by seeing the picture and assigning political values to it," said Hellenga. "As an illustration, if you notice the broken bottle perhaps that is because you are environmentally sensitive. There are several other paintings of mine around the gallery. The only other one you can see from here is a portrait of Senor Cartenga's vast wealth."

A few of the guests drew their breath audibly, seemingly taken aback by the artist's direct mention of his patron's financial standing.

They looked around for a moment until Senor Octavius broke the silence.

"Ah the devil you are Senor Hellenga. I see the painting of all the Cartenga wealth." He nodded towards a niche in the gallery where the central painting was of two young children and Margita.

"You are incorrigible Senor Hellenga," said Margita with a smile. "Shall I show you off to a few other guests?" she added. "Please excuse us."

"A subtle man, indeed," said the haughty guest, once the pair was out of earshot. "I must confess I was looking for construction cranes or a scene of damaged buildings."

"I had never met the man, though I had been alerted to his ways," said Octavius. "Margita Cartenga spoke highly of him and said he was a worthy person to know in the new normal."

"Artists are like football goalies," said the haughty man. "High strung, high maintenance and high on themselves."

"Sometimes they are just high." Everyone in the circle laughed.

"I too should mingle some more," said Octavius, with a smile. "I have to earn my master's keep. It was nice to meet you all."

He slipped away looking for Senor Cartenga and a bit more background on his pet artist.

As he worked his way through the gallery he managed to catch Cartenga's eye in passing, asking for a quick word and then for a lengthier private conversation after the event was completed. That was usually the case in these visits but he didn't want to miss out on this one.

He wandered some more through the gallery, joining conversations and sometimes merely eavesdropping while appearing to study a painting on the wall.

Information and an insight or two into existing conditions were invaluable, he knew. While our experience is limited to the past, it is the unknowable future to which we apply its lessons. It was this fluidity that fascinated him and in which he saw almost unlimited possibilities. Sometimes a chance remark, or a bit of tossed off local knowledge embedded themselves deeply into Octavius' mind.

Chapter Eleven   Baltimore

Mohammed Alambra motioned the three men to sit. He offered them hookah pipes as he took one himself. A young boy brought a tray of drinks.

"My brothers, I am troubled. We are at an impasse in our battle against these infidels. Too many of our best men have gone home we have not been able to strike more than gentle blows against these Americans."

"Too few, like you, are citizens. Too many have been forced to leave. As you know several have left with Allah rather than take the ocean voyage. They have gone down fighting. What would you have us do?"

"If they all must leave, we must organize a last offensive against the infidels. Can we manage a final blow in one month's time? Can we prepare for a final glorious stand in only 30 days?"

"That is not much time, imam. What would you have us do?"

"Battle to the last my brothers. Organize your groups to the last man. Wire apartments with explosives. Organize military strikes on soft targets, shopping malls, public transit, traffic jams, school and sporting events. Take down as many of the infidel sheep as you can. Spill their blood, make them fear interaction with us. Arrange it all for one glorious day before we are removed from their hovels."

One by one they nodded.

"We shall meet here again in a week to finalize our plans. How many people can we muster?"

"Many thousands. Quickly organizing for the most destruction is difficult but with thousands of attacks perhaps a million infidels will die. We fear not death. There is little else they can do to us."

"Let it be so, then. Allahu Akbar."

Each of the three men moved from the meeting room. One went north to a safe house in the Adirondacks where he called his lieutenants and had them draw up plans and gather ammunition that had been hidden away for such a day.

Another went west to the inner city of Cincinnati where he called together a war council. The third went south to Charlotte, North Carolina and brought together what was left of his trainees.

They all returned to Mohammed Alambra at the proscribed time and explained their plans, logistics and anticipated ready time.

"Excellent my brothers. We shall co-ordinate our efforts for June 7 two years and one week after the glorious attacks on New York and Los Angeles. Their guard will be down after the end of May. What will you each be doing?"

"Imam, I have organized three thousand soldiers from Chicago to Detroit to Cleveland to Louisville and Nashville and St. Louis. We will attack soft targets in threes and fours on the morning of June 7. My members have been instructed to hit more than one target and to plan for maximum strike force. All their apartments and places of employment will be booby trapped. I anticipate at least 50 kills per fighter and I have more than 3,000 in the field."

"Excellent."

"Imam, I have almost 2,000 soldiers under my command including several computer experts. We will arrange for a catastrophic systems failure in government and electrical networks on that morning. It is hoped that the failure will affect much of the eastern seaboard. I encourage my brothers to put some of their resources into bombing electrical stations and water purification plants. Without electricity these places will have reduced security. The failure will look like a cascading maintenance issue and they will drop their guard. I too will have my soldiers commit to multiple targets and a kill rate of at least 50 infidels per fighter before they melt back into society or go underground."

"Imam, I make the same commitments as my brothers. I have three other sub-groups who are working on this plan independently. One is in Atlanta, one in Jacksonville and another in Memphis. Between them I think we have 1,500 soldiers or more to do our work. Multiple targets, booby traps and attacks on electricity and water; each will do their duty to Allah on June 7."

The table was set.

The men took their leave of Alambra and returned to their homes, all the while thinking about their responsibilities to Allah. They quietly made arrangements to transport their families and warned their soldiers not to do the same, lest they tip off authorities.

"Well, something is up," said Arnie Spector looking at the monitor. "Keep that thing outta sight. We don't want to tip them off. Let communications know to keep a tight watch on their cell phones, emails and meetings."

"Inspector, we should take them out now. We can follow them on their travels home. Our agents can get them before anything is arranged."

"I know that but we want to get their networks. Big brass say if we can expose them then the deportation of undesirables will go much smoother. Reducing the protests is paramount. And frankly, that is the attitude even if some of their plots are successful, in fact some of them need to be successful in order to get our people on side, with a full appreciation of the threat."

"But even if we take out one of these guys now it could save hundreds of people," the drone operator said as he manoeuvred the drone down away from any sight lines as he flew it away from the mosque where the meeting had taken place.

"I know son, but we can't risk tipping them off. We have to let this play out and see what we can find from monitoring communications etc. You know most of their plots are very poorly executed. I always wondered why they weren't more creative or destructive. Except for 9-11 their plots are really small, compared to what they could do if they thought it through."

"I think they are planning a big one. All three of those guys are known as major organizers."

"They are, but nothing can be as big as the ones they've already perpetrated."

Chapter Twelve   **Pittsburgh**

Adnan Quireshi waivered again. He had been happy that he and his family had sought American citizenship after five years living and working in the US as a pharmacist. An Egyptian, he had seen the excesses of culture in Cairo and decided to move his family to America.

After several years of planning he had come to Pittsburgh and established three pharmacies just south of Pittsburgh in Harmony, Pennsylvania. Once steel towns Pittsburgh and Harmony had suffered difficult times in the shift away from steel but recently they had prospered as low land costs and infrastructure improvements had allowed great economic gains.

Immigrants like Adnan were part of the growth as he had worked very hard to build his businesses. He used middle eastern connections to gain a foothold for his business and had funnelled money back to the Egyptian based cultural groups which focussed on retaining their cultural touch-stones while in America and giving immigrants exposure to all things American.

Fittingly, Adnan had sponsored the Harmony Islamic Thanksgiving. He roasted turkeys and arranging for all the trimmings to be served at a huge feast presided over by local politicians and prominent citizens. It had gone over extremely well with his community and the greater area business community. He had felt a bit like the fictional Christmas Grinch, serving the roast beast, once given over to his new home and on side with the celebration but he still harboured a lingering doubt as to his place in it.

Adnan's young children beamed as they took part in an American tradition. Local citizens beamed as they felt they could be themselves with the new Americans. They passed on the feast of Thanksgiving even if the new Americans didn't fully understand it.

Adnan acquired his citizenship shortly after the second Thanksgiving event.

Two years later, New York and Los Angeles had been blown to bits. For a month Adnan kept his head down, tried to hide his accent and wore American symbols on his lapels.

Many of his local clients took to giving him strange looks. Some, apparently acknowledging his sympathy with Americans, some nodding to his obvious attempt at hiding in plain sight and others sneering at his lack of antipathy toward the infidels.

Adnan was concerned about his businesses when several young men of Middle Eastern descent made references to him as a cultural traitor, one who could not be counted on by Allah. Adnan sought to assure them he was an observant Muslim but one who did not countenance the violence. Two large men walked into his pharmacy and simply trashed a portion of his grocery shelves. They were in and out in 60 seconds but their message was received.

In the wake of the attacks on New York, Los Angeles and Norfolk government decrees demanded all the non-citizen Muslims leave the country. Adnan, a citizen, was concerned but apparently safe from the demands to leave. He received a letter from the Department of Homeland Security asking him for some detail about his life in the US; number of dependents, business or employment details, income, family connections outside the country and travel intentions for the next three years. Adnan called the government office and explained he did not want to have any trouble from local authorities nor from any local agitators who, seeing him walk into a government building would automatically assume he was an informant.

The nice lady at City Hall explained the need for the information and said he could mail it in or email it.

With nothing to hide Adnan complied by email.

A few weeks later he was behind the counter at his main pharmacy working the day shift. Adnan took turns with day and evening shifts in all three of his locations to better keep an eye on business and to get to know local conditions and his employees.

A large man with a full dark beard entered the store, stomped his feet to remove the snow, and looked up to the counter at the back. He made his way around the store, with his eyes constantly on Adnan at the back. Then he arrived at the counter.

"I'd like to speak with the pharmacist please," he said. Adnan was summoned assuming it was a question about meds.

"Mr. Adnan Quireshi?"

"Yes, can I help you?"

"Yes," said the man, as he quickly pulled his hand out from his pocket and handed Adnan a note. "I think you need to see this."

Adnan read the note carefully. It's first instruction was to keep a straight face and make it look as if the interaction was medical in nature. The rest of the note outlined a delivery that Adnan was expected to make two nights later. Then he was expected to hand the note back with a medical explanation.

Adnan read the note for a second time. He wasn't being given any opportunity to disagree nor were there any apparent consequences if he simply ignored the instructions. But he knew differently.

Adnan nodded slightly and handed the note back. "You just take it once per day. And if you forget, do not take double the amount. Just take the next day's dose."

"Thank you," said the bearded man as he took the note and made his way out.

Adnan could easily do what was asked. He knew that doing it would make him complicit in whatever this man was up to. Should he inform the authorities and endanger his family or should he simply comply and hope it went away?

Two nights later at another pharmacy location Adnan parked his car to start his shift. In the trunk he left six big bags of ammonium nitrate and a bag of amphetamines and strong pain killers.

As he exited the car he clicked open the trunk from the driver's seat. The latch disengaged but the trunk remained shut. Adnan went into the store. At the end of his shift he left the parking lot without checking the trunk. A small drone left the scene as well and followed him home.

Chapter Thirteen   Washington

"Alcoeur Islami, he's what's left."

"He's holed up somewhere in Central Asia. Nobody really knows, in fact nobody is really sure if he's a real person. All we have are communications which mention him by name and frankly with a name like that he might just be a mirage, some sort of idealized leader giving the remaining Muslims a figurehead."

"Something tells me we can't write this guy, or whatever he stands for, off."

"We have to keep him on the radar but right now I think he's more of a Russian problem than ours. Apparently he and a militia attacked a Tbilisi bus terminal last night. Anything that gets organized in his name seems to be directed at the southern Caucuses or Kazakhstan."

"The Russians would love to shore up their southern frontier with a buffer state or two. Any provocation and they're there in a heartbeat. This attack could be it. They've had great success with the hard hit and withdraw approach. In you go, show a lot of muscle and leave a strong impression of your willingness to return, should it be necessary. It's the lesson they learned after invading Afghanistan way back when. Subduing a place does not require your presence. It's been even more effective when they leave a few advisers or an active ambassador around after the big boys leave. Eyes on the ground and all that."

"We tried some of that approach but unfortunately we do not have the balls to follow up so the locals don't take us seriously and any order we are able to establish falls back into chaos soon after we back off. Anyway, don't tell anyone I told you. I'm on my way to brief the President right now and he's supposed to know first," he laughed. "It'll be department wide by tomorrow."

The two men parted, taking different hallways through the labyrinth of The Pentagon. Chairman of the Joint Chiefs, Major General Aaron Stewart passed through his office to make sure his car was ready. He pinned his Congressional Medal of Honour on his chest before leaving. He didn't usually wear it, but when he met with the President it was necessary - just a subtle reminder to take him seriously both politically and militarily.

General Stewart had won his Medal of Honour during the nuclear attacks of 5/29. He had been visiting the Naval Station at Norfolk to meet with Naval Commander Admiral Charles Nimitz, great-grandson of the World War Two admiral who had been Pacific Fleet Commander after Pearl Harbour. The nuclear attack on New York took place as the two men toured the Norfolk Station.

Reports of the attack spurred extra security around the Norfolk facility. It was Stewart who insisted that air patrols be increased outside of the Station's perimeter and that three unidentified cargo vessels be sunk.

That decisive action was mentioned in his Medal of Honour commendation but it was his subsequent actions which really earned the award.

The attackers were able to detonate the device off the Atlantic shore of the Station just before they would have been sunk by Navy jets. After the bomb exploded Stewart directed hundreds of Navy staff to safety and taking his own life in hand, ran to 10 vessels in the harbour and signalled the ships to move out of harbour and keep everyone below decks to avoid the fallout. This action saved thousands of lives, kept the ships out of the fallout zone, making them operable again very quickly.

Stewart himself had expected to succumb to fallout from the blast but he had shown no signs of radiation. His medal of honour was awarded, his bravery feted and soon after he was promoted to Chairman of the Joint Chiefs. There were some who figured the promotion was going to be short-lived as Stewart would not survive long. Many people wanted him to consider politics but he vigorously declined saying he was better positioned to use his experience and expertise in the military.

President Richard O'Day was very wary of General Stewart's popularity, feeling that despite the General's disavowal of politics he was looking over his shoulder should O'Day slip up in the public's eye. Certainly the General's public take-charge attitude contributed to that unease.

Stewart met the President in the Oval Office and outlined the intelligence on Alcoeur Islami. President O'Day believed Islami to be a chimera, a hopeful figurehead for a cultural group that had little home left, except for a generations long rebuilding project.

"You might well be right Mr. President however the US has suffered grievously when we have made assumptions and believed what we wanted to believe rather than the evidence before our eyes. He or his group is responsible for yesterday's bus terminal attack. Do not easily dismiss these martyrs - they still have the ability to bite us."

"Good advice General but what would you have me do regarding this ghost of a mujahedeen? At this point anyway, it appears to be a Russian problem."

"Do not forget Mr. President that explicitly Russian problems have a way of becoming our problems too."

O'Day smiled. "You know, that might be the ultimate statement coming from a State Department class on Russia. I'm stealing that one, General."

"I think we need more intel on the phantom. I would like to send in two small teams of Special Forces. One into Tashkent in Uzbekistan and another into what's left of Islamabad so they can sniff around in Kashmir, Afghanistan and even northern India."

"These are going to have to be very Special Forces if they are going to blend in there and not attract attention," said the President.

"Yes Sir. However I believe a small group with some support could gain valuable intelligence in those areas and help to re-establish our ground network there. That network has been neglected. If we happen to quietly eliminate some local issues along the way then it will have been a very successful mission. I expect to be there for a few months at least."

"Very well. Move ahead as you see fit."

O'Day was at first pleased that Stewart would appear to seek his blessing on such an endeavour but the more he thought about it he knew that Stewart could have simply proceeded with the mission under existing rules of command. Did Stewart have some other reason for seeking his blessing?

As Steward had predicted the intel on Islami was included in the next day's senior military and intelligence briefing. However the decision to send in Special Forces was not part of that briefing.

Navy Commander Marshall Wiertrzi smiled when he read the Islami info in the briefing. Stewart had been right again. He wondered why Stewart seemed to be taking an interest in him - at first he thought it was only because their offices in the Pentagon were relatively close by and they often shared the walk back from Joint Chiefs meetings. Certainly his boss, Rear Admiral Bruce McLeish, had casually asked him if Stewart had anything interesting to say in their walks through the building. Wiertrzi had been circumspect dropping a few crumbs but making sure not to give anything to McLeish that could be used against Stewart - not that there was anything specifically, save the odd bit of inside baseball or like yesterday a bit of higher level intelligence. Commander Wiertrzi was the Navy's top flyer and a close aide to Navy Chief of Staff McLeish.

He was very aware of protocols. The Defense Department had always been a hotbed of intrigue. Since 5/29 and the military and political convulsions which had come from those events, the intrigue was much thicker, deeper and more impenetrable. Loyalties seemed up for grabs, rumours and rumours of plots bandied about, some plausible others apparently far-fetched. It was hard to play it all straight as each officers background and connections were a big part of anything he said or did. And yet, playing it straight was imperative as loyalty was the currency with which everyone was measured.

He was sorting through his papers when an aide dropped off a set of orders copied to McLeish. He was to co-ordinate an armed drone and jet fighter cover force for a special forces group in northern Pakistan, orders of Joint Chief of Staff Major General Aaron Stewart. It was marked Top Secret on the outside of the envelope but QQQ - Top Secret inside - so as not to surprise or rattle the aide delivering it. He was relieved that McLeish was apparently aware of the order.

The orders said that the ground assets in the field were to be protected at cost and that the Navy air cover was their eyes and ears both offensively for their mission and defensively to maintain their presence and cover.

"That's a 24 / 7 cover half a world away for what, two months," Weirtrzi thought to himself. "Wow."

Chapter Fourteen   Washington

"That sure is a pretty impressive sight," said Peter O'Neill as he swung off 6th Street Northwest and turned left onto Pennsylvania Avenue. He was looking at the Smithsonian's Air and Space Museum, which he always visited when he was in Washington. His wife Amanda, seated beside him, thought he was referring to the US Capitol dome which swung into view straight ahead as they made their left turn.

"You are right Peter. It is an impressive sight and a pretty one as well," she said.

She continued to look at the street map on her lap. "According to this map, this is not the most efficient way to get to Foggy Bottom and the University. We might have even walked."

"I know but I wanted to do a bit of a driving tour of town, especially on a Sunday evening. It's quiet and the streets are empty. It's a great chance to move around quickly and get a better feel for the place. Any way we don't have to meet Congressman Bieritski for an hour and the restaurant is in a tough place to get to unless we arrive by car."

They swung around the Capitol Dome with Peter slowing down so Amanda could get a really nice view.

"Somebody on the roof is looking at us - look at the roofline and wave," Peter said. "We can't see them but they certainly can see us."

Amanda made a half hearted wave.

They passed the Supreme Court Building and the Library of Congress before heading west through the maze of federal office buildings south of the National Mall.

They passed the US Department of Health and Human Services, the Lyndon Johnson Building, the Voice of America offices, before coming upon a small group of fast food restaurants.

"Hey a McDonalds," said Peter, genuinely surprised. "Who knew that federal office workers actually ate during the day. I think these are the only restaurants we've seen on street level in our entire drive."

"Restaurants in Washington are pretty scarce in the central core. That's why we are meeting the Congressman at Foggy Bottom," said Amanda.

"We could have met him right here. Though I'm not sure it's even open."

They hit a wall at 6th Avenue Southwest when the road ended at the American Farm Bureau. Peter choked back a witticism aimed at agriculture, thinking it not really funny enough. A few twists and turns and they glided past the Federal Aviation Administration Building before finding the south edge of the Mall and rolling past a number of impressive public buildings. They motored past the Washington Monument, the Tidal Basin and eventually rounded behind the Lincoln Memorial before heading north to the University District.

Peter parked the car at a spot suggested by the Congressman between the Universities and they made their way by the directions they'd been given to a lovely old pub, once a house, that bordered the Chesapeake and Ohio Canal and was actually closer to Georgetown University than to George Washington U.

Inside the restaurant the Congressman was waiting for them.

"Peter," he reached to shake hands. "And Amanda," he held her hand while he moved to brush her cheek with his. "So very nice to see you." He directed them to a table in a small alcove in a far corner of the restaurant. Nobody else was sitting within two tables of them though the place appeared fairly busy.

They caught up on small talk and the doings of City Council in Buffalo and Peter's business dealings in procuring waste steel for his reforging plant in Buffalo.

"It appears that some hurdles have finally been cleared," said Congressman Bieritski. "Congress appears to have an agreement on some of the damage to New York meaning that reclamation projects can begin in a much larger manner than they have currently. We will make it easier to transfer title to whatever is lying on a property so licenses should be easier to get and most importantly environmental standards will be eased until the land is ready for re-use at which time the environmental standards are reinstated. It should speed things up considerably."

"That's good news," said Peter. "When?"

"A week, a month, soon," said Bieritski with a small smile. "Or perhaps a Federal 'soon'. I'm expecting two weeks before they can call the vote. Truth is, it's already been agreed to by each Party. They just want to get their credit-taking machines in order before the vote. I've been pushing for shared glory in the interests of speedy legislation."

"Your office will keep me informed?"

The Congressman nodded. "That is not the only reason I wanted to meet with you prior to your meeting tomorrow with the President."

Peter looked up from his menu with a quizzical look.

"I'm sure you are wanting to know the specials tonight," said the server, who had just appeared at their table. "We have baked tilapia in a lovely wine sauce with cilantro seasoned, seasonal spinach and vegetables. She spoke the tongue twister extra slowly. "We also have a 10 and 14 ounce New York cut steak cooked as you prefer and a lovely baked penne with chicken in a rose or cream mushroom sauce served with your choice of soup, and salad."

"Peter closed his menu," I know what I want. He looked at Amanda who was still diligently reading.

"So do I," she said after only the slightest pause. The Congressman concurred.

Once the server had all the details Peter asked the Congressman what else was on his mind.

"We'll it's exciting actually but I thought I should let you know prior to the President bringing it up so you wouldn't be caught off guard. President O'Day loves to spring surprises on people thinking they would love to be of additional service to their country. Sometimes they are too busy or have other issues that must be considered, so O'Day's staff makes a point of giving people a head's up in advance so they can properly prepare. They told me, so I can tell you."

"I'm intrigued," said Amanda.

"As well you should be, and will be even more when I tell you. It's actually a joint request. President O'Day is going to ask you Amanda if you could act as an unofficial assistant ambassador to Canada."

"Unofficial?"

"Yes, our current Ambassador has made some powerful Canadian enemies, particularly in English Canada and the President is hoping with you in Buffalo and your husband heavily involved with a joint industrial project between the two countries, that you might act in a manner which gets the administration's points to the Canadians in a constructive manner. You would have the full backing of the President and access to State Department resources. It's just that we don't want to be seen as withdrawing our Ambassador just because the Canadians have some difficulties with him."

"Well, yes I would be interested, but I need to know much more about this. How does the Ambassador feel about this?"

"Interest is enough. I can arrange for a State Department briefing and a meeting with the Secretary of State and the current Ambassador William Kenneth. You can actually decide along the way."

"As for the Ambassador he will be told of your involvement and connection to the President but he will not be party to your inside connections to the State Department. We don't want a joint Ambassadorship, nor do we want a snubbed diplomat making trouble. We just want him to have a 'good cop' that he can use.

"And you Peter, the President has plans for you as well," continued Beirinski. "Your industrial production is very important to the President. He wants to make is easier for you to expand your business into southern California to help clean up the cities of San Francisco and Los Angeles. He has spoken to US Steel executives and the Board of Directors of Dominion Steel in Canada. Essentially the President wants you to purchase the Canadian assets of US Steel including the plant at Nanticoke Ontario and those of Dominion Steel including their smelters in Sault Ste. Marie Ontario and use these assets to produce steel for rebuilding projects in the United States."

Peter looked at Amanda who had a broad grin on her face. "It looks like we will both be very busy."

"Frankly, the President is willing to arrange third party loans and whatever assets it takes to get these enterprises up and running quickly. And Amanda, as the wife of such an industrialist in Canada you will have easy access to decision makers up there."

Peter looked at Amanda. Amanda looked at Peter. He sighed. She smiled.

"It sounds like the challenge has been removed," he said. "This all comes on a silver platter. I can at least take some comfort knowing I've already done much of the ground work. I had much the same thought, seeing those industrial assets so underutilized."

"When the President says 'up and running quickly' what does he mean? What's the timeline here?"

"Yesterday. Last week. Even his staffers say the President formulates plans in his mind and waits for them to be executed without telling anyone about them. Then he comes in and wonders why nothing has been happening on the file."

"You can't move fast enough. In fact if you weren't supposed to meet the President tomorrow to start this task I would say you should be arranging meetings with Canadians to start this task. In fact a few phone calls might be a good idea - but wait until you have the official from O'Day before doing anything specific."

Chapter Fifteen   **Washington**

"Senator Findlay? The President would like to speak with you."

Findlay picked up the phone.

"Hello."

"Putting you through."

Findlay always smiled at the clash of protocol. The higher level official always comes to the phone after the junior official is already there. As a Senator, Findlay was acutely aware of the subtle expression of authority as he was usually the last in on any call. There weren't many officials who outranked him.

"Tom, Tom, I thought you said those Boston bastards were on-side," said the President. The protocol aide had done her job.

"Er, ah, Mr. President they assured me they understood the point of re-building New York and getting it back into being a functioning city ASAP."

"Well Massachusetts has just opened a motion in their state legislature to prefer Canadian dollars and UK Pounds to US dollars for government transactions."

"The currencies are all pegged Mr. President."

"I know that. But making it a legislated preference to use other national currencies is a blow of confidence against the greenback that we can't tolerate right now. Call in some favours, you have to get this reversed, or dropped or whatever."

"I'll do what I can, however, what they will want to help New York, is to get similar government support so they can be New York."

"Let them believe it if you have too. What they want and what will actually happen are two different things."

Two phone calls later it became apparent what the Bostonians would want.

"They want the major stock markets to headquarter in Boston," said Findlay to one of his aides. "How do we tell the guys in Chicago to back off?"

"Chicago is the largest city in the country now. They already have all the infrastructure in place for these exchanges - hell they did even before 5/29. This isn't going to work. What if we get Boston to be the kind of exchange back-up that Chicago had been before New York stopped functioning?"

"That might work," said Findlay. "Get me Jim Grange on the phone."

Grange was sympathetic but he had the burgers of Boston to deal with.

"Tom, I can pull some strings but without concrete federal action on Boston running hand in hand with federal plans to rebuild New York, it won't fly and frankly could kill my chances for re-election if I stick too closely to the feds."

"Jim the President is all over me on this. What you're proposing is a government initiative - your local businessmen likely don't care either way. The President is afraid the move will kill the US dollar, and I think he's right. With all our problems we don't want to fuel a currency crisis as well."

"Yeah, okay, but the President wanting to manipulate us is nothing new. New England is sick of it and we need a big win here. The business community is looking for some stability - word is the peg will come off the Canadian Dollar shortly. UK will likely follow. They pegged after 5/29 to show support and create stability in the wake of the destruction."

"I think currency support by the States is good for the country, Jim. Look, frankly, I'm trying to get set for a White House run. I could use your support and I'll do for Boston what I can. If you were with me on this you could be quite formidable in your quest to help the Northeast."

"As a running mate?"

"Yeah, Jim that's what I'm suggesting. Quiet for now. We get on the same page to help the country first and bring Boston and the Northeast along for the ride. I have already tried to convince a number of companies to locate head offices to Boston but the Atlantic has them spooked."

"What about Nashua or Burlington or even Worchester?"

"I got two to move to Albany and two more to Buffalo. But the preferred destination is Chicago or Pittsburgh - no Atlantic."

"They both have shipping access, if that's what they fear."

"Yeah Jim they do but you might notice that pretty much any big city has significant water access and I'm not sure Las Vegas would qualify as a national capital - but Denver might."

"Tom I've got to shore up Massachusetts and even the Northeast if I'm going to help you as a running mate. For that, I need some help."

"Get the currency bill killed and we can put some effort into that. Boston as a back-up exchange, maybe and possibly an enhanced Air Force presence for defence. The President has talked about decentralizing our naval assets to New York to avoid a single point of attack. I know you don't want Navy but you might consider Air Force."

As soon as he hung up, Findlay called the President to inform him that the bill would be derailed, though it would require some federal assistance to make happen. The President agreed.

The President announced that the federal government would increase the size of Westover Air Force Base near Springfield in Massachusetts as part of a plan to increase Military Defensive capabilities for the Atlantic Defence Force. San Francisco would get a similar Station as part of the rebuilding program. In addition the FBI's northeastern command was moved from New York to Boston - a fairly easy move as the New York offices didn't exist anymore. Nor did many of the agents.

Other smaller projects, offices and commissions were announced for the Northeast with an emphasis on Boston. The currency bill died in the State House.

Chapter Sixteen   **Malta**

First they came in rickety fishing boats. Refugees; men mostly, some women and children. A tide that swept up on Malta. The Maltese did their best to house the human wave.

Having established a foothold the refugee swarm continued with predominantly young men leaving their homes for safe shores and brighter futures as economic migrants coming to pave the way for their families. They were housed in hastily constructed camps around the main Maltese island. For months there was much coming and going from these camps as the migrants managed odd jobs, took on construction and agricultural work and became a part of the permanent countryside.

There had been little trouble between the migrants and locals. After the two initial waves of migrants there had been a significant slowdown in their numbers. The Maltese wondered what to do with these people as they did not have the resources to resettle them nor the broad economy to absorb them into society. They debated and continued to accept the small trickle of people who arrived on their shores, sending them to the camps where they were issued tents and some basic necessities and versed on the ways of refugee life.

If the Maltese wondered why the oil rich nations which dotted the Middle East never stepped in to accept refugees from Middle Eastern strife, it was never widely articulated. And yet as the numbers of refugees in the camps continued to grow so did the resentment of the locals to the rich countries which refused to help and to the refugees who seemed to take advantage of the soft hearted Maltese. Idle young men stirred up some trouble. A fight here, an attack on locals there. After some months of this, tensions between the two groups were high, with most Maltese demanding their officials do something about the human flood which had engulfed their island.

The Maltese asked French and Italian authorities for some help. Eventually some of the refugee families took up an offer from the Italian government to resettle in southern Italy. In those regions the old agricultural way of life was becoming a challenge as young people moved to the northern cities leaving many villages bereft of youth and a future. The problem appeared to be easing.

Late one evening, as dusk still hung over the sea, hundreds of boats appeared on the shores. Seeing a second wave of migrants the Maltese realized they would have to come up with a more permanent solution to the migration. They readied landing areas and prepared to do what they could for this wave of migrants, mustering their social services workers for a long night. As the absolute numbers of migrants had actually dropped many Maltese figured that their island nation was simply a way station for these unfortunate souls; the first spot of land they encountered once they shoved off from Africa.

As the vessels washed up on the shore the initial groups of migrants swarmed out of the ships, sporting flowing garb and duffel bags of possessions. They overwhelmed the processing lines that had formed with many unable to leave their boats as there was no room to make a landing. Patience was not holding as the sun went down but still the boats kept coming. However, in the dark, the people who landed were different.

They waited on the strand for a critical mass.

Armed with machine guns they quickly overwhelmed Maltese security forces, fired flares to signal the rising to the thousands of young men in the camps and by dawn had pretty much taken the island, save for a few small outposts of armed resistance.

They offered to remove anyone who did not want to convert to Islam warning that the island group was now part of the Caliphate and subject to Sharia Law.

Within a week many Maltese had fled to southern Italy where they were welcomed as long lost family. Some of the refugees who had moved to Italy were forced to return to Malta as Italians were worried about the sincerity of the immigrants after they heard about the fate of Malta.

Within another week, anyone who openly defied the Muslim take over was slain. The invading army was brutal and relentless - simply killing any-one who refused to submit. Often these killings were done to maximum public effect. Roasting people alive, drowning them in cages, cutting off heads on mass. The last areas of resistance succumbed without much of a fight as they simply ran out of food, water and will. No organized help came.

Three months passed and Malta was lost forever. Residents of Cyprus and Crete quaked, demanding protection from the EU and NATO. A few naval vessels moved into position and the EU sent a few battalions. Refugees of any kind were turned back into the sea or gathered up and ferried back to the African and Turkish coasts.

NATO declined to act at all. The EU made another pretense of talk but were more worried about their own borders.

Malta had been taken and converted.

Six months later, as the morning call to prayer sounded in the streets of the Maltese capital - six large transport planes landed at the airport.

Materiel had been funnelled into Malta to help secure the island nation. It came by ship and it came by plane. This morning, each plane sported the markings of Emirates Airlines. The six planes taxied to the terminal. The first in line turned to show its cargo entrance while the others remained ready in line to take its place and unload once the debarking of the first plane was complete.

The large hydraulic cargo door opened on the first plane and two Mercedes trucks piled high with boxes disgorged from the belly of the plane. Then two more.

While those in the terminal were watching, uncertain of what was being delivered, the other planes facing the terminal building, were dropping their cargo doors. Airport officials drove out to the planes and were met by the pilots and staff as they exited the plane waiting for local contact.

Airline personnel gave a friendly wave and beckoned the officials to meet them. The first vehicle rolled up to the truck which stopped. A man with a big smile jumped out and approached the car.

"My brother, where do you want us to drop our cargo of fresh fruits, vegetables and other foodstuffs? Do you have a holding area here at the airport or is it nearby?"

He turned to the man beside him. "Cargo section BB?"

"Yes, that will do. Are all these planes filled with food?"

"Take your trucks to Cargo section BB. It's around the far side of that building. It is well marked. There are several loading docks there. Are all these planes filled with food?"

"They are supplies from your friends to help the conquest." He turned to the driver of the Mercedes truck, "Radio the other planes tell them to deliver their cargoes behind that building to loading docks in Cargo section BB."

He turned back to the airport officials. "Lead the way, my brothers."

He got back into the truck and after a moment followed the airport vehicle to the cargo section.

Two more trucks emerged carrying boxes marked as foodstuffs. They followed the first truck to the Cargo bays.

"It is foodstuffs from our friends," a man in the airport vehicle radioed the terminal.

With deliveries of goods coming in most days, officials in the terminal were happy to take delivery of much needed supplies. Two more trucks debarked - these trucks had covered backs. They rolled slowly to the cargo section of the airport terminal. At precisely that moment, a wave of fighter jets flying very low, swarmed into sight. They were on the terminal in moments firing rockets at the terminal tower and taking out two small buildings along a runway where security forces were headquartered. Within a minute the signal was given and armed personal swarmed out of the covered trucks and entered the terminal building shooting as they went.

In the wake of the fighter attack people in the airport terminal quickly scrambled a resistance and moved into a defensive mode to ward off the fighter attacks. They had taken their eye off the apparently benign cargo planes at a critical moment.

Following the transport trucks, and lost in the confusion of the air strike, tanks had debarked from the forward facing planes and were quickly forming up a defensive perimeter around the airport. As soon as the last cargo was unloaded the first plane taxied and quickly took off. Hundreds of armed personnel swarmed out of the other planes following the armaments and heavy equipment. Thanks to their forward thrust into the terminal itself and the confusion sown by the fighter attack they quickly secured the airport. A band of airport security personnel attempted to put up a defensive stand but they were mowed down mercilessly.

Once empty the other five planes turned and took off in quick succession leaving tanks, soldiers, supplies and weapons.

An army of drones were deployed from the last plane as it left the air-space. Most were armed, all had eyes and ears. They flew to their pre-determined locations and sent a stream of data to mission control.

City officials called in armed personnel, organizing them in a warehouse near the shipping port. Several pickup trucks with anti-aircraft guns and others with heavy armor were made ready and given orders. Once they were clear of the warehouse, a rocket smashed into the mobile units, killing a dozen men. Two more rockets hit the warehouse destroying it and everything inside.

A second wave of fighters swooped into Malta and fired rockets into any potential command and control structures. Another group of cargo planes swooped in for a quick landing, disgorging their cargoes and turning to leave.

The drones continued to search for organized resistance and fired several rockets to neutralize threats before they could be organized.

Explosions rocked the city as bombing runs were completed. Fighter jets picked off command and control centers and security units with rocket attacks. Half of the original force held the airport while the other half - heavily armoured and determined to root out anybody who showed even the remotest link to resistance - poured into the capital and began a re-lentless house by house search. More cargo planes landed.

If the usurpers found resistance they simply set the buildings on fire. Those who surrendered were immediately taken to ships in the harbour. After 24 hours the ships set course for Libya. Once empty they returned to Malta and repeated the procedure.

More planes landed and several heavily armed destroyers appeared off the coast.

Within a week Malta was cleared.

Two days later Israel declared Malta a Jewish province saying it had been devoid of Maltese when they had removed the Muslim invaders. They began to heavily fortify the two islands and started to let the surviving Maltese, those who had fled to Italy, back into their homes.

A few Maltese agitated for a return of sovereignty but Israel was firm. There would be no return of the islands, they were now a province of Israel and anyone who continued to agitate would be removed and taken to either Libya or Italy. Maltese who could prove their ownership and heritage could resume their way of life, claim their rights as citizens but only under Israeli governance.

The United Nations condemned Israel. Israel issued a statement that the island had been taken and that none of the former Maltese were in residence when it occurred - therefore the land was forfeit. As the United Nations had ignored Israel's concerned about its Muslim neighbours prior to Israel being attacked with nuclear weapons, and had refused to even condemn actions taken against it when the nuclear strike had come - the Israelis declared that the United Nations had no moral authority in the issue.

Citizens of the EU and of North America sided heavily with the Israelis as they were simply in awe of the bold action and determination exhibited by the Israelis. In fact, Israel had remained so entirely under the radar since it had been attacked it had led many to believe it had virtually ceased to exist.

Certainly there were those who called out the Israelis for their heavy handed approach and demanded that they hand back the islands to the Maltese. The Israelis simply fortified the islands and took to removing any indication of their short term inhabitants. During the six months they were there the previous residents had taken care to remove evidence of any other prior ownership. Stripped of its history Malta began a new chapter.

Chapter Seventeen   **Washington**

"Small and nimble, that's the key there," said President O'Day.

"Mr. President, I think it's more about being bold and determined," said Tom Findlay.

"What is it a soap opera? Bold and determined, really?" O'Day had an unusual way of establishing his status. Findlay furrowed his brow. He had long ago determined that despite his condescension O'Day was treating him more as an equal rather than claiming automatic deference. Sometimes he had to remind himself of that fact.

"Well, it's not so much about the operation to remove the Islamic State or whoever it was that took Malta in the first place," said Findlay. "It's more about the determination to hold the islands, consolidate them as a province of Israel and refuse to budge on any public pressure. We probably should have seen it coming after their own country was reduced to ashes and nobody did anything about it."

"If they were reduced to ash, how did they mount such an effective campaign? How did the CIA miss this?"

"Obviously they were far more prepared for the ultimate attack on their territory than they even let us know. We knew they had some capacity to survive a nuclear attack of significant magnitude. But this goes well beyond survivability."

Findlay speculated, "I'm guessing they had something like this planned all along. In fact I wouldn't even be too surprised if they didn't engineer the Muslim takeover of Malta, to free it up to be reinvaded by them, with fewer political consequences. They might have gone after a larger island like Cyprus or Crete but that has political consequences outside of those places and they are larger and harder to secure and hold. Malta is nobody's colony and as such is a very ripe target for this type of operation."

"They must have a bomb proof city in Israel to survive this long after the blast and to be able to mount such an operation - there must be millions living in some sort of bunker."

"We simply cannot underestimate the Jews. They simply will not put themselves in any compromising position. They have learned not to trust anyone completely."

"Now, Mr. President that leaves us with our own concerns. As promised the good folk of Boston seem to have reattached themselves to the United States. Amazing what a little love will do. However we have lost Texas and word from our people in Atlanta is that the Cubans and Mexicans are cozying up to the southerners - mostly to divide up Florida and the Caribbean."

"I don't know what we can do for the old guard in central Florida. It's either all in to bounce the Latin influence out of the south or back off and consolidate our own borders. We could encourage Dixie to swallow Florida and keep the Cubans and Mexicans out. Their foothold is not a good thing from our perspective, as we have seen in California."

"Mr. President, I hate the idea of leaving loyal Americans out of the Union. I think we need to put the resources necessary into keeping Florida whole and removing the threat from Cuba. Jacksonville provides an excellent harbour for our Naval decentralization policy and we need to protect our military assets in Tampa. I know it is difficult but we must secure the east even at the expense of the west, at least in the short term. It is only California that is an issue. Arizona can hold its own at this point and the Northern Californians want no part of Mexifornia. The issue is our military assets in San Diego. I propose we begin the process of turning San Diego into a strong point that can be held and defended from the surrounding countryside. The military assets there are too significant to leave the harbour there to chance. Other than that we need to concentrate on the East for the time being."

"Well Tom, it's a plan and we are fairly short of anything else to even consider."

"I am also going to suggest that we worry less about racial and ethnic cleansing of our nation and that we put considerable effort into a cultural cleansing - in that way we might be able to entice Texas and the south back into the Union."

"How do we go about culturally cleansing America? I presume you have at least the outline of a plan."

"Mr. President we have to identify the core American values that have endured throughout our history and we have to relentlessly push those values, promote those values and punish anything other than those values. In no particular order they are - small constitutional government characterised by the rule of law, free enterprise, religious freedom, political democracy, and rewards for hard work and good citizenship."

"Yeah, those are easy to promote Tom," said O'Day sarcastically. "For this to work we need a small basket of things that are very specific."

"I thought you might say that. A ban on religion crossing over into politics with specific statutes and penalties for non-compliance including deportation, jail and heavy fines. It goes for every denomination of every religion and is really just a reaffirmation of the separation of church and state. Once your belief in a higher power crosses over into demanding that other people comply with the wishes of your faith - that is politics and therefore actionable. Politics are collective and end when they encroach on individual moral rights. We need to follow the constitution rigorously even and most especially if it causes pain to the federal government. It's a credibility issue. We need to reduce taxes on business as taxes are paid on income and eventually all corporate profits are plowed into increased business opportunities or income - both those things have advantages for society. Using the tax code for social engineering just encourages tax dodges."

"Can you draft something up on this. Please keep it very specific and very limited. If it's going to work it has to be unassailable and have virtually complete acceptance - otherwise the values they promote are not widely held. We need to make sure they are tested in non-activist courts."

"Now what about Texas?" continued O'Day. "There are reports that ranchers in the south have been shooting migrants in cold blood."

"Yes, I've heard that. Apparently they have made the point and are experiencing an almost total end to the migrant problem. Amazing what a little direct action can accomplish."

"Well the migrant problem is morphing into an issue on their other borders. Where they are less inclined to shoot."

" Apparently Albuquerque and points east want into Texas and many people south of Oklahoma City want in as well. The city itself is divided and there are threats on both sides. Texas is concerned about agitating us and they have a nice natural border already but the Oklahomans are pushing hard and the Texans don't really want to say 'no'. The New Mexicans are actually functionally part of Texas and have simply let Arizona deal with the migrant problem. According to my briefings Tucson is a virtual armed camp."

"And Virginia?"

"Most of the state wants to join Dixie. Only the extreme north around

Washington disagrees and that's mostly because its full of federal employees. Norfolk is a bit like Fort Sumter back in the day, as the locals are mostly federal employees or connected to the local economy which supports the naval station. They are happy with our clean up attempts. It might become Guantanamo north if things go badly wrong."

"Is it possible to tailor your American Values legislation to try to reel in Dixie and Texas?"

"Well Mr. President, I can sure try, but that gets away from the specific and simple approach and threatens to look too manipulative which would kill the whole package."

"See what you can do. Perhaps loosen up some of the Second Amendment restrictions we've put in place over the years, or killing them outright. And include some States Rights things for the South."

"That's what the strictly constitutional point was about but yeah, making it specific is probably wise."

There was a knock at the door.

"Come," said the President.

"Mr. President you are required urgently in the situation room."

The President rose and shuffled some papers. "If it's Texas, let the Texans handle it. After all they will shortly be an independent nation."

"I must insist Mr. President."

O'Day then moved quickly out of the office with the Secret Service man following in his wake. He motioned Findlay to follow him.

As the doors to the bunker opened O'Day could see the members of the Joint Chiefs as well as both Senators from California.

"Mr. President. In the last several hours an unknown force of heavily armed insurgents has moved through the southern California countryside sweeping it clear of inhabitants. They are insisting upon immediate evacuation of all properties and premises and are killing any citizens who resist."

"Mr. President, it can only be a Mexican backed militia or some sort of splinter group with covert backing of the Mexican government," said Martin Seafisher, senior senator from California.

"If the Mexicans are involved in any traceable way they know they will get war. Therefore, I cannot believe they are involved," said President O'Day. Have we been in touch with them?"

"According to our reconnaissance we are dealing with approximately a division worth of men and material - maybe 15,000 armed men and significant light battlefield arms and equipment. They moved across the border at Mexicali and Tecate before dawn and have reached the San Diego canyons and the Salton Sea. San Diego is in an uproar with our military awaiting orders on repelling the invasion. There are apparently local battles inside the San Diego city limits as much of that city is sympathetic to Mexico."

"We must protect San Diego," said O'Day, giving a quick involuntary glance to Findlay. "Send a squadron of fighters to search and destroy any large concentration of troops or equipment near San Diego. Be very careful of potential anti-aircraft missiles. Do the same for any force you find moving north towards or near the Salton Sea. We must make a very strong stand here or we invite it occurring again. For now, keep our operations within our borders. Once we have halted the troop movements investigate thoroughly the origin of these troops. I will issue a warning statement and we will proceed based on our information. Understood?"

"Yes sir," said every member of the Joint Chiefs.

"Mexico City is disavowing any knowledge of this and has offered to help and investigate on their side of the border. We have not heard back from the governors of two northern Mexican states."

Chapter Eighteen   **San Diego**

The seven plane formation quickly reached Granite Hills and swung out in a fan for a quick survey of the rugged countryside. The area was very suburban and it seemed unlikely that anyone would expend armaments to simply wipe the countryside clean.

"Happy Six to Blue Leader."

"Blue Leader copy."

"There is a large concentration of troops and equipment just inside the Cleveland National Forest Reserve."

"Bashful Five to Blue Leader."

"Copy Bashful Five."

"There is a string of armed men and some vehicles on I-8 between Granite Hills and the National Forest. Recommend a strafing run from east to west - highest concentration to lowest."

"Copy Bashful Five - a man with a plan. Form up five miles east and we will strafe with full array in flare pattern alpha."

All six planes copied the Blue Leader and the planes formed up in a battle line - a staggered line, slightly off center of their straight line direction, the F18s swung in from the north and south to catch the western direction of the highway and begin their run very low to the ground following the highway.

The first plane found its line, fired four rockets into a large group of vehicles and swooped up and away to the north. The pilot radioed that there were other concentrations of men and equipment off the highway hidden by camouflage tents in the scrub land. The second plane stayed low and fired its rockets into the scrub on the left of the road before swooping up and peeling off to the south. The third plane swooped in and repeated the rocket attack on the north side of the road. It peeled up and out to the north. As the last plane, Blue Leader simply fired a smothering rapid fire from his 20 millimeter cannons as he surveyed the damage.

"That will pin them down for a bit," he radioed command. "There are significant troops in the area and I recommend a quick bombing strike."

"Blue squad, form a double attack array Delta and commence attack run on the rest of the highway from Delta point Flinn Springs east and west. Southern section report any return fire and then return to base. Northern section reconnoitre troop movements south of Salton Sea once your strafing run is complete. "

The northern part of the squad formed up for another strafing run from Flinn Springs to the east while the southern squad did the same thing but moved to the west towards El Cajon.

Smaller units were hit mostly by cannon fire from the F-18s. Those moving toward the Salton Sea were fired upon by a surface to air missile. Coming in low over the National Forest after strafing the highway Sleepy Two was hit. The pilot managed to fly the plane to a much higher altitude and away from the area of attack but the plane began to break up and he was forced to eject over the forest, not far from the highway that twisted through it. His plane crashed in a fireball a couple of miles north of the highway. He landed softly near the top of a large rock outcrop perhaps 150 feet above the highway with a good view all around. Despite it being a National Forest, it was largely without trees. The pilot's rescue beacon emitted his location signal.

The rest of the squad had moved into a higher altitude as they passed by the National Forest and were able to evade two other missiles that were launched. A helicopter gunship was launched to rescue the downed pilot. He was in contact via a secure communications channel and was giving a steady stream of intelligence as seen from his elevated location.

A second squad was sent out to deal with the invaders to the east but wasn't able to inflict as much damage as word of the devastating counter attack reached them before the planes. A medium bomber was sent to the first point of contact and the area was levelled, more as a statement of intent than for the casualties it inflicted.

Choppers flew into attack zones as the army began its investigation. The dead fighters mostly appeared to be Latin American but had no identification of any kind, nothing Mexican, not even cigarettes or gum wrappers. All equipment was American made - but given the large arms sales over several decades, that was not a surprise. Some of the equipment was traced to Saudi purchasers but the Saudis said they had sold the vehicles many years before to other clients in the Gulf.

The only significant clue that was found was several of the men who were killed, while wearing the same uniform as the others, had one, two or three silver buttons on their right shoulders, suggesting rank. All of these men appeared to be of European extraction. DNA samples were taken to be compared against known insurgents.

As night fell the American military prepared for a second day of strikes and closely monitored any movements in the area using night vision equipment. Two helicopters were shot down in the dark, suggesting the insurgents had more sophisticated weapons than otherwise shown.

As dawn rose it appeared as if the entire force had retreated or melted into the scrub. There was no sign of them, save the burned out shells of vehicles and the corpses of those who had been killed in the counter-attack.

Military strikes were called in but the pilots found nothing to aim at. Helicopter and ground forces found plenty of abandoned buildings and a large number of refugees who had abandoned their homes at the command of the invaders.

"It's obviously an operation to support the Mexicanization of southern California," said Senator Seafisher at a hastily called national security meeting. "The attack alone is enough to drive most Americans to leave and head north to safe ground. That process was already well underway and now it will accelerate. If we do not counterattack the Mexicans and toss out anyone of Mexican extraction from southern California, the area is lost."

"Well we can't just blow up Mexico City because we are pissed," said O'Day. "Give me some evidence and I'll authorize a strong response. But without evidence, and with the Mexican ambassador purring in my ear, I cannot start shooting up Tijuana."

Chapter Nineteen

June 7th dawned cloudy with rain in much of the current and former United States.

All the pieces were in place. The army began to move.

Two white vans pulled up to opposite ends of a suburban shopping mall. Four men wearing long rain coats went into the mall, two from each end, and walked briskly to the center fountain. Four others remained inside the vans, moving the vehicles so they were only a short distance from the mall entrances while the back ends of the vans opened on the mall entrances. Once they heard the commotion inside they raised their weapons. As people began to stream out of the mall they calmly began to spray bullets into the mall exits mowing down the fleeing people.

The shooters inside the mall retraced their steps and moved in pairs to each main exit shooting and tossing grenades as they walked. Shoppers ran for the exits. As he walked, shooting groups cowering in storefronts, and tossing grenades, one shooter was killed. An older man, with close cropped hair, pulled a weapon and fired. The second shooter fired at him dropping him immediately.

As his companion was down he grabbed his gun and began to move quickly toward the exit. He sprayed fire at the fleeing people who were also facing fire from the other direction. Then he was shot in the leg. He looked down. Blood was seeping down his leg to the floor. Then he was hit in the arm and the chest. Then he knew no more.

A similar scene unfolded on the south side of the mall. And then it was quiet as the gunfire stopped. And then the shrieks of pain and the whimpers of death penetrated the swiftly quieting echoes of gunfire. Two vans drove away from the mall at high speed. One was caught by armed citizens who shot out its tires. The resulting accident saved them any need to expend additional ammunition as the van swerved and drove full speed into the side of a delivery truck. Both burst into flames and after only enough time for witnesses to register the accident, they both exploded into a 20 foot high fireball.

The second van reached the main road and slowed once it entered the traffic stream, quickly turning off onto a side street and then again to see if anyone followed. Then they proceeded to their second target. As they crossed a bridge over a busy highway they dropped four grenades onto oncoming traffic. Fifteen vehicles exploded and 25 more plowed into the resulting carnage causing a huge fire which engulfed the overpass. The fire burned for several hours and the overpass collapsed onto the tangled mess of traffic below.

The van moved to a local high school. The four men inside ran from the van to the school building and smashed or shot out windows and then tossed in grenades - one classroom at a time along both sides of the building. A local policeman had seen the beginnings of the attack and had radioed for help before leaping from his squad car and shooting two of the attackers dead. One of the others began to shoot back at him, pinning him down some distance from where the shooters had gone. Once they disappeared around the side of the building he got up and moved in the opposite direction, hoping to catch the attackers coming at him. He wanted to wait until they made their way around the building but he knew they were firebombing classrooms and he needed to stop it quickly.

He reached a corner of the building and cautiously peered around it. Right in front of him was one of the attackers - he shot him point blank as the man had little expectation of resistance at that point. The last remaining attacker put up his hands in surrender as he appeared to be out of bullets. The policeman approached him cautiously and when the man appeared to reach behind his ear to scratch his head he shot him without hesitation.

The policeman moved to each of the four bodies. Two appeared to be still alive. He contemplated shooting them in the head but settled on removing their weapons far from the places they had fallen.

He radioed the precinct to report but couldn't get through because of radio chatter from the other attacks.

As he spoke into his radio one of the attackers rolled over and tried to sit up. The policeman took two steps towards him and fired twice. His head exploded as the round caught him on the bridge of his nose. The second shot hit him straight in the chest and what was left of him was violently snapped back into the ground with a spray of blood and tissue.

All in - more than 1,000 people, shoppers, commuters and high school students were killed in three major locations. Thousands more were injured. Reports filtered in from across the state that there were many more attacks of a similar nature.

In Toledo Ohio a virtually identical attack was carried out at a local shopping mall. Attackers sprayed the downtown with bullets and firebombed several streets and highways. As the smoke cleared 17 apartments exploded taking much of their buildings with them and causing carnage beyond anything anticipated by local emergency resources.

Most attacks appeared to be less efficiently carried out but there were many that were even more devastating. It was the sheer numbers of separate attacks that simply overwhelmed emergency services and stunned citizens. Across Dixie there were 1,195 attacks carried out by 512 groups of attackers. Numbers were similar for the northeast and the Midwest.

When it was all added up more than 410,000 people were killed and an additional million people were injured, many quite severely. Death totals had risen every day in the aftermath as people with severe injuries succumbed.

While unconsidered at the time, the attacks reduced the number of religious and cultural militants and insurgents in the former United States. Almost all were permanently retired by police, armed citizens or premature explosions of their weapons.

Unfortunately a backlash was building in which many innocent foreign nationals were caught. In some places any type of non-standard dress, speech or action was greeted with derision, violence and where large numbers of people congregated, mob actions.

The shock of the attacks and their scope at first rendered the nation numb. As the scenes were cleaned up and the dead buried, as the survivors told their tales, the anger grew to a boiling fury. It took very little provocation for more mob violence to erupt. Even the peacemakers were attacked as sympathizers. Officials were attacked as those who had failed in their duty to protect Americans - even though most people had failed to heed the warnings and had failed to go public with their concerns.

Many innocents were rounded up by mobs and several were killed. Mob violence, once unleashed in specific cases was horrific. Most incidents were small acts of violence. Vigilantes scoured the nation, killing and destroying property associated with the attackers, their countries of origin and their cultural attachments. It was a short and violent episode, impossible to stop as groups appeared overnight and disappeared just as quickly. Anyone who did not appear completely innocent was dispatched with extreme prejudice. Even the innocent were targets.

Police arrested innocents for their own protection and governments moved where possible to quickly disperse the remaining targets. Non-citizens had been deported by the hundreds of thousands in the wake of the 5-29 attacks on New York, Los Angeles and Norfolk. Those that chose to remain now faced the wrath of the survivors.

Officials protected citizens in secure locations and made to deport anyone who showed the slightest sympathy for the militants. Those with extreme views risked the violence of the mob and would have been killed. Officials tried to rehabilitate the thinking of those naturalized American citizens who abhorred the attacks. Pretty soon it was evident that only those people who had several friends and neighbours speak up for them would be allowed to resume their former lives. And then only after some quiet period had passed.

Months and months went by as people were slowly allowed back into their communities. On the ground, in small towns and cities the United States had become a police state.

Chapter Twenty   **Oxford**

Edward Spenser cozied up to the bar. He ordered a Hobgoblin and looked about. The ceiling was very low. The ancient pub was laid out in a traditional manner with many cubbies and private areas brokered by walls and corners. There was plenty of wood, glass and velvet. Red and green velvet and gold lettering, too.

Spenser looked at his bottle of Hobgoblin and smiled at the guitar held by the goblin on the label. The label had been especially commissioned to promote an upcoming summer rock music festival. He rolled his left wrist open, shrugged his shoulder and stretched his arm until his shirt pulled back. Almost midway between his wrist and elbow on his forearm there was a small tattoo of a notched axe, with the letters AUW neatly inscribed. It was the same notched broad axe normally held by the hobgoblin on the bottle.

He shrugged his shirt sleeve back into place and with his right hand grabbed the glass of beer and took a sip. He immediately wanted more, but rolled the ruby ale over his tongue while taking a general look around the pub.

The Cape of Good Hope attracted mostly upper classmen situated as it was at the end of The High, with Magdalene College just the other side of the river.

Spenser wasn't entirely out of place in his dark summer suit. Too old to be a student, he might have passed for an instructor or some other faculty or administration type attached to the University or one of its many colleges. Oxford was a strange and yet compelling place. Almost no one looked out of place, even the summer tourists were a common enough site to be ignored by the permanent residents.

His remaining beer was approaching the halfway point when a noisy bunch of graduate students entered and made a big production of pushing a few tables together to handle their whole group.

As they were getting settled a youngish man, who might have been attached to the group came to the bar and sat beside him to his left. He ordered a Hobgoblin and put his hands on the bar so his cuffs pulled back. Spenser saw the notched axe tattoo on the inside of his left forearm. Then he put his hand in his pocket and the cuff covered it again.

Spenser waited until the publican had collected his money.

"A Hobgoblin? I'm amused every year by the guitar on the label. Who's headlining Knebworth this year?"

The younger man turned slightly to him and Spenser again rolled his wrist to briefly show the tattoo. "Yes, an axe for an axe on the label. Amusing."

"After the trouble in America, there are people fearing the same type of thing here. However our circumstances are more precarious and the solution not easy to implement. There are many who suggest a pre-emptive approach; ending all immigration, deporting all non-citizens and most evocatively, engaging in a Night of Broken Minarets."

"The reliance on citizenship is overdue," said Spenser. "However, a vigilante approach would leave a huge stain on our culture, one that most people would revile. Is there another way?"

"Some have suggested a return to state enforced Establishmentarianism - one church to rule them all - one church to bind them - the Anglican Church. It rubs many people the wrong way especially given the Roman claims to being the only mother church. However, it is in many ways, a gentler approach."

"And me - what is required of me?"

"You are to inform your contacts of the move to an Establishment church in the UK. For now you are raising the balloon. They would be encouraged across Europe to do much the same thing. Without Rome interfering it might actually play well to the predominately Catholic countries to establish a local Catholic church while keeping the hive at arm's length."

"Unless there is some really good reason not to do this, unless the great unwashed protest in the streets, it will occur in short order. I'll need you back here - he looked at his phone - in a month. We cannot wait. After America people are concerned that if a similar plan of uprising isn't already in the works here, it soon will be. We must be pre-emptive and strike before they do. My American contacts suggest events there went from planning to execution in only one month."

Spenser drained his beer. He nodded to the barman and moved through the pub, past the noisy table of students, past several couples. The generally younger couples were engaged deeply in conversation while the older ones were engaged in separate thoughtful concerns but doing it together.

Spenser started off down the street and then realized he needed to take care of some business. He doubled back a few dozen yards to the pub, and moved around to an alley in the back, through to the pub's detached facilities. Finding the correct door he moved into position facing the urinal. The door opened and a woman moved into the doorframe.

"Mr. Spenser, I thought I might find you here. You cannot be having a drink on your way to having a drink? What are you up to?"

He recognized the voice. "Ah, my dear, I thought we were meeting at The Eagle and The Child. I was just on my way there. Whatever are you doing here?"

"I saw you walking down the High in the wrong direction from our tryst. Must admit my curiosity got the better of me."

"Allow me to finish here and I'll happily escort you across town. I will answer any question you might have. I was inside speaking to the son of a London friend of mine. I'll introduce you to the young man should he still be here," said Spenser. "The young gentleman is the older son of a very old friend of mine. He works here at the University. My friend was once provost of New College. He now works for the Crown."

Spenser completed his task, and checked, noting that the young man had apparently left. He had expected that. He and his new companion made their way across the bridge past Magdalene College and along The High. They turned off the main street at the first opportunity preferring the less travelled streets in their quest for the Eagle and the Child.

"I always thought of this place as the inspiration for Shelob's lair," said Spenser, arriving at the front door of the pub.

"Not sure how I should take that seeing as you always insist upon meeting me here."

"Now Jennette, I was referring to the web of streets. Truth is I just prefer this side of town. There is more parking and it's easier for you to get here - the Ashmolean is just around the corner."

"Six blocks isn't around the corner but point taken." They ordered another beer for him - this time a lovely dark Guinness and a glass of a full red wine for her.

"Now tell me about your friend."

"My London friend or his son? There isn't much more to tell. We keep in touch and I usually drop into to see him when I'm in London."

"But you live there."

"London is a very big place. He lives in the southern suburbs just off the M25. He asks me to drop in on his son when I'm in Oxford as he has trouble getting here. Sometimes I deliver things to him - an envelope or magazine his father wants him to have. And I often have plans at the Eagle and the Child," he smiled at her.

"Or Shelob's lair," she took a matter of fact sip on wine, returning the glass to the table but left her fingers on the stem.

"I'm glad I'm here now. Unfortunately I have had a message from one of my suppliers and I cannot stay more than a day. I'm off to Germany and Switzerland."

"But we were going to take a week together - I've booked off work."

"Aye," he thought for a moment, "I had considered that. Why don't you join me. I haven't made arrangements yet, so we can do it together. I only have a few short appointments I need to deal with and we can take a week or eight days over yonder?"

"Really? Just like that?"

"Absolutely. I am sorry to have to change plans so quickly. It's the least I can do. As long as you aren't upset with me having to toddle off for a couple of short business meetings. Mostly stuff about supply lines and insurance arrangements."

"I'm skeptical of you Mr. Spenser and these alleged meeting times but if you are on the level it might be fun. Where are we going?"

"I have a meeting in Amsterdam. Another in Zurich and possibly a third in Venice. So we are going to Amsterdam, Zurich and maybe Venice. Any other places you 'd like to go? I don't mind moving about a lot for a whirlwind sightseeing tour or staying put for a few days in each place. It's strictly up to you."

She thought for a moment, "It would be nice not to move around too much. We should split the week between Amsterdam and Zurich and only go to Venice if your schedule takes you there."

"Okay. I had been thinking about taking the Chunnel to Amsterdam. So we will leave tomorrow morning from Kings Cross. Just let me connect to the Wi-Fi here and I'll book the tickets right now. Now how about something to eat?"

Chapter Twenty - One   Georgia

"Despite our concerns with the United States dollar we will continue to maintain the dollar as legal tender for all debts incurred in the Republic of Dixie. We will also continue with our plans to fully realize our own legal currency - which will operate at a one to one exchange rate with US dollars for the foreseeable future. However, Dixie dollars will not be printed, nor will Dixie engage in any deficit spending by its governments," proclaimed the announcement of Speaker Vernon Clemons.

Dixie dollars began to circulate but even the most ardent southerner was wary of holding too many of these dollars as the historic solidity of the US dollar seemed to be far more tangible than the new dollars.

"Ah, Ms. Gentle, Anne if I may . . ." he continued, "Mexico is most gratified with the apparent direction of the Dixie dollar. My President will make an announcement of recognition of the validity of the Dixie legislature and begin efforts to establish a full diplomatic protocol."

"I trust you have informed the Legislature and Mr. Clemons."

"Yes, I have. I simply wanted to provide you with the courtesy of knowing in advance that your efforts have borne fruit and that Mexico is an honourable neighbour."

"I hope that continues to be true Mr. Ambassador, I have heard some disturbing rumours of Mexican involvement with Cuban agitators in Florida. As you likely know much of Florida is interested in joining Dixie in its independence."

"Ah Ms. Gentle, I assure you Mexico has no designs on Florida. We have our own problems in our northern states - they require much of our resources but provide little back to the state in return."

"I have also heard disturbing news from California regarding a mini-invasion coming from Mexico."

"I too have heard that rumour. There is no evidence of official Mexican involvement. There is little doubt something serious happened there. Families are very worried and many have even moved away from California as it appears to be too volatile. We are cooperating with US authorities and conducting our own investigation as to who those rebels were. All that is known is they were a fairly substantial force and that they appeared like a mirage and melted back into the desert."

"On another note Ms. Gentle, as a demonstration of good faith, I have prevailed on the Spanish Ambassador to Mexico to meet with Mr. Clemons."

Clemons put down the phone. A cautious man, he wondered what was in these meetings. In two days he had received word that both the Spanish and Argentinean Ambassadors to Mexico wanted to meet him and open a channel to their diplomatic missions. Neither would commit to anything specific but did say this was a routine and concrete first step in establishing diplomatic relations.

Clemons began to get a creeping feeling that he was in over his head. Not that he would admit to it openly but so much of his current work was out of his realm of experience.

Clemons was the owner of a business insurance and employee benefit company that operated throughout the South. Based in Charlotte, North

Carolina it conducted extensive business in the Carolinas and in Georgia and had dealings in Florida, Alabama, Virginia and Tennessee.

Clemons had been very concerned about the weakness of the US dollar and the extremely high debt levels the US government had taken on. His involvement with government had been mostly based on the currency and debt questions. Prior to the 5-29 attacks he had been selected by the state legislatures of seven southern states to act on their behalf in lobbying Washington. When the attacks came he was riding a wave of southern concern and had used his position to call together a conference of Southern State legislators, ostensibly regarding the weakness in the US dollar brought on by the nuclear attacks. Southern congressmen and senators met among themselves regarding purely southern issues but they needed a leader who was not a Washington insider. Already in place as an approved representative of the southern states on monetary issues, Vernon Clemons was their choice.

At the behest of the seven state legislatures Dixie had declared itself a single block entity - more in the spirit of a new political party rather than a splinter group for complete independence. The independence angle took popular root and angered Washington. The ire of southern congressmen was raised by Washington's defiance and the southern members began talking about legislative independence. That talk quickly morphed into currency independence and quickly and without violence, Dixie was a defacto nation. It existed even though its borders were not firm, its legislature an amalgamation of state and US federal representatives, and it had no constitution or most of the other institutions of national government. Collecting taxes to fund the enterprise was high on the agenda. Most favoured existing taxes being funnelled to Dixie rather than paid to the US federal government. A decision on how to make it happen with the least upset was being debated.

Vernon Clemons was trying to take the whole bowl of unformed Jell-o and have it set as a firm whole without having a specific idea of what it should look like. He knew the difficulties that approach possessed but he also knew that espousing a specific idea was a revolution and he favoured the gentler approach of evolution.

Pretty much all of Dixie thought it should operate much as the US constitution did but without the US. They wanted a return to the federalism of the 18th century. So Clemons kept a lid on things, local mayors and long time elected officials took on a mantle of responsibility and nobody really knew where Dixie was going. Clemons was working on a road map using the currency issues he championed as the jumping off point.

He had most of the US federal representatives tied into a Dixie legislature but he was only the grease that made it work - he was unelected, though appointed by the majority of legislators themselves. They had taken care to make that appointment official through a vote. He felt at times like he was the commissioner of a professional sports league, presiding over unruly team owners at their own behest, and subject to dismissal at any moment.

It seemed a fair compromise as he had the legitimacy of their elections and their blessings of central power. However he could be removed at any time by their whim. He also had the backing of state legislatures and that dual legitimacy paid dividends on major issues but Clemons could see that on thorny battles he could be torn in two by divided authority.

He did feel an enormous responsibility to Dixie and the people of Dixie rather than to the various legislators who legitimized him.

Virginia was still an issue. Richmond and areas south of Fredericksburg were firmly with Dixie. However coastal areas were less sure and that coastal wavering was anchored by Norfolk and Newport News in the deep south east of the state. There were few natural boundaries and anything that was drawn appeared to be destined for conflict. That was the main reason nothing firm had occurred in Virginia though both state senators sat in the Dixie legislature and many of its federal Congressmen did also.

Northern Florida was in the same flux though neither Florida senators rubbed shoulders with Dixie. Some of the US congressmen representing northern districts did - and did quite enthusiastically. The western section of Dixie was its firmest border but while southern Louisiana was firmly in the New South it had its own agenda and had not formally joined the Dixie declaration, and Arkansas was a southern state with significant Texas sympathies. And of course there was the Kentucky question.

Clemons was content to ride the unknowable in Kentucky and Florida until some future time when it would become clearer. He was confident in Louisiana. Those legislatures were not among those from whom he derived his legitimacy.

"Even independent nations need friends," he thought to himself. "As long as the old US doesn't try to push the agenda we can remain on good terms. As long as Texas and Mexico and Cuba are all playing fair then we have a chance."

He breathed a deep sigh, catching himself on all the variables that had to remain favourable for Dixie to have a chance.

Clemons had cobbled together a small office staff as it became necessary. He was determined to keep his role small but needed an office dedicated to the task of being the center around which the spokes could radiate.

He had seconded staff members from each federal senator's offices to cover administration, communications, political issues, finance, policy and border issues. Now, with Ambassadors calling him, he needed a foreign service.

He reached for the phone.

"Anne, nice to hear your voice again."

"Ah Vernon, could this be about Ambassador Rodriquez?"

"Ultimately yes, I suppose. I've been so concerned about our local issues, governance, borders, currency, that I've ignored the foreign stuff. And frankly Anne, I am not very familiar with those workings. Do you know anyone I can get quickly to help out? I've got meetings in the next two days with Spain and Argentina. I'm not even sure I could point out Argentina on a map."

"You are the most honest politician I know, Vernon. Leave it with me. If I can't get someone here I'll get you someone to at least be your fall guy while you look for someone more suitable. Wasn't one of those Virginia senators head of the Senate Committee on Foreign stuff - Relations, Foreign Relations?"

"You are right again Anne. But I'm not much of a politician, I'm unelected save by the legislature so I'm not sure what I am, exactly. Can you make the call on my behalf? I hate admitting that I am struggling to keep up - better if they hear it from a Gentle voice."

"I will Vernon, and I will also send you a young man in our trade relations department that I just thought of - he has some foreign experience and at least will know where Argentina is. He might even know who the President of Argentina is. But you can only have him for a couple of weeks."

Jimmy Lablanc made his way across town to Vernon Clemons office at the behest of mayor Anne Gentle. He had been informed of the secondment, only for two weeks, by his department head at city hall - who didn't seem to care either way. He thought he was being seconded to the mayor's office but on arrival there was told he was to go to Clemon's office in Marietta.

Jimmy Lablanc was born in Canada but had come to Dixie when his American father had been transferred back to the Atlanta head office of the paper manufacturing company he worked for. His father's company dealings had taken him to many locations around the world and Jimmy had been in tow. He had absorbed much of what he had seen and used the experience to pursue a degree in international relations from the University of Georgia. He had taken the job at city hall, which his father had arranged, quite willingly as his responsibilities for trade relations allowed him to use his degree.

He opened the door of the low rise office complex and moved into the nicely appointed hallway complete with the obligatory sweeping staircase and hanging chandelier. There were two business offices on the ground floor, one an electrical supply company's administrative office and the other a local real estate law firm. Each flanked the staircase where there was a sign on a metal stand pointing up the stairs to the offices of Southern Caucus - Legislative Affairs.

Jimmy climbed the stairs and knocked, before opening the plain wooden door with a hand written - 'Knock and Enter' sign taped to it.

Inside, the floor plan was hodgepodge with cubicles extending in several directions from the central point around the door. There were three offices in the back of the open room. Two appeared to be meeting rooms and a third was where Jimmy was taken through the maze of desks and dividers to meet Vernon Clemons.

"That was quick. I just got off the phone with Mayor Gentle."

"It took me about two hours, so you must have had many things to talk about," Jimmy said.

Clemens eyeballed him, furrowing his brow and then lowering his eyes to look over his glasses at the young man.

"Okay, I asked Mayor Gentle for some foreign policy help and she sent you. I've got a scheduled meeting with the Spanish Ambassador to Mexico late tomorrow afternoon and another meeting with the Argentinean Ambassador to Mexico the next morning. I have spent zero time on foreign relations so I need a quick study on what they might want, what we might want and anything we can do in such a meeting to press our independence agenda - without being too heavy handed - we don't want to set off red flags regarding our actions - right now we are flying under the radar of a world gone mad. Time is our greatest advantage."

"You will have to work independently and quickly. I am getting a secondment from Senator Wallace's office next week to help on this file. We can talk about that later."

"Senator Wallace - he's on the foreign relations committee in Washington. Is there anything else I need to know from your end? Who called for these meetings?"

"They both did. However we made it known through Mexican Ambassador Rodriquez, our only firm diplomatic link, that we would ease the transition from the US dollar to the Dixie dollar if the Mexicans recognized our sovereignty. They have made that announcement and arranged these meetings. You should probably sit in with me at the meetings."

Two other staffers were hovering nearby holding sheaves of paper. Clemons said he wanted something to use as meeting preparation by noon the next day. He pointed at an empty desk and said that Jimmy could camp out there for the next few days as its owner was on assignment.

Jimmy moved to the desk, already mulling over things that might be of interest to the two ambassadors - potential trade issues, economic similarities and concerns, even the suggestion of sister city arrangements and cultural exchanges.

Chapter Twenty - Two   Texas

Jeb Ryan swung his Chevy pick-up into traffic as he exited the highway at Martin Street and headed east into downtown San Antonio. He passed a few low level condo buildings and then hit the maze of one-way streets that were comfortable only to locals. He didn't come to San Antonio often but he had been there enough to pretty much know his way around. Problem was sometimes the way around changed. He managed to find Main Street and turned south looking for a parking spot. A left on Commerce Street and a right on St. Mary's led to a hard left on Vilita Street and there it was, the public parking garage he was looking for.

He didn't mind a little bit of looking around while he was in town, it always amazed him on how much things subtly changed in the time between his trips to San Antonio.

His meeting was on the 12th floor of an old gothic revival tower right beside the parking garage. Not the usual type of building for Texas but with short notice, the meeting space served the purpose.

He found the meeting already in progress when he arrived.

"Just sign in at that table," said a bright, smiling woman in a summer dress, waving him toward a table with two seated attendants. "We just got started. I'm sure you won't be the last to get here. Some folks are coming from a bit of distance."

Jeb mumbled thanks, scribbled his name and details into the register and quickly took a seat. His two hour drive wasn't considered distance enough compared to some of the ranchers on their way. The medium sized theatre style room was nearly full. Despite there being some empty seats scattered around there were many people standing at the back and along the walls. It reminded him of a high school auditorium. He smiled at the determination of so many to have everything in front of them and the walls at their backs. He wondered if that was a Texas thing or if other people did it too.

"....I hope that answers the question. As I was saying, there is a reluctance to take on border duties, especially those kind of duties which involve shooting people by individuals on their own land," said the man at the front of the small stage. "Problem is, that is the most legally defensible and cheapest method we have available to us."

"Yeah but as I said, as residents, we are all too identifiable to the migrant groups moving through if we do it that way. We live there, we're sitting ducks, our homes will become targets," said a man in a weathered Stetson in the fourth row. "There are bound to be reprisals and some of us are going to get killed. We will have to set up our spreads as armed camps. Hiring private security is expensive."

"I hear ya. So the alternative is to have a deputized border patrol. Either we can pool money to pay for them or we can volunteer our time to man the patrols. Maybe a bit of both. We've got to be fairly ruthless so the message gets back to the Mexicans - 'Don't come. You are invaders. We will kill you.' I think we can all agree to that. I haven't heard anyone who disagrees."

Jeb figured it was going to come down to this. He just thought it would take more than five minutes for the ranchers to explore other options before settling on the obvious solution.

"What about both," said someone in the crowded room. A number of people voiced their agreement.

"Yeah. I don't mind defending my property. My herd is being picked off one by one as large groups are moving through. I have posted signs but my threats are toothless. I'd sure love about 20 guys on patrol for a few days. Once we set down the law I'm guessing I'd have no more trouble - at least nothing that me, my boys and our hands couldn't handle."

There was a general rumble of agreement. As it subsided a voice rose up from somewhere up front. Nobody could see who it was that spoke.

"For God sakes people. These are just people who are trying to improve their lot in life. Most of them are barely surviving in Mexico so they migrate north were there are at least some jobs - manual labour almost entirely."

"I don't begrudge them a life - but I don't condone stealing, rustling, trespassing and the like," said another. "If I never saw them or never had to clean up after them I might be able to look the other way. Thing is, I find dead cattle, see the remains of grass fires that kill livestock and destroy their range. I find corpses and garbage and my family has been threatened when we try to chase them off or call in the sheriff."

"It's gotta stop," said another voice. "Hell, they are taking over in California and nobody seems to mind. Let them go there. Heck, they appeared to be shooting first there. Sounds like justification to me."

A few voices rose up in support.

"How are they going to get there? It's 1,500 miles to California, give or take. Are you or your border patrol going to drive them?" said someone with a sneer.

Jeb listened as the meeting moved into the details of how the border patrol would work. It seemed do-able and a reasonable response to the issues at hand. An official from the new Texas government explained that legislation would be introduced to make it easier for ranchers to shoot first in these instances of migrant aggression.

The more Jeb heard, the more he thought there were a few plants in the audience who appeared to be siding with the migrants. He tried to pick them out but often their presence was only signalled by a voice with a counterpoint or one raising a legal or moral issue. It was hard to figure out who was taking the Mexican view.

The Texas official said the legislature would pass the new laws within four weeks and issue guidelines shortly after that. They asked that work be done to piece together local border groups and that ranchers in those groups be registered or deputized by local sheriffs to be protected under the new legislation. The meeting broke up as several groups formed around the presenters to voice specific concerns.

Jeb made to leave.

On his way out the front of the building two men approached him. He recognized one as a rancher who had sat near him.

"Sir, you were at that meeting upstairs," he waved toward the tower. As his sleeve rode up his forearm it revealed a small tattoo of an axe. "That border patrol meeting."

"Yes, I was," said Jeb cautiously.

"What if I told you that its more than just migrants moving through those border areas," the second man said.

"Nobody mentioned that at the meeting. If it's true then I'd say we need a lot more than just small arms to do the job properly," said Jeb.

"There are migrants, for sure, but they travel with others who have attached themselves to their groups as they cross. The migrants are happy for any help and the interlopers provide it in the form of supplies and intelligence."

"And for that they get what?"

"Cover. They are mostly Cubans and South Americans, Venezuelans usually, who are coming through to make trouble in Florida and Texas."

"What do Cubans care about Texas?"

"D'you hear about that trouble in Norman a couple of weeks back? Some people wanting into Texas so bad they shot up a federal office?"

"Yeah. It did seem strange that the Okies would want to shoot up a US federal building to get sympathy from Austin."

"That's because it was a pair of Venezuelans who shot the place up to stir up trouble, left a bunch of evidence of their 'Okies for Texas intentions' and then melted away. They are trying to weaken us by stirring up trouble."

"You don't say. If that's the case I'm afraid that me an' my boys aren't in any position to invade Venezuela."

The first man laughed. "Now that would be a sight. And you know, with a couple of strong boys you might well succeed. I've seen the Venezuelan's fight. Mostly just a bunch of scared mercenaries who can't get any other job. Venezuela thinks that the United States is constantly plotting to take over the place. They have oil. Meanwhile there's about 10 guys here who even know where it is."

"So what do you want me to do?"

"Just wantin' to let you know that it ain't only Mexicans and they ain't only economic migrants. I'm trying to get to know ranchers in the line of fire. Besides poaching they are coming here with murder on their minds - at least some of them. I am putting together a posse, my group has been hired by Austin to help fill in the gaps of our vigilance. I might turn up on your doorstep someday looking for a couple of strong boys, some guns, some help, sanctuary or medical attention," he grinned lopsidedly.

"Well, thank ya kindly for the information," said Jeb as he started to move away. "I'll keep that in mind when I'm trying to scare them off."

The second man reached into his inside pocket. "Here." He gave Jeb a card. "My name and contact info. If you find any of these people please hold them and let me know. I can have someone there to pick them up in less than four hours anywhere in Texas."

"Right now, I call the sheriff and he comes in 20 minutes, an' I don't have to hold them. Four hours means I'll have to track 'em or hold them. And that creates its own problems."

Jeb made his point but he did note that the apparent reach of this man and his group was fairly impressive.

"It's four hours anywhere in Texas today. Even a hundred miles from El Paso. In more populated places I might beat the sheriff. In a few months, I'm sure to beat him as my group gets bigger."

"You a bounty hunter?"

"Not exactly. Austin has hired me to help them with border problems. I'm not getting a bounty on people I bring in but bringing them in shows they hired the right guy. I'm not adverse to taking the heat from the Mexicans as they guy doing all the rough stuff. It keeps the retaliation off the locals and shifts it to me. And the only way they'll get me is to lay a trap or come after me directly."

Jeb nodded and agreed to make the call if necessary. He bid the two men good day.

He started back to his truck and turned to look at them again, but they were gone. He looked at the card - Emerson T. Boone - Federal Bounty Sheriff - United States of America - followed by a cell phone number. He flipped the card over. Boone Border Patrol - Official Agent of Texas Border Control - followed by a different cell number.

"Well," he thought to himself, "Emerson Boone might make some money off me, and I don't have to worry about the niceties of the law. Boone's connection to the United States got Jeb to thinking. The whole independence thing for Texas was new and odd, as people who were previously licensed by the US government simply assumed their credentials had validity. Until such time as Austin got around to addressing the issue, he supposed they still did.

Chapter Twenty - Three   Hamilton

Lake Erie opened up to the left and the river swirled beneath him as Peter O'Neill swung his car across the Peace Bridge and towards the bank of lanes at Canadian Customs.

He crossed easily and started towards his newly purchased properties in Hamilton, Ontario about 45 minutes away along the rim of Lake Ontario.

The highway swept him out of Fort Erie and through the countryside running parallel with the Niagara River. There was very little civilization visible until he reached the outskirts of Niagara Falls just before the highway swung north to follow the Lake Ontario shore. Hamilton was an old city situated on a once beautiful natural harbour at the extreme western end of the lake. Steel plants, docking facilities and general industrialization, once thriving, now aging and mostly shuttered, scarred the view. Continuing to travel around the lake's very built up shore brought one to the large city of Toronto another hour on.

The beautiful harbour in Hamilton was hidden by layers of industrial grime, crime and polluted slime. An old city, steel had been manufactured in Hamilton as long as anyone could remember. The huge labour pools that had tended those steel plants had spawned a criminal underworld far more sophisticated than one would expect in a small city, now about 500,000 souls thanks to a count of the wider hinterland still in its thrall. Government, medicine and education had taken up the slack of many of the lost steel jobs as that industry had died in the face of cheap steel from Asia.

The harbour was almost entirely enclosed, as a narrow sand spit reached right across the end of the lake enclosing the harbour, save for a narrow ship channel carved in its center.

The sand spit saved most of the polluted industrial water from mingling with the rest of the large lake, but it also resulted in a harbour that was particularly unclean. The occasional burn off of excess sulfur completed the hellish effect projected by the old industrial ruins.

Some years before, US Steel corporation had purchased one of the two functioning steel companies which called Hamilton home, it was part of a deal which allowed them to acquire the more modern Nanticoke Works on the eastern end of Lake Erie. Peter O'Neill had just completed the purchase of the other long running steel company in Hamilton, the Dominion Steel Works which included smelters in Hamilton and in Sault Ste. Marie, Ontario at the western end of Lake Huron near where that lake met with Lake Michigan and Lake Superior.

At the behest of the O'Day Administration he was about to complete the purchase of Stelco, the Canadian assets of US Steel.

Canadian officials had made all manner of noises when the plans for the purchase of Dominion Steel became known. They had gone apoplectic when O'Neill made it clear that he would consolidate the two steel companies. However all their concerns melted away when O'Neill said that he intended to operate the new company as a significant industrial concern rolling out new steel for construction projects across North America particularly for the rebuilding of New York and Los Angeles. While San Francisco need new steel, the city had been less damaged than had originally been thought, and many existing buildings could be saved.

O'Neill rolled into Hamilton to take part in a ceremony celebrating his purchase and to symbolically hire the first employees of the new venture. In truth he had been hard at work modernizing the old plants and was very close to production. His Buffalo plant was reproducing steel in a major reclamation project using huge amounts of steel claimed from New York, Los Angeles and San Francisco.

"We just keep expanding. I understand we will be ready to add a second shift to Buffalo in about a month and we should be able to do the same here and at Nanticoke in a few months."

"Well dear, as long as the trains keep running to bring us the waste products, things will move well. Are we stock piling scrap anywhere for the inevitable train problems? Weather or labour or something will slow us down at some point," Amanda O'Neill said.

"Of course. The Hamilton site is huge, wait till you see it. We are able to stockpile there. We are using Nanticoke to produce new steel and the Hamilton sites to reprocess much like Buffalo."

"Is it still your plan to shut down the Hamilton site?"

"Yes, that makes the most sense in the long run. Don't go mentioning that to the Canadians. They are suspicious enough of us. After the rush of reprocessing is done we will still need steel, but that can be handled out of Sault Ste. Marie and Nanticoke. Still, I don't anticipate closing Hamilton for at least a decade, assuming the estimates for scrap steel are correct."

The car hummed along the highway and neared Hamilton. Peter swung the car off the highway and onto a partly elevated road that led to the industrial heart of the old city.

"Truth is Amanda, this site is gold. Look at the topography. The Niagara Escarpment is right there on the left, the harbour is on the right and the downtown is just a few miles beyond the steel plants. Who would build a city with a steel plant in its downtown?"

"Canadians apparently. Pittsburgh was like that at one point right?"

"Now you are catching on. Then they cleaned Pittsburgh up and its old industrial heart is a beautiful cityscape. Imagine if we did the same thing here, once we no longer need it to reprocess steel."

"It would be like a Gold Coast or something," she said with a smile. Peter had used the phrase before. "Once the industrial sites have been cleaned up, the potential for this area is limitless. Large urban parks, where it is too expensive to do a complete environmental cleanup; high rise condos ringing the park lands, the escarpment right there and downtown only a few blocks away. And it's all right in the center of the Golden Horseshoe, a 150 mile long rim of development which rings the western end of Lake Ontario. This is a huge and very lucrative property development project. Likely one that will take a couple of generations."

"We can all dream dear."

"Actually I'm moving past dreaming and have hired a planner to scope out the needed land reclamations, environmental issues and to draw up a timeline of construction. This could be our biggest legacy my dear. We need to start slow and not tip anyone off as to the scale of development that we are planning. If everything goes right this city could tip the economic balance of the whole region to the west. It's already a megalopolis. It might rival any urban conglomeration in the world after I'm through with it."

The O'Neill's arrived at the plant's main office and were greeted by the general manager. They were ushered into a large meeting room where the press were waiting. As soon as he entered Peter was introduced and he moved to the lectern and microphones. He beckoned Amanda to join him.

"Welcome all. I hope you are as excited as I am about the growth of this company. That this is born out of tragedy and terror is unfortunate but while we here in North America remember our past we always look forward with anticipation. Hamilton will be the center of a new industrial revolution as we have added a significant metallurgical component to the manufacturing process. We have increased our research facilities five-fold and hope to utilize the new technology in ways we haven't even thought of yet. Already we have found a way to strengthen steel three-fold while making it lighter by 25 per cent. That has applications in the auto industry, in construction and in manufacturing."

There was an enthusiastic ripple of applause started by the general manager and taken up by other staff and employees brought in for the announcement. Peter beamed. He let the applause thin out.

"My wife Amanda has always been a fount of good ideas and a reliable measure of my business progress and our social conscious. You may know we have sponsored several medical projects in New York where we also have business interests. Today, I'd like to announce a similar undertaking here in Hamilton. We have spoken to local health care officials and will have a more specific announcement in a few weeks."

Applause cascaded through the room, this time more enthusiastically than before. Some of the assembled journalists raised their eyebrows.

"Also today I would like to announce our first hire in the newly refurbished plant. David Turner, please join me up here."

A youngish man made his way to the lectern from the second row of onlookers.

"This is David Turner. He comes to us from Hamilton Health Sciences and is the first employee I've hired. Mr. Turner is a human resources professional. He has overseen the hiring processes and necessary employee paperwork of Hamilton Health Sciences for the past three years."

Peter let that sink in.

"Obviously it is significant that our first hire is someone skilled at managing people, especially the hiring of people. Mr. Turner is needed because today, I'd like to announce that The Hamilton Steel Corporation will be adding a second shift to its anticipated operations. Applications for positions are available on line. We hope to have the shift operational in a few months."

The stunned silence gave way to happy applause. Even the journalists jotted down their notes with smiles on their faces.

"This is very much the start of something special here in Hamilton," said O'Neill. "Please join me and Amanda at a reception downstairs in the Niagara Room. I hope to have the opportunity to speak to everyone and will happily answer any questions from members of the fourth estate. Just follow the gentleman at the door who will lead the way."

People gathered themselves and made to leave the room. Two journalists moved directly to the lectern.

"Mr. O'Neill? How sustainable is this? It seems to me that all these feel good announcements are designed to allay the concerns of government officials that you will merely strip the steel plants of their machinery and move it to Buffalo?"

"No-no. My plant in Buffalo is small in comparison to Hamilton. I really can't expand there at all. It's a land issue thing. I am a New York guy, lived in the City for most of my life, so I wanted to bring something to the Queen City. However, the potential for the steel reclamation business is much larger than I initially realized."

A journalist interrupted him, "Thanks to the new tariffs announced by O'Day. You've got most of the American market to yourself."

"Those government charges simply level the playing field. The Asians generally don't have significant labour standards and are virtually without environmental standards. Steel tariffs are nothing new even in this freer trade era. O'Day has said with reforms in those areas from the Asians he would happily reduce or eliminate the tariffs on Asian steel. But as I was saying, there is significant opportunity in Hamilton as much of our infrastructure in Buffalo is aging and will need replacement over time. So the best option for growth, is to utilize the capacity for growth that Hamilton has already available. Off the record, I fully expect to add a third shift once the second one is stable and product is moving easily."

"A third shift?"

"Off the record please. For exactly the reason you suggested. And I don't want to go promising things I cannot deliver. That third shift will depend upon supply routes and demand escalating. However, we are already easily able to get raw materials and sell our product to cover the needs of a second shift. In fact, again off the record; we will likely shift some of the production at the old Dofasco plant into new steel while maintaining the older Hilton Works for reclaimed steel."

"Is there that much demand?"

"Have you been to New York?"

"I haven't but I've seen all the pictures and done some extensive reading," said the second journalist, a seasoned reporter who had been in the Hamilton area for his entire career.

"Well, you can report this; the US Congress has agreed in principle to a Bill that will streamline the insurance claim process and land ownership issues in New York, allowing us to proceed more quickly on steel reclamation projects and allow owners to rebuild."

"Are you talking about extending Eminent Domain?"

"No, that kind of government heavy handedness is not necessary. Really, the legislation is about streamlining the legal process around various land and insurance issues. There are people who want to sell their holdings in New York and they cannot due to environmental issues, outstanding insurance claims and even outdated survey information."

"What about radiation and fallout?"

"I suggest you take a look at how long it took the Japanese to rebuild Hiroshima. Fallout is very short term with the real dangerous radioactive material existing in only very, very small amounts."

"Remember gentlemen," said Peter, "the steel industry in North America was almost non-existent with regards to large industrial production. This plant here was making mostly finishing steel. The need for girders and construction steel has all of a sudden become very important. It's almost like we are back in the 1960s again steel-wise. Hamilton will benefit tremendously from that."

"How long will it last? It can't last forever."

"You are right, it won't last forever. It never does. However, I expect there are several decades of significant steel production necessary. Eventually, like most businesses the demand will shift. That's the way of the world guys. Truth be told, there is a tremendous opportunity for jobs, modernization, rebuilding infrastructure and retooling Hamilton. It shouldn't be missed. Even if steel or whatever comes next abandons Hamilton, this opportunity to remake the city must be seized."

One of the journalists turned to Amanda.

"Mrs. O'Neill, any hints about the hospital related project? When will the announcement be made?"

"I am working closely with Health officials here in Hamilton and will consult with provincial officials to make sure our contributions are in line with local needs and long term plans. I would love to announce something today, but there are a number of official channels we must proceed through if we are going to make our announcement in the next few weeks."

"Everybody has to get a piece of this, eh?"

Amanda laughed. "Now, not so cynical, sir. We don't want to announce something that isn't needed. Frankly, I understand US Ambassador Charlie Edwards is working on lending some technology to the project so we have to streamline things with him."

"Edwards? He'll just manage a bunch of platitudes and then tell us what the US is going to take from us. Now you have me worried again."

"I can handle Mr. Edwards," said Amanda with a smile. "I have it on good authority that he is really a big fan of Canada, just his job requires that he stand up for the US."

Chapter Twenty - Four   **New York**

There were places where you could almost walk from Manhattan to Brooklyn. The river had carved a narrow channel through the debris and there was certainly no solidity to the shifting mass of broken everything that clogged the East River.

And the cranes were working feverishly to clear the island. And while there was an effort to clear the river, it was solitary and lackluster as the water was managing it a bit at a time. The easiest place to get equipment in had been from the north and from the harbour. So cranes worked at both ends of the island and in Brooklyn cleaning up the mess.

Metal was reusable and prized. Some of the concrete could be reused as fill or as road material but there was just so much of it, even though most of it had simply been blown to dust in the explosion. What was recoverable was of so little value it was hard to decide if storing it was worth the cost. There were plans to use rubble for roads and foundations where possible. Eventually it was decided to take some of it to Jersey where it was stored in large piles to be crushed and used in future light concrete jobs.

After two years of squabbling and legal wrangles the work clearing most of Manhattan had been slow. Despite the troubles much of the lower tip of Manhattan had been scraped clean and cranes had cleaned up much of the northern sections, separating them into livable and unlivable buildings. Central Park became a construction yard - or a destruction yard as it too was strewn with debris in the north. The northern clean up was now engaged in the hard work of sweeping up.

The calls to relocate Central Park were loud and unanswered. Many people believed that the tip of Manhattan should be parkland, especially as it was the most difficult to clean up environmentally. Rebuilding of the city could begin fairly quickly in Central Park which, excepting the large storage areas that had been created there, was essentially untouched land, prime for development.

It was an idea that would not die. However, given the huge numbers of land claims and other issues that would be required to make the change, it had remained an idea only. As the land was cleared in the Battery leaving it fallow for a time appeared to be a good strategy. How owners could trade their parcels for land in Central Park, and all the details of where the park should begin and end remained nothing more than cocktail party speculation.

Working their way past Water Street to Pearl Street the clearing effort had found evidence of people, some of whom had survived the initial blast. Most succumbed within days buried in an avalanche of dust and debris. Those who had survived were always found underground as the surface was swept clean of what had been there. Anything left was underground and in some sort of concrete protected, steel reinforced space.

Once the initial shock of finding some of these victims wore off, it became evident that Manhattan was riddled with survivability as so much of the city was underground. As the clearing effort found the corner of Broad Street and Pearl and began to dig into the former Fraunces Tavern something remarkable was found.

There were 32 people found together who had obviously survived the blast. They were able to live for several months on supplies of the Tavern. They left written acknowledgement of the disaster and the probable cause, though they obviously didn't have any direct knowledge. They all died of starvation after many months of efforts to dig their way out. They were unsuccessful.

They had tried to communicate with the outside world but cell phone transmission was impossible and after a few days their devices could not be recharged.

The island had taken a grievous hit with the nuclear effects sweeping some of the buildings away down to their foundations while other buildings further from the epicenter served as pylons for debris to pile up against. Of course the fires had essentially destroyed everything else. In between was a steadily increasing amount of destruction the further one was from the epicenter. New construction had been proposed for the cleared spaces but legal wrangles and concerns about pollution had forced a halt to any actual building.

Block by block the city was being cleared. With the blessing of Congress things were about to pick up speed and it was hoped the entire island would be cleaned up in five years. That was going to require a constant stream of new demolition equipment moving into the area. Then came the clean-up of the Jersey side of the Hudson, and large parts of Brooklyn. It was a much needed boon to the economy.

Of course banks and financial companies were monitoring the progress as they had below grade vaults some holding vast amounts of wealth in gold, currency and other items. Some of this had already been recovered showing the world that it was all still there waiting to be uncovered. That first find did a lot to calm panicked markets and maintain financial stability.

However, the vast debt of the US government prior to the 5/29 attacks meant the US dollar was a very unstable proposition. While the economy did not cease to exist after the attacks the shift due to fear and instability was almost immeasurable. Americans were deeply in thrall to continuity bias, the belief that whatever is occurring and possible today, will continue to occur and be possible tomorrow. They seemed incapable of understanding that things that have never happened are able to happen if the conditions are right.

Never having experienced war or mass destruction, many Americans within the scope of the destruction had difficulty coping. To others in more distance places the destruction was abstract, an intellectual exercise on how to deal with life if certain aspects of life were removed. Some local markets like Chicago surged. Others took a hit and the US government spent huge amounts of money in the recovery and in military operations of retaliation.

The government had quickly determined its only course of action was immediate and significant retaliation, followed by disengagement with large parts of the world that were incompatible with American beliefs. Several courses of action had been explored and considered prior to the blasts in New York, Norfolk and Los Angeles due to the proceeding attacks on Israel and on Rome. So retaliation, when it came, was swift, without the usual hand-wringing and second guessing that had affected American foreign policy since the end of the Vietnam War.

And then came June 7.

The attacks across the US created such a surge of hatred and anger that it was impossible to contain. Restraint was gone. The United States launched multiple nuclear attacks on the Islamic World, destroying cities in Iran, Iraq, Egypt and Turkey.

The retaliation for the 5/29 attacks had been significant and restrained with only Mecca, Medina, Riyadh, Bagdad, Damascus, Teheran and several smaller cities hit. The overriding notion was to hit back much harder than the original attack to make the attackers acutely aware that their actions were going to bring considerably more pain to their own people than to those they attacked. In addition they were designed to stifle any co-ordinated response and end the perpetrators ability to make war.

With well more than a billion Muslims in the world a genocide was a logistical impossibility and would necessarily target large numbers of pseudo Muslims - millions of whom had never indicated an interest in violence. In addition, western belief in religious freedom, and in tolerance still held significant sway though most people now understood that without mutual tolerance there was no middle ground.

The shift in attitude was felt after the guerilla attacks of June 7 and led to a huge number of local retaliations. Whole families were shot to death in a wave of righteous violence that cleaned away the ethnic division in America.

Anyone left was quickly deported and what was left of the Islamic world was sealed off from trade, communications and technology and left to its own devices. It was the only rational approach that remained with even the usual western apologists quiet on the sidelines of public opinion.

There were fears with more than a dozen nuclear explosions occurring within days of each other that the radiation levels would become dangerous but those fears didn't come to pass.

Chapter Twenty - Five   **Central Asia**

The Navy covert teams went into Tbilisi and Islamabad in May.

They had slipped in by para-drop just north of each city and formed up their small teams of 12 people. In both cases six agents took on the offensive tasks at hand while the remaining six provided back up, eyes and ears and logistical support.

After making contact with local agents and discerning intelligence, the team in Islamabad decided a large meeting of mid-level jihadists was too much of a target rich environment to pass up. In addition it was being led by Mohammed Al-Silar, one of the men suspected of masterminding the nuclear attack on Rome.

The team scoped out intel on the site for two days before the meeting. They spoke to their informants and ascertained the best way to infiltrate. They disguised themselves as waiters and brought in rolling tables of fruit and rice and meat dishes to the meeting.

The event was taking place in a large meeting room upstairs in a private residence. There was security but given the location the guards were few and obvious.

The Navy team decided on a two pronged approach. The six man team would enter the meeting room and set up the tables prior to launching their attack. The other six would be divided between clearing the security detail from the building allowing escape once the deed had been done, and operating drones in real time, to launch rockets at the facility to complete the attack.

The teams moved into place. The caterers moved into the building and transported their wares upstairs into the meeting room. As soon as they opened fire on the jihadis the second team sprang into position and mowed down the security detail as they reacted to the shooting.

The attack went exactly as planned and 34 jihadis and guards lay dead before anyone realized there had been a covert operation occurring in their neighbourhood. Rockets were fired into the building to cover the escape and to finish off anyone who had survived the initial onslaught.

The navy team in Tbilisi conducted two raids - killed an additional 18 well known jihadists in their second attack and then retreated to another nearby city. After waiting eight days in a safe house they moved to the next set of targets - two more raids in Oms netted another 22 killed.

Islamabad had produced the same effect. Five raids in three cities and more than 60 dead jihadists. June 7th dawned in Islamabad.

"We are awaiting orders. I expect we'll be on the move in a day or two."

The satellite radio emitted a tone.

"Holy shit," said the normally dour munitions expert on the team, Captain Hollinger, reading the communiqué. "Massive radio traffic - attack on US imminent. Defcon 5 - pull out to staging area Alpha 8, await further instructions."

The team looked at each other and then all began to move to ready themselves to leave the safe house as soon as night fell.

Five hours later the radio came to life - another message.

"Massive Muslim guerilla attacks across US. Thousands and thousands of individual locations. Retaliation expected within 48 hours. Go to Alpha 8 and await transit."

"Holy crap. Here we are just taking out a few dangerous people and they are at home killing thousands of innocent people."

"It's getting harder and harder to decide who is innocent anymore," said Navy Lieutenant Ty Tanner. "They take the view that any American is supporting those who they determine are enemies. So every American is a target."

"Until now we have taken the view that only the perpetrators of violence are guilty. I think that is about to change boys."

Two hours later the team exited the safe house and was transported by van outside the city to a farm area.

"As they took their leave of their contact Tanner said, "Aziz, I think things are going to get very hot here very soon. You should quickly and quietly extract your loved ones and any members of your team you can. You've got about 48 hours to get out."

Their driver stared at them wide eyed.

"And then?" he asked.

"And then pray you have gotten far enough away. We will re-establish contact when we can, it may be many days. I will report your location and your help to our command. They will come for you should you want to be resettled."

Aziz nodded, "I was afraid it would come to this," he said. "I am ready. I can be gone in a few hours."

Three nights later, Aziz and his family were still getting settled on the same farm, wondering why they were taking this unusual holiday from their home in the city when the crop wasn't even ready yet.

The drone of planes started low. Barely noticeable above the insect noises. The sound started to grow.

After several minutes it was obviously not insects and through the moonlight it was possible to see several contrails.

A bright light flashed in the distance, framing the distant city, some 55 miles away. The rumble of explosions followed on some minutes later. Aziz gathered everyone together hurriedly and headed for the basement of his farmhouse. Just as he started down the stair he saw the reflected flash of light. He hurried down the rickety stair.

His wife looked at him. "Aziz is that what I think it is?"

"Yes, my dear."

"And you knew it was coming?"

"I did not know but I suspected after hearing a few things several days ago after those two terrorist attacks in the north of the city."

"And what did you hear."

"Apparently a number of our brothers who have gone to live in America let loose with attacks on civilians and innocents. The Americans have finally had enough."

"You heard all this?"

"Yes, my dear, most of it and the rest I just guessed at."

"You are a much smarter man than my brothers gave you credit for. How many did you warn?"

"I warned everyone I could who would heed the warning. Unfortunately those were very few."

A shock wave rumbled past the farm. It rattled windows upstairs but the distance from the blast seemed to be enough to lessen its effects.

"It's a storm papa," said his youngest child Aldeer.

"Yes, Aldeer a storm. A very big storm. Maybe the biggest you will ever see."

"Can we go upstairs and see papa?"

"No, my child. We should stay here safe for a while yet."

"How long is 'a while' ? asked his wife.

"Two days from now I'll take a look around. We should probably stay here for at least a week for most of the day. You will find sufficient food behind that door to last us many weeks."

She looked at him with a newfound respect.

"And all of this because you heard a few things?"

"No, my dear, we are here today because I heard a few things two days ago. This is all here because I know many things and because I can think."

Chapter Twenty - Six   **Southern California**

Hellenga had been hard at work. Ambassador Octavius had been monitoring his progress, he was a prolific and efficient artist. It was true that
Hellenga had been well supplied and provided with a framework for the
commission he was given - but Octavius was impressed with the zeal
which he brought to his work.

He had seen press reports of a dozen or more art installations, sketches
and paintings really, done graffiti style throughout Southern California.
Octavius hadn't worried about the exact nature of the artwork, he merely
instructed Hellenga to do some guerrilla art in high traffic areas and do it
with enough skill to have it recognized for its high quality. Hellenga was
free to do it off kilter enough to remain anonymous or to increase his
own profile by accepting the work as his own.

So far most of the pieces had generated local news stories as much for
their content as for the artistic curiosity of who was behind the work.

Hellenga had been suggested by those in the know in the local art world,
but he had been coy when questioned.

Behind all of the works lay the idea that Southern California was naturally
Mexican. Several of the artworks, especially the first few, made a chiding

or gentle reference to Mexifornia or Aztlan. The first, on a prominent highway overpass where the highway bypassed the ruins of Los Angeles, showed a Phoenix wearing a sombrero and rising from the ruins of the city which bore the word Aztlan.

The second and third were similar drawings of several people doing a good deed while identified as Mexican.

Ambassador Octavius had arranged to speak to Hellenga after meeting him at an art exhibit financed by his major patron Senor Cartenga, the owner of a southern California demolition and construction company.

"I read today that there is a new Aztlan mural, this one is causing a bit of a stir," said Cartenga, while he handed Ambassador Octavius a drink. "Lemonade with a touch of tequila and a bit of ice, as you like it."

"Thank you senor, it is always a pleasure to speak to friends and see them prosper."

"Aye, we have been shipping our scrap steel to Buffalo and one of my research engineers found a great formula for remolding the scrap concrete and building debris into an adobe style brick. We add a bit of polymer and some bonding agents. We have also pressed it into sheet forms, about four inches thick, which make a durable building material. Great for low rise homes and light industrial buildings."

"Are you part of the consortium that is rebuilding some of the Long Beach shipping facilities?"

"Yes, there are a number of companies involved but getting that facility back up and running will greatly help us with the rebuilding efforts. It appears we may have to relocate the facility a few miles north. So far radiation issues have been very small and entirely manageable. Hiroshima was rebuilt pretty quickly, LA will be too."

Octavius took a sip, and admired the taste, looking at the drink more closely.

"This is excellent tequila, my friend."

"So is that mural which has a few people upset in the Central Valley. Apparently, the mural was painted on the sea view side of several large buildings in San Francisco. It was quite a large installation and the article I read wondered how it could have been done without anyone noticing. It's an outline of California, 20 stories high, across several buildings, with Southern California painted like the Mexican flag, the central part of the state is taken up by a rendering of the Transamerica Building that looks remarkably like the Central Temple at Tikal and the north part of the state is emblazoned with Aztlan and the eagle symbol."

"The Americans don't like it?"

"No, but it wasn't even noticed until a freighter saw it as it was entering the Bay. It has to been seen from a particular angle only, unusual even for ships, otherwise it is only bits and pieces - the whole installation doesn't reveal itself unless seen from that exact angle. The ship had been on the Panama Canal run. The harbour hasn't been getting much traffic since the earthquake, though I understand that is about to change. The harbour facilities in Oakland have been repaired and will be able to take larger ships. Right now there are few ships making the Panama Canal run as most of the shipping comes in from the Orient and ships are not far enough south to see the correct face of the building."

"Is the Golden Gate Bridge open?"

"Yes, it never really closed. Apparently despite the size of the quake it was virtually untouched. The rest of the clean-up in San Francisco is moving pretty quickly as the damage was extensive to older buildings and concentrated on the south side of town. There are plenty of people still living in the area. Many of the downtown high-rises are abandoned as there are fears of collapse. Nobody noticed the artwork given the huge scale, really only visible at a distance. Many of the building in the north and west of the city are abandoned due to extensive damage. Clean up is centered on areas in the east and south side of the peninsula that were very heavily damaged, and in surrounding areas like Oakland and San Jose."

"So tell me, my friend, do you have anything to do with these artworks?"

"Now I am surprised at you senor, you are usually far more subtle," Octavius smiled. "I did not sketch or paint the pictures. But as supporters of a greater Mexican influence in southern California we all have our hand in the installations, as we talk about them, admire them and wonder what their significance is. Perhaps it is you who have commissioned this? You do know several artists through your gallery connections."

"Not me sir, and yet with you, I agree. Perhaps you are right. The artist is not important, though there is a subtle familiarity to the sketches. Perhaps the message and its reception are all that one must concern themselves with."

"I understand that there will be a media push on these bits of graffiti and what they mean."

"Well they are popular. Just yesterday my wife saw a gallery marketing prints of some of the images. She was looking to get a few to sell in her gallery. The artist likely will not press for copy right infringement."

Miles away Hellenga looked at the proof. It was exactly as he imagined but it didn't seem perfect. There was something wrong. He eyed it for a long while before deciding to put it aside and give it another once over tomorrow before the printer was expecting it back.

He wasn't particularly fond of the work he had done for Ambassador Octavius. Not because he didn't believe in the movement but because it lacked subtlety. Then he realized all his work lacked a certain undercurrent that famous artists had found and critics celebrated but nobody had ever put into any kind of words or tangible explanation. Like the strange brush strokes of Monet or Van Gogh. He had always been far more conscious of the composition, yet the most famous works of art seemed to

161

be a confluence of subject, style and subtlety of form that he had never been able to grasp let alone approach. He settled into a bit of a stupor, thinking himself a failure and trying to let the haze of his concern crystallize into some concrete direction or insight.

He just sat in his place stewing, contemplating nothingness and hoping for inspiration. It didn't come, but he liked the mental haze of staring at white walls and trying to pick out patterns in the play of the indirect light on the paint and the uneven texture of the flat walls.

He moved back to the computer terminal, provided his okay and sent the proof to the printer. He was done with it. It was, what it was, and so, perhaps was he.

He then settled back to look at the walls a bit longer and think of how the ad campaign was going to go over. His deal with Ambassador Octavius was now complete. He wondered if he'd see the man again or receive a message. Since their original meeting he had no contact. He wondered if he should keep up the program of graffiti or let it go.

His phone buzzed and vibrated on his desk.

He didn't pick it up but looked at it while the call went dead. No voice message. Then he received notification of a text at the same number. He stared at the device.

No he decided not to look just yet. He would wait. If it was the printer, he would have work to do and he didn't want any work right then.

He straightened up and moved out of his studio and started across the courtyard to his small attached residence. Northern Mexico was cool this time of year - it was the elevation. He had worked in this studio for several years, liking it because of the distance from his native California. That distance provided the perspective he needed when he thought about his home and its future.

The cool air hit him hard as he left the building. He decided on the spot that he was hungry and he needed something to eat. He didn't even go into his own residence, he just turned and walked down the path to the street and started the several blocks to a small restaurant he frequented.

Two sets of eyes watched him as he moved up the street.

"Why's he leaving? Who is he going to see? Did he call anyone?"

"There were no calls registered on his landline or his mobile. We asked him to await a visit on gallery business, that's supposed to be the code phrase. What the hell is he doing?"

"Perhaps it's innocent. Perhaps he didn't read the message."

"How could he not have. He must have his phone. Message him again. Use the code phrase again, and I don't know, something more obvious . . . graffiti . . . yeah mention graffiti, that'll get his attention."

The message was sent and nothing came back. Hellenga was still visible a few blocks up the main road. Better check out where he's going. It can't be far. Pull up a few blocks and then we'll follow on foot."

The two men, dressed as winter residents, got out of the car just as they saw Hellenga turn into a small Chilean restaurant. They followed.

Once inside they were waiting for their eyes to adjust to the dim light when a waitress told them to take any table they wanted. Soon they found themselves near the window so they could see the street. Hellenga had a seat at the bar and was just receiving a tall drink.

"Should we go speak to him?"

"No, let's just get a bit to eat and watch. We can catch him on his way back home."

Hellenga was obviously well known in the restaurant as the two men observed him joking with the waitress and being served something which didn't seem to be a standard menu item.

The two men finished their meal and lingered. Hellenga rose and left. He was followed.

A hundred meters down the road the two men had caught him. "Senor, may we have a word."

Hellenga stopped, looking a bit nervous. He was occasionally stopped by fans that recognized him. The two apparent tourists fit the bill.

"Yes."

"Senor, we are friends of Octavius, who had been wanting to drop in for a meeting tonight. You did not respond to our message."

"I don't always respond to messages right away, even if I read them, especially when I am hungry. I did not read any message and I am unfamiliar with this Octavius. How would I know him?"

The first man took a chance. "He is the Ambassador from Spain. He commissioned you to do some artwork."

Hellenga was uneasy. He did a poor job of acting surprised and oblivious. Octavius had merely spoken to him about the project and never suggested it was cloak and dagger in nature. These two appeared to know something but not enough.

"I am an artist, yes. But I have done no work for an Ambassador Octavius. Sorry gentlemen I cannot help you." Shaken, Hellenga made to retrace his steps back to the restaurant. It was far closer than his home.

One of the men reached into his pocket. Hellenga had been robbed once before by people posing as tourists, but they didn't appear to know anything about him, just that he looked like a good mark.

He broke into a run.

"Senor, we mean you no harm, said the man holding out a business card. I only have a card here with my phone number should you want to contact me for a meeting about an art commission."

Hellenga slowed. He looked over his shoulder to see a man with him arm extended holding something. He turned to decline the commission when two shots rang out. Hellenga fell. The two men fled in the gloom. One circled back to their car the other fled down a side street until the car came to fetch him.

"Well that didn't go well," he said once he got in.

"Is he dead?"

"Probably not. I'm not that good a shot."

"In the end it might serve our purposes," said the driver. "He knows that somebody knows what he is, what he's done, and who is behind it."

"That is, if he lives long enough to put two and two together. Either way this is getting back to Octavius and that does serve our purposes."

"We'd best get back and let them know what happened."

Chapter Twenty - Seven   Texas

"Oh shit. That's the call. Get ready boys. We've got us an invasion."

"Where? How many?"

"Getting that, just get ready. We're outta here - now."

Jeb grabbed his pistol and jumped in his pick up. It had a sealed container in the back with gas, some provisions, three shotguns and several hundred rounds.

They had been out a few times since the meeting in San Antonio. Texas had been true to its word and had quickly organized local ranchers and law enforcement into a rapid deployment force, ready to go whenever spotters called them in. He had heard stories of Emerson Boone swooping in to help but did encountered the man again himself. Drones on the Rio Grande had helped.

Both times he had been out they had captured a couple of migrants and turned them over to law enforcement. And both times Jeb had had the feeling that they had only captured a small group sent as a diversion from the real invaders. They didn't seem well prepared for a lengthy stay of living rough, nor did they try to evade capture. It seemed like they were trying to keep the Texans busy but others in the posse thought they gave up easily as they didn't want to be shot.

"Okay, got the co-ordinates. It's down by the Berry place. We are to meet up with the others and the sheriff will give us our assigned area to cover."

"I brought my own enforcement," said Billy Ryan, Jeb's number two son. He patted his rifle and then a handgun hanging from his belt. He relished these excursions. Perhaps a bit too much thought Jeb.

Within 20 minutes they arrived at the edge of the Berry ranch, which ran alongside the Ryan ranch, between it and the Rio Grande.

They were given their assigned area and took off, covering the area near the river.

"Damn, if the Mexies were spotted 40 minutes ago, they ain't gonna be around here no more," said Billy. "We ain't gonna see nothing."

As the words echoed in the cab two migrants popped up from the flood bank of the river, clutching a bag each, and staring right into the head-lights of the pick-up.

They both started in surprise and then hunched their shoulders, looking resigned to their capture. As Jeb opened the cab door a shot rang out. They could see a third man, who was partly shielded by the edge of the shallow ravine. With the shot he dropped back down out of sight looking to escape.

Jeb jumped up into the truck bed, grabbed his shotgun and took aim. The two men still stood there holding their large plastic sacks. The third had not shown himself again from under the rim of the ravine. Another shot rang out.

Billy stood in his open door on the far side of the truck. He poked his rifle through the 'V' made by the windshield and the open door. The second shot prompted two shots from him. Both the bag holders went down.

The man in the ravine had poked his head above the rim of the bank.

With the shots he fled back towards the river. Billy whooped and ran after him.

"Billy, stop," yelled Jeb.

"Billy, Billy, you don't know what's down there."

Billy reached the top of the flood ravine rim. "Oh! Shit," he said and dropped to his belly and rolled quickly back from the rim. "There's a bunch of them," he yelled back over his shoulder.

Billy rolled again and crabbed and ran like an animal away from the rim. A few shots were heard.

Jeb, moved cautiously to the edge. He could see a whole bunch of commotion in the shallow water. It looked like a school of piranha were thrashing in a frenzy.

He motioned Billy to roll the truck up to the edge of the rim. The headlights shone on a remarkable sight. Hundreds of migrants were running back through the shallow river as fast as they could. Many had already made the Mexican side.

Another truck rolled up beside them. The sheriff.

"Hi boys. Quite a sight. I saw them when I was back up the river maybe half a mile. I fired a couple of warning shots over their heads."

"I thought they were shooting at us. I fired back, got those two over there."

"We'll you were perfectly within your rights. You were here on Texas business, heard shots and downed a couple of trespassers. In fact the rest of them are certain to relay the message that Texas wants no more of their kind here and that we mean business."

"I heard the shots too sheriff," said Jeb. "I thought it might be a sniper lurking just under the rim of the ravine. Billy was sure scared when he saw the number of them."

"I wasn't scart. I just had to readjust my mindset, you know. Thought we had a half a dozen and then saw it was a whole town," he smiled at the older men and then turned and spat.

"Well, I'll call in the coroner. I'm gonna have to go slow on processing this. It's the first one we've had in our sector since the armed defence laws were put in place. Looks pretty straight forward to me."

A month passed. A few questions had come from the sheriff about the night of the incident but everything seemed on the up and up. There had been no additional migrant movements in their sector and in fact most of the frontier had appeared to be quiet.

Of course Mexico had condemned the death of two of its nationals. Texas officials had shot back that the Mexicans had better not be encouraging their citizens to migrate nor supply them with any resources, as there had been reports of migrants armed with light pistols and supplies enough for several weeks of living rough.

Mexico went silent on the issue. There wasn't much they could say in the wake of the strange invasion of southern California. The traumatized California population, many civilian deaths and denials from Mexico left a trail of mistrust. The media was rife with stories of the brutality of the invaders. The government knew it was much, much worse, as many people were not available to tell their stories. What scant evidence there was told it for them.

Several more months passed and the strange invasion of California receded from scrutiny as no real evidence could be found linking the invaders to Mexico. Stray text messages telling of a military style invasion, quick exits from dwellings and disappearances of hundreds of rural Californians told the tale of brutality.

Just as he was getting used to the quiet Jeb and the boys received another call to chase down transient migrants.

He grabbed his things, jumped into the truck where Billy and his oldest son Hank were waiting.

They drove to the meeting point and got briefed by the sheriff. "Small group, probably a diversion. The group was spotted by drone heading north through the eastern end of your ranch Jeb."

"North, eh Sheriff, now there's a surprise," snorted Hank.

"Sometimes they divert east or west once they cross the river, keeps us guessing. Tonight they are apparently headed straight north, probably want to move us away from the river where another horde is setting to cross. We'll be watching and waiting for them if they try."

There was some growling noise coming from the south and west. A few of the group looked that way with furrowed brows as the sheriff spoke.

"That's a funny sound. What is that? We got a large group down there patrolling? I thought you wanted Sullivan's group to go that way. Maybe it's already covered."

Then the men heard a whirring. Jeb looked up into the sky and caught the sight of a drone flying up against a cloud still illuminated by the sun which had dipped below the horizon.

"Well the drones is looking around, any idea of what they see?"

"They appears to be looking at us."

Then the low whistle of a shell was heard freezing the posse. It exploded behind one of the pick-ups spraying dirt everywhere.

"Shit, sheriff. Call it off. They think we're the migrants," yelled one of the posse who had all hit the dirt.

The sheriff was on his phone.

"It ain't us boys," he yelled over the whine of a third and fourth shell.

From over the ravine edge crawled a line of mechanized armoured vehicles, each sporting a howitzer like gun emplacement in the rear.

"Holy shit, run."

Every member of the posse ran, jumped in trucks and sped away.

Hank was first to the Ryan truck, started to roll but waited for Jeb and Billy to jump in. The exodus cut them off. Jeb waved Hank to go. He jumped into the bed of a nearby truck with Billy.

The driver headed out off-road into the scrub with the main lights off. Hank had been one of the first to leave and was using the main ranch road north. Small arms fire was thick punctuated by the occasional shell blast.

Once they were out of immediate danger Jeb motioned the driver, a man he immediately recognized from local posse meetings and who's father he had known, to head toward his ranch home, 15 minutes drive away. He got on the phone and warned his wife to start packing essentials. They would leave within minutes of his arrival.

Then he got on the phone to the sheriff. His phone was busy so he left a message.

A minute later the phone rang.

"Danno, what can I do?"

"Shit Jeb, I dunno. I reported to the central command. They already had wind of it. I was just confirmation. It looks like a similar invasion to the one in California a few months ago. It doesn't appear to be Mexican but I can't believe the Mexicans are innocent in this. They couldn't have just materialized in the shallows of the river. Austin is going ballistic - no check that, they can't go ballistic, they don't have any nukes. But they are mobilizing everything they've got. Want us all far away as they are going in with airstrikes. Hope to drive them off quickly. Some people are speculating that they will melt away by morning."

"Take care of yourself. Stay out of the fight and sit tight. This will likely be done in six to eight hours. Then the recriminations begin. Austin is going to be one shaken up bees nest. It ain't going to be pretty."

"I'm gonna bail on the ranch tonight but hopefully can get back there tomorrow. That place will go feral in short order if they ain't nobody there to tend it."

"Be careful Jeb. Surely your stock can wait a night. I'm sure there will be official news in a few hours. You'll likely be back by morning. In Cali they got 50 miles inside the border. You got your boys with ya?"

"We jumped a ride. Billy's with me but Hank took off in our truck. Hopefully he heads for home. We could use that truck to help haul stuff outta there."

"Don't worry about stuff Jeb. If this is like California the invasion is particularly brutal. It wasn't widely reported but invaders there simply executed anyone in their way."

"You be safe too Danno. I don't know what you saw but I saw at least a dozen of those gun trucks. There could have been personnel in there as well."

Jeb's ride dropped him at his home. His wife was remarkably composed.

"Well you had to expect them to fight back," she directed Billy and Jeb to a couple of cases of supplies and a large wooden box. "Get that on the Chevy and we are good to go. Where's Hank?"

"I was hoping he'd be here by now. Billy see if you can raise him on his phone. Meantime let's get these things loaded."

Pretty soon the trucks were loaded and they were ready to move out. However Hank had not arrived nor could they get him on his phone - all they got was an out of service message.

"Can't imagine there is much service available for these things," said Jeb looking down at his own phone. He was starting to get an uneasy feeling. "He likely hiked it up to town to give them a warning."

As he considered staying for a few more minutes he heard the whoosh of jets flying overhead. They seemed to come from the north and east and moved off south.

"Wow, that was fast. It was less than an hour ago we were shot at."

There were some concussions of discharging explosives in the distance.

"Should we stay here pop?" asked Billy. "Seems like they've got it under control."

A second wave of jets passed overhead.

"Boy I'd like too but I think it is foolish to remain without more info. And we can't defend the place with just the two of us. If a few of those transports got here we'd have no chance to stop them and a smaller chance of escape if we were it's only target. We can come back at first light after we get a sense of what happened."

Jeb left a note for Hank should he come after they left. The two trucks pulled out.

Chapter Twenty - Eight   **Harmony**

Muslims fled. Some, long time residents, citizens for decades toughed it
out. They had nowhere to go, no home country to flee to. Any remaining
family relations in their native lands were distant and scarce.

They remained out of sight, removed any manifestation of their religion
and kept a very low profile. People still noticed them, and kept their distance. Even their closest associates made it obvious they didn't trust
them and would be much happier if they left.

Adnan kept going to work every morning. He had faced some angry locals. His pharmacy had several broken windows, one location had been
totally trashed and he quickly reopened with the assistance of some local
church groups. He blamed no one.

The streak of religious freedom was deep in Americans and even in the
face of significant evidence, personal fear and foreboding, church groups
were determined to help those who they felt were innocent and perse-
cuted.

And yet, it seemed to Adnan that the worm had turned. Long standing
American citizens complained that American Muslims did not condemn
the violent actions of their co-religionists. At this point thought Adnan, to

stand up and condemn the acts still put a target on your chest. And, he thought, when the situation called for it, members of the religious mainstream did not condemn the violent reaction of their friends, family and co-workers who rioted against Muslims.

Several area Mosques were trashed. Across the country it was uncommon for a mosque to have weathered the storm without damage. In fact, it seemed that the only time they were left alone was when they announced plans to close of their own volition.

Non-citizen Muslims were being deported. Members of that cultural group were being encouraged to go where their religion and culture were welcomed and tolerated as the capacity for toleration of Muslim atrocities had ended by their own actions. Mosques were being bulldozed and the slate of toleration wiped clean.

Adnan held on. He was a citizen. He knew many citizens well. Some came to his aid with vocal support. They encouraged Adnan to disavow himself of the violent actions committed by Muslims. He did to anyone who would listen.

With so many dead it was uncommon for people to not have some very direct connection to the violence, the deaths, the injuries and the terror of June 7.

Adnan had been visited by authorities. He appeared to have passed their test but was warned to keep a very low profile. Those government types were right on top of things, he thought. He wondered what role his supply operation had played.

A month after the attacks, as emotions seemed to be calming, but while the aftermath of the massive attacks was still raw, Adnan went to work as usual, though he now mostly stayed in the office behind the high pharmacy counter. Several of his employees had quit. Some could not manage the social stigma of working for the enemy while others quit in terror of being injured or worse in an attack on the store. While most of the vandalism was done at night there had been a brick thrown through a storefront window in the middle of the day.

The front window had been repaired and without a threat or customer rant or even minor violence for over a week, Adnan was beginning to think the worst was over.

His cell phone rang. It was his wife - his own name and home number were displayed on his phone. Going over a column of numbers Adnan distractedly clicked open the connection.

"Adnan, Adnan, they have the house surrounded and they are breaking windows," his wife frantically yelled into the phone.

"How many? Are they angry?"

"Yes, yes, many, many people and they are yelling things I cannot understand. Oh, it's on fire. Help!"

"I will call the police and I'm coming right away. Put the fire out or get out of the house."

"And walk right into the mob. They are in the back as well. They don't want us to leave."

"I am hanging up to call police. I will be there."

Adnan hung up the phone and quickly punched 911. He gave his address and described the situation, the fire and the mob. He ran to his car and sped for home. After he cautiously ran a red light a police cruiser gave chase. Adnan did not stop, hoping to bring the police with him to his home.

He looked in his rear-view mirror and the policeman on his bumper was pointing to the curb side of the road, telling him to pull over.

Adnan gestured 'no' and waved the policeman on, to follow him. The policeman seemed to get the message and followed with his lights and siren engaged.

Two more blocks and Adnan would be at his home. He turned off the main street and then made another quick turn up the hill on Federal Street. He could see a small billow of smoke at the end of the road. He rushed up to a few on-lookers who seemed curiously disengaged, like spectators of some foregone conclusion.

The house sat at the highest point of elevation on the street, which climbed the hill and turned to go back down it after passing Adnan's home. The house was an older bungalow with a yard carved into the slope of the hill which became too steep for reclamation 60 feet behind the building. A few trees punctuated the streetscape, turning the once working class neighbourhood into something a bit nicer. Despite the age of the neighbourhood, the homes were well kept and some had substantial additions.

"Is the fire out?" he asked the closest bystander.

"No. I thought that siren behind you was the Fire Department."

The policeman walked to Adnan briskly.

"Where is the Fire Department? My wife called, said there was a mob of people trying to set the house on fire."

The policeman quickly ascertained the nature of the incident.

"Did you call 911?"

Adnan nodded, "The Fire Department is on its way - standard procedure. Now let's get a look at the house."

The policeman stepped up to the front door. He opened it up and smoke poured out from the upper third of the doorway. A rush of air momentarily stopped the flow.

"How many are home?"

"My wife for sure and my youngest child, he is just a little kid."

The policeman thought for a second. Come with me, let's check out the back of the house, that's where the fire should be. They ran around the back and as predicted the back was fully engaged though most of the fire appeared to be inside the building. Air rushing through a broken window was fuelling the fire. The policeman thought again, listened and heard a distant siren. They ran back around the front.

"I am going in. You stay out front and direct the Fire Department."

There were still dozens of the curious hanging around the house in twos and threes. Nobody appeared to be doing anything except observing.

"I should go in. I know the layout of the house."

The policeman thought for a second and then agreed. Okay, we stay down and we head directly for the most likely place they could be. At the first sign of smoke issues we have to get out immediately or we die."

"Go, I'm right behind you."

Adnan plunged into the smoke filled door, taking four hard steps with his lungs full of fresh air before dropping to his knees to stay below the smoke. He entered the kitchen yelling for his wife. The inferno seemed to be at the back of the home in the living areas. If she was still there she was likely dead, but he had to check quickly. He crawled to the back room entrance and quickly scanned the room from the floor. Fire engulfed the back wall. The heat was blistering. He forced himself to remain long enough for a scan of the room. Nothing.

He turned and left, crawling out of the room as he was beginning to choke. He stopped in the kitchen to try to clear his lungs, but it wasn't working. The heat was intense and felt stronger in the hall than it had when he first passed that way. He stood up and made a plunge for the back bedrooms. Four more steps and he dropped again to get the clearer air down low to the floor. The bedroom area was covered in a thick layer of strong smelling smoke down to the tops of chairs and other furniture.

"There, there in that heap of clothing. There are two shoes sticking out."

It was not their usual laundry collection area. He crawled over as fast as possible and rustled the pile. He moved some garments. His wife flopped her arm, she was holding the baby which appeared lifeless, it's eyes rolled back.

Adnan grabbed the child and handed him to the policeman. "Go."

"I'll get her," he choked.

The policeman was at his limit for smoke and was coughing deeply. He tucked the child under his arm like a football and ran like a defensive line-man on an audible looking for the front hall. Once there he dropped to his knees took a deep breath of reasonably clear air, got up and made a last run for the door. One, two, three, four steps and he was still sur-rounded by smoke unable to see. He took another step and passed out, pitching forward and with his last thought, rolling to his left so he would-n't land on the baby. There was an audible gasp from the crowd, when he emerged from the smoke filled doorway, but nobody moved.

Adnan, grabbed his wife under her arms and tried to crawl backwards. The smoke had almost gotten a hold on him as he pulled and dragged and fought his way towards the front. She was unresponsive.

Adnan stood and simply grabbed her wrist and started to pull and churn his legs as fast as he could. He needed air, so he dropped to his knees, dipped his head down and took a huge gasp. It wasn't far down enough. He filled his lungs with smoke and began to choke. He tried again, this time more successfully. He rose and took another step and another coughing and choking, gasping for air.

Outside a fireman had given the policeman and the baby straight oxygen from their own respirator's supply. A third firefighter donned his tank and moved into the home. Others began to douse the home with water. The firefighter moving into the main hallway behind the front door, tripped over Adnan and his wife. He radioed for help and soon the bodies were carried out and the rest of the unit had moved into the home to get water on the flames in the back parts of the house.

An ambulance arrived on the scene.

"Serious smoke inhalation for the officer. He got out just in time with the child - looks about two years old. You want to take over treatment on both - they aren't dead but the baby looks like it might soon be."

Emergency para-medics worked feverishly on the child. Soon a cough, and a sputter signalled some success. The child was transported to hospital. The policeman responded somewhat better to oxygen, and emerged from unconsciousness appearing almost no worse for wear. Except he was much worse, his breathing very shallow. He appeared to be completely cognizant, even asking after Adnan and his wife and asking that his wife be informed he as okay.

He was also transported.

Para-medics had a long look at Adnan and his wife. She was dead. Likely she was dead, or past the point of recovery even as Adnan dragged her down the front hall. Adnan, was unconscious and was breathing very shallowly. Then he stopped breathing. Efforts to restore his aspiration failed multiple times. The paramedic covered him with a sheet - matching the cover that his wife had.

During the drama local interest had remained at the level of curiosity. Nobody left and nobody seemed to come out to add to the crowd. After the ambulances left the crowd began to disburse in twos and threes.

Police canvassed the neighbourhood after learning the basic circumstances from the 911 call that Roman initially made.

Nobody seemed to have seen the angry mob. They all said they were neighbours, describing their locations relative to the fire, and said they came out to help only becoming spectators when it appeared the fire was too large to stop with buckets and garden hoses.

One man said he tried to enter the home but did not see anything and believed the home empty. He did not want to take any more chances with the smoke and he cleared out. His still smoky clothes pointed to the likely truth of his story. Another pointed to the garden hose he had been futilely spraying on the back of the house.

The investigation of the home pointed to two accelerants likely from bottles of gasoline thrown through the back windows on either side of the house.

There were no other family members living nearby and very few willing community members to rally around what was left of the family. After spending some time with local foster families the two surviving children were sent to Egypt to live with Adnan's younger brother and his family. The house was ploughed under and eventually another built in its place and the memory of the incident remained only with those old enough and guilty enough to remember.

Chapter Twenty - Nine   Texas

In the clear light of a south Texas dawn Jeb and Billy arrived at the house.

Everything looked peaceful but some things were askew. Evidently there had been some presence at the house during the night.

Jeb exited the truck and made his way to the house. A single shot sounded and something bit him hard just above the left elbow.

"Get down, Billy. I've been shot."

Jeb thought for a moment. He made a quick call to the sheriff and explained the situation. There doesn't seem to be much fighting so I'll bring a few boys around. Be careful.

"Have you heard anything from Hank?"

"No Jeb, not yet, but I have a bunch surveying the damage from last night and we'll see who pops back into the light now that things have simmered down. Meantime wait until I bring reinforcements. Are there any vehicles around the house?"

"Just looking at that. Can't see round back yet but I don't see any," he told the sheriff.

"Billy, you circle around the house going that way," Jeb pointed to his right. "And I'll go from this side. Don't get too close. We are just scouting. The sheriff is on his way with some boys."

"Okay dad, coming back here, or meeting round back?"

"Back here. We just want a good look at the whole place so we can tell the sheriff when he gets here. Careful. Keep your distance. Don't do anything without telling me."

Another two shots were heard and one impacted a tree behind them. "Best move this truck back a ways.

"Once the truck was tucked partly behind a nearby willow tree, the two men started their mission. Billy dodged to another tree and scanned the area around the house.

Jeb moved toward the barn. Then he realized he didn't know if anyone was in the barn. He decided to circle the barn as well. He drew another shot as he scampered across the open ground. His arm didn't really hurt, in fact he had forgotten it almost immediately after being hit.

He shrugged off his light jacket and felt around for a wound. There was a bit of blood but it didn't appear to be flowing or even seeping into his shirt. He touched the wound. "Ah, there it is," he thought. It was painful to the touch. It appeared as if he had only been winged. He put his jacket back on and started toward the back door of the barn.

"Gotta find out if the barn is clear." He stepped gingerly through a small door built in the back side and let his eyes adjust to the low light.

A few horses shied, and clomped around in their stalls. So far so good. No voices or any indication of humans. He moved to the main door and flicked on the power. Lights sprang on everywhere. But there was no sound. Even the horses seemed to be holding their breath.

Jeb ran to the back of the barn and moved up into the loft. Nothing. He used the height to scan the rest of the building. Nothing. He moved back down to the main floor. The only way to know for sure was to look into every room. One side was divided into three sided rooms, open to the central section of the barn while the other had a row of completely enclosed rooms for storage, administration, and tools. He quickly checked them - nothing. The barn was clear. He stayed in the office room at the front which had a window which faced the yard and the house across the compound.

He couldn't see Billy anywhere. Either he was well camouflaged or hidden around the side of the house.

Jeb was considering his next move when he heard several shots, some quite closely packed together. Then Billy came sauntering around the house on the barn side.

"Pops, I got 'em," he yelled out. "Three guys loading a truck with our stuff."

Just as Jeb let down his guard a shot sounded. Billy went down. There was still someone in the house. Billy was still for a few horrible seconds then he rolled behind a farm vehicle. Jeb breathed hard and motioned to him about his wound. Billy reached back and tapped his left shoulder blade but didn't seem too worse for the wear.

He grinned a big grin and then went down again. Jeb could see a large red spot on his shirt. He fumbled for the phone.

"Sheriff, Billy's down. He got a few of them but someone holed up in the house shot him in the back. He said there was a truck in the back and they were looting the house."

"Okay Jeb, I'll get an ambulance. Is Billy moving?"

"A bit, he went down a minute ago but now he's propped himself up against a truck in the yard. Looks like there's some blood."

Jeb was contemplating his next move when the sheriff rolled up the driveway slowly. There was no gunfire to greet him.

Jeb telephoned him saying he was in the barn and there appeared to be someone in the house. Then they heard the sounds of a truck moving off. They ran around the house to see the pickup perhaps a half a mile away across the open country behind the house. A couple of bodies lay in the dirt. The sheriff jumped in his truck and gave chase. He motioned one of his men and Jeb to stay and secure the house.

"Room by room, be careful. Listen, take your time. But I'm guessing there is nobody there."

Jeb entered the familiar house and began the room by room search. It had been ransacked entirely. Everything was jumbled on the floor and anything portable of value was gone. Jeb and the deputy found nothing and retreated to the yard to see if they could get any information on the pursuit. The sheriff had just pulled up and the truck with Jeb's belongings rumbled over the uneven ground before getting on the blacktop in front of the barn and coming to a halt.

"Got 'em and your stuff. There was three more of them but they look like banditos rather than smugglers or military. I'm guessing this bunch was just along for the ride when the para-military guys invaded. They were hoping for some easy pickings."

An ambulance rolled up and they bundled Billy aboard. One of the para-medics remained behind and cleaned and treated Jeb's arm.

He took a look at the three invaders behind the house and then rolled out with the sheriff to see the bodies of the robbers left in the scrub.

"That appears to be the last of 'em. You have some clean-up to do. Me, I'll send the coroner around to collect up the dead. Para-medic said Billy'll be alright. Apparently got it right on the bone. Gonna have some recovery time, but it coulda been much worse. That kid of yours has a thick hide."

"Thanks for coming sheriff. Billy thought he'd got them all when he ambushed them loading the truck. I'm guessing he'll learn a lesson from this."

"I was hoping he a learned it from the Night of the Piranhas down at the river," said the sheriff. "He jumped in there a bit quick too. Gotta admire his spirit though."

Jeb asked about the invasion the night before.

"Sounds a lot like the one in California. Military precision and equipment but not as big. No insignia of any kind and a quick hit and run affair. Some are speculating it was a diversion to allow a lot of people in without being seen. Border guys are investigating.

"I do have some bad news though Jeb. Hank didn't make it."

"What? How do you know."

"Some of our guys found him in the truck he tried to drive away. He was on the road outta there and they mowed down a bunch of our guys trying to regroup. The truck sustained a direct hit from a shell. I'm really sorry Jeb."

Jeb just hung his head. One son dead and the other rushing to hospital to patch up a serious wound.

"Thank you sheriff. Where is he? I'm going to have to tell his mother."

The sheriff reached out and touched the top of Jeb's shoulder. They've got him in the morgue in town. Frankly Jeb he's in pretty bad shape. Direct hit to the truck. You can see him if you want. He had some ID on him so there is no need to identify him."

"I gotta do it. I gotta see my boy." Tears were rolling down Jeb's face though he refused to acknowledge them.

"Take me there sheriff, please - I don't think I can drive just now. My trucks 'as been a bit shot up recently."

"Sure I will Jeb. Do you want to tell the missus?"

"Best do that face to face sheriff and before I see my boy. She's gonna want to see him too."

The tears got larger, and Jeb swept them aside once. He was silent on the drive to town, though the sheriff relayed details of last night's fighting. All Jeb could think about was Hank as a little gaffer, running around the pasture pissing off the cows, laughing and giggling but taking Jeb's warning to stay in front of them or to the side to avoid being kicked.

"We got a few of them as they advanced but the jets knocked out a bunch of those AVs quickly and the rest just melted away. Some people think they might be in hiding, either in barns or in pre-built underground compounds - they disappeared that fast. There were only wrecks of seven of them and by all accounts there where at least twice that number. There are patrols out and we've doubled up on drone surveillance."

Jeb arranged to meet his wife in town. As soon as they met she asked after Hank and Billy.

Jeb tried to hold it in.

"Billy's in hospital. He got shot in the back clearing people out of the house. He's going to be okay. With Hank, I have some bad news."

Before she could react, he added, "Hank didn't make it. He was shot up trying to get away from the invasion. Sherriff said it was a direct hit on the truck."

She made him explain every detail of the invasion and the attempted escape. He relayed the situation about the house as well. She took it all in and then leaned in to him to rest her cheek on his chest.

"This has not been a good day for the Ryans," she said, with a sniffle.

"Now I'm going to identify my boy and make arrangements."

"An I'm coming with you."

"Are you sure. Sherriff said he's pretty banged up - direct hit and all."

"Jeb, I'm his mother, I have to go. I have to see my boy, even if there isn't much to see. I have no option."

"I feel that way too," said Jeb, nodding and steeling himself.

They arrived at the morgue where officials tried to talk them out of even witnessing the body, reiterating that identification had been found with the remains and it was conclusively Hank Ryan.

"I have to see my boy one more time," said Mrs Ryan. "Lead the way."

The attendant moved them through the building into an examining room. On the table lay a body covered with a white sheet. It was obvious that much of the body was not in its usual configuration. Some just wasn't there. The attendant pulled the sheet back over the head and held it in place just under the chin. Despite his efforts it was apparent that Hank's head was positioned on top of his body, it really wasn't attached, as there were two small blocks on either side to hold it in place.

"Oh," gasped Mrs. Ryan with a long, jagged intake of breath. The attendant pulled the sheet back up.

"I'm very sorry, but I have to ask, "Is that Hank Ryan?"

"Yes," said Jeb. "That's him."

Mrs. Ryan reached out to touch the head under the sheet. "Oh, my. There is nothing left to hug."

She broke down. First a deep wail and then tears, a deep outpouring of her motherly tie to her little boy. Hank wasn't little any more but to his mother he might as well have been a curious toddler, with a smile on his face and a first-born's desire to please his parents.

Jeb gently pulled her away from the table and held her tightly. Her silent sobs racked her body punctuated by an audible gasp from time to time as her body shook.

"My boy, my boy," she started to say and Jeb moved her towards the

188

door.

"I think she needs a sedative," said Jeb.

He and his wife moved into a waiting area and sat down. She leaned against him still sobbing. Her sorrow was almost unbearable. The sedative took hold and her sobs eventually quieted as she drifted into sleep.

Jeb was numb. She had grieved for both of them and he simply shook with remorse and regret. Tears rolled down his face but he made no effort to wipe them away. His mind would not stop replaying a couple of incidents of Hank's childhood. One when he had a big grin after soaking his brother Billy with the hose and another when he repeated that same grin after he first drove the tractor and made a squiggly but serviceable furrow. It was a distinctive smile that he kept his whole life. Not just a happy look, it was an uncontained display of joy.

"My son, why did I send you off? I just wanted you safe and away as quickly as possible. Why did you stick to the road?"

With nowhere to go, his sorrow building exponentially, Jeb took one of the other sedatives the morgue staff had given him and he settled in to thoughtless sleep with his wife and he, holding each other up while sitting in stiff, industrial, plastic chairs.

Morgue staff saw them there and one of them threw a blanket over them. Many more dead were being brought into the facility in the aftermath of the previous evenings' invasion.

Chapter Thirty   Europe

"It's not ethnic cleansing - it's cultural cleansing."

"And this is going to achieve it?"

"That's the plan. Got a better one?"

"When is the announcement?"

"On Sunday, makes sense. On Sunday, the EU will announce that Christianity, both as Protestantism and Catholicism are state religions in specific nations and no others can exist."

"Do Jewish leaders know this?"

"Yes, and we've been very upfront with them saying they are free to practice behind closed doors but any outward sign of non-compliance with the established religion will result in deportation."

"And they trust you?"

"Not at all, but they have few other options, save to join their co-religionists in Israel or Malta. Look, it's not meant as a forever and they know that. It's meant to sweep away the Muslim scourge. That blood culture is defined by its alleged faith which proscribes dominance over everyone else. It's got to be excised and this is the best way."

"As long as it's a negative construct it might work, but the minute you demand that everyone comply publically, it will be an issue."

"We're going Elizabethan on this - you have to be onside publicly, but you are free to your own devices in the privacy of your own home, unofficially even Muslims too."

"How many people have been consulted?"

"Actually a remarkable number. Leaders, spiritual leaders, business people such as yourself. Not surprisingly the Christian churchmen were quite enthusiastic."

"And we will be cleaning up some of the more liberal aspects of our street life. This is where it gets a bit dicey. We know immoral things will continue to be done and by forcing them under cover we risk losing some sense of control. But condoning everything anyone wants to do has not produced a just or equitable society. Social liberalism is a farce of misplaced social license, leading to a cesspool of moral freedoms that nobody envisioned that anyone would want to claim. It's no wonder the socially conservative types refuse to out the fundamentalists. So which is best, putting a lid on vice and at least insist on playing straight in the public sphere, or letting everything go any which way, which appears to lead to more vice and poor choices?"

"Well we've moved towards personal choice for decades. It has its value."

"Yes, but when your rights and my rights bump into each other then rights are meaningless. We need to impose some sort of social limit to help keep society on the up and up. Anyway, I'm not here to argue the merits of this policy. What's done is done."

Spenser left the hotel feeling a bit uneasy. He had been an early proponent of the re-establishment of national religions to battle a crumbling culture. However, it didn't seem right that to secure freedom, a nation had to impose slavery of conscience on its citizens. However, freedom to live your life only exists if everyone lives that freedom. Imposing faith at the end of a curved sword was different from imposing it officially but not actually. Spenser dreamed of a simple, elegant and defensible solution to the clash of cultures - but that solution remained elusive.

He walked down the street, beside a lovely old canal, in Amsterdam, on his way to meet his date. Well she was more than a date, they were travelling companions of a sort. She was an old girlfriend from his Oxford days. She was married, divorced and married again, then widowed. He had looked her up when he heard that her second husband had died. They kept close touch and he visited her whenever he was in Oxford which he made sure was quite regularly.

She had worked at the Ashmolean Museum for many years.

"So what was your big meeting about?" she asked.

"A product that I'm involved with distributing that will be a 'must have' in every household."

"A kitchen device? A bathroom product? What is it? Do I want one? Do I need one?"

"No, no. None of the above. Suffice to say it will be coming out shortly and I will have a hand in its distribution. You already have one, and I'm not sure if this new version is any better than the old."

"Such riddles. It will be announced next week? I'll wait and see."

They moved to Zurich by train. The trains weren't entirely safe but they were much safer than travelling long distances by car. There were underground groups of radicals that acted as bandits and insurgents. When the attacks came nobody was sure who was behind the violence. It was almost impossible to secure thousands of miles of highway. Authorities had a stake in making sure the trains ran.

They arrived in Zurich and spent a day touring the small downtown area where the Limmat River reaches the Zurichsee lake. They spent most of their time in the Banhofstrasse and the Town Hall district on opposite sides of the river but did visit the Swiss National Museum.

"I simply must see the museum's unrivalled collection of cuckoo clocks," said Jennette with a laugh. Spencer laughed too.

He knew she was a museum junkie and was constantly on the lookout for innovations that she could use at the Ashmolean.

"Okay, but if we go there, I get to pick the restaurant."

"Okay, you can pick the restaurant. As long as you pick something I like."

He laughed. "Oh, you'll like it. It's a mountain climbers theme. Lots of yodelling and cuckoo clocks. Bits of rope, hammers and pinions," he joked. "The menu is all boxed up for carrying."

"It's the height of chic?"

"The height, yes. Chic - depends on your perspective."

The two had reached the door of the museum. Spenser bought their tickets and they went in.

"You know how I am with Museums. Each person has to move at their own pace. If I want to look at a Roman coin with Claudius on it for three seconds longer than you, it gets very uncomfortable for both of us."

"I'm not here professionally, I'm here to enjoy the museum with you," she said.

"And I'm here to enjoy the museum. Just don't get wound up if I wander off. I have a very tangential imagination in these places. I'm not at all linear and I sometimes get very annoyed with the spacing, pacing and arranging that museum curators impose upon us poor plebes."

He gave her a deep look, challenging a response. She knew better. They had had this conversation before.

The pair began their journey through the main floor. After an hour Spenser spied Jennette and suggested they take a break with a little snack or a cup of tea.

Jennette agreed. As they were moving toward the restaurant through the main lobby of the museum a man ran out of one set of doors. His hands and arms were covered in blood and he held something about 18 inches long and the width of a ruler. He looked about wildly and then made for the main exit. A siren had sounded and three overweight, out of breath museum guards charged through the same door from which he had come and seeing him, gave chase.

"Stop that man. He has stolen an exhibit." Even in German it was pretty obvious what they had yelled.

The three guards did everything they could to make their pursuit look good but they were in no shape to give proper chase. Spenser and Jennette had been near the center of the space when the bloodied man ran past.

The siren still rang as the guards re-entered the museum, having failed to catch the thief. They quickly sealed the entrance and started a protocol to screen everyone who wanted to leave.

Spenser quickly moved to the tea room and grabbed a pair of seats knowing they were going to be some time. He was able to make his order for tea and a few biscuits known despite the wailing siren. It stopped as he received his change.

"The only German I know is from movies and television," he said to Jennette. "I pretty much knew what those guards were yelling - though I must admit it took a moment for it to sink in. Does that mean that in every film in English the Germans are yelling at people to 'Stop!' "

Jennette laughed. "You have a way of putting into words exactly what I have been thinking."

The next day, Spenser left Jennette to explore a few chic clothing shops while he attended his meeting.

"I don't think we are going to have any unrest here in Switzerland. Rather the opposite. Re-establishment has been going on here for many years - though quietly, unofficially and with virtually complete support of the people."

"I wish I could say the same for the rest of Europe," said Spenser.

"You might be surprised Mr. Spenser. It's actually a rather simple, elegant solution to our difficulties."

"I always preferred an end to travel and discourse between Western countries and a basketful of nations who sow discord and seem to have one thing in common which we needn't name if we simply point to their apparently secular manifestations as governments and countries."

"A plan, to be sure, but one that does not rid us of the problems we already have."

"It doesn't have to be a one-pronged plan. There is room for other measures."

"Perhaps I should take the time to mention to you another issue which has arisen. You may have heard of the robbery at the Swiss National Museum yesterday."

"Yes, I was there. I saw the thief run."

"Interesting, you will have to tell me more once I am finished. The man stole a small object. About 18 inches long and three centimeters wide and high. It is covered in hieroglyphics and is apparently Assyrian in origin. The object was found in the Valley of the Kings about 100 years ago, not long after many of those tombs were discovered. Similar objects were found in four other tombs including Tutankhamen. All from about the same time period - when the Egyptians moved to an institutional sun-worship of Akhenaten."

"It has only now come to our attention that some middle eastern group is trying to acquire all these five pieces. One went missing from a Museum in Cairo about a year ago. Another disappeared from a display case in the Louvre in Paris and now a third has been stolen from the museum here, yesterday."

"Assyrian, but coveted by Middle Easterners. Wasn't Assyria lost in history by the time our Middle Eastern friends started to put their society together?"

"A good point. However, according to our intelligence on the matter from those who are trying to get these pieces, there are five of them. And once all five of them are together, they actually fit to form a five pointed star. The inscriptions are supposed to be the instructions on how to build a very powerful weapon. Sounds like hocus pocus, a little Ark of the Covenant-ish, but remember many of the ancient artifacts are quite real and very much what they claim to be."

"Where are the other two pieces?"

"One is in the Royal Ontario Museum in Toronto. Until now, these pieces had only been seen as small decorative things, suitable for display as religious tokens."

"Where is the fifth piece?"

"It's in Oxford at the Ashmolean."

"I take it they have been pulled and are under heavy guard. Just in case, you know," Spenser smiled.

"Yes, steps have been taken to secure these pieces, as it was only yesterday that it became apparent exactly what we were facing."

"Not that we really know anything, just that we aren't taking any chances."

"Quite."

The man turned his left arm forward and shrugged his jacket up his arm to consult his watch. Spenser didn't have to see the ax tattoo on his wrist to know it was there.

"I must wear a watch, as the damned cuckoo clocks are notoriously inaccurate. Especially the ones outside. I've always wondered why Swiss watches were so incredibly accurate. It dawned on me that the cuckoo clocks are terribly inaccurate, more decorative artworks than actual timepieces. So the watches are particularly accurate in compensation."

Spenser smiled, "So we are all set for the announcement, and no trouble expected. Did I really need to come all the way to Zurich to get that?"

"One cannot be too careful. We are trying to communicate face to face as much as possible. Other forms of communication have a way of going astray or being intercepted. I believe our friends in Venice will want to know what you know. As well, can you please deliver this small package to them. I remind you, you are supposed to be conducting business in Switzerland."

"Oh, but I am. I am making sure my lady friend remains happy. That's important business. I also made a visit to my two largest suppliers. Just a social call."

Chapter Thirty - One   Washington

"Ultimately, Austin was thankful for the help with the invasion," said President O'Day. "They may have made some noise about nation to nation communications but the newness of their 'sovereignty' makes it difficult to react quickly. Who are we supposed to call? They were pleased we were there to help."

"It's amazing what a squadron of F-18s can do, especially when they are determined and the enemy is defined."

"But they just melted away, just like California. Do we have anything definite on the California invasion?"

"No, Mr. President. As you know, what little evidence there is, points to some Mexican indifference and to some combination or co-operation between Venezuela and Middle Eastern elements."

"Are we going to be able to get anything more definitive than that?"

"Probably not, not unless there is an additional incursion. We are now much better prepared and ready to discern origins. Remember back when Russians annexed Crimea, they were there in force and able to operate for weeks without anyone being able to absolutely point fingers. It's hard to start an offensive war without strong evidence," said Senator

Tom Findlay.

"I have heard some intelligence reports that there are more and more Cubans in Key West. There is speculation that Americans of Cuban origin are purchasing Key West properties and that Cubans are making their way to Key West by boat. Once there, they are brought into Miami and ultimately disperse throughout Florida."

"Crap, the borders are just too porous. We've got to stop these incursions at the source. Do we need to teach Mexico a serious lesson?" asked O'Day. "Or Cuba?"

"That's a serious step Mr. President. Certainly we will need some sort of provocation and some clearly defined goals for any operation on our part. There is some satellite evidence of camps and military presence in parts of Northern Mexico. An offensive operation to remove these camps risks a stronger reaction by Mexico."

"That's what we should do. What are they going to say, 'You can't blow up my invasion camp'? General, do you have a recommendation on this - please do not be afraid to stray into policy and issues of state on this - it is much more than just a bombing run we are considering, should events escalate."

General Aaron Stewart, Chair of the Joint Chiefs of Staff, had been called into the Oval Office for this conference. He considered the question posed to him.

"Mr. President, I would like to have more time to consider the implications of this. However, my first thoughts force me to consider the stance of Texas on this. Do we have fly over privileges? Does Texas want such an aggressive approach since they are likely to bear the brunt of any reprisals? Will Texas join with us in a joint operation? What is the status of our installations and personnel in Texas? Certainly I can make the necessary preparations for a quick strike and for the need for any follow up, up to and including a complete invasion of Mexico. Logistically the quick strike can be ordered at any time as it falls within our operational parameters. An invasion would require more lead time."

"Okay, please move ahead with the quick strike - is a week enough preparation to be ready for likely reprisals and to get the ball rolling on logistics for anything more substantial?"

The General nodded.

"Okay, strike in one week - give or take, just give some regard to operational advantages - please keep me informed up to the minute on the timing and results. I don't anticipate anything further from the Mexicans or anyone else but we need to be ready. Thank you General Stewart. Oh, and US federal government property is still US federal property in and out of Texas. We have initiated negotiations on our bases and equipment. Until then it's all ours. Don't ask for permission just apologize for any inconvenience."

The General nodded and left.

"Mr. President what about a message to the Venezuelans and their allies?"

"Tom, I am aware of those issues but I think that is for any escalation in the situation."

"Mr. President, it is possible to do it all at once so it is accomplished without escalation?"

"Let me mull it over, what are you suggesting?"

"I was thinking about a clandestine strike on a Venezuelan naval vessel, even one in port, to highlight their vulnerability. Doing it at the same time as the Mexican strike makes a very strong point and gives the appearance of a one and done reprisal."

The President nodded slowly. "Yes, Tom it would."

Six days later three squadrons of fighters supported by six B-52s and several cruise missiles hit three quickly constructed camps spread across Northern Mexico. The day before a US Navy submarine slipped into the harbour in Venezuela and attached four mines to the hull of a Venezuelan helicopter launch destroyer.

During the airstrikes a satellite signal tripped the mines and the destroyer was sunk with four large holes in its hull. It was salvageable but only barely and only after it had been dredged up from the bottom of the harbour.

The cruise missile strikes in Mexico were completely unexpected. They were followed by carpet bombing of the camps by the heavy bombers, ideally deployed for this kind of attack. Squadrons of fighters swooped in to mop up anything that escaped the missile and bombing runs. Several attack helicopters landed in the aftermath with scores of personnel tasked to comb the wreckage for evidence, computers and anything else that would lend itself to understanding the issues better.

The men stayed on the ground for almost eight hours covered by F-18s. They were extracted only when it became evident that the Mexicans were soon to arrive to investigate the incident. They had wisely stayed away in the immediate aftermath and made the timing of their arrival in the area well known.

Evidence of Venezuelan involvement was overwhelming. It was on computer hard drives, it was with many of the personnel at the bases. The Venezuelan connection was obvious right through the highest levels of the Venezuelan government - though the operation was designed to be clandestine.

It appeared that while the Mexicans were involved it was not a government sponsored operation - in fact it was done through only some parts of the Mexican military and with the co-operation of two Northern Mexican state governors who made sure their interests looked the other way. Through the scrubland in northern Mexico, looking the other way was a way of life. Likely there were kickbacks or some sort of financial reward involved.

The Middle Eastern connection was there as well, through Venezuelan operational notes. The Venezuelans were controlling the operations but using Middle Eastern volunteers to do the grunt work of the invasion. Most disturbing was the suggestion that the invasions in both cases were meant to scare the border populations into leaving and were set up as diversions for other groups and materials to gain entry to the US or for-mer US for the purposes of internal guerilla activity.

While the operations had been a success, Washington and Austin could not help but feel that the worst was yet to come, especially in light of the June 7th attacks.

Chapter Thirty - Two   **Marietta**

"We have to step up."

"It's not going to be as bad as all that."

"I cannot see the US rolling over the same way they did for Texas. We have a bit of history here."

"Yeah, but O'Day is no Lincoln. He will not force the issue. He does not want a hostile neighbour and would likely be happy to see the Florida issue handled. There have even been quiet suggestions that we could buy the US bases at Tampa and Pensacola. They want Florida handled and they can't afford to do it. We want Florida handled and we cannot afford not to."

Vernon Clemons sat back heavily. The three US senators were on the other side of his desk.

"Look Vernon, if we can settle this peacefully it brings a lot more stability to Dixie and then we can tackle constitutional and political legitimacy. All of us have US senator terms which are up next year. We have to find a mechanism to maintain our political legitimacy."

"First things first," said O'Day. "How do you propose we move ahead."

"It seems to me," said Alabama Senator George Caleb, "that we have diplomacy and geography on our side. And now we have Florida Republican Herb Chartaway who has stated publically that Florida belongs with Dixie."

"Wonderful yes, but how do you propose we proceed?"

"Have Chartaway publically declare his intention to sit in the Dixie legislature. That will provide any signal the locals need to state their case either way. We have several newspapers in the area strongly on side with Dixie. Once Chartaway sits with us the pressure will fall strongly on Florida's other senator Bill Scott."

"It'll be hard for him to resist joining our caucus as his state will be effectively cut in half and he is getting only lip service from Washington," said Caleb.

"It seems a prudent course. You know gentlemen I am most concerned that we proceed carefully and predictably," said Clemons. "We are not fully separated from Washington yet and we want to allow that separation to continue naturally so that eventually it is fait accompli."

"It pretty much is - especially as Washington is trying to scoop some cash for its assets in Pensacola and Tampa. They understand the argument that locals paid for all the federal improvements over the years but a lot of things in those naval and air stations can be moved out on a moment's notice."

"So if we buy, we buy the weaponry as well?"

"If we don't get it, why buy it? Fat lot of good a naval station does with no ships, or an air base without planes and pilots."

Clemons remained still. The point was made but hanging in the air was the need to get loyal southerners to take up the manned positions in the new military. He realized in order to proceed he would need to designate a military commander for Dixie. And that was a major step away from the

204

old US. It would have to be handled very gently.

"What about your meeting with the Mexican ambassador Rodriguez?"

"It was pretty formal," said Clemons. "After all he had an agreement to fulfill. In fact, I think that recognition and the virtual quiet on the issue from Washington, may have pushed our Florida friend Senator Chartaway into our camp. He was headed there anyway but a little push moves things a bit faster."

"After all the Mexican sniffing around I think they will back off southern Florida for a while. The Cubans have taken up the slack though. I'm told Key West is being overrun by people literally drifting in from the island. There's enough sympathy from Key Westers that there hasn't been much uproar," Clemons said.

Two days later Florida Senator Herb Chartaway told the Jacksonville press he was going to sit in the Dixie legislature for the rest of his term and would seek re-election to his role at that time.

Jacksonville took the news matter-of-factly. The Panhandle wondered why it took so long but support for the move dwindled the further south one asked the question. South of Daytona Beach the public mood might have been resigned, as many people saw what many in Dixie saw, but they were not happy about giving up their allegiance to the old United States, especially as so many had emigrated from the rust belt.

And predictably the pressure on Florida Senator Bill Scott did increase. He was courted by the Dixie contingent. He was leaned on by Washington which simply did not want to deal with negotiations in public. And he was pushed by those in Central Florida who wished the whole thing would go away. Southern Floridians appeared split between Dixie and the status quo, especially the Cuban contingent who benefitted from the lack of cohesion. They could more easily push their own agenda which was to take as many illegals as possible to puff up the Cuban numbers making any democratic expression more likely to favour them.

"Look Bill, with half the state already in Dixie and the other half being invaded from Cuba, you have no choice but to side with Dixie on the condition that they end the problems in Key West."

"I know. However all my support comes from Floridians who came here from mid-Atlantic states. They are all pseudo Yankees and not too inclined to side with the rednecks. Have you ever seen an angry Yankee? The British did and they sued for peace."

"Don't be so dramatic Bill. The Yankees haven't got their dander up for 250 years. The most they've risen is to flee the north for Florida and Texas. They are Floridians now. They understand our need to secure our borders and settle the question of unity. With Dixie in the middle we aren't even part of the contiguous states anymore. It's time."

"Yeah, but can I get re-elected as a Dixiecrat?"

"Who is going to run on a 'Return to Washington' platform? Nobody. Hell every politician in the old US has run against Washington for 50 years. Now you can take Florida into the south on a ticket of maintaining good relations with our northern brothers."

"Okay, so how do we do this?"

"The best way is to signal the likelihood first," said his political aide, Justin Jancovic. "When asked you say you are considering the new political landscape and are consulting across the state including the north - makes you look inclusive and indicates your likely move."

"Assuming there isn't an uproar or some other political backlash, you can announce your intentions to join the Dixie legislature with your colleague Senator Chartaway in about a month. Just toss in a promise to work with both the Dixie and US governments to maintain dual citizenships and you are golden."

"And so just like that Florida is part of the South," said Scott.

"Just like that, it moves into a cosier relationship with Dixie. Remember it's a big coup for Dixie's legitimacy to have Florida and it works geographically. We have a fair bit of negotiating power, especially prior to your announcement. We need to use it," said Jancovic. "South Carolina has little choice but to join a southern caucus. As partial outsiders we always have a choice. As rebels to the Union the southern guys cannot clamp down on our foibles as they have to maintain that their own right to secede is legitimate. Puts us in a pretty good spot thinks I."

"Okay, so get me a little unrelated press time in Orlando."

"Will do boss." Jancovic thought for a moment. "Anyone there you want to honour or get your photo with? Other than Mickey Mouse, that is."

"So I'm guessing the real independence will be established in a year or so when we all collectively re-run for our offices but outside the Union, or inside the Dixie Union?"

"Gotta watch the rhetoric - Dixie Union is a charged phrase, and we can't call ourselves a Confederation. We've got to come up with something more palatable."

"Just add that to the list. There are so many things to do, it appears impossible to achieve within the timeframe we have," said Clemons.

"So hire a few people to help."

"I thought maintaining a limited sized government was a major reason for our secession?"

"More charged phrases. We have to tiptoe through all of this."

"That's what I've been saying. In reality we appear to be moving quickly on the ground but we keep our rhetoric in check and hold open the possibility of rejoining the Union to keep a lid on things."

Chapter Thirty - Three　　　　　Malta

Malta was an armed camp.

The Israelis were steadfast that Malta was a prize of war which they seized.

Many Maltese had moved to southern Italy after they fled the Islamic invasion of their island. While the Israelis welcomed anyone back who could prove property ownership many Maltese simply remained in southern Italy.

Many thousands pressed their property claims. They secured their ownership and sold, using the proceeds to build a new life in Italy. In many ways they blended in fairly easily with the Italians who were desperate for population growth and renewal after generations of people leaving for the New World.

The announcement that Christianity was going to be a national religion throughout Europe rankled many in Italy because they were nominally Catholic and preferred to think of their faith in those terms. Others were upset as government appeared to be imposing upon their freedom of conscience. However there was little organized opposition as even the hard line liberals understood the choice was necessary to restore cultural balance. As some nations did not allow freedom of conscience no nation could welcome the hardliners and expect to survive.

With its economic turmoil and general disorganization after World War Two, Italy had never been a major destination for emigrants. Certainly there were some pockets in the north, but the relatively poor conditions in the south and Italy's weaker social state programs kept most non-Europeans more interested in France and Germany when they emigrated to Europe.

The emigrating Maltese, now blessed with abundant land and opportunity, took to the building of their new homes with relish. Local markets were jammed with agricultural produce and towns and cities burst with new ideas and renewed enthusiasm.

Spenser and Jennette had been in Venice when the re-establishment announcements had come. There was little stir. People seemed please that continental security was at long last, being taken seriously.

They walked through the narrow streets, poked in glassware shops and among other fine goods, and negotiated the bridges and canals. Spenser arranged for a gondola ride along the Grand Canal stopping only once to deliver the small package he had been entrusted with in Zurich.

They glided along the canal, waving occasionally to passersby, and trying to keep up appearances as photographers were quite interested in their presence in the foreground of their tourist shots. Spenser could not help but be drawn back in thought to the Ashmolean.

"My God, my dear. We are going to be in half the world's tourist photos of Venice. Good thing we are supposed to be here and aren't hiding from anybody - we'd be found in a moment," said Spenser.

Jennette laughed, "Perhaps we should look surprised in some of the photos. We'd give people a bit of a laugh when they get home and look at their holiday shots."

"Now I was thinking the same thing. Next time someone points a camera let's do a bit of play acting, you know, surprise, bashfulness, using your arm to artfully hide your face; that sort of thing."

"I'm glad to hear that we are supposed to be here. With all your cloak and dagger meetings I was beginning to think you were a super-spy rather than a businessman with logistics problems."

"I am a super-spy my dear. But I'm just supposed to be in Venice. In fact, this gondola ride is my way of very publically being in Venice," he looked at her with a dour look. "In fact all the digital processing units around Europe will capture our images and lock us in as having been in Venice on the Grand Canal . . ." he looked at his watch . . . ."at precisely 2:37 p.m. on September 15th, in the Year of our Lord 20 . . ."

"Oh, stop it," she said with a giggle. He too broke out into a broad grin.

"Yes indeed, a super-spy. Spenser, Edward Spenser. On her Majesty's Secret Service, gliding the canals of Venice in search of a good meal and something to drink."

"Once we get well past the Accademia Bridge we'll take back to land and find a nice restaurant for dinner."

"We haven't even passed the Rialto yet, how long is it going to be?"

"I reckon another hour, more or less if we want it to. We only must inform our most excellent gondolier."

The gondolier turned towards them at the sound of his profession but gave no indication he was following their conversation, however lightly. He liked to maintain the illusion for his customers that they were alone on the canal.

"Sir, how much longer to the Accademia?" Spenser asked.

"Ah, sir, ah," said the Italian struggling with the language to prop up the illusion. "Ah, Accedemia, ah bout another hour sir. Would you like it longer or shorter?"

Spenser smiled. The man had been listening.

"That is fine, thank you."

"Jennette we can search out a museum or two past the bridge. Remember the Italians eat very late and restaurants will not be ready for us. At least those restaurants at which we want to eat."

Spenser mulled over how to subtly bring up the Ashmolean and the Assyrian artifact. Jennette was looking at her phone for messages.

"Now you hate it when I look at my phone but there you go with yours," he said light-heartedly.

"It's been buzzing a bit," she said scrolling through messages. "Anyway you have your nose in yours at every meal. I just check mine once every few days."

"That's the difference dear, I'm on a working holiday and you are simply on holiday. I have to make sure my meetings are still on so as to minimize the amount of time they take."

"And Edward, you have done a wonderful job of that," she said still looking at the phone. "Oh, oh. That's not good."

"What? Is your mother okay?"

"Yes, no, it's not that. The museum was robbed yesterday. Isn't that odd. Just like the robbery we saw in Zurich. A smash and grab in the Assyrian section. They aren't sure if anything was taken. Asking anyone with even a tidbit to pass it on. I'll just remind them I'm on holiday," she said tapping out a message.

Spenser felt his whole body tighten up at the first mention of the robbery. He knew what it was before she even detailed it.

"When did that message come in?"

"Just recently. There's been a few of them. That's why I checked. There were several buzzes."

Spenser realized that there was little he could do or would likely be asked to do. Still, he wanted to know more from the Ashmolean but Jennette hadn't been there anyway. He decided to take a chance.

"Is there any indication from your colleagues that the robbery we witnessed was in anyway related?"

"Yes, the Curator has asked for details on the pieces in the display case that was smashed and said that other Assyrian cases be emptied and stored for a time as another robbery targeted Assyrian artifacts."

"How would you know that?" she asked.

"It's just that at my meeting my Zurich supplier said that the news had mentioned the Swiss Museum robbery was one of a number of museum robberies which had taken place in the last while."

"The art world must have a demand for Assyrian stuff. I know a lot of it was destroyed in the run up to 5/29. Many of those areas overrun by the fundamentalists had anything destroyed that suggested a history other than Islam. I guess that drives up the price."

"It appears everyone is okay. Jeremy cut his hand on some broken glass trying to grab the robber," she was reading her emails. "And he twisted his ankle in the ensuing chase."

"I take it that is some new Jeremy, not Jeremy that I know from last year's Christmas party, the older gentleman who is in charge of security for a couple of floors? That Jeremy wouldn't chase after anyone."

"Quite. This Jeremy is a young man who started at the Ashmolean a couple of months ago. His family is from Jordan, but they have lived in Britain for three generations. It was his grandfather who emigrated. Jeremy has a particular interest in Petra and has been involved with setting up an exhibition of Petra artifacts."

Spenser thought he should pass that bit on to his Zurich contact. He wondered if there was more.

"What does this Jeremy's father do?"

"Oh, I don't know. He's not involved with the university or the museum as far as I know. He's some kind of businessman in Oxfordshire. It's never come up, other than in the natural curiosity to know if he was placed at the museum by some high ranking Oxford academic or administrator."

"Well, I hope he recovers quickly. At least he tried to stop the thief."

"I wonder why he was on that floor at the time. Usually he'd be in the artifact rooms or in the administrative wing making exhibition arrangements. He must have been checking out all the Petra stuff we have on hand. Of course those rooms also house some Mesopotamian artifacts as well."

The gondola glided on, past the fish market, past the produce and fruit and under the Rialto. The gondolier had slowed going under the bridge as tourist cameras were clicking.

"Keep smiling dear, we won't be here for long."

With that the gondolier pushed with a little more vigour and had them past the bridge and out of the way of camera shot within a few minutes. They resumed their leisurely glide down the canal which widened considerably past the bridge.

"Just around that bend," said Spenser pointing far ahead to where the canal took a dramatic left turn. "And the Accademia is only a quarter mile past it. We won't be able to see it though, its hidden around a second slight bend in the canal to the left. "

"While we have the boat we should get dropped at the end of the canal at the Basilica of Santa Marie. We can look around there and then make our way to the Peggy Guggenheim Museum for a bit before finding a late dinner. Sound good?"

Chapter Thirty - Four   **Italy**

Like all airports it was chaotic.

They made their way to their gate for the flight back to London. Situated north of Mestre, the sister city of Venice on the mainland, Marco Polo Airport was not as busy as some European airports but it was not large either, making mornings a bit jumbled as all the flights tried to get away on time.

Spenser and Jennette took a shuttle across the causeway connecting Venice to the mainland and swung north through Mestre to the airport.

"Not the most romantic way to leave Venice," said Spenser as they crossed the causeway.

"There is no romantic way to leave Venice."

"I suppose you are right. I hope you've had a good holiday. I know I've enjoyed it."

"Yes, except for your meetings, and they were mercifully short, I did enjoy getting away from it. The Museum is a bit dry sometimes, though I expect they will still be talking about yesterday's uproar."

"I expect you were secretly pleased to spend a bit of time shopping on your own, though I'm not sure you bought anything."

"I did buy a nice blouse. I like to have something to remember the trip."

"You mean that lovely glass paperweight I gave you is not enough?" he laughed.

"That is more long term," she said. "It sits on my desk with a bit of magic of its own. The blouse is a bit of Italian style I can pull out whenever I want. I can take it or leave it."

The shuttle deposited them at the airport and they made their way to the proper gate. Taking the train back to England was almost as expensive, slower and there was a risk of terrorist attack. Spenser was not sure of the effect the re-establishment edict had had in the banlieues. Italy was a bit out of the way of violence due mostly to lack of serious numbers of Muslims. France was different. Already there were rumours of battles with police in several major French cities but he hadn't been able to get too much official information.

"Come dear, this is our gate. Let's pass customs and we can get a coffee or tea in the boarding area. I expect we have 45 minutes before we board."

They passed through customs security easily with Spenser being given an extra two questions about any business he had conducted while in the EU. They were questions he had been asked many times before.

They were directed behind the customs desks and through the doors into the waiting lounge. As they were passing into the waiting area a commotion broke out down the main departures concourse. Spenser stopped just short of the doors to look back down the long open area.

There were shouts. Then there was the sound of mass movement and shortly after that concussive pops and breaking glass. The mass movement became a torrent and the screams and commotion increased exponentially in only a few seconds.

"Quickly, in here," said Spenser as he herded Jennette into the inner waiting room. Inside was a scattering of passengers and carry-on luggage. Most people had a coffee or drink in their hands and were trying to manage their possessions to get settled for the wait. Everyone looked through Spenser at the door through which he had just come.

He turned to follow their stares, acutely aware that everyone had pitched forward in their seats, on hair trigger alert. The running people began to thin out almost as quickly as they had materialized. Then there was a shout and a volley of shots from near the customs area just outside the lounge door.

Spenser directed, in fact almost pushed a curious Jennette to the side of the room, out of direct line of fire through the doors.

"What is going on?" she said as she only partly resisted his directions.

"I'm sure authorities are taking care of it. It sounds serious. Likely we will be delayed."

There was another volley of shots, this time from far down the concourse and the commotion stopped. Sirens could be heard.

The public address system cracked to life with a burst of Italian. Then English, "Please remain calm. Anyone who can should exit the immediate area around Gates 35-38. Flights from those gates will be redirected. Please consult the departures board for updated information.

"Flights from all other gates may experience a slight delay. You may be asked to re-clear customs and you may be approached by police or airport security and directed to other waiting facilities. Please take their direction swiftly."

The instructions were repeated in French and German and then the whole cycle was repeated.

"I expect it was a terrorist attack. A frontal assault on the airport. Those gates are right opposite the main doors to the departure concourse."

A number of people flooded into the waiting area. They could not have all just cleared customs. Several of them appeared injured with bloody hands or clothing. Two or three people looked shell shocked and once able, simply slumped to the ground upon reaching the room. Several people began to lend a hand to the injured. Others merely stared in awe at the unusual sight before them.

"We are going to be here a while," said Spenser.

However within a few minutes an announcement was made asking passengers for London to begin boarding.

"They must be trying to clear us out."

As they passed the check point two airport officials stood and scrutinized everyone carefully. Once aboard and disengaged from the gate, two security personnel made their way up and down the plane asking customs questions all over again.

Several people asked what was happening and only received an answer that they were going to London on time, that extra security precautions were in place and that the pilot would provide more details shortly.

The plane taxied down the runway and cleanly rose into the air, making a rapid ascent, banking sharply north east and was soon over the Alps.

"And you thought our holiday would be pedestrian," said Spenser with a grin.

"It was pedestrian. We walked everywhere!" Jennette smiled. "I wonder what happened exactly and how many were hurt."

"I think we are best out of there though we may be flying from the frying pan into the fire. If this is a reaction to the re-establishment edict, we can expect this type of reaction all over Europe. It could go on for many months and how it will play depends on official reactions."

"I am of course concerned with the number of violent Muslims but any I know are very nice, respectful, and very much a part of Englishness."

"Really Jennette. I'm guessing the Muslims you know either are happy to be in Britain or have never had to choose between their cultural brothers or modern, multicultural British."

"It is our background as an Empire which seems to make us tolerant of other seemingly outlandish ways of living."

"It is our live and let live nature, that makes us strongly tolerant of outlandish people and which grants them the right to be outlandish, and fully expects that they have no desire to insist that anyone else be outlandish with them. However, many people do not agree that our tolerance and our culture are superior. They think our culture is decadent and that our tolerance is weakness, that only their version of what is right and good is, well, right and good."

"But how can we change our belief in tolerance so completely?"

"Because it isn't shared."

The plane had leveled out and people had calmed now that the chaos was behind them.

"Ladies and gentlemen," said an English voice. "I am your pilot, Captain David Cook. I'm sure most of you saw or heard some of the commotion back at Marco Polo. We were asked to depart quickly to make room for emergency services. I have been told by Italian authorities that several people were killed and perhaps 50 injured due to a terrorist assault on the front gate of the departure concourse by a small band."

"There was no warning, no demands made and police and security were able to neutralize them quickly preventing additional injuries."

"We will be around to your seats asking if anyone aboard was still in the concourse when the attack occurred. For those that were, officials have asked for statements to be made to help the investigation, things like timing, viewpoint, or any other details you can provide."

"I was right," said Spenser.

"Quite the investigative journalist you are," said Jennette with a forced grin. "A terrorist attack, who would have thought?"

Spenser was scrolling through some web news on the personal screen built into the back of the forward seat. He pointed to the screen.

"Ah yes, terrorists. And the news source here says there were several attacks yesterday in Britain including an attack in central London when terrorists sprayed bullets into the crowd waiting in line to get into Westminster Abbey. And in France there were running battles in many banlieues near Paris, Marseilles, Lyon and Strasburg. It seems that re-establishment is not being accepted as smoothly as many had hoped. In fact it is bringing out the crazies, making them easier to identify."

"How many were killed? Anything in Oxford?"

"The news story is not terribly specific, just 'Attacks across Britain' with the only specifics being the drive-by shooting of tourists at Westminster. According to this, there are 149 confirmed dead, many more in hospital. One hundred and forty nine! It appears they drove by with at least two vehicles and doubled back and shot again. Some of the victims were from a school group from Northumberland."

The two were silent for some time until a stewardess leaned in to ask them a few questions. They confirmed they had cleared customs and had been in the boarding waiting area and had not seen anything except running people and those who entered the waiting area just prior to the flight being called.

"Are we on time for Stansted?"

"Yes, we actually should arrive there just a bit early due to our quick departure. I'm told there may be a bit of a delay processing everyone through customs due to the unusual nature of our boarding. Also, don't be surprised if your luggage didn't get onboard. It will be coming on the next flight and should arrive within two hours of our arrival. Easier for you if you can wait or it will be delivered by the end of today to anywhere in London you request," she smiled and nodded and moved to the seats behind them.

"We can wait. I'm in no hurry to get back to Oxford," Jennette said.

"Yes," said Spenser thinking. He was due back in London by the end of the day and was wondering if he should suggest they stay a night in the city or if he could make the back and forth run to Oxford to get Jennette home.

"I have a meeting in London tonight. Perhaps we should find a hotel and stay. It might be a nice way to cap off our trip. I can drive you home in the morning."

"I was hoping you would stay tonight in Oxford. What time is your meeting? We could leave after that, as long as it's not too late."

Spenser reached for the screen to scroll down for more news. His tattoo was exposed. "We can do that. My meeting is scheduled for the end of the work day. Five p.m. in the city - talking to some bankers."

Jennette had seen it plenty of times on the inside of his left wrist. She never failed to wonder why he and his college mates would get such a simple, cheap tattoo in such an obvious spot after one evening of revelry. It seemed so completely unlike Spenser to do something so rash and so obviously permanent.

"You go to your meeting and we can meet for dinner in London, or if it's not too late we can drive back to Oxford for dinner. I can use the after-noon to visit my sister in Hampstead. Perhaps I will have the baggage delivered there."

The plane landed without incident. Jennette called her sister who was delighted to have her come and spend the day. There was a particularly close questioning at customs but nothing they said appeared to interest the questioners and they were soon on their way. They shuttled into the city, shared a lunch in Canary Wharf and parted with a kiss, after Spencer got directions to the Hampstead address for later.

"Now don't be surprised if Lydia asks us to dinner. She's a fabulous cook and with the kids underfoot never gets a chance to entertain. Of course the short notice may kill her initiative. We'll just roll with it."

"Yes, that's fine. Do let me know. There are nasty things afoot. Remember curiosity killed the cat, avoid commotions and stay clear of anything unusual," said Spenser. Jennette disappeared into the Tube entrance.

Spenser moved about London for much of the afternoon, checking on suppliers, talking to insurance companies about premiums and assuring his distribution network that products would arrive on time and without liability for them. There was a notable increase in security in most public places - a few extra police, a few more suits with eyes and he even spied a flash of a sniper on a City roof.

After a few phone calls he made his way to the City and got off the Tube at Bank Station. He made his way down Cheapside, and with the spire of St. Mary le Bow in the distance, he tested his Cockney with a few mumbled phrases before turning left on Queen Street and left again on Pancras Lane. He could have gone down Queen Victoria Street and turned into the pedestrian walkway but he liked to see the church when he was in the area. He entered the Green Man pub and made his way to the bar.

Spenser ordered a Hobgoblin. As the publican took his money he looked over Spenser's shoulder and made a short, curt nod.

"Sir, the man you are here to meet, is seated at that table over against the far wall behind you."

Spenser thanked the barman and rose to change seats. He recognized his drinking partner.

"And so it goes, Mr. Spenser. Things have not been as smooth as we had hoped. Though we have been able to isolate a number of insurgents and neutralize them. What you have seen, are only the small percentage that went undetected."

"Like Westminster?"

"Aye, like Westminster. We were moving in on them. In fact our raid was only a few minutes late. Remember, we don't want casualties but understand to flush out insurgent elements they will happen, and they do serve their purpose of galvanizing the English public into understanding the depth of our problems."

"Not the most noble approach but I guess we don't have the luxury to be noble anymore."

"Aye, Mr. Spenser, nobility and generosity of spirit got us into this mess. Now some will pay a terrible price for our willful ignorance."

"And what am I to do now?"

"We need two of your shipments to move through France in a few days time. They need to have sufficient lead time to attract major terrorist attention. We will be lying in wait."

"It's a suicide mission for anyone on board."

"Not suicide, we will be there on the trains in force. But there is significant danger. We hope to take down a lot of terrorists and weapons. The chief danger is we will not know when they will strike. But they will strike. And you cannot let on to anyone, even the security personnel that you know of the situation. Regular security must be in place or it would look odd to potential attackers. We will simply attach several cars to the train with our men inside, heavily armed and ready to go. We will also be watching the train and be ready in force, from the air if necessary, for any attack."

"My business will suffer if my products are attacked."

"Everyone's businesses will suffer as we make our way to a scouring of our shires, and in this case the French countryside."

"I usually travel with my trains."

"Then you must travel with these trains or it will look unusual."

"I cannot be in two places at once."

"We will make those arrangements. The trains need to be sufficiently close together to attract our enemies and not tip off our hand."

"What about the Assyrian artifacts that are being stolen?"

"I understand you were in Zurich at the time of the theft."

"And my lady friend works at the Ashmolean and was notified of the robbery there. Apparently they have four of the five pieces."

"Yes, I think it's a bit of hocus pocus. We have detailed photographs of each piece and are looking at them to determine what may make the finished star so attractive to certain elements. The last piece has been moved from public view into a very secure area at the Royal Ontario Museum in Toronto."

"That doesn't seem too secure. And they are considering the value of this artifact through photographs? So only our top people are looking at this?"

"Yes," laughed the man. "Only our top people."

"And what have these top people ascertained, if anything."

"Not much as yet. It appears that the writing suggests some sort of communication with God, should all five sections be connected. It didn't appear to help the Assyrians, as they disappeared a long time ago."

"May be they mislaid the device."

"Maybe, or maybe it is merely a depository for a series of affirmations or social laws that bring peace. Often bringing peace and stability to society is construed as bringing the presence of God. Only the violent think they can direct God's will or his power to their need. There is a suggestion on the staves, the five sections of the star, that speech with God will bring and enforce lasting peace. Maybe God tells them to stop trying to force their will on everyone. Remember, our top people are on it."

The two men worked out some of the logistics and timing of the train runs. Spenser left with a promise to meet again in the same place in one week.

Chapter Thirty - Five   Mexico

The bright light shone through the window. It bounced off the floor and reflected on the walls and ceiling. The room was mostly white - a hospital.

Hellenga remembered two men who had encountered him, asked about his dealings with Octavius and then someone shot him. He tried to sit up and saw the back of a well dressed man in the window.

"I'm so glad you have finally woken up Senor. I cannot stay much longer, my business in Mexico City has been delayed as much as possible."

Octavius turned from the window, bathed in the bright light which shone through it, and moved to sit in a chair beside the bed. The light was so bright to Hellenga's long closed eyes that he had to turn away with a squint.

"Why did your men shoot me?"

"My men?"

"Yes, they said you wanted to speak to me about our deal and when I became frightened at their persistence they threatened me and shot me as I ran."

"Those were not my men. We're they Americanos?"

"Yes, at first they looked like tourists. You know the kind that are un-threatening except for their large numbers when they demand hamburgers, fries and very cold beer," Hellenga forced a smile.

"Senor, I have been wanting to speak to you but no, those are not my men. This is most troubling. They appear to have tried to scare you away from our public relations campaign."

"I guess if it was you behind this then you would have shot me by now. How can I keep these goons off my back? I want justice for my people and our home. I do not want violence. And what further do you want of me?"

"I can assure you that if I wanted to speak with you I would simply call. Our campaign may be somewhat clandestine, but that is more because of me than you. As Ambassador I cannot be obviously engaged in activities subversive to my diplomatic recognition."

"So they shot me because they wanted to send you a message? They knew your name."

"So they may have. And for that I am sorry. Your desire to find justice through understanding is not always shared by those who believe they have a stake in the outcome. I am sorry to have exposed you to this. You must lay low for a while, remain inactive for a time while I do some investigations of my own. You cannot stay in Mexico or in California either. Your homes will be watched. I can arrange for a wonderful holiday in Spain if you like. A few months should do."

Hellenga accepted, saying he wanted to retrieve some things and would go as soon as he was released from hospital.

"Your wound was deep but non-damaging though you did lose a lot of blood. You have been here for a week healing. I can arrange for you to leave whenever you are up to it. I have posted a guard for your convenience."

"My convenience?"

"He will leave whenever you ask him to. He will escort you to my villa in Spain. Somebody wants you to stop our campaign. Let's allow them to have the victory in the short run."

"So you will continue?"

"Yes Senor, with or without you, I will continue to strengthen Aztlan's Spanish heritage. It will be returned to us eventually. However, I have no wish to let you martyr yourself to the cause. Non-violence and patience will achieve our goals much better and more permanently than blood."

Two days later Hellenga found himself in a small villa on the north coast of Spain, not far from St. Sebastion de Compostella, a medieval monastery and historic pilgrimage destination.

The villa was a postcard in itself. There was a small staff on hand as it was Octavius' retreat where he usually spent only a few weeks per year. He had promised to be there after his Mexico City business was complete.

The villa sat on a cleft in a hill side about a quarter-mile from the Atlantic Ocean which appeared peaceful most of the time. Hellenga settled in, taking one of the smaller bedroom suites on the upper floor. He tried to find out who might oppose his campaign and began to search sources of news stories about his art installations in Southern California. He found a very angry op-ed in the San Francisco Chronicle, reduced to a small tabloid in the wake of the earthquake, that called out Mexico's art community and the diplomatic corps for allowing the incursions of graffiti to occur.

The editorial was not subtle about blame and called on those involved to come forward and state their aims and purposes in the light of day and not to cower behind graffiti or subterfuge.

Hellenga composed an email to the Chronicles editor outing himself but he decided not to send it until he spoke to Octavius.

So he convalesced for another week, much to his own satisfaction as he did not realize how weak he still was from the shooting. He was in no hurry for Octavius to arrive.

And neither was Octavius. His meetings in Mexico City were a bit more cloak and dagger than he had let on. Many Spanish speaking countries were represented at a formal gathering of their kind but it was the informal portions where things got interesting.

"I for one am very pleased with this stirring of Aztlan spirit in California. Word is the natives there are restless. The Americans want to leave the United States and the Mexicans want to complete their re-conquest. The only question is do they formally join Mexico or begin as a breakaway Republic of Upper Baja California, or some such thing. That would provide some cover for Mexico City and perhaps would give the US some comfort that they were not being invaded."

"But they already believe that, given the two attacks they have faced by a shadowy military force."

"I know those attacks were not sanctioned in any way by Mexico City. They were clandestine paramilitary operations designed to pin American resources down, to jar the US into acceptance of its new regional power status and to get some insurgents into the country in deep cover should they be required in the future."

"And how is it that you know so much, my friend?" asked Octavius.

"I have firsthand knowledge. You, Senor, want to work too slowly. Our re-conquest should be completed soon. Your methods won't find with success for perhaps a generation or two."

"Maybe, but they would still find success by your own admission. I prefer success as a fait accompli rather than a violent struggle which produces equally violent enemies and long term suspicions. Your way fuels resentment, my way gives us Aztlan without any real fear of reprisal. How do you think they took it away from us in the first place?"

Octavius continued, "Those attacks have simply raised their awareness of what we were already accomplishing. Please do not do it again. Another attack and the US could well annex Mexico, or set up a puppet government. It is still a very formidable country. And now they are more likely to use unexpected methods to achieve their aims. Perhaps more so as they have filtered dissent to all the breakaway sections like Dixie and Texas. Texas has no desire to grow in size as to Texans its plenty big enough. However in a fight the Texans will side with the US to secure their frontiers. Even if it means installing the US on their southern frontier."

"Then I encourage you all to formally recognize Dixie as an independent nation. You should also consider relations with Texas, even if they are informal. I have already spoken to several Texas legislators about Spanish co-operation. We have much in common," said Octavius.

There was a murmur of consent around the table. "Perhaps you are right Mr. Ambassador. If we work together we can slowly pull the old US apart and maintain reasonable links where necessary."

"Change must be sustainable and accepted or it will simply be the fuel of future violence."

Chapter Thirty - Six   Washington

"Ah, so nice to meet you Mrs. O'Neill. I understand through the State Department that you can help me out, especially on industrial issues."

"Mr. Edwards I have heard much about you from President O'Day. He warned me about you," she said with a big smile.

They were standing in a lovely room with a view of the US Capitol Building in the Canadian Embassy in Washington. The Canadian Ambassador held these receptions regularly to introduce business leaders and policy makers to their American counterparts. The O'Neills had attended several of these events but this was the first time Ambassador Edwards had been in Washington and been able to attend.

Ambassador Edwards made a small grimace, remembering the meeting he had had that morning with State Department officials at the President's insistence. The Ambassador was still miffed that the President had not met with him in person.

"President O'Day warned you? It's nice to know he remembers me. I only had a chance to speak to his men at State. Once you've been assigned to the great snowbound nation to our north, it is easy to be forgotten. Nothing much ever happens there. Oh, the locals think they are on the edge of wild events, but the truth is they are looking through the window at the storms while we trudge through outside, fending off this monster and that bogeyman."

"It sounds like you've given this quite a bit of thought."

"Yes, perhaps I'm going native," Mrs. O'Neill. "I do very much like our northern neighbors. After a time with them you begin to see their point of view. And I am beginning to assign a larger importance to the swirl of events in Canada than those events should otherwise deserve. It goes with the territory I guess. Same thing happened when I served in South Africa."

"No doubt in the barnyard the sheep are all very concerned with their sheep-iness and sheep-doings, even if the rest of the animals in the yard cannot tell one sheep from another."

Edwards smiled a tight smile. He had received a directive from President O'Day that Mrs. Amanda O'Neill would be a valuable asset in his work with various industrial factions in Canada, especially in Ontario where her husband's business interests lay. A career diplomat he knew he must keep this O'Neill woman occupied or he could have a huge mess to clean up. Non-diplomats usually didn't fare well in the often touchy world of talk between nations. Even if they spoke the same language, the dialect was different enough to cause misunderstandings.

The last special envoy to Canada had nearly brought the countries to a diplomatic impasse when he suggested the President would demand that all business in Canada be conducted with the US dollar. It had started with a private conversation with the President who had expressed exasperation with the Canadians' determination to maintain their own currency despite a dozen reasons to abandon it. That special envoy was recalled to Washington shortly after the issue died down. He was now an analyst of post-industrial issues, in a State Department office that nobody ever heard of - one step up from a placement designed to park his ambitions permanently.

Amanda excused herself and wandered off in search of the finger foods. Diplomatic affairs were either conducted as huge formal dinners at horrific hours or slight affairs with finger foods and cocktails. Either way they messed terribly with one's metabolism as following days were consumed getting one's digestion back on track.

"And for Mr. O'Neill, the clean up continues unabated I imagine," said Edwards.

"Yes, it will for many years. I have just returned from California where I have secured arrangements to extract waste steel and metals from the twin disasters in California - Los Angeles and San Francisco."

"I must say I have heard them referred to that, but that was before the earthquake and 5/29."

Peter O'Neill smiled thinly, he understood why many people did not take to this Ambassador.

"It appears as if the Canadians are keen to have our western steel come to Sault Ste. Marie. The train links are excellent and they can ship the finished steel products by ship through the Great Lakes. There is ample industrial space in the Sault for storage and expansion. The winters are a bit of an issue. Any chance getting the Canadians to agree to a slightly longer shipping season on the Lakes?"

"I have been working them on that Mr. O'Neill. Be assured that you will be the first to know if I achieve anything, after the President of course."

"Thank you Ambassador, have you any timeframe on this effort?"

"This is statecraft Mr. O'Neill. It will proceed as fast as the Canadians want it to. They do appear motivated, as the jobs you are bringing to the Sault and to Hamilton are considerable."

"Perhaps you could utilize my wife's help on the file. Simply let her know how you want to proceed and . . . "

"Now Mr. O'Neill, we will have to leave some of these negotiations up to the more seasoned diplomats. She may be very helpful getting us a meeting with your counterparts north of the border who could help us pressure the Canadian government into seeing things our way. Slow and steady works best. I cannot tell you how many deals and diplomatic efforts have been killed due to a misstep or a perceived insult."

Mrs. O'Neill strode through the crowded room bringing a well dressed young man in her wake. She rejoined her husband and Ambassador Edwards with a deep huff and puff from her exertions moving through the crowded room.

"Whew. Mr. Ambassador, this is Mr. Lyall. He is with the Canada Center for Inland Waters in Hamilton, we met at our companies' announcement. I asked him at the time about Great Lakes shipping. Well Mr. Lyall, why don't you tell him."

"Sir, Mrs. O'Neill said at the opening, that they, O'Neill Steel, would want to ship their products by freighter as much as possible, given the shipping costs and huge demand in New York City. So I crunched the numbers and it appears that we can open the shipping routes about 10 days early and close them 10 days later, as long as everyone knows that ships can be caught in a quick change in weather and may have to be held in a frozen port for the duration. Given that they are useless in winter anyway - it seems a reasonable thing, though there maybe some additional costs to wintering on the Lakes. We will have to issue a first round of closure times - ie those times where ships can be assured of free entry and exit from the Seaway, and a second closure date, where we cease to operate the locks to allow ship movements."

The Ambassador tilted his head back over his shoulders. He was silently taking in the information.

"Have you discussed this with your Department of Foreign Affairs and all the necessary agencies?"

"We have not gotten the sign-off from everyone yet, but the Seaway is on -side, and all the affected Ministries have given approval. We just need a few of the tardy to sign off and we are good from our end. I have verbal agreements from them, just not the paper proof as yet. Our US counterparts have warmed to the idea and apparently they are also on-side," said Mr. Lyall.

"Yes, I imagine they are. Mrs. O'Neill was very persuasive regarding the economic impact, particularly to Sault Ste. Marie. This idea of an informal or partial closure was inspired."

Chapter Thirty - Seven   Washington

"Everything appears okay but it isn't. Chinese officials say they are going to begin to cash in their treasuries."

"We've been fighting like hell to stabilize and now this. We can't keep making stick save after stick save. The pressure has got to come off."

"Truth be told, unless there is pressure the Fed just keeps pumping it up. There has to be pressure in order for the Fed and the government to behave responsibly."

"After all the Chinese can't completely cash in. If they did the Yuan would rise so high they'd never get their value out of our treasuries. Our biggest problem is the movement away from the US dollar for international settlements."

"And the Chinese are doing that too. Maybe it's time to tariff the little bastards."

"I know the President is thinking seriously of imposing a tax on imports from nations that are not tied in with our free trade system. That means China."

"Well it's about time. How long have we let those guys act like robber barons, without standards in labour or environment or product quality, while robbing our intellectual property and marketing savvy?"

"It's got to be eased in. At first symbolic and then gradually tightening until we get some of our manufacturing back and/or the Chinese decide to play by the rules. We have to open free trade negotiations. They will still have a huge labour and environmental advantage even if they do impose standards and improvements. If they go slow on that stuff, real progress will take a long time."

Grange shifted uncomfortably in his chair. "You know the goddamned Texans and the good ole boys in the South are digging into our good will. Both had currencies pegged with the US dollar and both have strict monetary controls which make their currencies more desirable, or it will in time, as those currencies gain acceptance and familiarity."

"We have some time. Those currencies may gain acceptance in their local markets but it will be decades before they are internationally accepted. With our economy in the tank you know manufacturing in China has taken a big hit. That's why they want to cash in the treasuries. They need the money. President O'Day is mulling over a big change. He's considering going cashless and ending the use of paper money and coins. He is also thinking of issuing a new currency, one that is pegged at $100 US dollars to 1 new unit. The thinking on this is a super strong currency for internal US transactions only to counter the Dixie Dollar and the Texas Buck," said Findlay.

"Hummm, it sounds intriguing, but doesn't the Federal Reserve issue all banknotes?"

"Yeah, but the President says they are largely on-side. They still regulate interest rates and would have control over the currency."

"Yeah, but what about the Congress having control of the currency? Remember it was the Fed that allowed inflation to eat up about 97 per cent of the value of the dollar in the last couple of generations. Under

Congressional control the new currency could be kept whole."

Findlay turned toward Grange. "Jim, that is likely the way it will go. Not sure I have much faith in Congressional control. The track record there is a bit spotty, but what alternative do we have? If it's proposed for the Fed, public opinion will push it to Congressional control. The chief fear will be that the Congress will not be able to control itself."

"Tom, without the Dixie liberals and the Texas big spenders we should be able to maintain control through tight money legislation. The Fed won't be able to manipulate it and it will eventually supplant the US dollar. Do you have any idea how much money is counterfeited?"

"Probably a lot, but if money is only on computer screens counterfeiting will be almost impossible to police. There isn't a program anywhere that cannot be hacked or manipulated or co-opted. It seems to me that a misplaced zero on a computer screen is a lot more dangerous than a bunch of physical paper making its way into the monetary system."

"This whole money thing is tough," said Grange. "There really isn't a satisfactory explanation of money. Economists for hundreds of years have never really been able to figure it out. And through history all forms of fiat currency have failed. It's just human nature I think, to try to manipulate perceived value to your, or your government's advantage."

"Okay Jim here's the heads up. I think the President will enact legislation to kill paper money. He will keep coins and likely issue new, larger denomination coins, $2 and $5 to help bear the burden of small transactions. It will force all the cash out in the open and will kill criminal organizations, counterfeiters and hoarders. It should streamline taxation and tax collection. The plan is to announce it with a tax cut to highlight the illegal ways cash is being used to by-pass the tax system."

"Holy crap - what about the parallel currency?"

"I think he'll float the idea but back off and let the change to a cashless economy do its work. That alone should firm up the dollar."

Chapter Thirty - Eight   Black Sea

"And whatever you do, do not hit St. Sophia. In fact don't let anything get near it. That's a command from the top, the very top. It is the symbol of the Orthodoxy. Keep it whole or your life is likely forfeit."

Everyone in the room gulped in a bit of unexpected air and looked around at each other. The small, windowless room was full. All the chairs were taken, people lined the walls and many simply melted into spaces they could find with the last few spilling out the only door. There was a map on one wall and very little space for anyone to move about to point things out on the map.

"It's actually not that hard. I have seen the reconnaissance and studied the maps, there is a wide area of park land around it. Just avoid shooting or dropping anything in that perimeter."

"So you looked at Google Earth and we're supposed to buy that?"

"Yeah, pretty much," he said with a wicked grin. "It's a damn sight more accurate than our own maps, which are from the middle of the Cold War."

"There you go comrades, you have your assignments. We engage at first light. Make your preparations and your peace. While I am confident in our victory, some of us, through accident or divine design will not return. Good luck, and accept my thanks on behalf of the Mother Russia. We will prevail and be free at last."

The men dispersed; some to eat, some to sleep and others to write letters to loved ones. The ship which had been moving southeast through the Black Sea under half steam, went dark with the sun and turned hard west, going to full power. By the first hint of dawn they had covered 300 nautical miles and were in position. Volleys of planes launched from three ships, formed up and sped west. As the full light of the rising sun touched St. Sophia, the sneak attack began.

Cruise missiles proceeded the air assault. Hard on their heels fighter jets swooped in on military installations at either end of the Bosporus, and the Dardanelles in the west. Troops were landed by helicopter at first with troop ships coming in on their heels.

Much of the command and control areas of the city were heavily bombed and the airport was captured with a full scale assault. Several Turkish fighter jets were able to get off the ground but they were quickly dispatched.

By noon the Russians had captured the European half of Istanbul and had almost completed the set up of a line of defence to the east of the city between the Black Sea and the Sea of Mamarra including the Omerli Barraji, a man-made lake in the middle of the peninsula. The Russian zone went from Alacali on the Black Sea to Pendik on the Sea of Marmara, an area of about 25 kilometers wide by 45 kilometers north to south.

Simultaneously they attacked Turkish military installations on the Bulgarian border and secured the northern side of the Dardanelle passage into the Mediterranean.

To the relief of everyone, St. Sophia remained standing as Russian troops moved through the city securing locations, quelling violence and passing out leaflets.

The Russian president issued a statement of congratulations to his troops on behalf of Orthodox Christians everywhere that the city of Constantinople, taken by the Turks in 1453 had been retaken from the infidels after nearly 570 years of captivity.

The Russians moved relentlessly to root out all Turkish influence in the Constantinople zone. They allowed anyone who wanted, to go back and forth between countries peacefully. Remarkably most residents of the area took little notice of the attack and subsequent subjugation of their city and region.

Even the Turks, while furious, were simply unable to mount an effective defence and were obliged to essentially cede control of the area to Russia.

The Russians were content with their ability to secure the city and to have full access to the Mediterranean. Troops flooded into the area, bureaucrats were as thick as weeds and soon life in Constantinople returned to normal.

Russia had accomplished this with few lives lost, with little outcry from the international community and with almost no dissent from within.

The Turks were in no position to complain given the destruction of their Muslim brethren around the world. The French and the British were unconcerned and the US effectively held its breath as Russia took on what was left of the organized Muslim world and won.

The Russians began to build huge defensive installations along their new eastern frontier with Turkey. While Turkey remained belligerent they could not win a fight with Russia and were reduced to diplomatic complaining. The Russians were firm in their resolve and unwilling to negotiate. They counted on Muslim Turks to filter back into Anatolia on their own and encouraged Russian and Slavic immigrants to fill the City, making the former Istanbul a less desirable place to live for the remaining Turks. The Russians knew that they could build and plan for decades and perhaps generations before the Turks would come back looking for the reconquest of the city they had taken and held for more than five centuries.

A new normal was descending on the world. Russia ascendant. The US cowed and scattered but still able to bite and perhaps more willing than usual to remind the world of that fact. Dixie, Texas and California battered and moving into new ways or returning to old. Muslims reduced to scavenging their civilization or what remained of it. Europe still trying to combat the troubles they had imported.

And yet the ripples of all these changes had not been completely felt. China, Japan, and a score of other countries would feel them soon enough. Economic forces were realigning. Military forces were redeploying. Ideology was shifting and politics was the means of revolution.

The old ways had been swept aside. The new way forward had been indicated but nothing was settled. History had taken a major turn but history still dogged everyone.

Impotent for decades, the latest geo-political seismic shift had effectively killed the United Nations. International diplomacy had a void to fill as a new order began to form. The Canadians proposed an English language commonwealth, centred on the five large English speaking countries - Canada, England, Australia, New Zealand and the constituent parts of the United States including Texas and Dixie. India agitated for observer status.

Other countries clamoured for a place at the table, countries where English was widely spoken. However the main group realized that it wasn't about language but about culture and they only wanted English culture to be represented. If they were committed to one another, they had to share values. It was through this group that the US was able to maintain its light grip of hegemony around the world.

Chapter Thirty - Nine   **Southern California**

He came without fanfare.

Mexican President Alphonso Miguel Carrerra drove up to the US border
and presented himself as an ordinary citizen of Mexico coming to California for the day. He was asked a few of the normal questions and admitted
without incident.

One of the cars loaded with his retinue of hangers on were questioned a
bit more and only then did US officials understand that the Mexican President was in California.

However there was no quick reportage up the chain of command - border
guards thought his entry a bit unusual but put it down to his strong stand
against elitism, a stand that had gotten him elected twice in a country
with a huge gap between the rich and the poor.

Once past the border Carrerra's small convoy of cars moved north into
the San Diego suburbs. It was the start of a busy day for Senor Carrerra.
First he was scheduled to meet with a grassroots Mexifornia group which
advocated the slow, legal annexation of California back to Mexico. He
spoke at the event for several minutes on family and business ties to
Mexico, trade and the free movement of people.

"Senor Presidente we have seen the effectiveness of the underground campaign to rouse our people to support Aztlan," said a large, balding man dressed in an old suit. "It is that type of constant messaging, subtlety, that gets into the blood of even the White Americanos, and makes them realize that California was not always a natural part of the United States. It works."

"Thank you for your comments, Senor Arranga," said Carrerra. "As you likely know we cannot be seen to be obviously meddling in what is still officially US territory. I have seen photos of the art installations, and read the newspaper reports. We have conducted some investigations of who or what is behind this campaign, as it is obviously carefully staged and funded. As yet, we do not know who it is. We must be careful to walk the tightrope between knowing and supporting their efforts. Some of my advisors suggest it is better if we do not know who is behind the campaign."

"But Senor Presidente, with all due respect, you are here today without official US sanction, when your visit becomes known it will cause huge ripples."

"Yes, Senor, that is part of our plan. We want to ingrain our presence here in California under the skin of the Americans and in a very quiet way. I have no public events today, I am simply travelling to meet with some friends to ....renew acquaintances."

Carrerra looked to his chief of staff, who was standing to one side.

"You might note there is no security today, no trappings of the office, save these lovely people who insisted upon coming along," he waved generally to his right where several members of his staff and his official photographer stood. "I am here to see friends."

"I understand that this visit will be leaked and that your presence here is a powerful signal to our people of the changing landscape, however, there will be consequences with the Americanos."

"Si, that there will. But they should be short term, and will fall far below the effectiveness that my visit today will provide. When you sell a car at your dealership, do you care who you sell it to? Do you treat every customer equally?"

"Yes, but we need something more concrete."

"I thought your group advocated patience. Remember, if we take baby steps, suggest that nothing in everyday life will change once California joins again with Mexico, we will not only prevail geographically, but also economically and culturally. To be frank, senor, waiting a bit, laying the groundwork, gives the Americanos the opportunity to rebuild California for us, at their expense; and all without hard feelings."

The balding man, nodded sagely.

"And all of that doesn't mean you should slow your efforts," said Carrerra. "Aztlan will come back to us, of that I am sure. But we must prepare it so that coming back is as natural to the inhabitants as Baja is to us."

Carrerra shook a few hands, moved through the small crowd and was gone. He repeated the meeting five more times that day in areas around San Diego, imploring Hispanics to treat the Americans as they would treat their own, to give them no fear of a change in government.

He was asked about the invasion but could only shrug. His government has worked furiously to find the perpetrators and had a fair idea of who it was, but took no official action, nor made any complaint when the Americans and Texans took their own actions.

As he left the final meeting place, a medium sized restaurant in the city of San Diego proper, he was met with a small group of US officials who insisted he speak to them.

"Just tell Mr. Carrerra that Michael Watson, the US Undersecretary of Defence - West, at San Diego Naval Station, is here to say hello."

Carrerra saw the limousine adorned with US flags as he exited the restaurant and was shaking hands with people who had come out to see him. He had actually expected a visit earlier.

He jumped in between local meeting organizers and the US undersecretary Watson.

"Mr. Watson, it is a great pleasure to meet you sir. I am Senor Carrerra, here to meet some friends and share a meal," he tapped his stomach. "Is there anything I can do for you?"

"Ah, Mr. President, this is most unusual, and we apologize for not providing you with official security and route preferences," said Watson. "However it is usual that we be informed of these visits in advance in order to insure your needs. It appears the notification of your visit was . . . . misplaced."

"Yes, it is a bit unusual Mr. Watson, but I have done this before, I like to speak to my friends first hand and like to forget that I am bound to Mexico City and chained to my office," he said. "Now that you know I am here I invite you to accompany me, should you like. I only had one more stop planned. I wanted to go to Los Angeles and see my friend Senor Cartenga, who is in the recycling and construction business and share a drink before heading home. We went to school together. I had hoped to keep this low key, just me meeting with some old friends."

The border guard who admitted Carrerra had kept his entry into the US to himself until a few hours later when his shift ended. He knew that Carrerra was a ranking Mexican official but did not know he was President. It was the addition of several people entering the US with Carrerra that made him wonder just how important an official he was. In his shift ending report he mentioned the small group who had entered the US as being unusual but had triggered no unusual responses to standard questions nor any reason to deny them entry.

The shift supervisor had seen the entry an hour later as he was sifting through the shift reports and mentioned it verbally to the Customs Chief who checked the record for photo ID and immediately recognized Carrerra. He double checked by matching the security video to his passport. The shift supervisor considered what to do, weighing the advantages of doing nothing with the difficulties he would find himself in, if his inaction was ever to come to light.

He mulled over his choices while completing his reporting tasks and then called his boss, the border point sheriff. Getting through to his aide he explained the situation. At first the aide did not believe him but when he did, the immensity of diplomatic issues at hand caused a minor storm. Informing his boss the district border control and immigration office chief, phone calls fanned out up and down the chain of command. Eventually a US Senator's office caught wind and they phoned the US Secretary of State. Watson was the highest ranking US official within three hours drive of San Diego. He was briefed on what to do, and dispatched.

Most career bureaucrats would be scared of the layers of protocol involved in calling the Mexican President out, but Watson saw it differently. He merely wanted to have Carrerra acknowledge his breach of protocol and agree to a security detail. Official Washington could deal with the rest of it.

"Unfortunately Mr. President, once the word gets out that you are here in the flesh, there will be many people who would like to meet you," Watson said. "As you can see by the crowds who have come to your 'private' engagement you really need to be much more discrete. I will happily escort you to your final engagement and then assist your return back across the border."

Carrerra had no choice but to agree to the official US help. He dutifully attended a small reception put on by Senor Cartenga and then left for Mexico. Carrerra crossed the border without incident. However many people in his party, including his chief of staff, his photographer and several prominent members of the Mexican press corps were detained for additional investigation, as they had obviously been there in their employment capacity and had not declared their intention to work while in the US.

American officials confiscated cameras, notebooks and other work related paraphernalia before releasing the offenders with a stern warning and a 12 month US travel ban.

"Mr. President, they have confiscated all the photos and our notes on local figures of importance."

"Ah, my friend, you are still too young. I had our photographer Jimenez give me his camera's memory disk and I took photos of two pages of names from your assistant before crossing the border. I expected the Americans would take action, but they would not come after me directly. Next time, talk to your assistants before coming to me to confess your sins."

The chief of staff smiled broadly. "I am still learning Uncle. You are a bit more experienced than me in these matters. But I am learning."

Carrerra beamed, "You are your father's son, Juan, he would always learn the lesson, and learn it well, but required a sting to remember it by."

Watson reported his encounter to an assistant to the US Secretary of State who requested a detailed follow up report for the next morning, saying it would be going to the Secretary and eventually to President O'Day.

"This is a significant breach of protocol. I must have that report, with every detail, as soon as possible and no later than 3 am Eastern Time.'

"That hairless Chihuahua has gone too far," said O'Day when he got the first verbal report. "First they look the other way and allow military action against us and then Carrerra thinks he can go campaigning in San Diego. I want strong action. I can hardly wait for the full report."

"Yes, Mr. President I will have State Department officials considering all possible responses as part of the official report. It will be on your desk first thing."

"That's going to be 7 am."

"Understood."

Phone calls were made and Mexican and Hispanic specialists at the State Department were roused from their beds to put together the necessary report. Watson, toiled away on his report, finally issuing it at 12:30 am California time. He decided to stay up, awaiting the inevitable calls for clarification and additional detail.

State Department specialists went to work on the initial verbal reports and then tore apart the written report to find out who Carrerra had met with, for how long, and who else was present. They started to work trying to get details on what was discussed and if Carrerra was forced to deviate from his agenda at any time.

"Woo, shit," said Matthew Clark, a State Department information analyst. "This points to a major open air rally that Carrerra was forced to abandon when we showed up. Apparently the Aztlan group had fired into over-drive and was putting together a large rally in Los Angeles for Carrerra to speak to. Look, there are drone photos of some of the crowd gathering and here's a copy of the email that went out about the event. Once we got on to him, it was all called off. They even had a small stage built where he was supposed to speak."

The details were included as part of the report to O'Day.

"Yes, sir, Mexico looked the other way, but they didn't attack us. Others attacked us, and along the Rio Grande they attacked Texas."

"Yes, yes, of course," said O'Day. "However this is a stunning breach of protocol. We must take serious actions. Diplomatic actions at this point, though."

"The most serious would be to withdraw our ambassador. Sending theirs home would be a slightly lesser response. There are any number of similar actions that could be implemented with lesser officials. A stronger response would be to close the border."

O'Day mulled. He read the report through twice, mumbling that the Mexicans were being provocative, that this breach in protocol was obviously planned as a public relations exercise and that the Mexicans were being duplicitous.

"Close the border for two days to do some routine maintenance, give everyone 48 hours notice of the closure," said O'Day. "Send a strongly worded diplomatic letter to Carrerra directly through his Ambassador and insist he deliver it himself, in the letter tell the Ambassador he is not welcome back in the US until after the border maintenance is completed. After two days of the closure, announce it will be closed indefinitely as maintenance upgrades are more extensive than anticipated. Then keep it closed for two more days before announcing it reopening about 11 am on the fifth day. Have a ship at San Diego Naval Station inadvertently lob a live shell into Tijuana on the afternoon of the re-opening, claim it was an accident. That should get their attention. Make sure you target something big but empty - we don't need to kill anyone - yet."

Chapter Forty   Oxfordshire

"Have you ever read Matthew Arnold's Dover Beach?"

"Why yes, yes I have. Long ago in school," answered Jennette.

"I came across it recently and you know, our world seems to have descended into a "Dover Beach" phase, a melancholy resignation of what is possible, what is probable, and how hard it is to gain and hold good and virtuous things."

They drove fast through the dark countryside, the road well lit but everything beyond the road covered in darkness. A few lights twinkled in the distance but they were few and indistinct. The low hum of the engine and the sound of the tires eating up the roadway were the only noises save their voices.

"I guess I should read it again. You are especially thoughtful tonight. Did your meeting not go well?" she asked.

"Truth be told, I have to accompany one of my shipments by train from Bern to London."

"Is that so bad, boring maybe, but not particularly bad. You've done it before."

"Yes, but this time I expect there might be trouble."

"How would you know that?"

"I don't for certain, just that I have to ship a larger order than usual and I've been very lucky for many months as everything has gotten through with little problem. There have been threats, nothing new there. It's kind of a fatalistic approach I suppose but I am not looking forward to it."

"You hire security for these things, why do you have to ride?"

"Because you can't always be sure of the security. Yes, the train may get through but there could be enough product missing that the profit is taken out."

"Well do be careful," she said. "Don't go charging off into the night to rescue a chocolate bar or a leather purse - empty or full."

They were on their way back to Oxford after a lovely meal at her sister's in Hampstead. Spenser took to her sister's husband, a sports enthusiast who was not interested in the usual professional and high level sport competitions but rather revelled in the small doings of his children's games and teams. To hear him talk about the nice efforts and the talents of a bunch of near teens on the football pitch or cricket ground was at once boring and exceedingly touching as he took more pleasure in a nice touch by a weak player than he did in a televised highlight that had everyone talking. If professional sports were the reality television for men, then minor sports were their soap operas, as little details piled up into interesting story lines.

After taking their leave, Spenser drove Jennette to Oxford and left early in the morning to return to London on his way to Zurich. His flight landed midday and he spent the rest of the afternoon readying his shipment. He could not shake the feeling of foreboding he had, though he had made this train run many times. He knew something was going to happen this time but did not trust fate to ensure whatever happened would turn out well.

Oxford was a much different place at first light, where London was the same only a bit less crowded. Oxford was misty, quiet, and weighty with only a lone provost on a bike or a bakery worker heading to his oven while the water on the river slapped gently on the wharfs, docks and sides of punts. You heard things in Oxford that went unnoticed through the height of the day. London was not any quieter it was just that you could hear the auto horns more clearly.

In London the streets were busy, people that supported the vast army of citizens who descended upon the center of town were already in their places getting ready for another day. Enough people worked early or stayed late that London was London around the clock. Tourists flocked, businessmen walked, and everyone talked and talked while occasionally being mocked by everyone else.

Spenser made his way back to the Green Man pub.

"The plan is to have only a skeleton security crew otherwise it would look strange. For the same reason we will go with only one train. One train that's a bit longer than usual but not two as we had originally thought. The logistics of defending two trains was too big to overcome. As the train proceeds to Reims on its way to Calais we will stop in a train shunting ground about two kilometers from the center of the city. It is at that point I expect the attack as the train will be immobile and will appear largely unguarded and escape routes for the attackers are easy in a built up area. We will have two cars, one fore and the other aft, full of heavily armed military personnel. At your signal they will exit the train cars and converge on the center of the train. You will have to give them precise instructions on where the threats are - likely a strong guard will be set up for those looting the train and there will be some rebel presence at the head of the train to control its movements."

Spenser took this all in and prepared to leave for Switzerland in the morn-ing. He would hook up with the train the following day and it would arrive in Reims in the early evening.

He travelled without incident and left with the train shipments as scheduled. He even made the rounds of his suppliers, as he normally would just prior to a departure.

Hours later the train rolled along the track only a few miles from Reims. Spenser retired to a sitting area inside a special freight car reserved for security. He had taken in the last of the Alps and resigned himself to a long wait as the train made its way through the gently rolling hills of Alsace and into Champagne country. He told the security personnel that there might be trouble at the shunting yard and warned them to be ready.

The train took the final bend slowly getting instructions from the shunting yard command to take a particular track.

The train stopped on an open rail line. The small official security detail fanned out fore and aft. A yard manager manually disengaged the last 15 cars and signalled the tower that he had completed his task. The train was commanded to move forward and then come back on a different track to connect to 10 other cars going to London.

The train lurched into a slow roll forward, switches were engaged and the reversing train was now six tracks to the east on most easterly shunting track in the yard. The 10 cars were positioned at the south end of the track so the reversing train could latch onto them and then continue north to Calais. This was all according to the plan - the armed detail were in the 16th car from the end when the train had disengaged to begin its manoeuvres.

The process of moving six tracks over, across that many switches was laborious. The train had to go particularly slowly to make sure its weight engaged the switches. Any single mistake could hold the train up for hours so it slid backward under the watchful eyes of several stevedores.

Just as it cleared the last switch, the light signals changed warning of an incoming train. The second train moved quickly into view, coming into the station. It was evident to the yard workers through the signals that the train was coming in through the track immediately adjacent to the London bound train.

As the train slid in beside his train, Spenser sent his commands to his two defense units. His train was completely cut off from a line of sight from the main control tower by the arrival of the new train.

Freight doors opened on the side of the new train visible to Spenser and instantly 20 men were out swarming the Swiss train. They formed chain gangs and quickly emptied several of the freight cars from the new train, putting the goods into empty freight cars on Spenser's train. Spenser held his command instructing his security to do nothing.

Then Spenser's train began to lurch forward and move slowly out of the station.

The rebel gangs weren't going to attack the train, or had they already? Surely they weren't satisfied with the theft of the goods in only two freight cars? Spenser tried to contact the engineer. No response.

Then it dawned on him; they planned to steal the whole train. They must have overpowered the engineer. Spenser relayed instructions to his security team to stay hidden and allow the train to move. He tried to contact the engineer again but received no response. He was thinking fast, expecting to be taken to a rebel held warehouse somewhere between Reims and Calais. He informed the hidden military personnel to remain quiet.

It did not take long for the train to exit the shunting yard and then switch off the main line. Shortly after leaving the shunting ground, it slowly rounded a bend and switched off the main line into an industrial side rail only a few miles from the station shunting yard. The train pulled directly into a large warehouse, where the cars could be unloaded out of sight five at a time, the train moved and five more cars unloaded.

Spenser allowed this operation to commence. He relayed details of the operation to his contact and asked for re-enforcements.

The first cars were unloaded without incident. The train moved deeper into the warehouse to unload a second set of freight cars. Still Spenser held his hand. Then the train was moved again for a third set of cars to be unloaded out of sight, inside the warehouse facility. It was these cars which housed his security contingent. He informed the military that they would spring their trap.

At his command, once the train had stopped, two freight cars erupted. A score or more of heavily armed men, exited the train and began to sweep the perimeter for rebels. Several went down immediately. A dozen were trapped in or near the train trying to unload it. They made motions to suggest they were surrendering. The military personnel had secured the outside of the warehouse and placed the rebels between Spenser's armed security and their own squadron. They very aggressively ended any perceived threat.

Spenser's security men moved to the front of the train in the melee. They secured the engine, killing two rebels and two officials looking at maps. They then swept through warehouse office facilities making sure there were no surprises for the military to contend with. A small group of re-bels tried to flee the facility but re-enforcement personnel lay in wait and shot them as they fled.

A few minutes later everyone gathered inside the warehouse to assess the outcome.

"An excellent job Mr. Spenser. We have about 65 rebels dead. Our boys were able to get a few who were trying to flee after the operation at the shunting yard was complete."

"I was a bit surprised by the second train coming in. This looks like a much more sophisticated arrangement than I had been anticipating," said Spen-ser. "It was supposed to be a bit more Wild West, like a frontal raid on the train."

"Yes, but they wanted the goods and that takes planning. Two of our boys are pretty shot up, but they'll recover. They took the hits and allowed the rest of the squad to clean up. The rebels certainly were not expecting more than the usual token security resistance. This should stop these train raids for a while."

"How can we ever recover Europe?"

"I'm not sure we can, Mr. Spenser. But we must try. The first step is to establish our determination, the second to show little remorse in direct combat situations and the third is to try to encourage the invaders to leave our countries."

"The results of this raid will be published far and wide. The 65 dead will be investigated and their families likely deported if there is any evidence their activities were known or supported. This is a new phase of our resistance to the tide. Operation Roland's Voice will not cease until all the violence is quelled and all the rebel activity stopped."

"So Operation Roland's Voice is a formal government policy? Will it exist for a long time?"

All the attacks we have suffered, all the innocent deaths, murders committed to scare us into submission have finally resulted in a very strong determination to fight back and fight to the last. The re-establishment decree is the social and cultural attempt to end this clash of civilizations without bloodshed. Operation Roland's Voice is a back guard approach to battle guerilla war with guerilla defence and to remove the blot on our society quite aggressively."

"Oh there will still be outrage at our tactics but in truth they are necessary as our enemies fight without rules of engagement and seek to use our desire for peace against us. They have seriously overshot our ability to look the other way, to seek peace first. Now we will have our peace by eradicating the disease."

"So it begins here in Reims?"

"So it begins here on this night. There are 15 move counter raids occurring this night all over France, Belgium and The Netherlands. I understand the Germans were preparing something similar but they would not formally commit to our terms. Perhaps they have taken a more severe approach, however, knowing their leaders it is most likely a softer more conciliatory approach, a last chance to end this issue without violence. The German people will applaud our approach and my fear is that they will take matters into their own hands in vigilante groups. They have a bit of history of that. By trying to avoid it, they actually make it more likely to occur again."

The raids across Europe were very successful outing thousands of active rebels and scores of rebel underground members. A follow up two months later was a series of clandestine military attacks on the banlieues in many larger French communities. Strangely most of these were resisted strongly when they occurred, but peace was quickly established as the remaining residents of these areas did not resist. The result was a reduction in the rebel population and a movement toward the government - those who owned property and wanted to stay began to integrate into everyday life. They were forbidden from attending public services and many resorted to private or secretive mosques, but the aggressiveness of Islam was stamped out, at least in the short term.

Governments had resorted to these aggressive tactics to quell local populations from acting as vigilantes. It worked well though the Muslim threat remained and there was an undercurrent of disengagement in certain areas of cities.

Jennette heard about the raids and knew Spenser had been involved. She secretly harboured an admiration for his bravery and determination to face the violence head on, yet she continued to wish the violence away ascribing a peaceful nature to everyone, regardless of events, cultural background or experience. The Muslims she knew were peaceful people just getting on with their lives. Spenser knew the rebels to be far more aggressive, using the majority of peaceful people as a springboard to bolster their ends.

As the Muslims slowly withdrew from Europe, either voluntarily or by being pushed, Europe was forced again to find its own identity, having been swallowed whole by the multicultural approbation of its own culture. Europe needed to remake itself in its former image, with a clearer understanding of its own often violent past and its newfound violent determination to maintain itself.

Chapter Forty - One   Austin

He looked up for the report and shook his head. "Aww crap. More unrest on the river."

"Well at least they want in. It's a happy problem."

"Yeah, tell that to Washington. We don't need problems with Washington. We need peace and quiet so we can slip away quietly into history. Having those southern counties of Oklahoma agitating to join in creates a distraction we don't need."

He put the papers on the desk, put his elbows on the table and hunched forward in his chair to rub his eyes.

The two men sat in a large formal office in Austin. They were the grease that moved events in the Texas government. They wanted to have a firm hand but a light touch, an approach that was usually difficult to achieve. Nation building required a strong arm and a big push.

"God almighty I get to hating desks, telephones, computers and offices sometimes. I wish I could just get out and saddle up and go for a bit of a ride. Maybe shoot a few gophers, pick off a couple of birds for practice and just let all of this go."

He took a deep breath and let his shoulders down, sinking a bit into the chair.

"Don't we all, or at least all of us who grew up in the country. We are here to protect that stuff, you know? Don't forget the southern battle and that infiltration of agitators. Do you think they could be linked?"

"Shit, you know, you might be on to something. I always wondered what the A-rabs and the Venezuelans figured they could do with a couple of score of agitators."

"We saw a few raids and skirmishes as they fanned out north. I always thought we got most of them. Maybe the military guys were just a distraction."

"So far ignoring it has worked. Let them want to be part of Texas. We can like them, we can have a special privilege for their citizenship of Oklahoma, like a waive through at the border, but we can simply not act on any annexation or anything else. Washington would flip and we don't need that problem."

"Our relations with Dixie are not bad - there doesn't seem to be the same level of agitation on the border there, though I'm half convinced the buggers north of Baton Rouge already figure they are Texans and that Louisiana is just a bit of East Texas."

"Our new currency is gradually gaining hold but we are having trouble getting any traction with it outside of Texas. I expect that's not unusual. These things take time. People are just more comfortable with the US dollar, even if it is full of holes."

"It's getting holier by the day, as every other currency seems to be in steep decline. Seems crazy, the least stable currency on earth stiffens up when people get worried. It's propped up by its own weakness. Watch out for something else, perhaps something unconventional to start to gain favour. I have heard of some transactions taking place in Swiss Francs. The whole electronic currency stuff makes it easy and makes it less tangible and I think leads people away from trusting anything. Cash seems to be king - and Swiss cash is high on the list."

"We keep plugging the strength of the Tex-o or the Alamo or whatever we are calling it this week, and the fact that it exists as backed by Texas land holdings. We are almost at the stage where we have to revalue it compared to the US dollar. The dollar is sinking even though other currencies are sinking faster. The Tex-o has strength inside Texas, especially far from our borders, but it is almost valueless outside our borders. Bottom line is Texans get it and trust the value but non-Texans see it as just other manipulated currency."

"The rubber hits the road where the two currencies clash, where one person takes in Texo's and pays out US dollars, or vice versa. As long as that occurs, even unofficially, we have a viable currency."

"The next meeting of the currency board will address the issue of letting it float against the US dollar. Might be some short term pain on exchanges but long term gain if people see how steady it is."

"But it isn't that steady against the US dollar as that currency is inherently weak, it just looks strong against most of the other world currencies. Fricking Washington is only off our backs because they have their own internal problems and we are considered a wayward state - a problem they will address later. I think they will take on Dixie first, as they still have some significant border issues with Virginia."

"I'm hearing loud noises from the northwest, Oregon, Idaho and that bunch who are unhappy with the yoke of Washington but largely afraid to do anything about it - likely because they have no history and don't know what could be done. The Starbucks crowd up there thinks that Seattle is a major terrorist target as a US city but would be left alone outside the US. Then there are the hundreds of thousands of liberal minded independents - who want their cake and too eat is as well. US cash to prop up the social network but a leave us alone attitude when Uncle Sam comes calling. Makes for a volatile mix."

"I'd love to punish the Venezuelans for their part in the raids, but I know we can't afford to do it alone nor do we want to conduct a joint exercise with Washington. How about something covert? Shit, they are doing it to us."

"I'm not sure Texans are really good with covert action," he laughed. "I think we need to set unequivocal terms and then do what we say we are going to do. So far that seems to have worked. Nothing more has happened now in what, more than six months."

"Even the god-damned Mexicans seem to have backed off. That look-the-other-way stuff was bullshit - they have no credibility."

"Hey, Mexico City took out those governors and set things right pretty quick. Even quicker than we would have."

"Well somebody took them out."

The two men were sitting in an Austin conference room. The governor's aides had finished their presentation on the state of the new country - outlining many of the same issues the two former US congressmen had taken up in their conversation.

As they rose to leave the room they may have believed most of their conversation was accurate in its reflections on the situation. The border with Oklahoma appeared benign enough but that type of quiet is often a mask of activity beneath the surface. Chance and opportunity occasionally take center stage in statecraft, advancing changes that may have come slowly or not at all if not pushed forward by events.

A large number of Oklahomans were sitting that day at the Texas border in long lines of cars and trucks. The bright sunny day where the few clouds could be mistaken for aging contrails helped to lighten the mood among travellers forced to wait to get into Texas. So far, the United States had not imposed any border controls on those leaving Texas.

People were used to quick and easy access to Texas, even after the Texas Republic had been declared. All they had to do was pass a Welcome to Texas sign on the highway which flicked by at 70 miles per hour. Oklahomans had been making deliveries and doing business in Texas for generations. New Texas border protocols had gotten tighter after the raids in the south and many of the Oklahomans were not happy with the waiting.

There had been much grumbling and a bit of agitation with some in Oklahoma suggesting similarly tight terms for Texans travelling north. However the US was playing the Texas border like the Europeans had done with the European Union, where borders simply vanished. Texans were allowed to pass into Oklahoma without restriction. Local conditions were calling some of the Texas imposed protocols into question.

"There is a lot of US money swirling around that border. What if we insisted upon Texo's - it would piss everyone off for a bit but it would give our money a lot of credibility," said one Texas congressman to anyone who would listen. The roundabout question of currency rose often among his colleagues.

"We need to make that move at the same time we float. Then there is good reason."

"What about an exchange incentive?"

"No that's been done to death. As soon as you devalue your currency to encourage it's use you have set a value that you don't want. It's counterintuitive to many but a strong currency represents a strong country and leads to a belief in the underlying strength of the currency. Look at the US dollar. For years it was the strongest currency on the planet and still commanded value even though everyone knew it was seriously inflated and oversold. It's really hard to shake that perception of underlying strength."

"Yeah, but every other currency is in the same boat. Makes it easy to fall back on the Greenback."

"I do note that the US dollar is much more desirable in cash though."

The line of cars snaked back from the five kiosks set up on the highway. Most people were resigned to the wait but a few were unhappy.

A pick-up truck rolled up to the kiosk. "I was born in Texas, what am I havin' to wait for?" said the driver without waiting for the border guard to speak.

"Sir, if you want to ask those in front of you to move aside due to your place of birth, I have no objection. If you want back into Texas, why don't you move your home and family back and join us? We'd love to have you. Other than that I'm just here because Texans want me to be here."

The man dropped his chin to his chest like he was working up the courage to say something. He turned his head to kiosk, and brightened his look. "I was fixing to be in your face. But no, I understand. It is a new world and I gotta get used to it. Maybe I will come back to Texas. Anything special I have to do?"

"Nothing that I know of. We haven't been given any instructions other than to keep out undesirables. I'm guessing if you showed up here with a moving van full of stuff they probably ask a few questions. Your birth certificate should be answer enough."

There was an explosion. Then another.

Both the driver and the kiosk attendant felt the concussion and ducked instinctively. They were in the last kiosk on the western edge of the installation. Two kiosks to the east were destroyed along with several cars in or near the bays.

People exited their cars and ran to the side of the asphalt roadway and jumped down a small embankment into the dry gulch of the ever-changing Red River, fanning out away from the Interstate.

No more bombs went off nor was there any other noise save the panicked commands to get away from the scene and the crackling fire of burning fuel spilt in the explosions. A few minutes later the sound of sirens came from the south, in the direction of the Texas town of Burkburnett a few miles down the highway.

Some of the solo travellers moved towards the fires and managed to pull several drivers out of their vehicles and pushed a couple more cars and small trucks away from the immediate threat.

Car parts and other bits of debris littered the asphalt plaza. Several small fires burned. There was mostly silence, as mercifully casualties were either unable to cry out or were too shocked to speak, and those who leaped away from the carnage were silent in their escape.

A single voice remained to direct those who leaped to help. It was calm and deliberate.

"I had better check the kiosks," said a tall, lightly bearded man with a rancher's tan, wearing a heavy t-shirt, blue jeans and a light jacket with a University of Oklahoma logo on the breast. He was wearing baseball cap with a unrecognizable design.

He moved to the center of the line of kiosks. A few other men joined him reluctantly. As he approached the middle kiosk he pointed to his right deliberately sending the less willing to the kiosks that were still standing.

"Take a look at those two. They are damaged but not much more than blown out glass. I'll check over here," he said moving to his left.

Two men and a older boy looked grateful for the direction and quickly agreed to investigate the least damaged part of the border crossing.

The first one reached the blown out window and looked in. A long sharp shard of glass was stuck in the throat of the border guard who was slumped on the floor, partly under the back counter of the kiosk. His legs were bent unnaturally underneath him. His jacket was off his right shoulder and he looked right at the men who encountered him. He gurgled and a line of blood exited the corner of his mouth.

"Oh shit," was all the first responder could utter. The man in the kiosk blinked, tried to say something and then the light went out of his eyes. The wound in his neck continued to leak but after a few seconds the flow became only a trickle.

The young man had quickly moved to the last border hut on the right. The windows were broken but the border guard appeared unhurt, sitting on her stool facing the front window.

"Ma'am? Are you alright?"

She sat there for a few seconds, obviously processing the question. "Uhm, uh," she sighed heavily. "Um, yes, I am okay." She shook her arms to see if they worked. A deep breath in and then out, and a shake of her head and she appeared to make a decision to return to the present.

"Yes, yes, I am okay . . . fine. How about you?"

"Well, ma'am, I much better knowing you are okay. Can I help you out of there?"

She looked around her. The glass in the kiosk windows was broken on all sides but appeared to have cracked and fallen rather than been blown into the kiosk. A pick-up truck had just cleared the kiosk beside her and must have provided a bit of cover during the explosions. That truck had continued to pull through and then had stopped about 50 yards into Texas. The driver stopped and sat in his truck. A man who had seen the dying border guard moved to the truck after determining there was nothing he could do for the man in the kiosk.

"Hey, are you alright?" he asked through the half open window.

"Yes, I am, but I am mightily pissed off. My truck has been damaged, my day changed irrevocably. People who were counting on me will have to adjust to me not being there and I have seen firsthand what we are facing. And what's worse I don't rightly know what it is."

"Can you get out of the truck?"

"I think so, but I've been trying to start it and I'm not sure why it won't turn over."

"Put it in neutral and I'll push you out of the way. Those sirens are sounding louder. Then maybe we can see about getting you operational again."

"Okay, thank you kindly." And they moved the car over to the west side of the plaza on the Texas side.

The east side of the kiosk line was worse. The most easterly kiosk had taken a direct hit, almost as if the bomb was right beside it when it blew. The kiosk was essentially gone with only the jagged bits of the bottom structure still there. The kiosk itself had been blown to pieces, most of which littered the river bottom scrub to the side of the highway. There was no sign of any body at first glance.

The man in the Sooner's jacket worked his way to the east, after quickly ascertaining the situation in each kiosk. He came to the second kiosk from the east. It had suffered much the same fate as the first, however, vehicles on either side of it had kept the force of the explosion from going side to side forcing it forward and back. There was little left. The torso of the attendant was 20 yards into Texas, blown there alone without arms, legs or head. The man scanned quickly for the head and covered it with his jacket.

He moved back to his own vehicle, grabbed a few tarps out of his trunk and placed one over the torso he had found, weighing it down with bits of debris.

The sirens sounded louder now and looking up he could see a line of emergency vehicles moving towards them from Texas.

A couple score of people milled about in the dry bed. Some had moved back to their vehicles. There were a few at the back of the line that were drivable. Others were severely damaged.

As the emergency vehicles rolled to a stop the last of the tarps were being held down with some heavy debris. Another explosion rocked the area. One of the initial blasts had been wired with a timer for a second bomb to go off.

There wasn't much more damage to make, though the explosion did stir up what was already there and it scared all the curious back to their distant refuges.

The man, now without his jacket was hit by a spray of shrapnel. Most didn't inflict any real injury save one piece of jagged steel which lodged in his upper arm. He gave a short cry and then reached over with his left hand and removed it. He moved toward the emergency service personnel and told them what had happened.

Emergency personnel reached a lurid scene. They called in bomb disposal units and waited. Soon a steady stream of people approached them for advice or treatment of minor and occasionally significant wounds mostly from flying bits of kiosk.

"Who would do this?" asked one man to anyone he encountered. "Who would do this?"

Chapter Forty - Two   Los Angeles

"We need to declare independence," said Hellenga. "It will quell the unrest in the south and provide a starting point for the future."

"Yeah, and it will also bring down the wrath of the Americans and our independence might be very short indeed."

"They have nothing. They won't come. There is nobody left who wants them here. They aren't going to shoot their own residents and they won't want to interfere with self-determination," said Hellenga. "That's why independence is so much better than asking for an annexation by Mexico."

"Ok, a reasonable approach would be to conduct a referendum. Then you might get some traction."

"Okay, you might be on to something. Let's set up a referendum."

"Yeah, but who is going to 'administrate' the referendum and eventually the new nation? Assume you can get a vote, assume it is without controversy, who will direct the apparatus of government to begin acting independently?"

"Good questions. I think if we declare a referendum to be operated by local municipalities, the new administration would emerge from the leaders of the pro-Aztlan movement that are currently elected officials in those municipalities. Right now we are engaging with Southern California municipalities to help fix issues of mutual concern. That group becomes the upper level government by default. Nobody would challenge it as it is unfunded, already elected and merely acting as starting point for Southern California issues. They referee the move to independence, and remember that the referee runs the game."

"An interesting proposal. It still needs a front face - someone to call for the referendum and someone to chair that vote - not necessarily the same person. And that person must remain neutral."

"I will call for the referendum and our municipalities can run it jointly," said Hellenga. "This is a vital first step in gaining our independence. You are right, we need credibility from our residents, and with our process, if the rest of the world is to believe our validity as a new nation."

Hellenga designed a series of murals depicting local administrators acting in concert on behalf of their towns - local concerns being addressed by local voices to strengthen Aztlan for its residents. He arranged for other artists to complete them and organize their installation. The call for a referendum was echoed by a series of columns and news articles that Hellenga submitted to local newspapers and radio stations.

Finally Hellenga announced that the decision to hold the referendum and if approved the mechanism to determine its wording would be accomplished at the meeting of municipalities. The news was received well, with official responses saying that people had a stake in the way they were governed, but with a real word of caution about independence.

The meeting was held in Los Angeles. The referendum was passed, though the delegation haggled over the wording for many days. There were a few new buildings in LA but by far the largest was the recycling warehouse where all blast materials were taken to be sorted for reuse or refuse.

The main delivery floor was cleared and a makeshift meeting room set up, with several hundred chairs and a lectern with a small public address system. Journalists from across the state attended the historic meeting taking up as much space as the delegates.

Eventually, what emerged was a direct but cautious question, "Southern California counties south of but not including the counties of Monterrey, King, Tulare and Inyo should become an independent nation. Yes or No."

Local issues were also discussed with several pro-Aztlan issues sprinkled into the mix. Delegates voted for a common pictograph to be adopted for most signs across southern California towns. The plan to add Spanish words where appropriate, passed without debate. Hellenga assumed that 'appropriate' meant on every sign.

American law passed in Congress in the wake of the 5/29 attacks had set precedent for quickly determining land ownership in destroyed areas, but the assembly discussed making it easy for neighbourhoods to be packaged into a single land holding with a three year window where new property must lie fallow and a further four years upon which claims could be made to be paid by the purchaser and an additional 13 years upon which successful late claimants would receive compensation from a fund set up through the collection of development charges. Unless title could be proved through a proscribed set of documents the state became the landowner with a mandate to sell the lands to interested buyers. After 20 years all claims were voided and any money left over from the compensation fund would be used by the municipalities for environmental remediation of unclaimed property which the municipality could then sell at its discretion.

That passed with little debate.

A third measure passed with little comment. All debts were payable in US dollars or in a mutually agreed upon amount of oil, gold or copper.

The assembly dispersed with an agreement to reconvene in a month just before the referendum period was to become official to assess the fairness of the referendum process and give it the green light or postpone it if necessary. However, as soon as word about the referendum leaked out the two sides began forming up.

"And that was the most important thing. We are back together in a month," said Hellenga.

"Yes, but according to some of the press questions, it appears that the State government wants to have a voice in the process. They want to convene every municipality in the State. Perhaps they will force a wider referendum on keeping California whole?"

"Let them, we won't go. The north and central parts of the state can make whatever decisions they want, but without the participation of the southern counties they are handicapped. These successes are vital to having a credible referendum. And frankly, if they simply mirror our question, authorities might be surprised by the result. Many northern Californians would be happy to lose what they consider the troubles of the south."

"With a win in our vote independence will already be an accomplished fact. That the South runs on its own, completely differently than the North and with a significantly different culture, is already obvious and widely acknowledged."

"Ah, my friend, do you really think this whole thing can be accomplished without violence? I do not see Washington letting go of the jewel in its crown so easily," said Octavius.

"I do hope so. Remember that this jewel you speak of is tarnished, splintered and without beauty at the present. That's why we must strike soon before rebuilding takes hold enough to produce a land like the old California."

"I'd like to see more entertainment being created here, like before the blast."

"Yes, there is some, but it is mostly Mexican and Spanish as producers have moved here in search of the talented people who survived. Many of the facilities, sound stages, film and sound processing locations were far enough away from the blast epicenter to survive. Long Beach is still a pretty great setting for a disaster film."

Hellenga laughed, "If a blast zone wiped clean of strip malls and palm trees isn't disaster enough. Actually New York has more recognisable features still in place, bridges, some buildings and the river. But it's too cold there to film all year round."

"Many have moved to San Jose, Las Vegas, or Phoenix. Orlando has grown exponentially by offering good terms on development and housing. I understand the CGI studios are bursting with people rendering old movies into three-D versions of any celebrity who was killed in the blast - there's enough work in that alone to keep the entertainment companies in business for years. That's why so many are so surprised to see the devastation in LA first hand when their favorite shows are still going strong."

"I must say, I did notice that most big time studio productions of the last couple of years have been full of British actors - never really wondered why - until now. That explains all the costume dramas."

The destruction of Los Angeles was more complete than that of New York, and yet, because of the size of both cities, much had survived, mostly due to geography and to the sprawled form the cities had taken. Los Angeles was spread out. And while some of the outlying areas had not had much damage due to the nature of the narrow canyons, and the main lay of the city, about 15 kilometers from Long Beach Harbour where the blast had occurred had been devastated as it was a flat coastal plain.

Remarkably what was considered downtown Los Angeles survived though the buildings were heavily damaged, mostly with broken windows. Outlying areas to the north, Pasadena, Hollywood, Beverly Hills and Burbank were largely unaffected except for the large loss of life to the south and the recalibrating of society. Carson, Torrance, Huntington Beach, Cerritos and Westminister were utterly laid waste. There were many that believed that overall the loss was about as little as could be imagined from a nuclear blast as many in the blast zone were lower class neighbourhoods with significant social problems. While few would acknowledge the apparent advantages of the blast there was a widespread nod and wink when some suggested that the explosion of a bomb in Long Beach was a plot by the Illuminati.

Most of Los Angeles' richer neighbourhoods survived. Most of the country was horrified by the devastation but the city actually thrived even if the piers at Long Beach had to be rebuilt at Marina Del Ray. The shipping center at Long Beach was simply too important to the California economy to be abandoned.

Chapter Forty - Three   Central Asia

"Imam, we are being pushed back on all fronts. How shall we proceed?"

"And yet we resist, my friend. We must invoke taqiyya and hudna, and use our time to retrench in our homelands and grow strong in our new territories in Europe."

Al-adori smiled. He knew his Imam, Alcoeur Islami was right. The only way to end the vast retreat was to wave the flag of peace - to appear to integrate into local populations, as the Muslims in Britain had done for 50 years, and to avoid agitating but grow strong, numerous and await a more suitable time to rise up.

"Al-adori, my friend, call our brothers. We must sup together and speak of jihad and our strategy of peace."

"Yes, my Imam. They await you. Several more are still to come but have sent messages asking us not to wait as travel is difficult."

The two men walked through the compound and into the main hall of the mosque. The room, which had been loud with conversation quickly fell silent once Islami's presence was noted. He moved to the front of the crowd and raised his hands.

"The blessings of Allah on you all for hearing my call. We have made significant progress in our efforts to convert infidels to our calling. And yet, they resist and fight with terrible vigour. We must, it seems, lull them into a trust, a trust where we wish upon them the blessings of Allah, the joy of jihad to convert infidels to the wonders we know. We have declared hudna, a truce in our conversion of dhimmis, for perhaps a decade, to allow these infidels to see the wonders and truth of an Islamic life. They have only seen the wild determination of Islam to help them to Allah. They need to experience the softer persuasion of our people to convince them that Allah is the one God and Mohammed is his messenger."

The room was silent. Heads nodded. Eyes glistened.

"I call on all Islam to recognize the need for taqiyya in explaining our change of heart - because there is no change of heart, my friends, for Islam will never change its heart, its determination to bring Allah to all. And yet, we must convince the dhimmi that coming to Allah is their choice - for even though it is told that all men will join with Allah, with these Europeans it appears they must be persuaded rather than converted. It is more effective if they come willingly. We will engage in this approach as a hudna, which we will reconsider in a decade, after we determine its effectiveness."

"Join with me for a time. Speak with me of your struggles. Let me help you in your work for Allah. When you return to your homes, you will take up the cause of Islam with renewed vigour, with a long term approach to our jihad. We will reclaim our traditional lands. I call for all Muslims to visit our rebuilt Mecca during this hudna to reaffirm our desire for a better world."

The room erupted in cheers. Al-coeur Islami held his hands up, palms in, then he clasped his hands together. He made this gesture to every part of the room and then departed, with a quiet command to his lieutenant Al-adori to bring to him anyone who wished to speak to him. Al-adori circulated the room explaining to those in attendance where they could find food and directing those who wanted an audience with Al-coeur Islami to wait for him to guide them to his chamber.

Soon several men were seated around Al-coeur Islami taking food and talking.

"Imam, this hudna is part of a larger plan?"

"Yes, we must remain in these lands we have claimed for Allah. The only way at this time is with hudna, a strategic truce and by invoking taqiyya to have the dhimmi believe we have acceded to their wishes of integration with their infidel societies. We will still practice Islam, just less obviously, in their shadows, to allow it to grow roots, to convert locals and to move into all aspects of local society - government, business, entertainment, administration."

"How far should we take this hudna?"

"As far as required to end the battles against Allah. Remain as visible as you can without stepping on the dhimmis toes. We want to remain and grow Islam and will choose our time of renewing our jihad, our struggle to convert the infidels."

"So it will be different everywhere?"

"Yes, Allah has willed it. We will become almost invisible in Europe. We will appear to flood back into Arabia, Persia, Afghanistan and Pakistan. We will go quiet, go soft in Central Asia, remaining a strong undercurrent in social discourse. We will end the insistent push in Africa, and try to co-exist with local populations, while insisting that Allah be accommodated and respected. We will defend our place in America by insisting upon our freedom of religion and that we only want to worship Allah in our own way."

"Will it work Imam?"

"Allah will guide us, my friend. We will retrench. We will succeed. Allah has willed it. We will bring our way to all infidels, who are so determined to exercise their freedoms that they break Allah's laws, they are decadent, they are immoral, they are disrespectful. I still cannot understand how these infidels cannot see the truth of Allah, the justice of his way, the messages of Mohammed. I am filled with dread that our hudna will allow the infidels to practice their terrible irresponsible freedoms upon the world, but I take peace that it is the only way to finally end their terror."

Al-coeur Islami had days of discussions with Muslim leaders from all around the world. In some places, such as Indonesia, very little had to change with the declaration of the hudna. In others, where Muslim populations were strong they took a softer approach to convert by example. In Europe and America they were instructed to remain if possible, where citizenship extended several generations, and to bear the pain of the infidels battle against Islam - for surely the infidel would not take the battle to places it could not see.

Al-coeur Islami made an announcement of infinite hudna, calling it a truce for as long as is necessary to bring the world together. He called for Muslims to respect the laws and traditions of the lands where they were living and to bring jihad only as a personal struggle to achieve a more perfect world.

He insisted that Allah would prevail and that he was prepared to take a different approach to conversion, to demonstrate Allah's long term view and eventual victory of minds and hearts. He called for all Muslims to peacefully join their brothers to make a better world.

He moved to a newly built mosque in the ruins of Mecca. He reestablished the Kaaba, the black cubed House of God at the center of Mecca and Islam. He celebrated the Hajj inviting Muslims to the pilgrimage and to stay to help rebuild Mecca.

Many Muslims took him up on his pledge and moved to help rebuild cities in Arabia. The Western world waited. Governments were pleased that many Muslims appeared to be leaving Europe. There were many voices saying it was only a strategic surrender, but there was no stomach for continuing the battle, and once the threat was removed, people seemed satisfied that it would not return. Those Muslims remaining in America spoke with no accent, dressed as locals and refrained from any outward demonstration of their cultural loyalties.

And yet it was an uneasy truce as governments were in place to push the Muslim threat away. In some cases the local Islamists remained outside the law and conducted hit and run raids as they believed Al-coeur Islami was a dupe of the West. With the removal of many Muslims, voluntarily and by persuasion the threat was much diminished but the battle was not won.

Chapter Forty - Four   Washington

"Mr. President, we have an agreement by all on our borders. I think it can pass Congress. I'm quite sure it will result in some on-going battles, in court only I hope, though possibly of the shooting kind, this is Virginia after all, but once done it will be done."

"So we have a new state of East Virginia? And we have what, a billion lawsuits to settle?"

"Now sir, a billion is a bit much, more like many thousands," said political aide Jimmy Fenton with a smile. "And frankly we can likely settle most of them with a blanket payment to each affected landowner."

"Why is it Jimmy, that every political solution requires the spending of lots of money?"

"Well Mr. President, that is how we have appeased people for decades. In fact, our currency, our ability to persuade, more than freedom, democracy or capitalism is really money, US currency is currency I suppose."

"So are there any changes to the final draft in Virginia that I don't know about from the briefing?"

"No sir, the State of Virginia was firm on their wants but willing to make some concessions based on our shared history. Your determination to maintain good relations paid dividends in the negotiations. Using the rivers as borders where possible was fairly straight forward, especially once the Virginians realized we were very serious about protecting our assets and creating an East Virginia."

"So it's the Shenandoah River in the north and west, to the Rappahannock River then pretty much straight south across open countryside, where most of the lawsuits will be, to the narrowing of the York River and then south again to the Chicahominy River across the James River and south to the Great Dismal Swamp. South through the Swamp to the current Virginia state line and east to the Atlantic."

"That's it sir. We keep Newport News, Hampton, Norfolk and the Naval Station there, and maintain open land access through to Washington and Baltimore. Essentially the Atlantic Shore of Virginia and northern Virginia becomes East Virginia. Bottom line was Dixie wanted Richmond, no surprise, and they didn't want the huge number of US federal bureaucrats living south and west of Washington to be in their territory. Again, no real surprise there."

"Once Dixie conceded that if they could split from the United States, then parts of what might be Dixie could split from it, things proceeded rapidly. We won't have any difficulties with river borders, but the southern sweep, east of Richmond is going to be trouble - but mostly it will be costly trouble rather than violent trouble."

"And all the other border disputes?"

"Mr. President, they were mostly solvable with a handshake. The Red River separates Oklahoma from Texas, notwithstanding the violent provocations in that area. Nobody really knows who is fighting for what. Arizona is firmly with the United States but it is the borders of New Mexico, which appear to be leaking into Texas, and California, through which the Mexicans are pouring people and propaganda. Those are the primary concerns."

"We are leaving the issues to local conditions and maintaining what exists. Northern Californians want US border controls in the south, even if the southerners don't care, and they want US military presence to protect them, just like the Arizonans."

The call for a referendum in California is troubling as we expect the Yes side will win fairly easily. We need to work up a response to every possible referendum outcome prior to the vote. That could range from protecting our assets in the event of a Yes sweep, to frankly, protecting our assets in the event of a No side win."

"What about Florida?"

"As we spoke about before, it appears Florida is a lost cause. The two US senators have declared for Dixie and we used that chip of interest in Florida to get the concessions in Virginia. I imagine they have the same view - that they used the lost cause of Virginia to get our concessions in Florida."

"It's a much different United States of America now Jimmy," said President O'Day. "I protected the Constitution and preserved the Union, just with a few less members. At least we are on friendly terms with our new neighbours and they are fully aware we would welcome them back into the Union if they chose."

"Frankly Mr. President, history will record your gentle handling of this difficult situation, from the attacks on our cities, to the guerilla attacks on our borders, to the determination of some Americans to pull away from our central government. Your establishment of an annual governors meeting between all jurisdictions in North America went a long way to preserving something of the old Union. Including Canada and Mexico in those meetings was key, if the pundits and opinion columnists are to be believed. It reminded the Canadians and Mexicans just how different their neighbours were, making additional succession less likely."

"Well thank you Jimmy. We have done our best in very trying times - I will leave this office in less than a year, believing strongly that I have done my best."

"I believe that most of the current candidates for the job agree with you. Not one has suggested an alternative approach. Politically, taking a strong stand against any of our former countrymen, is a huge mistake. Leaving the stars on our flag is a hopeful sign as well."

"Tom Findlay won the New Hampshire primary for the Republicans or New Federalists or whatever they are being called these days. It appears to change by state. His hinting around Jim Grange and appearances with the Massachusetts Governor seemed to seal the deal, sir. Findlay has been rightly seen as a strong supporter of yours and a strong advocate for the continuation of the gentle approach to the Union. His success reflects the popularity of your approach."

"His major opponent appears to be Art Mansia - the former mayor of Kansas City, who favours a sale of US assets to Texas and Dixie rather than your approach, that the citizens of those places paid their share for Federal assets within their borders. As you have said, the issue is more one of military reach and strategic importance, hence your compromise between the Norfolk Naval Station and military outposts in Florida."

"Well, Findlay should win but it would be nice if he had a running mate from somewhere west of the Mississippi. There is a whole country out there that feels pretty isolated. We should get a better feel of that with the little tour we are planning out there. Have we nailed down the itinerary yet?"

"Still working on the details though Mr. President. You are making an appearance at the San Francisco Chinese New Year's parade, the Super Bowl in Seattle and some Denver events. I'd really like to get you in Phoenix and maybe Vegas. I don't think any sitting President has ever visited Las Vegas. Perhaps we should make two visits. You can do the final of March Madness in Las Vegas at the end of March and maybe we can work in a Denver event at that time."

We are going to tour San Francisco and see the amazing progress they've made since the earthquake. It was a scary few months for people there but much of the city held up remarkably. Once debris was cleared away the city began to function again very quickly."

"I understand some of the largest buildings are still derelict."

"They are Mr. President. In fact that's one of the things you are doing out there. Two large office towers are being re-opened. Having you on hand would be a huge boost to the locals and to California in general."

"Why aren't there any Californians in the presidential race, in either party?"

"We might find that out once you are there. California is feeling mighty put upon by the Mexican influence in the south, by the destruction of much of LA and by the dislocation of the earthquake in the Bay Area. If it wasn't for so many southern Californians fleeing the south, the Bay Area may not have recovered so quickly. Remember 22,000 people lost their lives in that quake and there was a huge amount of infrastructure damaged."

"You'll be meeting with the Governor, the Mayors of several Bay Area cities and several farmers in Sonoma and the Central Valley. Easing federal water regulations have helped the farmers considerably. They are looking for some guarantee from the US that we will capture all the water from the Colorado before the Mexicans can get it."

"That already happens."

"With the Mexicans pushing their interests north, the farmers want to make sure it continues."

"I think we need to push the narrative that Findlay and Mansia are looking at California with interest and for potential running mates."

"A worthy plan sir," Jimmy opened a map of the new Virginia border. "Here is the agreed upon border. All the land owners have been consulted and most have agreed to be on one side of the border or another. As you can see we managed the entire White Lake area and its drainage hinterland on our side, and we gave up some of the Upper York River drainage areas to get the border up to the main navigation areas. I believe Virginia thought the areas north of these wide rivers would be too hard to administer as there are few bridges across the widest sections of all those rivers. It gets a bit tricky south of the James but it's mostly rural through there, so we used the Brackwater River north of the North Carolina border and then a series of local creeks to try to find a natural break. For the most part it worked but we still have a few people to satisfy."

"What about you Jimmy, what are your plans after all of this?"

"Well sir, Findlay has been sniffing around. I told him that I would get involved with the National campaign after the convention, so I guess I'm doing that, if nothing else changes. I have been contacted by a few Congressional districts back home in Ohio but I haven't really been interested. All that mucking about in the quagmire of political minutiae is not terribly attractive once you've spent some time flying at a more strategic level."

"Let me tell you Jimmy, elected politics is the most satisfying thing there is, and also the most horrible as you have to balance political necessity, political reality with electability in trying to satisfy the most number of people with the best long term approach. And the whole thing is balanced on such a short cycle - only two years - that it is almost impossible to think long term, the absolute requirement for success."

"A good summation sir."

"Where will we be in a year, Jimmy?"

"Right where we are now sir. Just a little bit more firm on some things, a little bit less firm on others and with a new view of the kaleidoscope of problems that face us. And it will be someone else's problem."

O'Day laughed. "A kaleidoscope? When have you ever seen a kaleidoscope?"

"I never really have sir. It's just a figure of speech now. I know what they are and have seen a demonstration of them on the web."

Chapter Forty - Five   **Florida**

"I guess that makes me a good ole boy," the old man cackled.

"Not quite Lev."

"Well I've been whistling Dixie for 10 years. And I sho nuff ain't no damned Yankee."

"Lev, you are neither young enough to be a 'boy' and while you've lived in Florida for a decade you spent most of your life in Jersey, and you are Jewish. You are ruled out in every way. And, it isn't even official yet, just a lot of politicos fishing around to save their own butts."

"Morrie, you are my best friend, we've known each other in Jersey from the time we were kids . . . ."

"Fourteen years old, first year of high school. You were the slick fielding first baseman I was looking for . . . "

Lev nodded, remembering. "Yeah, I had to make that team twice, once for me and once for you. If I didn't scoop up your throws from short you'd a never made that team," he laughed. "And now after all of that, we're southern boys. Maybe we should take in a NASCAR race or something? You know once the suits decide to move they are as good as moved, until

287

something better comes along."

"Northern Florida wants in. Lots of ties to Dixie. The south is run by the Cubans. Central Florida is still in play. Everyone here is from Jersey."

"And New York, and Massachusetts, and Pennsylvania and Ohio."

"What is that, a railroad?" Morrie laughed. "Anyway, I don't think it's going to change much for us."

"Now that Bill Scott is with Dixie, it might as well be everything."

"If he's smart he'll extract as much as he can out of Washington before cozying up to Dixie too much."

"Morrie, I think he's pretty much got all he can get. That would be everything. Apparently Washington has even ceded the naval station at Tampa and a couple of air bases. Frankly, O'Day is pretty smart about this. Don't let anything official happen just go with reality on the ground and maybe the good will generated, will help in the future. As I've always said, the future isn't written yet and it takes a long time to commit it to paper."

"It doesn't take the papers long to print it, just one day."

"That's the past Morrie. Sort of like me scooping your throws to first."

"I'm thinking your scoops got you on the team. You needed me to make you look good. You could hit too I guess."

"A bit," said Lev. "I just remember that I was a very tough out. Coach of Stuyvesant said that. I remember being real happy about it. I sometimes wonder what would have happened if I went for big hits rather than reaching base. Scouts like first basemen that can hit big."

"You did it sometimes Lev, like when we really needed it, you tried for it. Worked out some times."

"Those are the ones I remember. That and the senior year league championship."

"You struck out with the bases loaded."

"I know, but I should have been bunting. Coach never called for it but it was the right play. Kipper on third with all that speed, me with good bat control at the plate, one out, down one. We would have tied it at least."

"He trusted your bat."

"I know, but bunt was the right play given the game situation. He went for the win, I would'a gone for the tie. I always thought it was in my head too much and that was why I struck out. It's a regret of mine - one of several thousand, or none."

"I know what you mean Lev. If I had to do it all over again I would have to be conscious of the choices I did make to be sure I wouldn't make them again. It's like, I know how it worked out this time, so I wonder how it would have gone with different choices. Not that I really regret them, given the same circumstances I'd probably make them all again, except of course, the ones that didn't make any difference or have any impact in the end, but I am what I am. It would be nice to see what would have happened with different choices in some spots."

"You are rambling Morrie."

"Well if we are southern boys now, I have to practice my rambling and whittling. Maybe we should go hunting or something?"

Lev laughed. "Hunting golf balls maybe, or hunting down a deal at the Mall."

"So you don't think anything is going to change?"

"Not for a while. Everybody has to lay low and let the whole idea of an independent Dixie sink in. The good ole boys won't know who to moan about without Washington looking over their shoulders."

A trio of fighter jets took shape in the distance. The low roar tipped those poolside to the flight in time for them to look up and see the delta formation flying fairly low overhead.

"Are those ours now. Still have US markings, but are they Florida's jets, Dixie's jets or Washington's jets?"

"Good question, let's just hope that for the mean time all those groups are on the same side. I'm guessing they are just answering to their local commanders. When the orders eventually come from Washington to take commands from whoever, they will likely be given the right of transfer to other units in the north. Maybe that's already happened."

It had. The jets were on regular patrol for Dixie, having been ceded to the southerners in the Border agreement. They would continue to fly with US badges for the foreseeable future to maintain the illusion of continuity. Transfers north had already been approved and some personnel had moved. The patrol was looking for Cubans coming into Florida by boat, or even Mexicans who had been reportedly entering the state through the Gulf.

People were relatively relaxed as the major changes in jurisdiction had been soft peddled. However state officials were very concerned after the Texas and California invasions from Mexico. Especially with close ties between Venezuela and Cuba. Cubans were entering Florida through the Keys in droves, finding willing residents throughout south Florida to give them cover and get them jobs in the central and northern parts of the state. The locals thought they were helping out dissidents and fellow countrymen to get a better life. What they didn't know was that an invading army was moving with the migrants, hiding among them.

Patrols caught hundreds and they were removed and deported. But until the discouragement for entry was steeper, they would still come.

Caches of weapons were moved into place as the invaders grew in strength. They worked as gardeners, day labourers and in fast food restaurants waiting for the appointed day.

Everything was centered on an abandoned theme park outside of Winter

Haven. Weapons were transported there. Transport trucks were hidden inside buildings. Cuban insurgents started to gather there.

A satellite launch was scheduled for a Friday in March with the rocket leaving Cape Canaveral on Florida's east coast at 8:30 am. Central Florida was abuzz with tourists who wanted to see the launch and locals who knew it would be spectacular.

Just before dawn the transport trucks at Winter Haven loaded - they took small arms, several heavy machine guns and hundreds of Venezuelans, Mexicans and some Cuban illegals in 21 transports and headed east toward the launch.

The transports were printed with the logo of several food supply companies and national beverage brands. At 7 am, as dawn was breaking the convoy neared Orlando. It turned off the highway and entered Disney World along Buena Vista Blvd. A truck stopped at Interstate 4 and Florida State Route 429. Another truck continued north on Route 429 stopping at State Highway 192. A truck stopped at each of the next five exits along Interstate 4.

The remaining transport trucks moved into the park taking up strategic spots outside of resort hotel areas, particularly in the southwest where several resorts were clustered, in the east around another cluster of resorts and at the iconic Contemporary Resort. They waited.

At 8:30 am there was a low rumble, even at Disney World, 50 miles away. The burning fuel of the large rocket soon became visible on the horizon and it slowly climbed into the sky leaving a contrail of smoke and water vapour and steam in its path.

With all eyes pointed skyward zero hour had come. The transports all opened and troops poured out. They commandeered intersections, and effectively controlled access to the whole of Disney World. They captured hotels by gaining control of the access points and sending armed troops into the large lobbies.

Several people were shot dead resisting causing others to move to the safety of their rooms or cars. Two buses were shot up when they failed to stop on command. The buses were moved into place as road blocks.

Command of the whole of Disney World was complete within an hour with hundreds and thousands of tourist families hostage to the invaders.

A communiqué was released. "The government of Florida, and the joint governments of the United States and Dixie will cede south Florida from Marco Island to Lake Okeechobee along Route 76 to the Atlantic south of Port Salerno to the Government of Cuba."

"We have taken a large portion of Central Florida to enforce our will. We have para-dropped a large number of men and equipment into areas where we have taken control and along border points of the Everglades Province of Cuba. All people in the occupied zone are safe and will be released unharmed if our demands are met. If you do not agree to our truce we will be forced to eliminate your citizens from our occupation zones commencing in two hours."

The Governor of Florida was given the news of the takeover as she was leaving the scene of the rocket launch. She was in complete disbelief.

"I have to see this. Take me there."

"Governor, we have law enforcement on the ground that confirms it. Two police cars tried to break up the road block as it was beginning to be formed. They were all shot - four local policemen dead - as scores of armed men swarmed their cars. These intersections aren't just held light-ly, there are reports coming through 911 that there are some heavy arms - large ground based machine guns in place at several of the intersections and even some of the transports being used to shore up approaches to nearby buildings where the insurgents have holed up to disguise their numbers. They apparently even have anti-aircraft weapons.

North of Atlanta Clemons's heart felt like it had stopped. "Have senators Chartaway and Scott been notified?" he said slowly. "What about

Washington?"

"Washington said they are able to help if we request it."

"I don't want to go there. Independent nations don't require help."

His aide looked at him lopsidedly.

"But I can't rule it out. Two hours, that isn't much time to respond."

He thought for a moment. "Issue this . . . "Dixie and its citizens believe in the will of the people, not the will of the armed few. We will commit to a referendum on the status of south Florida with consultation with the Government of Cuba. However, we will not be coerced into this action and will defend any aggression on our territory. Sign my name."

"Sir, we have just received a communiqué from President O'Day. He says the United States can cripple Havana in less than two hours from Guantanamo Bay. It is a long standing contingency plan, though they would require our help from Tampa and various air bases in the area."

"Any word yet from the two Senators?"

"No sir, this is all less than 45 minutes old. The two hour deadline is rapidly approaching."

An aide rushed in. "Sir I don't know what to make of this - we just received word from Havana that this is not a Government of Cuba action. They said they expect it is a Venezuelan led coup with some Mexican influence - much like the invasions of Texas and California last year."

"Great, first they take responsibility then they disavow it. Who do we fight?"

Clemons phone rang. It was Senator Scott. "Vernon, you've heard. We must acquiesce - give them what they want. Once they leave central Florida we can re-negotiate. We have to get them out of there peacefully. Thousands of lives are on the line, the economy of the whole of central Florida is at risk. Anything other than a peaceful resolution to this and our tourist industry is dead. Our credibility can wait."

"Thank you for your suggestion. I am going to consult with Governor Anderson. She and I will issue a joint statement."

He put down the phone and turned to an aide. "Please let Senator Chartaway know what we are doing. I will of course take his call, should he want to speak to me."

Clemons dialed Governor Anderson's personal cell number. "Debbie, its Vernon Clemons. You know what's happening? I have issued a statement calling for a referendum on south Florida's future but saying we will resist aggression. O'Day has offered a military response on Havana from Gitmo. The Cuban government disavows any connections with this."

"I'm right here on Interstate Four," she said. "I was nearby when we heard about the insurgency. These people are heavily armed but it is a light invasion. Yes, they could kill many thousands if they had a mind too. They are heavily in control inside the park. We have drones in the air and are getting a flood of 911 calls with information. However, we could never coordinate a counter attack that would eliminate the threat - if we try we will have huge numbers of casualties and a dead tourist industry. We have to get them out of there at any cost. I think we concede to their demands and should ask for more time to negotiate the withdrawal to the south and warn that any violence must be answered for."

"Okay, my office will co-ordinate with yours on a joint statement. Let's see how serious they are."

He hung up.

"Get the right Rodriguez on the phone," he snapped. "The one from Mexico. If those bastards have anything to do with this, oh man."

The Ambassador spoke with Clemons disavowing any involvement at first and then, after closer questioning and a few threats, he made it clear there was no involvement from Mexico that he was aware of or had been privy to. He began to have his doubts privately, as the invasion description matched a war-game format that had been tossed about Mexican diplomatic circles in the event of a need to threaten Washington. The apparent plan matched too well with the actual event. However Rodriguez kept this detail to himself. He wondered if this event signalled a coup of sorts in Mexico.

The appointed hour came. Everyone held their breath including those stuck inside the hotels who were watching events on television.

A man clad in military fatigues but without insignia moved to the front of the Contemporary Hotel. He was broadcasting live on You Tube.

"You have not seen fit to agree with our position. South Florida is already majority Cuban. We simply want to speed the already inevitable process. He turned slightly - 'Now' " he said with a downward chop of his right arm.

A few seconds passed and then a series of explosions rocked the iconic hotel. As the smoke cleared it was evident that entrances had been dynamited including the monorail entrances halfway up the sloped structure. Without question there were many dead.

"We insist upon your honorable word for our orderly repositioning along the new border with north Cuba. Until we have an agreement, we will continue to remake our new territory."

Clemons watched the broadcast and was stunned at the violence. Clearly these people were unwilling to negotiate.

"Look, Cuba disavows this invasion. Mexico says it has no involvement but the Ambassador seemed nervous and clearly knows more than he's letting on. We have to get those people in there to safety so we should agree to a withdrawal and then attack their convoys as they advance south. We will have to take a chance that they do not have a strong grip in the south and will not be able to take it out on people there."

295

"That appears to be the only repercussion as nobody is on-side with these guys - except maybe Venezuela and they aren't answering. Anything we do under duress can be disavowed. Agree to their terms with the caveat that a referendum must be held on annexation of south Florida to Cuba. If we don't push back a bit they will suspect something. This is Texas and California all over again. If we attack them they will melt away. If we attack them after they've left the resort then our people are safe. Once we find out who they are we can retaliate."

"You are right. Any indication that they have taken aggressive positions in south Florida? Shall we consult with Washington?"

"No, we need to do this on our own. Make the arrangements. Let the military know the plan and have them draw something up quickly."

The capitulation agreement was transmitted to the insurgents who transmitted an agreement on terms and said they would be begin their withdrawal shortly. A few hours passed and they began by packing up their transports and sending half of their force south while the other half remained guarding major hotel areas inside Disney. News of insurgent action in Miami trickled back to the command post.

The first half of the operation was underway as dusk came.

"We will attack when the next part commences its movement to the south. They will likely back off another half of their contingent and either hold the hotel areas lightly or back off and only hold one with the remaining troops."

"We are prepared for both scenarios?"

"Yes, and our military says either way is okay by them. Heavy concentrations make for quick work and lighter concentrations will make easier going. SWAT teams are in place to take on whatever group of insurgents remain. they are co-ordinated with law enforcement in the Miami area. They do say to prepare for some civilian casualties. If the remaining troops fight back they could cause some significant damage."

The second group left the Disney area, leaving one large group remaining at the Port Orleans / French Quarter resorts which stood side by side on the east side of the property. It was one of the largest hotel / resort areas within the Disney property, with thousands of vacationers in residence.

Dixie military waited until the second continent of invaders was nearing the first contingent. They guessed that the remaining insurgents would have their guard down and that the two groups of invaders who had moved south would be fairly close together, making an inviting target.

Helicopters moved into Disney from the west leaving scores of troops on the ground, making their way east, checking on each hotel and getting closer to the eastern location of the French Quarter. At the same time the air was filled with jet fighters, some light bombers and scores of helicopter gunships which moved into a position to attack the retreating main contingent.

"We have just received word from Miami that hundreds of heavily armed men dressed in uniforms without insignia have surfaced in that city and are taking control of key installations and institutions. Our people there are laying in wait for our command."

"I knew there would be a rat here, it all seemed too easy," said Governor Anderson. "We can't call off the hit. Let our people in Miami know there is going to be blood - a state of emergency is to be declared, curfew, lockdown, anything to keep citizens off the streets. Our local police and any military you can scrounge need to take charge of the city, block by block if necessary. Do we have any idea of the size of the invasion force?"

"No, all we have is multiple reports of the armed men taking charge of water, electricity, television stations and major intersections."

First the helicopter gunships swooped down and laid a withering fire into areas occupied by the retreating troop of insurgents. Then they downed quickly and let off several hundred soldiers with orders to wait for the next two rounds of airstrikes before moving. At that point they would be able to radio for additional gunship strikes on specific targets.

The jet fighters came in from the darkening east. They produced a wide range of destruction, as pilots were able to use their night vision and infrared goggles to identify troop groups. The lit up areas produced quality targets for the light bombers who concentrated on vehicles and on troop concentrations in the almost swamp like conditions north east of Marco Island.

The soldiers moved forward and were able to find small groups of fighters and eliminate them. Back at Disney the ground forces battled what was left of the invasion troops who fought hard against the Dixie troops inflicting heavy damage on several hotels. A final stand occurred on an island in the lagoon at the centre of Port Orleans. Insurgents, not willing to be captured tried to hole up on the island but were discovered as the resort was cleared. The final gun battle left eighteen dead men in or around the pool complex at the center of the island. There was significant damage to the hotel complex and several dozen dead tourists. Disney was already moving parties who had booked that hotel away to other accommodations and making arrangements for repairs.

Hundreds of Disney patrons had escaped the violence as they ran from the occupation. However many more were dead or wounded in the explosions at the Contemporary Hotel or as the terrorists tried to impose their promise when the army and SWAT teams moved in.

When morning broke, the clean up began. At Marco Island however, there were far fewer dead than had been anticipated. Either the insurgents had melted into the night taking many of their dead and wounded with them, or there simply had not been very many of them to start with. Reports suggested many hundreds were killed but in the daylight only 73 bodies were recovered, none with identifiable markings. At Disney there were only 22 insurgents accounted for - while CCTV cameras and other reports suggested there were several hundred armed men in control of the resort at the final stand.

It had taken nearly 24 hours. And the repercussions would be felt for years.

Chapter Forty - Six   **California**

"Why not run for office my friend?"

"Because politicians have to say things they do not believe or even care about to satisfy voters, and because I am really just a one-issue person."

"When the time is right, when that one issue is all-important then it is time for the one issue man to facilitate change," said Ambassador Octavius. "Now is the time and you are the man. Aztlan is real. It always has been. Now it is real to a majority of people who live there."

"And what would you have me run for? I am very effective at greasing the wheel of change. One need not be elected to have political influence."

"My friend, think big. As a senator from southern California you would wield tremendous influence and be able to sponsor legislation, and make actual legal change."

Hellenga leaned back in his chair. Reached for his tea and took a slow sip before returning the cup to the saucer.

"Yes, the ability to bring legal change would be good. However, what about taking on a Congressional seat, much easier to get elected and it still has the ability to bring legislation?"

"It does, but the enormity of a senate seat cannot be overlooked," said Octavius. "And frankly, you are the only activist well known enough to win election."

"Where would I get the money? I'm apparently already a target, why should I invite trouble? Frankly the referendum will achieve our goal. We do not need political clout on the inside. After the referendum we are the inside."

"A referendum, when was this arranged? I have heard nothing about it," said Octavius.

"Just yesterday, it has been big news in California."

Octavius was thinking quickly, this curve was hard to process.

"My friend, it is your destiny to lead on this issue. Lead from within. Then there is no trouble in itself, but you are fighting for the cause of Aztlan. And I am helping to facilitate justice for members of our cultural family, strictly on my own time and for my own pleasure."

The artist took another lengthy sip of tea. He looked to the ceiling and chose his words carefully.

"I am an artist. It is true I have used my efforts to promote our cultural heritage in Southern California and it is equally true that I am desirous of a return of our voice in our affairs. However nothing can be accomplished by force no matter how determined, how powerful or how its directed if those being pushed are unwilling. Short of killing all opposition to the last man, woman and child, our desires must match the desires of a large majority to effect the change we seek. A referendum is the quickest way to that goal. I can run for office. I can continue my influential efforts outside of government. At this point I am not sure what is best for Aztlan. I don't know if anyone is or if that discussion has even been entertained as it has always seemed so far away. Should Aztlan be a separate State in the US? Should it be a province of Mexico? Should it be independent? There are advantages for each. It is this question I want to explore before I entertain any plan to legislate it."

"As you wish my friend. I believe you will eventually attempt election. It may be your voice that quells the thunder of violence as this change is made. It may be you who answers the questions you just posed. It may be you who answers the bell that our people are ringing?"

"Or not, Octavius, or not. I am not a person given to fights. I am merely someone who adds his weight to the mass of opinion and desire. I lean strongly for Aztlan to have its recognition. If enough people lean with me, then perhaps we can topple the existing structures of government."

"I favour independence," said Octavius. A new nation, a highly industrialized, world leading, new nation with ties to two strong cultures, but an independent mind."

"And at this point I am unsure," said Hellenga. "The weight of Mexico is strong. It's history is partly our history. The weight of the US is stronger. It's will is the wall we must scale. It may be a necessary step to become a State of the US on our own, to gain trust of residents first before embarking down the path of independence. The US would not allow a direct annexation by Mexico and I believe most Hispanics in Southern California would not want to kowtow to Mexico. There is a reason they left that country."

"Wise words my friend. Know this; I am here to help you help the cause of Aztlan, no matter how you decide to lend your effort. I can get you money should you need it for elections. You might consider an Hispanic media presence. I can get you money for that as well."

"As always your support has been wonderful Mr. Ambassador."

"Careful, for me Hellenga. In this I am a private citizen. I do not hide my support for Aztlan but I would prefer to be anonymous in the backroom of this endeavor. I like my job. I like its perks and I want to keep them."

"Have your investigations found any link to the attempt to kill me?"

"No, it is troubling. On the surface if seems only some unfortunate street violence. However, the mention of my name, and the obvious knowledge of your activities points to a political play but by whom and for what, I have not been able to uncover. It seems unlikely that the American CIA or some Mexican agents would target you so ineptly. Frankly, if it really were them, you would be dead."

"And if it was the CIA posing as street violence why would they so obviously tip off that they were not street violence by way of their knowledge of your affairs? If they wanted to scare you it seems a more direct and civilized approach would have a better effect."

"I have sold my studio in Mexico and now live and work exclusively in California. I have used the security detail you have generously provided. I am certainly a bit distressed that this cannot be explained."

Chapter Forty - Seven   Venezuela

Two cruise missiles dove down from the sky as they approached the northern coastline. They were flying at mach two as they homed in on their targets.

The tracking software adjusted their courses to pass by the sheltering islands and move up the inlet. They passed over the headlands where the inlet narrowed and flew the remaining five kilometers low over land slamming into the Petroquimico Santa Anna Campus across the water from Maracaibo, Venezuela.

The two concussive charges destroyed the refinery's separation towers, tore apart office buildings, industrial refining facilities and set hundreds of thousands of barrels of oil and oil by-products on fire. The initial explosions did much of the damage but ongoing explosions, as fire worked its way around the facility, accounted for a huge amount of additional destruction.

There was no official reaction. The local press treated it as an industrial accident. The foreign press followed suit. They remained open to the possibility of terrorism but no evidence was ever presented and the Venezuelan government did not point fingers publically even after their investigation.

Venezuelan officials looked closely at the evidence.

"We have security footage of two cruise missiles, though they do not have markings."

"Americans? What ships were in the vicinity?"

"There were several warships in the area, say within 500 miles, the range of most of these missiles."

"It could have been a number of different countries involved. Perhaps one of them delivered the missiles by proxy."

"It has to be the Americans. By not identifying or making any public statements they are giving us the option to avoid retaliation and any escalation. It is obvious they know about our involvement with the raiding parties in California, Texas and now Florida. They are being quite aggressive."

"So were we. We can avoid all out war if we choose, and that appears to be the best option. However, we do not have to curtail our activities, just know that now we will face retaliation and this from a country that has used nuclear weapons when it sees fit."

"Have we not succeeded in our goals? Our raids have destabilized the Americans, they are far more worried about making peace with each other than with engaging in our affairs."

"I agree Miguel, we do not want them to join forces against us. We took our actions in separate places to give them a sense that not all is well among their own borders. Now Dixie does not trust the Cubans, Texas does not trust the Mexicans and California doesn't trust its own southern population. Our goals have been met."

"We still have agitators in these places. I believe they should still stir up resentment and mistrust."

An aide knocked urgently on the closed door.

"Come."

"Sir, we have just received word from our assets in Mexico that two northern governors of Coahuila and Sonora have been deposed by Mexico City and arrested."

"We need to get them out."

"Yes, we will. Mexican justice is notoriously porous. We will have them handled before sunset tomorrow. We do not want them talking. Our agents know what to do."

"Tell our agents in Oklahoma, Texas, California and Florida to lay low for a while. They will receive further instructions in several weeks."

The aide nodded and left.

"We cannot afford to go all in against the US or its chipped off bits and pieces. We have to continue our policy of sowing mistrust so they can never again be as strong as they have been."

The two men agreed to meet for an update at noon the next day. They returned to the same unassuming office building.

"I have news. We have the former governor of Sonora. He is on his way to Caracas. Our agents were able to hijack the car that was taking him to a secure facility. It appears as if the Mexican authorities did not even question him. Unfortunately the governor of Coahuila was shot and killed trying to escape. There was a gun battle and he was hit in the crossfire."

"Our agents?"

"They escaped and are short only ammunition. That poor devil, he was trying to carve out a little fiefdom in the North."

"Has Mexico City approached anyone in the diplomatic community?"

The Mexican ambassador to Dixie has been closeted with Vernon Clemons for much of the last several days. He is likely trying to convince Clemons that Mexico is not involved even if the arrests of two governors suggest otherwise."

"How long until our refinery is rebuilt?"

"Perhaps six months. We are able to transfer most of the refining capacity to other facilities. In fact, the destruction gives us a chance to upgrade the technology at Santa Anna, something we were needing to do anyway."

"We will set our assets in Florida and Oklahoma to work in a little while. They need to keep at the agitation without drawing too much attention. We want to create some additional inner turmoil. Perhaps we can spearhead a misinformation campaign to keep the Cubans and the Floridians apart and to keep the US great plains unhappy with their neighbours in Texas."

"Something along the lines of Hellenga's work in California?"

"Yes, like that but perhaps with a fresh approach. Hellenga is a US citizen and deeply committed to the Aztlan cause. If he knew who was behind his activities he would likely have a stroke. His abilities and our needs met up perfectly. We have to find the right approach to keeping Texas busy with Mexico and South Florida busy with Cuba. Octavius is likely to have figured some of this out - he is likely a lost asset for us, though he may encourage Hellenga to keep up his pressure in California."

Chapter Forty - Eight   Toronto

"Bloody construction . . . . "

"Yeah, this one's been there for three days now. Must be some trouble with pipes deep down."

The two men were sitting in a car on Bloor Street in uptown Toronto. A portable metal fence was woven with orange fabric and set up in the curb lane on the south side of the street about 75 meters west of Avenue Road. Cars waited to snake around the obstruction with nary a construction worker in sight.

"You think they'd actually be working on it at least. This is a killer spot for traffic."

As the car rolled slowly past the three meter square enclosure there was nothing to see save a hole in the pavement and the top of a ladder descending into the depths.

At the bottom of the pit two men toiled in the city services conduit. The first struck something solid.

"It's not a rock, there it is," he said to his partner. Sinking the pick deep into the dirt just above the spot he'd already struck something hard.

Sure enough, he struck something hard again and pulled the dirt away. Now a flat facing surface was revealed. They both began clearing the dirt away.

"Just like he told us it would be."

The two men cleared more dirt revealing a corner of concrete. They wired it with dynamite. The sound of a series of small explosions floated up to the street through the hole but was swept away and lost among the traffic noise. Returning to the bottom of the hole they quickly cleared the way.

"We must move quickly, no telling who heard what and when they will come to investigate. The smaller of the two men slipped into the new hole in the wall and dropped down onto a table in a large storage room full of racks of shelves spaced in neat, efficient rows.

"Ahmed, you know where to look."

Ahmed, immediately felt the cool air in this temperature controlled store room of the Royal Ontario Museum. He smiled broadly. He moved into the shelving units and quickly found the one labelled Assyrian Artifacts. He moved down the row looking for a particular number - and thanked Allah that the kaffir were so meticulous. He found the correct box number, grabbed the carton and moved quickly to the table where he handed the box through the hole. His partner took it and quickly scrambled up the ladder.

There was no indication their intrusion had been noticed. No alarm was sounding. Nobody was pounding on the door. However, Ahmed knew his partner was only fulfilling his job, moving the carton away as quickly as possible. He was supposed to stay and fix the hole in the concrete as well as possible and use dirt stored in a small dump truck, two blocks away to hold everything in place. He crawled through the hole back into the service conduit, put a few sheets of plywood up against the hole, braced it with some heavy stones they had kept in the hole for this job, and shoveled some dirt up against it. Without more dirt to cover the breach temperature controls in the room would give away their entry.

His quick fix completed, he climbed out of the hole and moved off to get the dump truck. Upon returning he tipped the ladder in so it did not reach the rim, and started to dump dirt, stones and other refuse down the hole. Upon refilling it he left the warning fence up to make it look as if a paving crew would return to finish the job. He gave a friendly wave to a motorist who offered to let him edge into the left lane and he was gone.

Ahmed dropped the truck off in another construction zone a mile or so away, and made his way to the safe house near College and Brunswick.

He arrived on foot, having taken a very winding route to the house, walking past it three times as those in the house watched to see if he was being followed. A quick text and he moved up the path and into the front door. Once inside he saw a large man holding a slender stick about half a meter in length. At his feet was the carton, opened with its contents spread around.

"I've got to take pictures of it and send them to Jerusalem. I leave with it tomorrow to take it to them in person. They should respond in a few hours to authenticate it. If it isn't the right one we have to go back."

"It's the last piece of the star. I have studied it for 10 years. This is the right piece."

"I cannot believe it wasn't more closely guarded. Surely they've figured out what we are trying to assemble. Our other acquisitions have not been so subtle."

"The infidels do not believe in the power of Allah. They do not understand the power of this thing. Soon they will see it for themselves."

On the other side of town another group of men were meeting.

"They got it eh?"

"Yep. Now we just have to put out a little news item about a missing item at the museum, downplaying the theft, suggesting it's art collectors. Overnight we should fix the road. Let's put up a serious security show on most flights tomorrow."

"The piece is leaving via Montreal?"

"Yeah apparently, but we will track him as they drive to Montreal and then fly from there to Cairo, then Cairo to Jerusalem."

"Let's hope they don't cotton on to the fake."

"Why did we fake it? Why not just secure it or even destroy it?"

"Brass thinks it's a great way to keep them occupied. Tracking it we can track their networks and expose them. And, if they go for it we can reveal the fake and pull their faith right out from underneath them at an appropriate time. Plus we are studying the thing. We have photos, as these things are catalogued very specifically."

"What's the inscription say?"

"The one they have contains a call to spread Islam to all people while promising jihadis the inner knowledge of Allah. Thing is, it is Assyrian, or about 1,000 years older than Islam. I'm not sure why Al-Islami thinks its Islamic in nature."

"Maybe they know something we don't."

"We'll that's always a possibility but I'm inclined to think they constantly underestimate us. Slow to anger and all that. I used to wonder why our special forces didn't undertake more operations against them. Then I realized it's because they don't want to teach them anything. That's why everything is done high tech and with subtlety."

Al-Jeru took the artifact with him and escaped Canada as planned. He arrived in Jerusalem and sauntered to customs - after all he was an Israeli citizen. He was visibly nervous and triggered an extended baggage search and questioning. He told border security that the artifact was an old family memento that he was bringing back home. Officials let him pass.

The artifact was quickly handed over to a prearranged contact in Cairo and was making its way to Jerusalem over land. Soon, thought Al-Jeru, all five pieces would be united and the message revealed. He took great pleasure in his part in this affair.

When he arrived at the house he saw the five pointed star assembled from the pieces collected from the Ashmolean, Swiss National, Cairo and a small museum in Italy. The piece arriving from Canada completed the star and revealed the complete message.

Reading along the top of the point from the right side of the star the message read in Assyrian hieroglyphs . . . . "The truth and power of god's law," then down and to the right, "Will be brought to all men," and then up to the top of the star, "And applied to them equally," and down to the left, " And those who struggle with god's will," and back up to the right point, "Shall be blessed with god's knowledge."

The light flickered. They all looked at it and their eyes widened.

"How do we use its power?"

"That is unknown. Triggering it. Aiming it. Controlling it. We must learn its uses. There is no rule book or product manual."

"The truth and power of god's law, will be brought to all men," said one of the men in the room.

And applied to them equally," said another. "And those who struggle with god's will, Shall be blessed with god's knowledge."

The light went out, and them flicked back on. A power disruption. In the distance a roll of thunder thumped against the sky.

"Perhaps we should be more careful with this. Perhaps we should take it apart . . . for safety. Let Al-Islami discover its secrets. He was the one who bid us to fetch it piece by piece."

Two men sat in a control room.

"Well that went well, now we have to wait for Islami and then do it again."

"Fricken parlour tricks. Next thing you know we're going to have to learn card tricks or how to saw a lady in half."

"At least we aren't trying to stone her."

"Look, I thought we were supposed to be putting a wall around Islam to let it feed upon itself. We should just ban people from certain countries from ours and forget about them. If they want Islam they can have it, they just can't export it anymore."

"I'm thinking that's the idea. But we have to give them something to fix-ate on, or they will never stay behind the wall making their plots. They are supposed to be laying low for at least 10 years. I think we'd like to see a couple of generations at least."

"Is there any other writing on the star?"

"Yes, the same message is written on all the faces of the rectangular piec-es. We have people trying to interpret it with other starting points. They are even reading it backwards."

"What does the actual piece say that we still have?"

"The big boys didn't pass that on. I'm guessing if they thought it was im-portant they would have made plans to capture the whole thing. A little 'power of God' can go a long way in a pinch," he laughed.

Chapter Forty - Nine   **Buffalo**

"Go talk to Charlie Edwards and make sure in the end it's his idea, even if it never was and you have to do all the work."

"I know Charlie can be a bit difficult. It seems like he takes the Canadians' side when talking to the State Department, the US side when talking to the Canadians and his own side when talking to anyone else," she said.

Jimmy Bierieski laughed. "An excellent assessment my dear, I think the President chose well. Have you anything on the bridge proposal?"

"I was speaking to the local member of parliament and put it in his head that a separate commercial traffic depot, like a weigh station, some distance back of the border might help clear trucks for the crossing without letting them get all backed up on the bridges - Niagara is very busy, you know."

"Any ideas are good places to start discussions. Was he receptive?"

"Yes, I think he was. Within a mile of the bridges in Fort Erie and at Queenston there is a tremendous amount of undeveloped farmland on the Canadian side. If we helped pay for a combination customs inspection, truck stop and service center we could make the bridges much more efficient. Then we wouldn't be so worried about having to expand their capacity when there is very little space in which to do so."

"It would be nice to have that commercial activity on the US side - you know, more jobs for Buffalonians, and all that."

"Find the land Jimmy, find the land. Right now the Canadians appear to be open to the idea and of course they see the opportunities for development on all that empty land."

"Don't forget, the approaches to Queenston might seem empty but those berms hide large water reservoirs for the power plants. You have to get back a little further from the border, but you are right, there is land there too."

"Of course the Rainbow Bridge in Niagara Falls is just a write off for commercial vehicles," she said. "It's far too developed and in any case there isn't a big appetite for 18 wheelers swinging through the tourist areas."

"As long as its Charlie's idea it might work."

"I don't need the notch in my belt with the State Department. I just want to be able to get our steel across the border a bit easier. Unfortunately the shipping accesses are pretty small for our needs so road and rail make the most sense."

"I'm hearing that Albany isn't too happy with us upstate guys, as we have been carving out some good commercial connections in Canada and with the money guys in Chicago. Albany is tied pretty tight into the Washington, Baltimore, Philadelphia, and Boston matrix," Bierieski said.

"Those guys all think they are the Centre of the Universe in the New United States. They aren't interested in anything but their own dominance. Problem is the commercial interests in Chicago and the growing economic power of northern California and the northwest are pulling away from them. Seattle is practically a Canadian city. San Francisco and the Bay Area is essentially an independent country. We haven't been able to do much for them regarding their southern neighbours."

"Well that is something I'm not sure I have much influence in. Peter has some connections out there with the reclamation business, but San Francisco isn't as lucrative as was first thought. The locals have managed to make repairs in many more cases than we anticipated."

"What about Chicago?"

"The jihadis never did anything to it. Though you could argue it was destroyed by the Democrats long ago. I do have a few connections with money people there, or at least Peter does. What do you have in mind? Or should I be talking to the State Department?"

"Funny you should mention Chicago and State. The President asked me to ask you, outside of the knowledge of the State Department, if you could ask the bankers there to build stronger connections to San Francisco, mostly in the commercial loan areas - a satellite office of some of the larger lenders, etc. He's looking for easier credit terms - easier defacto terms, rather than forcing it through official channels. Frankly, he told me he's worried about a growing independence movement there. He's also worried that the Eastern boys are dominating too much without giving any consideration to the west coast. Findlay is strong but he is too regional and his winning with only half of the country on side is bad for the future of the Union. He's spoken to Findlay about it and Findlay is going to call for Eastern interests to help finance California problems."

"I can certainly do that. Peter has been doing it already."

"Obviously this is political, quietly done and not any of the business of the State Department. Charlie Edwards would about faint if he knew what we were doing."

"What does this have to do with Canada?"

"Right now, several Canadian banks are moving into the California void. It's not that we don't want them there, it's that we don't want them to become the major players - that might fuel the independence movements. We need eastern interests as the major players and champions of

California recovery. It's good politics."

"So you want me to encourage the Chicago commercial interests to move into California big time while I warn the Canadian banks that it isn't such a great idea and make it all seem like Charlie Edwards' idea even though he would not really like it? Is he involved in the western independence movement?"

"Ah, Amanda, so very perceptive of you. Charlie is a Stanford man. He moved east decades ago because Washington is there. He now appears to have leanings back toward California - and he doesn't like eastern political influence getting too strong in his old home."

"So who am I working for in this . . . ?"

"The President. He just won't acknowledge that. Remember, this is all commercial on the surface the political undertones are just happenstance. Work your Chicago commercial interests. Work your Canadian connections to have them back off California. Work Charlie to see the value of new investments. If this begins to look political you have to back off."

"So who is going to win the Oval Office?"

"It might not matter, many of our same challenges will still exist no matter who wins, they just take a bit of a different tilt. State finds you very valuable. The new President will be apprised of your position to be an asset. And I enjoy having lunch with you . . . and Peter when he has the time."

"He said he was going to try to get here for a drink after his meeting." She looked at her phone. "That's any time now. I think I'll have a cheese tray. Would you like some?"

"Yes, yes I would. Perhaps another glass of wine too. I have a few questions for Peter about the need for improved transit access to the steel plant."

"Sorry I can't help you with that. I think he is concerned about improvements to the Interstate access as well for overland shipments. There have been some improvements to the old Buffalo - Pittsburgh Highway but once the route approaches the southern tier the highway has not been modernized and the route is too slow unless we are taking product to destinations in the western half of the state but east of Pittsburgh. And that's a mighty small amount of steel."

"You appear to know a lot."

"Not so much. I don't know any details. You need Peter for that. Truck weights, road allowances, bridge heights, some routing in the southern tier - the devil is in the details, and Peter knows the details, so he knows where the perils lie."

"Can I tell the President you are on side with him?"

"Absolutely, anything I can do to help him get the country back on track is worthy of my time. I've just got to think a bit on how to keep Charlie Edwards at bay, or better yet, on side. I'm thinking the soft pedal approach with the Canadian banks is likely best. A bug in their ears at various cocktail receptions and the like. Only trouble is we won't know the effectiveness of that strategy for many months. In fact, I'm attending a reception in Toronto in a few days where there are sure to be some bankers. If I let slip a few well chosen words in the right ear, I might be able to get their attention. Ah, here is Peter."

Peter entered the restaurant and looked around for a familiar face. She waved to catch his attention. He told the wait staff he knew where his party was and with a nod, he was given the opportunity to walk through the room.

He sat down heavily. "Oh, my it's nice to finally sit down. It's been a busy day already and its only just past one."

"I was just mentioning to Jimmy some of your concerns about transit approaches to our waterfront operations."

"Yes, you must have received my letter detailing most of it. Let me catch my breath and change gears for a moment. I'm fresh out of a meeting on steel purification and reusing rubble for foundations. Complicated business, what with rebar, on site re-manufacture of stone products, it doesn't make commercial sense any other way, engineered stone can be wonderful but it's a bit tough to work with."

He ordered a small salad, a glass of wine and nodded happily when the cheese tray was presented. My starter and your dessert!" he laughed. He took a deep breath and a small bite of cheese.

"What plots were you two hatching? No don't tell me, it has everything to do with keeping Chuck Edwards happy and looking good."

Amanda smiled. That's about it. Apparently I am wanted to help smooth some commercial lending into California."

"That would be good. I've been trying to get that to happen for a while now."

"This time there are political consequences, rather than merely commercial ones. It should help you finance your operations a bit easier there."

"I like to know these things so I don't step on Amanda's toes. But generally I prefer to stay out of the partisan politics."

Chapter Fifty   **Germany**

The night was quiet. A few cars moved through the streets, mostly people going to work in bakeries and restaurants, people who had to be at it early, as they provided services for the army of people who trampled through their nine to five.

A couple of cars were parked alongside an ancient wall. A shuttle of people moved from a doorway in the wall to the cars and back, loading them with their tools of the trade.

Soon both cars were full and the drivers and passengers got in and they glided off into the darkness. They had heard the edict, lay low, remain in place, our time will come.

Europe was in the process of shedding unwanted migrants. The first, voluntary phase was complete and hundreds of thousands of migrants had been escorted back to Iran, Iraq, Turkey, Pakistan and Egypt. Most of those who went quietly took their $2000 Euro payment and left willingly, as they had not intended to stay even when they arrived. The second wave, those who left because Europe was no longer a welcoming place for migrants were steadily moving on.

There were still large banlieues in most European cities, areas where

Muslim influence had been strong and had been on-going for many years, sometimes generations. In some of these areas they had been harmless to their hosts but others had been a destination of choice for jihadists and revolutionaries seeking to advance the Islamist cause. They were often no-go zones for locals and even police.

Tonight's mission was not to kill or destroy in the name of Islam. Tonight's mission was to maim Islam. Underground groups had formed in many cities intent on using the jihadist tactics against the remaining Muslims.

Franz and Albert were in one car. The trunk was full of Molotov cocktails. They would target two mosques and a street of Muslim grocery store in the urban hinterland. The other car was similarly loaded and they had their targets in another direction. The two prongs of the assault would be co-ordinated to begin at the same time.

Having scoped out both mosque locations Franz and Albert had already decided upon their method of attack. They parked their car on a back street, moved toward the mosque from its rear with four gas-filled bottles each. They dropped their masks into place, threw a towel over two security cameras, scaled the wall and approached the mosque. They found a little copse they had previously seen, stuffed the bottles with rags, lit them and ran to the building - Albert going left and Franz going right.

Franz threw his first bottle against a window but it bounced off without breaking. He moved to another window and saw it was protected by a mesh screen. He pried the screen off, stuffed the bottle in and pushed it through. He heard the rush of incoming air as the bottle broke and the fire flared up inside.

He ran to another window and did the same thing. He then saw a covered doorway and threw the last of his bombs under the archway and ran quickly back to the car. He jumped in, removed his mask and Albert joined him moments later. He fought the desire to peel out, and expertly glided the car down a hill in neutral before engaging the engine and driving off. Within a minute they were gone from the neighbourhood.

"Shit, the windows were covered," said Albert. "I didn't see that when we came by last week."

"It's hard to see. Did you get anything inside?"

"Yeah, two. One of the others I tossed up on the roof and another exploded underneath the first window. You?"

"About the same. My first one was still burning when I left, hadn't exploded yet. Got two inside and hit a doorway with the last. Didn't think to toss it on the roof."

He swung the car down a dark and quiet commercial street, full of small groceries, bakeries and Halal pizzerias. He told Albert to get ready.

"Okay, I'm slowing down. Fire off all the Molotovs we have, let's set the whole block up. I'll double back for the other side and then we are out of here."

The car slowed and Albert tossed bottle after bottle through store windows, into storefront doors and up onto the roofs. Two blocks down Franz swung the car in a large half circle and they moved a bit quicker down the same street dealing destruction on the other side of the street.

"And now for the other mosque."

"I don't know. I think we are trying a bit too much, you can already hear the sirens."

"Yeah, but the mosque is five miles from here."

"The police might be assigned to guard it once they figure out its not random. And there aren't a lot of cars on the streets."

Franz thought for a moment, "Okay, you are right, better to fight for another day. Let the others know we are backing off."

"We still have a small box of cocktails left in the trunk. Too bad there is nowhere to use them. "

The pair drove back to where they started and removed the extra box of cocktails. They both showered to get the smell of gasoline off them and then they went for breakfast.

The sun had risen and the traffic was up as they moved to a restaurant a few blocks away. The radio news made mention of the fires last night across the city. They only mentioned one mosque specifically and also the arson attack in the commercial district.

Franz and Albert had their breakfast while watching the parking lot. Their companions were expected. A police car pulled into the lot and parked beside them. After a few minutes the policeman entered the restaurant. He spoke to the waitress and waited. Franz and the group were acutely aware of the policeman and tried to keep an eye on him without being too obvious about it. The policeman was handed two bags and he left the building got into his car and drove off.

"Just getting the boys at the station a bit of breakfast, I guess."

Franz and Albert finished up, paid their bill and started to leave. As they arrived at the car, a police car rolled up behind them, blocking their way.

Franz motioned Albert to get in while he looked at the policeman. The officer opened his door slowly, adjusted his cap and jacket and walked around his car.

"Son, I was here a short while ago and noticed that your car has a strong smell of gasoline."

"Yes, sir. It does. I have a small leak in my gas tank, I think. I rolled over some loose stones yesterday and noticed the smell myself this morning. I had a previous engagement for breakfast and am now on my way to the garage to have it repaired."

The officer stood motionless for a moment. "Fine, he said. Please get it taken care of - a large leak is very dangerous."

"Yes, sir."

The police car moved away and Franz eased out of the parking lot and went the opposite direction. He made for a car wash facility and put the car through the most thorough wash available. He even used the scrubber on the inside upholstery of the trunk area. A little soap and a fair bit of water, he figured it would dry if he left the trunk up once the car was out of sight.

Albert texted their companions to take the same precaution.

Theirs was the fifth such attack on Muslim areas in the last nine months. Muslims were complaining but those complaints fell on mostly deaf ears. Years of terrorist attacks had taken their toll of sympathy and the Muslim complaints sounded hollow.

Some families drifted away from the ghetto areas, determined to stay in their new found homeland but equally determined not to become victims by presenting a large target for hoodlums.

The attacks were officially decried but were never investigated too closely. The hit and miss nature of them left very little evidence and nobody from the public was volunteering any information of unusual movements or suspicious activity prior to the attacks.

Muslims without a history in the country heard the message and began to leave. Others liked their familiar surroundings and decided to keep their cultural affiliations quiet. The re-establishment of Christianity had provided a centering point on which to balance the culture. Several ancient symbolic festivals were renewed and caught on with vigour as cultural Germans, French, Dutch, and Italians were moved to declare their solidarity with one another through the ancient practices. Many towns adopted an official Passion Play at Easter as a spectacle of their affiliations.

Italy had its own problems, as the Maltese who had moved into the south after being forced from their own country had supplanted the Italians in many small and dying villages. The land bloomed as the Maltese used their skills on larger parcels of land than they were used to, even if it was suitable only for limited agriculture.

Believing the renewal a blessing, the Italians had welcomed the Maltese. However, there was a growing disquiet among Italians about the invasion though all were forced to admit it was positive even if it was quite jarring. Northern Italians hadn't taken much notice of the plight of their southern brothers dismissing them, as they had for years, as unproductive wastrels. The agricultural bounty wrought by the Maltese changed that thinking quickly.

Some Maltese had drifted back to their island and reclaimed property. While the Israelis welcomed them back they were very clear about their new sovereignty and made returnees very aware of how the country would function in the future. After the trauma of invasion, many Maltese were quite happy to wrest back some local control while giving up the security of the islands to a very determined Israel. After the initial invasion it was obvious that defence of their islands was not high on their list of skills. The Israelis were very firm in maintaining the agreements with returnees. They respected the contracts and enforced them, to the point of deportation of those in violation.

Despite being surrounded by destruction, ruined cities, smashed infrastructure and broken peoples; despite being hit with multiple nuclear strikes and losing half its area to nuclear pollution and half its population to nuclear attack, Israel was remarkably strong. The nuclear attacks had provided a buffer around its remaining settlement areas. The Muslim invasion and destruction of Malta and its population had provided the Israelis with a more defensible land base.

Muslim countries such as Jordan and Egypt had faired reasonably well in the cataclysm as they had been moderate and more concerned about the posturing of their Muslim neighbours than anything else. Saudi Arabia was no more. The Saudi royal family did not survive the destruction of their country and the influx of a new population from Central Asia.

Turkey still existed on paper but it was a land of local governments without any real central authority. Kurdistan had been born and remained as there was no one able to resist. In truth both the Iranians and the unofficial Turks liked the idea of a Kurdish buffer between them and were content to know that with all three of them there, no lone country was likely to dominate the others for generations.

Europe was rapidly changing, from an immigrant friendly zone to an immigrant no-go zone, from an open society of laws and liberal morals to a much more determinist society of specific moral codes, less moral ambiguity and laws that were propped up by the ancient moral codes.

Appeasement had been destroyed and the lesson learned for the second time in a century. The cataclysms that had occurred had set the terms of the apparent peace for many years.

Chapter Fifty - One   **Korea**

It happened the first time in 1952. Then it happened again.

Fifty divisions of Chinese troops crossed the Yalu River and invaded North Korea. In 1952 they had been saviours to the Communists who had had their victory over the south snatched by US troops fighting under a United Nations mandate. This time they were saviours to the citizens of the Hermit Kingdom, a secretive, paranoid society existing almost entirely outside the normal day to day of the 21st century.

It was simply easier to take over the country, install a Chinese - friendly government and pull North Korea into the mainstream than it was to continue to have constant border issues and a nuclear armed loose cannon attached like a lamprey to its north east coast.

The Chinese divisions crossed the river followed by a general call to North Korean military units to stand down and allow the liberators to restore order. A general curfew was ordered and a grocery shopping day declared two days later - assuming all fighting had ceased. It did very quickly. A few fanatical units, loyal to the Jong regime, fought anything that moved but within a few hours calm had fallen across the country fuelled by an anticipation of liberation. Two days later the grocery stores were full, food was plentiful and cheap and the coup was completed.

Quickly, the Chinese put together plans to get the country onto a sound social footing, reopening universities, announcing plans for several manufacturing plants, and reducing the size of the military by converting most of the soldiers into policemen or corps of engineers workers.

The UN presence in South Korea had been on high alert for several weeks when the anticipated order came to stand down and resume a normal posture. Officially, the UN was guarded about the Chinese invasion, decrying the aggression but in private they lauded the Chinese for taking charge of a potentially dangerous situation. The United States was careful to hold up its pledge to protect South Korea from invasion and to make reference to the Chinese action as provocative while warning about other areas of friction.

The Chinese were not done taking advantage of a weakened US. They announced plans for joint talks with the Taiwanese - talks they had apparently insisted upon. Diplomatically the US let them know that they would defend their Taiwanese allies. The Chinese knew that the US did not have the capacity to wage war on the scale necessary should the Chinese determine that an invasion was the right action. However, the Chinese were quite confident they could pull Taiwan back into the fold given time and diplomacy.

Their new form of government and its adherence to more open market conditions meant that the divisions and fears of the past had begun to recede from Taiwanese society. However, the determination of the island to be its own master had not.

The Chinese were pushing their dominance of the South China Sea in the face of significant diplomatic pressure. They had heavily mined many of the approaches to their string of sand island bases and while warning the international community, they actually hoped for an incident to relieve the tension.

They got one. A huge explosion ripped a large hole in the USS John S. McCain, a modern destroyer equipped with tomahawk missiles and several helicopter gunships, which had been sent to traverse the South China Sea to maintain freedom of navigation in ostensibly international waters.

The Chinese immediately radioed the ship to offer help. They had been sending a steady stream of warnings about sailing in Chinese waters and regarding the heavily defended nature of the sea lanes in the area.

The US issued its standard diplomatic warnings and determination to maintain international sailing rights according to international accords. The Chinese didn't even raise their level of military preparedness, in the wake of the incident, simply offering to tow the ship out of the area or into one of their ports as a guest of the Chinese until arrangements could be made for its reclamation from the area.

The US refused to send the McCain to a Chinese port, after which two Chinese warships shadowed the damaged hulk as the US Navy began emergency repairs on the open ocean. Those repairs were completed in a few weeks and the McCain limped away to a rendezvous with a Hawaiian dry dock.

The Chinese might have been pushing their sovereignty but the US was virtually helpless to fight back. All that remained was to refuse to officially acknowledge what was an established fact on the water - the South China Sea was rife with the Chinese Navy. None of the local players were pleased, but neither did they have the ability to make any real impact on the reality of it.

Certainly those in northern and western Philippine Islands like Luzon, Mindoro and Palawan were concerned as the Chinese were now virtually on their doorstep in the Spratly Islands and on several build up atolls sprinkled around the region. The Vietnamese were none too happy with developments other than the fact that their long standing local battles for fishing rights were now more understood around the region. They were very concerned about skirmishes on their long border with China where there was much open to interpretation. In many areas the Vietnamese - China border followed the meanderings of a river but with Vietnam holding both sides of the river within their jurisdiction making for a very porous and poorly defined area.

The international community saw the South China Sea standoff as a battle for Chinese hegemony and a claim on natural resources. The Chinese saw it the same way.

China continued its policy toward Tibet and other western areas - essentially a colonization approach, slowly integrating areas into the greater whole of China. It also continued to buy up land in Africa and South America for industrial agriculture and natural resource extraction. In some ways large tracts of these continents were essentially part of China as locals neither cared nor had the capacity to invoke their national jurisdiction but were content to hand over control for the cost of land or a rental payment.

As the United States writhed in its own existence and battled with its future and past, the Chinese simply got on with exerting their control where necessary and their influence where control was impossible or too costly.

They began to buy property and businesses in Hawai'i. Too often Chinese nationals ran into competing interests in these quests to gain a stronger foothold in Hawai'i. The Japanese had much the same idea. The two sides eyed each other and drove up prices as they competed to purchase key locations and profitable businesses. Hawaiians took their good fortune in stride, happy to make sales above market value to anyone who would pay. The Japanese were less thrilled with the new competition from China - for generations they had been moving slowly into Hawai'i and gaining influence.

Chapter Fifty - Two   Ankara

"So now we take it into battle."

"But how does it work?"

"Faith my brother. Even if we test it first, it will diminish its power as we will have shown doubt. Our faith must remain strong."

Alcoeur Al-Islami lifted the five pointed star and held it by two points tilting the top point as it to aim it. "We carry this, recite the words of Allah inscribed upon it and march to battle," he said. "With faith, we will be invincible."

A month later the insurgents were assembled. They had infiltrated the porous border of a crumbling Turkey to gather near Ankara. The demonic state of Turkey, on no one's side but their own, was all that stood between Al-Islami and a true Caliphate. A Caliphate stretching from Mecca and the sands of Arabia, through the Persian Gulf, to the Caspian Sea north of Teheran and deep into Afghanistan where local warlords had agreed to join Al-Islami in a loose coalition. Even much of Pakistan was listening to Al-Islami and watched to see if he could tumble the last piece of his Caliphate into place. Egypt and much of northern Africa was already converted to his influence, though pockets of local resistance remained, which Al-Islami expected to fade away with the establishment of the Caliphate.

"Imam, the battle groups have assembled as you asked. Half are hiding in the Odtu Ormani in the south of Ankara. Another quarter lay in wait in the Karakoy Ataturk Ormani in the north and the rest are in the city awaiting the call to arms."

"Let us go and join them. We bring the 'Faith of Allah' to battle. "

In Washington the President was apprised of the changing situation.

"Mr. President, we have noticed large numbers of insurgent fighters and weapons being moved into Turkey. Our reconnaissance suggests they are gathering in Ankara."

"General Stewart, what do we think is happening?"

"Mr. President, it appears that our plan to provide the jihadis with a 'Battle Star of Allah' has succeeded. According to our intelligence, the 'Battle Star' was forwarded to Al Coeur Al-Islami, the defacto leader of all Muslims in the aftermath of 5/29. He has called for the Caliphate to be completed by toppling what is left of the Turkish government. He plans to use the power of the 'Battle Star' to achieve his victory. Our agents say he is in route to Ankara now to meet jihadis who have gathered in secret in and near the city - primarily in National Forests and garden areas north and south of the city."

"Your recommendations on this General?"

"We are in a position to launch an air strike as two battle carriers are in the Med. We have long range capacity if necessary from the Gulf and Admiral McLeish can speak more specifically about that if necessary. Conferring with the other Joint Chiefs, however, we recommend standing pat."

"Why?"

"Mr. President, there is no United States' vital interest at play in this. Should the attack be repulsed, the Caliphate will have to wait. Should it succeed it will be announced, but nothing in particular will come of it as Al-Islami must rebuild his world and make the Caliphate something other than a wisp of history."

"Excellent. We will monitor this situation?"

"Absolutely Mr. President. We want to know what happens and maintain our intelligence on any growing or potential threats to us or our allies. I am convinced it will happen eventually, but with this move by Al-Islami it appears he is more concerned about his own power base than attacking us. We may not see any threat from the Middle East in a generation or more."

"Please ensure that satellites and some high flying drones are on hand to observe events in this battle. Inform our intelligence assets on the ground and have them report back when the heat dissipates. Please keep me informed of events as required."

"As always Mr. President."

O'Day left the Situation Room. He very much enjoyed the tension there, knowing the decisions made would have a huge impact on events a world away. While he considered those decisions closely after they had been made, he was content to take the Joint Chiefs words to heart, and accept their advice, along with the advice of the Security Chief and Secretary of Defence.

He felt it was his job to probe their thoughts, to open up discussion in areas that had been dismissed and to generally make sure every option had been considered and given proper weight. Once a decision had been made for action the form taken was virtually never anything other than what Stewart and the other Joint Chiefs had recommended.

Al-Islami's battle plan was simple. The chief danger in it use was the al-most complete lack of large scale battles engaged in by the jihadis under his command. They were much more used to hit and run attacks, small scale offensives and larger scale insurgent movements.

This battle would use both tactics while leaning heavily to the former style of attack. Insurgents had been informed about taking key government and institutional targets. Government buildings, banks, cultural institutions were all invaded by small groups of heavily armed men. They burst into buildings shot anyone who made any attempt to question them and secured their site to await further instructions.

In this way dozens of the most important sites in Ankara were in Al-Islamis hands by noon. Specially armed men descended on cultural sites and wired them before blowing them up, destroying most of the artifacts of modern Turkey. They commandeered the local radio and television stations and broadcast their control of key sites and their efforts to eradicate Turkey and turn Anatolia into a province of the Caliphate.

The Turkish Army had been focussed on its new frontiers with Russia and along its border areas with Azerbaijan and the new and unstable Kurdistan. In a panic they were summoned to the capital. In the afternoon of the first day of battle, Al-Islami gathered his forces in the south, hiding in the Odtu Ormani, and marched north into the city. As they approached the city center he held the 'Battle Star' forth and intoned its message.

"The truth and power of god's law will be brought to all men, and applied to them equally, and those who struggle with god's will, shall be blessed with god's knowledge."

People came out of their dwellings and into the streets as if pulled by a strong force. They came out to listen. Al-Islami entered the city and stood at the Mausoleum for Kerman Atturk and recited Allah's message from the Battle Star once more, television cameras trained on him. He asked everyone who could hear him to go to their local mosque and beg Allah for guidance in helping to establish for all time the Caliphate of Islam.

"There is no god except Allah, and Mohammed is his messenger."

Imams throughout Ankara were instructed in the glory of the revolution, the call of the Battle Star and how Al-Islami took the city without firing a shot on local military. There was no mention of the gun battles with security and the hundreds of civilian deaths visited on the local population by the shock troops who had laid in wait in various institutional locations the morning of his arrival.

"Remember Imam, glory is yours along with the Caliphate, and Al-Islami who is the Caliph, our new messenger of god. He brings the word of Allah and all fall at his feet."

Within two days all resistance was ended, more with a whimper than a shout. Those who would fight for Turkey simply saw the result, saw the movement to support Al-Islami and melted away in the night. They joined family members and otherwise disappeared into Turkish society, simply saying when asked that they had no capacity to battle the obvious Caliph and rejoiced at his arrival.

"The power of the 'Battle Star' is real, my imam."

"Yes, my brother," said Al-Islami. "It's power is subtle. I do have faith that if necessary it would engender fire and kill our enemies. It is what we need it to be. In Ankara it became the power of persuasion, of inevitability; the power of faith in Allah. It is our most powerful weapon and has further uses in uniting our people and building our new Islam."

In Washington President O'Day was briefed on events.

"Mr. President? Al-Islami entered the city holding the 'Battle Star' before him and took the city without a shot. Turkish resistance is collapsing and Islami has declared a Caliphate with Allah to appoint the Caliph by divine decree. Our agents tell us they are working hard to have Islami decreed by popular choice. There is no other potential leader, but they are working hard to establish the cult of personality around Islami," said General Stewart.

"The Joint Chiefs believe we should shoot up Al-Islami's headquarters in

Baghdad and in Ankara, using a significant air raid. If nothing else it will lead many to question the validity of Al-Islami and his divine claims. Leaving a seed of doubt among the populations will pay dividends later."

"General Stewart can we convene in the Situation Room in 10 minutes to discuss this?"

"Absolutely, Mr. President. I will inform the rest of the Joint Chiefs and your National Security Advisor."

The group gathered deep within the White House complex.

"Here is some drone footage of Al-Islami's march into the city. He commands a formidable ground force, but it is significantly light on armaments and heavy weapons. Note the large number of hand held rockets and hand held ground to air missile launchers. Here is the force coming from the north. They met in the city center and proceeded to the Mausoleum where Islami made his declaration. It appears as if the Mausoleum was off limits to the cultural strippers. It is the only significant landmark of the former regime that is still standing. Some pieces of museum displays are making their way out of the country as word got out pretty quickly in cultural circles that they needed to bug out."

The large screens displayed overhead shots of the invasion and switched to archival footage of museum pieces and displays alongside a map of the city showing the key locations.

"It is here and here," said General Stewart as two circles flashed on the screen, "where we believe Islami is headquartered. The one closest to the city center is an operations center and the other one is a residential area, where Islami is staying in the large home of a Turkish billionaire and industrialist."

"How would we attack?"

"We do not believe that there would be much resistance to a short, powerful air strike as they simply are not expecting it. We should go with

NATO markings - to spread the blame for the attack and because it is politically defensible given NATO's ties to the former regime. We are talking
about a single sortie with full engagement from both the Stennis and the
Ronald Reagan - about 175 fighters equipped with four rockets each."

"All that for a slap in the face raid?"

"Sir, we believe that we might get Islami. If we do the single generation of
peace we are likely to enjoy may stretch beyond two generations. The
Joint Chiefs believe it is worth a shot."

"And failure to get him?"

"Means very little. As a one shot deal it will almost be forgotten, save in
the minds of those who we need to be most uneasy about Islami's total
control of the new Caliphate. We can essentially seal them off from the
rest of the world. We can let them fight and kill each other."

"What if they emerge from this exile as a formidable foe?"

"We will monitor them Mr. President. And history has a way of bursting
out in unexpected ways. In either event we will know our enemy and continue our preparations for any threats we see in the short and long term."

"I suppose we have some rebuilding and healing to do as well. Let's do it."

Two nights later, wave after wave after wave of fighters came over Ankara and Baghdad. They unleashed their rocket payloads trained on their
targets and returned to their carriers. A single plane had crashed due to
malfunction rather than anti-aircraft artillery. The pilot managed to bail
out of the plane before it came down in a remote area south of Ankara. A
task force was quickly assembled to recover the wreckage to prevent any
reverse engineering by the Caliphate. No chances were being taken and
no enemy was to be taken lightly. The rescue and recovery mission was
almost as well equipped as the original raid.

Al-Islami had retreated from the city and watched the attack on Ankara
from a nearby aquatic sanctuary. He was unsure where the tip off on the

attack had come from, but it had come through a trusted source. Several on his immediate staff who were expendable had been killed, the billionaire's home destroyed.

He watched with an entirely blank mind as the explosions light up the sky. Allah would protect him. Allah would protect all who needed and deserved protection. These losses were inconsequential. He would go to the destroyed buildings tonight, to emerge from the wreckage of the central operations location tomorrow morning as an almost mythic figure - the embodiment of Allah on earth. This he knew.

Chapter Fifty - Three   Washington

Findlay strode back and forth across the carpet. When he first entered the Oval Office, years before, he was intimidated by the rug and the Great Seal of the President, he hated to walk on it. Now, with O'Day's presidency winding down he hardly noticed the design.

"I as much as promised Jim Grange the vice-presidency."

"He's a reasonable man. Ask him what he wants or better yet, ask him for advice on how to bring the west in. If he's honourable, he might suggest it himself and then you can gratefully extend to him whatever cabinet post he wants. It's for the good of the country. We have to tie the country back together or it may not survive. California is feeling very isolated. This Aztlan thing is very big."

"I heard the Texans are establishing border controls. Word is they will allow Oklahomans in with just driver's licences," said Findlay.

"Louisianan's too?"

"I'd expect that. Wonder how it will play with the Dixie guys?"

"Frankly we are exploring the same things in East Virginia. There is just too much back and forth to make requirements too difficult for people or commercial interests."

"We still have our problems. I understand Hawai'i is feeling the effects of a separatist movement. According to our intelligence it isn't very strong as anyone who thinks about it for a moment realizes an independent Hawai'i is a ripe target. Same with Alaska, though some of those guys are cozying up to Canada," said Findlay.

"They always have. I've always seen that one as Yukon getting cute with Alaska. The Alaskans like the attention. Let's face it they have more in common with each other than they do with their respective national governments."

"Arizona is going to continue to be a problem. The west is a whole bunch of problems, and our northern border is becoming more ephemeral. The bottom line is we are still the most powerful country on earth. We just have a few more partners - or seen another way, states-rights groups have won for the meantime. Who knows what the future will bring."

"It's a whole new world. Russia is fighting its own Muslim invasion. We seem to have subdued ours just in the nick of time, before it became an irreversible problem. Europe is cleaning up after a widely advertised party. China is fighting its own internal battles. We are no longer the world's policeman. More like the world's jail guard. You know it's been more than 75 years since the end of World War Two. Seventy-five years! When World War Two started Americans were the same amount of time distant from the Civil War."

"Time doesn't stand still. Everything is in flux, always has been, always will be. Will the United States of America have the same borders in a generation as it has today? Most assuredly not. But who knows what they will be and what conditions of history will create those new borders."

"We have to worry about today. I need you to work with Art Mansia - he can't win the primaries but he would be a good running mate."

"I'm not so sure if the mayor of Kansas City would bring California into the fold. I have a different idea. Assuming Jim Grange falls on his sword, what about Hellenga?" asked Findlay.

"The activist artist? Are you crazy?"

"Am I?"

"He's been an agitator out there for Aztlan. He's been the underground voice of the movement."

"And he's gone legit. He's become a bit of a statesman since he was shot. He's been driving the local county governments together. I'm sure he doesn't want southern California becoming another failed state. Especially after the two northern Mexico state governors were arrested for treason. Remember all the Mexicans in California left Mexico for a reason."

Findlay continued, "I'm thinking that Hellenga on the ticket, with a platform of bringing in Southern California as a 51st state, and Puerto Rico as a 52nd, could be a perfect way to pull the strings together."

"What are the chances that Hellenga would go establishment?"

"You know, I have fished around a bit. He's open to the idea. He fears the violence that annexation or independence might bring. He simply wants the way cleared for Hispanics to buy into the country and not always be on the outside looking in. With the right arrangements I think it can work. California is already a state - this just recognizes the reality on the ground and firms up our position which is getting weaker and weaker in the area. And with the rebuilding of Los Angeles, we have ready-made reasons for growth."

I have my doubts Tom that hiving off the problem part of California is going to lead to more unity," O'Day said.

"There is precedent. We divided Virginia from West Virginia because they had different interests and each wanted a louder voice which they couldn't have with competing interests in their own state."

"And Grange? Will he be happy in cabinet?"

"You know, I think he will. Especially with a little sugar on it and a choice of portfolio. In some ways, say, Secretary of State, is a more powerful position than Vice President, especially if the Vice is a person who is unelectable on his own."

"I have spoken to Hellenga," said Findlay. "Don't discount his abilities. He will appeal to the whole liberal blue state group - an artist with an agenda to help a minority group. That stuff plays big in New England and in some of the big cities."

"Have we done any polling on this?"

"That's the next step. And I need to talk with Grange - we need a face to face - I'll ask for his advice and desire should all options be open to him."

Three days later Findlay found himself in a Boston restaurant waiting for Jim Grange. As a candidate for the nomination Findlay was a well known person. If that wasn't enough the security personnel that travelled with him tipped off those nearby that someone important was on hand. Even the maitre'd seemed to know exactly what the conversation was going to be about. Or at least he thought so.

"Jim, so nice to see you."

"And you Tom. I was expecting this social call," he said with a hint of resignation.

"Oh it's more than a social call Jim. You know the conversation we had all those many months ago? I need you and your advice."

Grange immediately perked up. Findlay started in.

"Look, I'll lay it out. I offered you a shot as my running mate. It still stands. However, given the difficulties we are having out west, I was wondering what you think we might do to shore up support out there? And my offer has grown. For your council and support, I would be willing to offer you any cabinet spot you choose."

"How about two?"

Findlay paused only for a second. "What do you have in mind?"

"Well, played the right way the Vice job is tempting, a real spring board, especially in troubled times. Ambassadorships are nice but ultimately more for retirement minded people. Obviously State has to be in the conversation but Treasury is where the action is going to be in the next few years. I'm looking at both - holding both posts at the same time and obviously a fair bit of influence at the cabinet table."

"That's pretty much unprecedented."

"In modern times, yes, but these jobs were often handled two at a time in the early days of the republic. And truth be told, we are back in the early days of the new republic. It's a challenge, yes. But it's also an excellent fit for the way forward."

Findlay thought for a moment. "I think you are on to something. What about getting the west back into the fold? They seem to be peeling away."

"Well, there's the Vice job and that could go to someone in California, the northwest, or even Colorado - whatever you think will pull the most support. Barring some utter catastrophe you will win. People want stability and O'Day has done a solid job keeping things together, or letting them break apart peacefully, depending on who you talk to. You are seen as a big part of that. I think the retaliation attacks in Mexico and Venezuela went over particularly well with the public as they wanted to see us fight back and stand up. The June 7th stuff was unforeseen by anyone and actually helped galvanise public support for our efforts at re-establishment of our culture."

"Okay Jim, they are yours," said Findlay. "However, I'm going to need significant public support from you and I'll need you to get your electoral troops together. We have considerable work to do lining everything up. Even though I do believe the Presidency is mine to lose - I have no intention of losing it and every intention of doing the right thing for the country. I will need you to draw up say eight to 10 policy points for the campaign. We are likely to focus on only three or four, but good ideas won't be dismissed and might even make their way into the main thrust of the campaign."

"What are you going to run on?"

"At this point nothing is carved in stone. I have other people drafting up their wish lists. I believe we need to re-establish our industrial base and that likely means some form of tariff protection, either monetary or ethical, such as no products can be imported where certain standards of labour and environment have not been met. Yeah, difficult I know, but something must be done. Also I am interested in financial reform, likely through a financial system that cannot be easily manipulated by anyone, that means government too."

"That's the federal reserve system and that's what we have to eliminate," said Grange.

"Or fix, though how to do that isn't immediately obvious. If you have specific ideas on this pass them on. We need to keep any and all manipulations out of the marketplace - stronger investing rules, stronger rules on capital formation and retention and a stronger approach to enforcement. Seems to me when existing rules are stretched or broken there is never any consequence - a little jail time for some very rich men might have the desired effect."

"I will give those thoughts some attention and get back to you in a week or so. The nomination will be wrapped up in short order and we will head to convention and then into the general election. In addition I will try to come up with a few names for Veep."

"Great. So how are the Red Sox doing? They started off great but faded -

a few injuries seemed to be their downfall."

"It wasn't injuries Tom, it was defections. A few big players figured they were done for at the first sign of trouble and they asked for trades. That just ripped the clubhouse all to hell. Nobody felt they could trust anyone and all the problems on the field translated into a lack of trust in each other and the future of the club. The mix of veterans and up-and-comers this year was great, but they threw it all away. At least for this year."

The two men chatted amiably about their non-political lives. Grange had a summer place in north western Maine where he liked to go - the fishing was top notch. Findlay was a baseball fan quietly favoring the Orioles but publically waffling between the Pirates and the Phillies. Truth was he preferred the American League. Even his own staff hadn't noticed that he mostly attended Pittsburgh and Philadelphia games during inter-league play.

Chapter Fifty - Four   Switzerland

"It's not possible it is?"

"No. Remember your history. Even Charles Martel was only able to push the Muslims out of France. They stayed in Spain for 400 years. We are able to hold them at bay here and there, sometimes for many generations, but we haven't the stomach for genocide."

"Even if we did, there's more than a billion of them and they are everywhere. What we need to do is convert the fundamentalists into finger pointers rather than have them as righteous warriors. The fundamentalist Christians in the United States are like that - and mainstream Americans worry what would happen if they got power or the balance tipped so that the fundamentalists thought they could force their hand."

Edward Spenser and Franz Bergenheiler shared a table in a Zurich restaurant. Spenser was again making product shipping arrangements. Insurance and security premiums remained high but several months had passed since the last major terror incident.

"So it's fundamentalism of any sort that is our enemy?"

"It appears so. Look at your Nazi Party, they were ethnic, cultural and ideological fundamentalists - we call them fascists for lack of a better term, but they certainly took society in a direction which ultimately proved destructive."

"A painful time for us. So much of the time even today, it appears that attitudes toward society and government are cultural and that encouraging the basic cultural norms to continue is the safest way to proceed."

"I think that perhaps Burke had it right. Our cultural norms are always in flux, it's the nature of human progress. However they need to evolve, to change slowly, rather than change or move in large increments. The culture has to pull along the institutions rather than the institutions leading the culture."

"The fundamentalists want to pull everyone along in their wake, and the majority are not ready or do not subscribe to the fundamentalist approach. It appears that moderate everything is the best approach, and that slowly, everything evolves very slowly to reset the field and redefine what is moderate."

"So how do we defeat Islam? Islam doesn't have that same belief in cultural evolution. It believes in violently assimilating anyone in its path."

"So we have to be equally determined to keep that approach out. Violent assimilation is not an option. We are a nation of free willed people. They can change but they cannot be forced to change. We have to be equally determined to oppose fundamentalism - on its own terms, with extreme prejudice. We did not defeat Nazi fascism by brushing it off, keeping it from our shores and tut-tuting it. We destroyed it utterly. I'm not sure we have the cultural stomach to do it again - though our approach to 5/29 and June 7 showed we can get roused if necessary."

"The Americans have much of this figured out. The problem is so many of them don't want to believe it was figured out 250 years ago by their own countrymen who set up their Republic. They want to be heroes today and come up with a wonderful solution. The US Navy was virtually created to fight Muslim pirates. This isn't going to go away, it can only be held back."

"Problem is, we allowed it to get so strong. By treating it as a civil disobedience rather than a war we gave them the feeling that they are more successful than they really are."

The waiter came to their table after Bergenheiler caught his attention with a little wave. "Can we both have a shot of Scotch, please?"

"I have only recently taken to Scotch, what's your recommendation?"

"Aye, laddie, a little Lagavulin is perfect. It's rough going down but oh, so satisfying. What's the occasion?"

"It appears that our gambit to re-establish Christianity has paid off. Islam has moved on or gone underground and Christianity has enjoyed a bit of a renaissance. Churches are being used again and Christian denominations are proliferating - some might even say coalescing around a newfound approach - the personal exploration, led by churchmen through services. It's actually quite remarkable. A bit of freshness has blown through Christendom. I wonder how long it will last before the fundamentalists knock it down or take it over?"

"There were go again. It's the fundamentalists that bugger everything up."

"Not true old friend," said Spenser. "The fundamentalist whiskey makers are true to their art. This dram is perfect. I think it goes well with the mountains."

"And a touch of celebration. So far the Islamists are at bay. Intelligence chatter suggests they have gone silent. Perhaps we've stopped them for a generation or two."

"Yes, perhaps but the damage they wrought will be difficult to correct for decades. It can only be hoped that the damage imprinted on European brains and we will avoid this kind of stealth invasion in the future."

"You know, sadly, I think the Islamists have some of it right, some of our cultural excesses were and are very damaging to our society," said

Bergenheiler. "There are few children being born. We have become culturally and morally relativist. Personal responsibility seems to have faded. Perhaps that is why the Muslims were able to have the success they did. Long term success of our culture requires us to look at ourselves like the fundamentalists did and try to correct the worst excesses of our libertine approach - marriage and family issues are at the forefront. Financial irresponsibility next. Remember Plato said that given time people would turn liberty to do what they want and feel into a license to do all sorts of social wrongs, attacking things that have been established through perhaps thousands of years of cultural heritage. My own father was not a churchman as he did not like the excesses of the church, however, he saw the social and cultural value in the Ten Commandments and the thousands of years of experience that they represented."

"Unfortunately the success of Islam has provided them with a similar belief in the primacy of the Koran. How does one differentiate?" asked Spencer.

"It's the violence. To violently impose is the wrong approach. Certainly believers can expel anyone who does not subscribe, but they can only expel within their jurisdiction - and that does not include territory for a religion, as religion is supposed to be an ideal not a place."

"How does one build that ideal into the culture? For it to work in the long term it has to be sacrosanct, above debate and a universally accepted truth. In the end, it's all about the Golden Rule - do unto others as you would have them do unto you."

"That's the question isn't it? How to get it into the culture? And why does Speyside Scotch taste so much better than the rest?" He shrugged and took a small sip. He settled back in his chair and let a smile slowly crease his face.

There was silence between the two men for a few minutes.

"Are the night raids any better now in Germany?"

"They are in France I know. The French were pretty quick to turn and clamped down fast. It's one thing to retaliate, another to take pleasure in it. In Germany we are less likely to take the authoritarian approach. That has left the door open to some shadowy groups. Fortunately for today the Muslims seem more concerned about keeping their cultural alive in Germany even if it is mostly underground. Keeps the violence down. Unfortunately that could be an issue in the future as it appears Islam isn't knocked back as far in Germany as it is in France and the Netherlands."

"What about the Nordic countries?"

"Only Sweden let things get out of hand. They face significant changes and adjustments in Malmo in particular to get things back on track. The good news is they have finally recognized that their Swedishness is valuable and worth preserving. For a while there they didn't seem to see that. Even they got tired of tolerating the intolerable."

"It's going to take time to see how the remaining Muslims move forward with their lives. Already our cultural lack of interest in Muslim countries is having an effect. Except for a few tankers at a few ports we have almost no contact with Muslim countries and some of them barely exist anymore. Saudi Arabia has just become Arabia. Syria seems to be broken up with some of the cities governing themselves and forming little alliances. I guess they are part of the caliphate now, even if they do not publically acknowledge it. Northern Iraq is under the control of the Kurdish people who appear smart enough to hold the territory and bide their time rather than declare a cultural victory and draw the wrath of their former masters. Iraq and Iran barely exist anymore in the way we think of countries as the various Islamic denominations fight for territorial control only after they manage to survive. The former Gulf States are holding the barbarians at their Gates - as they are the only prosperous Muslims left."

"Our actions are only going to fuel resentment."

"Yes, but I'd rather have a cultural resentment without the means to do anything about it, rather than cultural resentment with a fundamentalist streak of righteousness. Remember, we set up many of these divisions after World War One. That fuelled much of the trouble. Fundamentalism is a problem which has always come back - and as I said at the start - genocide isn't really an option. We have to keep them at bay, and hope that eventually they will alter their viewpoint. Though with the Koran trumpeting the need for violence it's hard to knock them off their approach," said Bergenheiler.

Chapter Fifty - Five   **Cincinnati**

He realized it was a shot only after Hellenga fell.

The campaign was nearing its end. The Findlay - Hellenga ticket was popular. Campaign events drew large numbers. The Democratic challenger, a former governor of Minnesota, Ethan Grass, was presiding over a party that was breaking up.

Both major political parties in the US had undergone revolutions in the years since the May 29th attacks. The Republicans had adjusted the best, adopting a strict constitutional approach which squared with public feeling on how best to rescue the republic. The Democrats were split between those who wanted an end to federalist government by handing almost all powers over to the States, and those who wanted to carry on with the libertine social and financial experiments that had failed so thoroughly.

Grange sat in his study in his home in Boston. He had been at the rally, preferring to blend in with the crowd to hear the banter between those at the grassroots level rather than hear the political pundits and pollsters and opinion makers try to tell him what was happening.

It was something he had made a career of, understanding the street, the regular guys, his constituents first and not the special interest groups or the lobbyists. His position inside the Findlay campaign but virtually unknown to most of the voting public afforded him the luxury of being in the crowd without attracting attention, especially in those events outside Massachusetts. He was recognized in a Rhode Island rally and had a wonderful conversation with a few interested Democrats who had wandered into the rally out of curiosity.

Two days before, he had attended a rally in Dearborn, Michigan. He had stood with the crowd during Findlay's stump speech so he could watch people's reactions - he had heard the speech dozens of times, often more than once a day.

As Findlay spoke, there appeared to be some disgruntled people in the crowd, who took exception to Findlay's call for economic sacrifice to help rebuild New York and Los Angeles. It wasn't a call to transfer funds, or for more taxation, it was simply a call for economic opportunity in those areas to help strengthen the country.

Hellenga had reluctantly accepted the proposal to run alongside Tom Findlay, after Findlay explained his future support for a new State of Southern California. The artist-activist was standing behind Findlay, with a few local dignitaries, mostly the mayors of suburban Detroit and some nearby small towns.

In the middle of Findlay's explanation of economic stimulus to help fuel the rebuilding, Hellenga put his hand to his chest and fell down. In the commotion the shots, and there were two in rapid succession, were heard only in the memories of the incident after Hellenga fell.

Sitting in his study, Grange wondered if that effect was due to the differences in the speed of light and of sound, based on where he had been standing. It was then that he realized he didn't know where the shooter had been. Findlay had stuttered momentarily and then continued for a few more words before the confusion behind him, and the growing belief it had been a shooting, brought out security who surrounded him and whisked him off to a safe spot before transporting him from the venue.

Hellenga lay on his side in a growing pool of blood. His eyes staring up at the circle of onlookers. He said, "I only wanted fairness and a peaceful voice for my countrymen. A peaceful voice . . ." and then he said no more.

In the commotion the gunman was missed. Several people on the stage pointed to the rafters of the old theater where the lights were located as the source of the shot. The bright klieg lights made it impossible to see anything on the catwalk in any detail. The shooter left his gun and a pouch with several unused rounds. He or she apparently fled by a route well known to him or her, and encountered no security personal who had been delayed by the nature of the shots.

Officials soon wondered if the shooter had actually escaped or merely blended in with the crowd after the shooting. All exit doors were well covered by security personnel and nobody had attempted to leave in the immediate aftermath of the shooting.

Investigators swarmed the building and refused to let anyone leave until they had been spoken to and had had their hands and arms tested for gun residue. People slowly trickled out of the theater. Nobody was found with any residue though some were detained for lengthier questioning after the initial round. Most of those had admitted to being in the bathrooms at the fatal moment.

Hellenga was dead, thought Grange. Now what? Findlay had already solicited his advice on what to do. Grange had deferred to have some time to think. He couldn't get past the obvious approach to offer his services as Findlay's running mate which is why he kept thinking about the speed of sound and light, and the dying words of the artist, who he had come to admire during the short campaign.

He thought the best approach for the last few days of the campaign would be to announce that Findlay would name the likely replacement for Hellenga after the election, as if Hellenga had died after Election Day. There were legal questions and a tacit understanding that even if a new running mate was announced that ballots would not be altered in time.

He did not want the Vice-Presidency, he had already made that clear. Time was required to find the best person. The issue should be treated as if the Vice President had died in office and a replacement was required, which meant the Senate was required to agree with the choice.

And while it seemed obvious that the shots were meant for Findlay, how could a shooter with a high powered rifle miss from that distance. Hellenga was immediately behind Findlay, but a shot from the rafters that hit Hellenga was actually far off line if Findlay had been the true target. Who exactly would want to kill Hellenga? Grange could not conceive of anybody who would want him dead. He had played a central role in the Aztlan movement and had agreed to run for office as a conciliation to bring Southern California's Hispanic heritage to the forefront, as a supporter of a new State of Southern California within the US. he had come to believe it a better solution than annexation by Mexico or complete independence.

As American companies moved into Northern Mexico at a greater rate prosperity had followed and the north had become much more integrated into American concerns.

Grange wasn't entirely sure if the north of Mexico might not eventually leave their southern brothers and separate into a new nation. Mexico had its own problems that an independent Southern California would only encourage.

As Grange and Findlay and the Republican brain trust tried to figure out what to do, Hellenga's killer was in Madrid. He stood a short distance from Octavius as King Felipe VI draped a medal over his head.

"For services to the state, I award you with the Real y Distinguida Orden

Española de Carlos III (Royal and Distinguished Spanish Order of Charles III) and a yearly pension of 10,000 pesos."

Octavius and his body guard left the reception hall. "A difficult thing my friend and yet a mighty blow for Spain."

"Sir, despite my training and years of skilled marksmanship I would not want to do that again. The margin for error was so small. I had only a very narrow path through the crowd of people on the stage. It was a miracle that everything went according to plan. If anyone had moved it might have gone much differently. Dignitaries were whisked out of the arena very quickly and nobody even suspected."

"But it did not go differently, my friend. And now, Hellenga has placed his life as a martyr in the service of Spain as the faith in Aztlan grows and the strength of the Americans wanes. Their attack on Maracaibo's oil refineries was simply the most recent in a long list of attacks and provocations against our brothers. Weakening them is necessary."

"What is next Ambassador?"

"I have much work to do in Dixie and in Texas. I must work to pry those new countries away from Washington. It is not a short term task, in fact it will never end. But sowing the seeds of discord and distrust will keep the Americans off our backs in Latin and South America."

"In fact I travel to Atlanta next week, to offer the Mayor there some advice and intelligence regarding her city. Atlanta is the defacto capitol city of Dixie and she must consider strongly if that is what she wants for the long term, because it is possible now to have an influence on where that capitol should be."

"You my friend, stay here, rest and take a holiday. I have it from the King that you will be reassigned, a promotion into the intelligence apparatus - I expect as a top level agent with some administrative duties. I urge you to take the new job and grow in your knowledge in the service of Spain."

Octavius flew to Mexico City where he met with President Carrerra.

"It is too bad about Hellenga. He was one of my favorite people. I first met him at an art show in California."

"Yes, but his death greatly weakens the United States position in southern California," said Carrerra. "I still do not entirely understand why he accepted the place on the ticket with Findlay. I'm guessing he had some other people who took his political endeavours as a sell out and had him killed."

"It was not widely known but he had been attacked before and shot. He identified the shooters as New York types who, from his description, did not appear too professional. They were never found nor any motive ever really understood. Hellenga thought it was Americans opposed to his support of Aztlan. It might just as well have been a robbery gone wrong with no political overtones."

Carrerra leaned back in his big, ornate leather chair, situated behind a large dark oak desk. "Yes, Mr. Ambassador I was aware of the shooting of Hellenga, and of his pro-Mexican leanings, especially when it came to California. In fact I took great pains to make the US Ambassador and Texas officials understand that Hellenga was a US citizen and used his studio in Mexico as a holiday home. He had no sanctioning from the government of Mexico or me. They were not convinced as apparently their investigations showed some degree of sophistication beyond that of an activist, even a very well financed activist. His connections in California were investigated as well to try to put the picture of his influence together."

"He was close to the Cartenga family, who own the large demolition and construction company in Los Angeles."

"Yes. But who financed his activities in California?"

"It could have been any number of people or national players," said Octavius. "Even me. Though I am more inclined to believe it was the Venezuelans. The attack on the oil refinery suggests the American's thought so too. After all it was them who benefited most from a weakened US and a confused California."

"Certainly that is where most of the circumstantial evidence points. And while the Venezuelans are none too subtle they are only rarely that directly stupid."

"Oh, please do not sell the Venezuelans short on stupid Mr. President. Their obvious involvement with your northern governors and the terrorist attacks in Central Florida suggest a world of stupid that we haven't even imagined."

"And yet, if Hellenga was in their debt why would he agree to be on the presidential ticket?"

"Perhaps he was a Manchurian Candidate, a Venezuelan plant into the upper echelons of the US government."

"Perhaps, perhaps. Well Mr. Ambassador what can I do for your King?"

"Mr. President, Spain is wondering about the instability in northern Mexico and looking for some detail on your quick handling of the situation."

"We want no trouble Mr. Ambassador. It was up to me to contain the northern problem. We already had enough instability on our northern border. American investments into our economy there are large and we do not want to cast doubt on our good neighbourliness. Hellenga was a concern of ours, and Venezuela a larger concern. The US may be wounded but it is still a behemoth capable of taking countries, topping governments or inflicting huge economic carnage. While we have an interest in our people in southern California, indeed all over the United States, we are quite content to have them treated as equals and have their voices heard locally in the way they live, the taxes they pay and their ability to move between countries freely. Tomorrow things will be different. And there are a lot of tomorrows."

"So I can tell the King that Mexico is pleased with the status quo as they fear the threat from the US is diminished and the Americans are much easier to deal with?"

"Mr. Ambassador, you can tell your King whatever you want. Thank you for your visit."

Chapter Fifty - Six   Moscow

Mother Russia contemplated its next move. How was the next 200 years going to look for the Motherland. What did Russia want it to look like?

The Russian President sat at his desk, a map of the world spread on top taking the whole surface of the large lacquered oak desk. The desk had been in the Kremlin storage for many years, a Romanov desk perhaps or the desk of a high ranking general from the Great Patriotic War. The President only knew that the desk had survived as he had, for many years leading a weakened Russia back to greatness.

The unexpected attack on Istanbul had cemented his reputation as a bold, unpredictable calculated risk taker. If the Byzantines could hold it for 500 years of constant plotting, then the Russians could hold it indefinitely. They had already begun to denude the city of more than 500 years of Muslim rule - minarets were removed, mosques changed to Russian Orthodox churches, new symbols abounded reminding citizens of the city's heritage, of its Roman and Byzantine roots and of its similarities to Russian orthodoxy. The Russians were giving the city a special status, like Hong Kong was to modern China.

Hagia Sophia was cleared of its exhibits and it was renamed the Orthodox

Church of St. Paul and St. Peter a direct reference to Moscow's famous onion dome at the Kremlin. Defences were strengthened and much of the Muslim population was encouraged to leave. Opportunities knocked and the city flooded with Slavs from the Balkans looking for the former greatness of their ancestors.

Turning from his conquest the Russian President gazed over the former Ukraine. The eastern section of that former Soviet Republic was now firmly in the hands of Mother Russia. It was the cradle of Russian civilization, perhaps as necessary to the Russian psyche as New England was to the American.

The Dnieper River formed much of the border between Russia and the independent nation of Ukraine with the Trubizh River, a tributary of the Dnieper, forming the border as the river approached Kiev.

Satisfied with that the President gazed into Central Asia and knew he was pushing the Muslim threat from those areas around the Caspian Sea. Many central Asian Muslims were moving south to lands where Muslim populations had been reduced. Iran, Iraq and some of the former Saudi Arabia were being repopulated through migration.

The Russian President looked at China. So far the two countries had been on friendly terms, largely because their goals had been similar without overlapping. China was extending its influence to South America and Africa and southern Asia, while Russia was content to firm up its needed hegemony in Europe and central Asia.

The Russian President furrowed his brow when he looked at the Pacific Rim of Asia. The Chinese had carved out a significant sphere of influence into south Asia and were expanding island by island into the Pacific. He saw the Hawai'ian Islands in the middle of the vast ocean, still American but perhaps not as firmly so, and yet he could not really conceive of them as Russian.

However, he did not really want the islands to fall under the influence of either Japan or China. Japan was already making some economic inroads into the islands business communities, building hotels, upgrading roads and generally trying to find a place for a significant Japanese minority to grow into what was already a fairly fertile Japanese garden.

He moved his eyes north. Alaska, that was his final frontier and yet he felt it was beyond his current grasp. He resolved to make as many cultural inroads as possible to keep the ground open to some form of Russian influence in future generations. He had done much the same thing in the Baltic States of Estonia, Latvia and Lithuania - parlaying a Russian influence into a distant Russian protectionism - an implicit big brother should those small countries need help in any way. He poured Russian cultural financing in and kept his military far away.

"Do not gaze too longingly at anything Vlad," he murmured to himself. "Just ensure our resources shore up the gains we have made. If the current map of the Motherland remains intact for the rest of the century you have done your job, restored the Motherland to its rightful, respectful place and ensured your legacy. If some of our former brethren in southern Asia return to the fold then so much the better. We must have buffer states and we need them to be voluntarily friendly - even if we encourage their submission, with emigration, economic ties and brotherhood in difficult times."

A sharp knock came on the large, decorated oaken doors to the office. The official entered, and marched up to the desk before speaking.

"Mr. President we have had a report that the US Treasury has voided the US dollar and is re-issuing new dollars at 100 old dollars to 1 new dollar. They will be doing this to all deposits and money parked in US accounts. They will be issuing new paper bills but only in five and twenty new dollar denominations."

The importance of this move did not escape the Russian President.

"What about our Treasury holdings?"

"Treasuries must be cashed at the penalty rate, unless they come due today; so much of our reserve is lost. Current US cash must be exchanged in the next seven days or it is worthless."

"Those bastards. They have reduced our holdings but not eliminated them, meaning that to retain any value we must go along with the New Dollar or we risk everything."

Not unexpectedly an entirely similar situation was playing out in Beijing. The President of China was assessing his nation's situation given the huge geopolitical changes of the previous few years when he was interrupted with the announcement of the issuance of a new American currency.

"Ahh, we anticipated this move but not in time to divest ourselves completely. Go to the markets, spend whatever Old US dollars we have on property, companies and on physical assets. You have only a few days before the market for such things is destroyed."

Within hours the markets crashed as the value of hard assets skyrocketed, tied only to the ability of those to cash in the Old US dollars used as payments.

"Give the Americans credit. Actually, it might take a while for them to get that again. No, give them a nod, by only revaluing their dollar but not actually changing its name this revaluation will fade from the public memory in a few years as prices stabilize. All of as sudden their coinage gains huge value in some ways balancing off against the loss of value due to the 100-1 revaluation. The big winners are those who keep coins."

"In one stroke the US has rescued its fading star and we are largely powerless to stop it, save by insisting that they use our own currency to pay us with."

"Yes, but they don't buy anything from us anymore. Their economic troubles have devastated our manufacturing economy."

"I fully expect tariffs to be announced shortly."

"That could lead to war."

"I am afraid it might. But will we be fighting them to open their markets? That seems farfetched. Or will we be fighting our own people who want work, food, shelter and a future?"

"The Americans have pincered us. We thought we had the upper hand with their treasuries. Now their recklessness becomes clear. They never had any fear of us destroying their currency as they were ready to destroy it themselves."

In Europe the American move was viewed with distaste and distrust in most capitols but some, the more pragmatic, realized the US had completed an end run, a flanking attack on those who would try to control it through its currency. Yes, the US would face some difficulties on this, and they would face distrust for decades, but they had effectively thrown off the shackles of their economy and taken back their global dominance.

Nations and boardrooms around the world were waiting for the other shoe to drop as once the US Dollar had been breached then nothing was sacred and any decisive movement could be the wrong play in a rapidly changing world.

The announcement had been made at the end of business on Thursday in Hawai'i or about 10 pm Thursday night in New York. The rest of the world's economy writhed for a day as the import of the announcement sunk in. US markets would rise to the news and the news that there was a banking holiday until the following Tuesday.

Three days later an uprising occurred in Istanbul. Fish markets were not opened and shoppers protested the lack of food and lack of Russian interest in the welfare of the local populations. As local Russian authorities called in military units to put down the rioting, remnants of the Turkish army struck the frontier in the east. Without Ankara and without Istanbul there was little left for Turkey. They tried a final gambit to push the Russians out. The Russians gave way initially while they recalled the local military to fortify their positions.

The Russian military governor issued an edict. Rioting in the city would cease by 6 pm and all residents were to observe a curfew and remain in their homes until further notice or the fish market would be destroyed and other protests would be handled quickly and harshly.

The Russian military fired several salvoes of cruise missiles from ships anchored near Sevastopol. These missiles hit Turkish cities of Ismil and Bursa as well as the Black Sea resort of Karasu. The cruise missile attacks were followed within hours by bombing runs aimed at infrastructure. Within a day Russian paratroopers had secured the airports and the Russian infantry groups had moved east to new positions along the Sakayra River. Several Turkish Air Force planes attempted an attack but where quickly subdued. The Turkish thrust went silent and the rioting in Constantinople ended.

A few days went by with the Russians hardening their defences but no further attacks from either side. The Russian Ambassador was summoned to the Turkish President's residence.

"Mr. President, I am here at your request."

"Mr. Ambassador you must convey to your President the determination of my countrymen to regain their city of Istanbul and to end Russian aggression in Turkey."

"Mr. President, my President has conveyed to me to tell you that you no longer have any jurisdiction and that any non-Russian cultural influence in Constantinople will be removed. He has issued an edict asking all citizens of Turkey to leave the city and relocate to areas in the east. Your unfortunate attempt to push Russia away from the Orthodox city of Constantinople has required us to build a larger defensive zone. Until then we were content to allow Turks who owned property in the city to remain - your aggressive actions have precluded that consideration. Good day."

The Russian Ambassador inclined his head slightly, and turned and strode out of the room.

Faced with battles in the west, the loss of Ankara, battles with insurgent groups in the south east and an increasingly unhappy populace the Turkish President sat down heavily, unsure what to do next. His appeals to NATO had already gone unanswered. There was little of his country remaining.

The Russian Ambassador reported to his own President.

"Mr. President. He appeared quite stunned. As you know, our commanders in the field suggest that the Turks have no more offensive capability and frankly, only a small defensive one. These Turks are not Russians in any way and the further you get to the east of the Bosporus the less likely you are to encounter a Slav. In fact there are few remaining on the Asian side of the water. I suggest a fall back from Bursa and Izmir in the south and make the Sakayra River our new frontier, at least it signals our non-aggressive intentions - we have what we want. The only wild card I see here is the possibility of coup and the unknown intentions of any rebels. It is essentially suicide for any attack on us and with our cultural cleansing of Constantinople, it will increasingly become pointless to want the city. Deep down the Turks know they held a foreign city and have now lost it."

Chapter Fifty - Seven   Washington

"Our approach is three pronged. First we must impose tariffs on any manufactured wares that do not meet our standards for environmental protection and fair wages. Second, I reiterate my campaign pledge to monitor events in the Middle East and Central Asia but to have no involvement with countries in that part of the world, no trade, only the most basic national relations, no immigration. Americans are free to go where they are allowed and Americans will determine who is allowed within our borders. And third, I will pursue a policy of balanced budgets made possible by a fundamental reduction in the size and scope of government."

Tom Findlay had been elected President of the United States. He had a monumentally difficult job, to keep the Republic viable, to entice stray parts of the former country to remain under the American umbrella even if they operated separate governments, and to remain a vital and strong country despite the setbacks it had endured.

"My first act as President will be to put forth a Vice Presidential nominee for confirmation by the Senate. We in the United States must return to the rule of law and the guidance of the Constitution. "

The campaign had been difficult after the assassination of his running mate, the artist and activist Hellenga. However, the good will that Hellenga's selection had gathered was maintained during the election and Findlay emerged with a large majority of state pluralities. He lost Colorado, Wyoming, Montana, Minnesota, Michigan and Maine. Voters in new border states like East Virginia, Missouri, Nevada and Tennessee all appreciated his even handed approach to their new reality - where he maintained an open door to any and all states that voted to return to the union, while keeping movements between the states easy for local residents. He hadn't had to do much arm-twisting with Texans or Dixieites as they wanted to keep economic connections together.

"My second act as President will be to call together a meeting of all North American nations to build a strong defense zone. Most of this is already in place but new protocols need to be developed to ensure a seamless passing of information and responsibility."

I want to assure citizens of the United States that I am concerned about all aspects of our Republic from foreign policy and international relations, to governance, to economics to managing the rules of civilization. And to all Americans I pledge to be on your side in defence and in rebuilding the institutions that bring us together through our long shared history."

Findlay stood on the steps of a Capitol on a mild spring day with throngs of people gathered. He praised former President Richard O'Day as a commander in chief who held the nation together despite its scars.

My mentor, President O'Day, will have his legacy reviewed and his actions turned over and examined from every angle. I am confident that time and history will find in him a note perfect response to the horrors we endured and the fears that have gripped so many of our people."

"And while I acknowledge that some of our brothers have decided to take on the mantle of their own affairs, they need to know that they will always have a home here in the United States, and that I fully expect they will return to our community of states - secure in their new independence. In time it may be possible and indeed preferable to sponsor a Continental Congress to examine the issues we collectively face and to address them together."

"My running mate, my friend, the renowned artist Angel Bolivar Hellenga, a patriot of California and the Hispanic people, paid for his desire to build bridges rather than exhort violence - he paid with his life. But his life has paid for our understanding of the place California has in everyone's mythos - it is the long sought golden land of youth and opportunity."

As he spoke he lifted his left hand in the air a gesture to pound home the point he was making. The white cuff of his shirt pulled back and revealed a small cartoon axe tattooed on the inside of his left wrist.

And then the ceremonies were over and the hard job of the future for a broken land was begun.

"So Jim do you want the Vice-Presidency or should I offer it to Vernon Clemons?"

"An intriguing idea but I don't think he'd take it. He'd say that as Vice President he could protect the South's interests but once he was gone, the South's interests would remain."

"How do you know that?"

"I already asked him."

Findlay laughed out loud.

California was rebuilding. New York was rebuilding. Europe was rebuilding. The frayed sinews of western civilization were being stitched together, wary that their 100 year, perhaps 2000 year reign as a dominant civilization had come within a whisker of ceasing to be. It had been saved by the existential determination to be the master of one's own affairs. It would continue to exist only on those terms. It could not be stage managed by governments, but only by the collective will of the people to maintain their own freedom.

The shade of tyranny had been turned aside. The cost however was high. And, the end had not yet been found as the seeds of this battle had laid the foundations of the next one.

But now there was resistance to giving away anything of our cultural freedom. The world was ravaged, ravaged by its own hand, the hands of those who called it home. The determination of people to live their way, to be unconquerable in the face of their desires, was again demonstrated. Never had a people been subjugated who did not desire the result. Civilizations had been destroyed, laid waste and turned to dust but not while there remained anyone who opposed the inevitable.

Westerners did not flee their problems but stayed in place and fixed them.

To destroy the desires of Islam, one would have to destroy Islam. Or Islam would have to change its own focus. The only hope for the redemption of Muslim peoples was for they themselves to understand that they wanted to take a different path. And in the path of that goal lay hope, and fear, and an uncertain future.

- END-

Characters

Richard O'Day - President of the United States

Jimmy Fenton - presidential political aid

Tom Findlay - Senator from Pennsylvania - candidate for Republican Presidential nomination

Jim Grange - Governor of Massachusetts (Findlay's political friend and suggested running mate)

Art Mansia - Mayor of Kansas City - Republican candidate for President

General Aaron Stewart - Chair of the Joint Chiefs of Staff

Marshall Wiertrzi - air navy commander and Naval attaché at Pentagon to Admiral McLeish

Bruce McLeish - Rear Admiral in charge of Navy

Charlie Edwards - US Ambassador to Canada

Robert Bieritski - Buffalo area Congressman

Amanda and Peter O'Neill - steel industrialists, she is a special assistant of the US Ambassador to Canada

Jeb Ryan - Texas rancher

Billy Ryan - Jeb's younger son

Hank Ryan - Jeb's older son

Alphonso Miguel Carrerra - President of Mexico

Miguel Octavius - Spanish Ambassador to Mexico

Margita Cartenga - wife of reconstruction company owner - operator of Galleies du Baja Nord in Palm Springs California

Angel Bolivar Hellenga - Californian Hispanic artist and activist

Edward Spenser - English businessman

Fritz Bergenheiler - German businessman

Jennette - Spenser's girlfriend and employee of the Ashmolean Museum in Oxford

Anne Gentle - Mayor of Atlanta

Vernon Clemons - speaker of the Dixie legislature

Alabama Senator - George Caleb

Florida Senator - Herb Chartaway

Florida Senator - Bill Scott

Senator Scott's political aide - Justin Jancovic

Debbie Anderson - Florida Governor

Ambassador Rodriguez - ambassador to Dixie from Mexico

Mohammed Elambra - Washington imam

Adnan Quireshi - moderate Muslim pharmacist - American citizen

Alcoeur Islami - head of Islamic caliphate

Hank and Cheryl - microwave plant foreman and his wife

Paul sub-foreman

Ethan young employee

Mark an older employee

www.ingramcontent.com/pod-product-compliance
Lightning Source LLC
Chambersburg PA
CBHW071507260626
47170CB00002B/293